Praise for Brian Moreland's
Dead of Winter

"With *Dead of Winter*, Brian Moreland breathes disturbing new life into an ancient horror legend. Crisp dialogue, riveting action, and a skin-of-your-teeth pace. Wow!"

—Jonathan Maberry, *New York Times* bestselling author of *Patient Zero* and *Dead of Night*

"*Dead of Winter* had me breathless. This is one hell of a great read."

—Nate Kenyon, award-winning author of *The Reach* and *Sparrow Rock*

"Brian Moreland writes a blend of survival horror and occult mystery that I find impossible to resist. A thriller that hits every nerve with perfect accuracy."

—Joe McKinney, author of *Dead City* and *Flesh Eaters*

"A gripping blend of supernatural and historical thriller. Moreland boldly enters the realm of dark legends and evil magic."

—Scott Nicholson, author of *The Red Church*

"Grisly and terrifying. Moreland spins horror and history into a truly savage yarn."

—Joseph D'Lacey, author of *Meat* and *The Kill Crew*

"Grab a warm blanket and throw another log on the fire, and delve into the terror that only winter can snow down on the soul."

—Aurora Nominee Suzanne Church, author of "Destiny Lives in the Tattoo's Needle" and "The Tear Closet"

Dedication

Dedicated to Mom and Dad, for their love and support, and inspiring me to live my dream.

Acknowledgements

I wish to thank all those who supported me in getting this book written and published. Thank you to my agent, Betty Anne Crawford, for all that you do. My editor, Don D'Auria, for giving this book a home at Samhain Publishing. My friends in my writers' circle: Bridget Foley, Lisa Glasgow, Max Wright, Pat O'Connell, Paul Black, and Erin Burdette. Mark Pantak, for his wonderful success coaching. I wouldn't be where I am today without Mark's insights. My soul brothers, Neil Pflum and Greg "Magick" Bernstein. My mom for reading my earlier works and our brainstorm sessions. My dad for his wisdom and encouragement. Betsy Torman for her feedback and enthusiasm. Nancy McGinnis for sharing her knowledge of the Ojibwa tribe.

About the Author

Brian Moreland writes novels and short stories of horror and supernatural suspense. In 2007, his novel *Shadows in the Mist*, a Nazi occult thriller set during World War II, won a gold medal for Best Horror Novel in an international contest. The novel went on to be published in Austria and Germany under the title *Schattenkrieger*. When not working on books, Brian edits documentaries and TV commercials around the globe. He produced a World War II documentary in Normandy, France, and worked at two military bases in Iraq with a film crew. He also consults writers on how to improve their books and be successful. He loves hiking, kayaking, rock climbing, and dancing. Brian lives in Dallas, Texas, where he is diligently writing his next horror novel. You can communicate with him online at www.BrianMoreland.com or on Twitter @BrianMoreland.

Dead of Winter

Brian Moreland

SAMHAIN
PUBLISHING

Samhain Publishing, Ltd.
11821 Mason Montgomery Rd., 4B
Cincinnati, OH 45249
www.samhainpublishing.com

Dead of Winter
Copyright © 2011 by Brian Moreland
Print ISBN: 978-1-60928-663-7
Digital ISBN: 978-1-60928-649-1

Editing by Don D'Auria
Cover by Angie Waters

First Samhain Publishing, Ltd. electronic publication: October 2011
First Samhain Publishing, Ltd. print publication: January 2012

Part One

Predators and Prey

1

December 15, 1870
Manitou Outpost
Ontario, Canada

It was the endless snowstorms that ushered in their doom. Each day and night the white tempests whirled around the fort, harrowing the log houses with winter lashings. At the center of the compound, the three-story lodge house creaked and moaned. Father Jacques Baptiste chanted in Latin and threw holy water on the barricaded front door. Above the threshold, a crucifix hung upside down. No matter how much the Jesuit priest prayed, the Devil would not release its grip on this godforsaken fort.

Something scraped against the wood outside. Father Jacques peered through the slats of a boarded window. Tree branches clawed violently at the stockade walls. The front gate stood open, exposing them to the savage wilderness. It also provided the only path of escape. If by chance they made it out the gate, which way would they go?

The priest considered their options. Beyond the fort's perimeter, the dark waters of Makade Lake knocked plates of ice against the shore. Crossing the frozen lake would be a dead man's walk. Last week, two of the trappers fell through the ice. The only way out was through the woods.

Father Jacques shuddered at the thought of leaving the fort. The trappers had fortified the outpost to keep the evil out. They hadn't counted on the savagery attacking them from within. He prayed for the souls of the men, women, and children lost in the past few weeks. Last autumn, the French-speaking colony had been twenty strong. Now, in midwinter, they were down to four survivors and not a crumb of food to split among them. How much longer before the beasts within completely took them over?

"Forgive us, oh Lord, for our fall from grace." Father Jacques sipped the holy water. It burned his throat and stomach like whiskey. "Cast out these evils that prey upon us."

Behind him, the sound of boots approached from the darkness. The priest spun with his lantern, lighting up the gaunt face of a bearded man. Master Pierre Lamothe, the fort's chief factor, wore a deerskin parka with a bushy fur hood. His eyes were bloodshot. He wheezed.

The priest took a step back. "Are you still with us, Pierre?"

The sick man nodded. "Just dizzy, Father. I'm so damned hungry."

Father Jacques knew the pains of hunger. Each passing day it pulled his flesh tighter against his ribcage. "We'll find something to eat soon, I promise. Here, take another sip." He offered the bottle of holy water.

Pierre took a swig and winced. Seconds later he stumbled back, rubbing his eyes.

"The burning will pass." Father Jacques grabbed his wrist. "Remember our plan?"

"Yes... check on the horses."

"We must hurry. Now may be our only chance." They removed the barricade from the door. A long staircase led down from the second floor to the snow-covered ground. "Bless me, Father." Pierre raised his shotgun and stepped out into the blizzard. He all but disappeared in the white squall. The only parts visible were his hood and the outline of his shoulders. Father Jacques nervously watched the fort grounds. At the surrounding cabins, wind howled through shattered windows and broken doors. When Pierre reappeared at the stables, the priest released his breath.

Please let the horses still be alive.

The chief factor pulled a horse out. The poor animal was so thin its hide sunk into its ribs. As Pierre threw a saddle on its back, he raised two fingers, signaling that a second horse was still inside the stable.

Father Jacques closed the door and clasped his hands. "Thank you, oh Lord."

Someone tugged at his cassock. He looked down to see a small, French-Indian girl. Pierre's daughter Zoé had tousled black hair and large brown eyes that had kept their innocence despite the horrors they'd witnessed these past few weeks. The girl held a tattered Indian doll to her chest. "I'm afraid, *Père*."

Father Jacques touched her head and gave the most comforting smile he could conjure. "Don't worry, Zoé, the angels will protect us.

Here, you need to bundle up." He fastened her fur parka, pulled the hood over her head.

"I want Mama to go with us."

"I'm sorry, Zoé, but she's too sick. She would die out there. You, your papa, and I are going to ride out to the nearest fort. Then we'll send help back for your mother."

The girl frowned. "Noël says you're lying!"

Father Jacques glanced down at the Indian doll. One green eye stared back. The other eye was a ragged hole. Since Zoé had stopped eating two weeks ago, she suffered from dementia. She spent most of her days whispering to her doll. Father Jacques wanted to rip its head off. He squeezed his fist. "Noël is just afraid like the rest of us. Now, pray for forgiveness for speaking to me in that manner."

"Sorry, *Père*." Zoé crossed herself and bowed.

"Now, drink." He gave the girl the last of the holy water. She drank it and winced as if it were castor oil.

Outside, the horses whinnied. A shotgun fired.

Father Jacques dashed to the window. He searched the fort grounds. A saddled horse ran in circles. Where was Pierre?

Behind the wall of whirling snow, more shots were fired. Then came a scream. Pierre stumbled out of the mist. Blood spouted from the stump of his shoulder. He was missing an arm.

Peering out the boarded window, Father Jacques screamed at the sight of blood gushing from Pierre's shoulder. As the wounded man stumbled up the front steps to the lodge house, the white mist rolled in from behind and swallowed Pierre. His scream was cut short.

"Papa!" Zoé ran toward the barricaded door. "Let Papa in!"

"No, move away from the door." Father Jacques grabbed her hand and backed away.

Outside, the storm wailed. Snow blew in through the cracks of the boarded windows. Footfalls charged up the staircase like thundering hooves. Something rammed against the front door. The hinges buckled.

Zoé shrieked.

"Back to the cellar!" The priest pulled the girl through the dark corridors of the lodge house. Behind them, the front door crashed open. Terror stabbed Father Jacques' chest with icy pinpricks at the shattering of windows and splintering of wood. Growls echoed throughout the lodge.

They're inside!

Zoé released a high-pitched shriek.

"Stay quiet, girl." The priest led her down the cellar stairs. The swinging lantern slashed the darkness with a pendulum blade of light.

7

Brian Moreland

Scratches and streaks of crystallized blood glistened on the steps and walls like a gallery of agonies marking the descent to hell.

They ran into the dark cellar. Father Jacques brought down an iron bar across the door and shoved crates against it. He took the child's face in his hands. "Hide, quick."

The girl crawled inside a nook stuffed with fur pelts. She hugged her doll to her chest. Father Jacques pulled a deerskin blanket down over the nook so Zoé was fully hidden. "Don't come out no matter what you hear."

A raspy voice whispered, "Father..."

The priest aimed his lantern at a row of beds. The storage cellar had been converted into a makeshift hospital. In three beds lay twisted corpses. In the closest bed, an Ojibwa woman was lying beneath the quilts. Wenonah Lamothe, Pierre's native wife. She was too delirious to know that her husband was dead. Her skeletal head rolled back and forth on the pillow. Teeth chattering, she coughed clouds of frosty air. Her long, black hair now had streaks of white. Her skin, normally reddish brown, had turned fish-belly pale, with white scabs and ghastly blue veins. She looked to the priest, her bloodshot eyes pleading him. "Help me, Father."

"I'm sorry, Wenonah." God had failed her. Failed them all.

The Jesuit picked up a silver cross with a daggered tip. "I cast out all spirits of Satan."

The woman tied to the bedposts growled like a wolfhound.

Father Jacques stood at the foot of Wenonah's bed. Her thrashing body smacked the headboard against the wall. She laughed and moaned, blue tongue licking her lips. She kicked off her quilts, thrusting her hips upward, spreading her bony legs for him. Remaining steadfast in his prayers, the priest raised the holy dagger over the Ojibwa woman's chest.

Wenonah glared with fiery eyes.

Zoé yelled, "*Mama!*"

"Stay hidden, child." Father Jacques stumbled back as a wave of emotions coursed through him. Anger. Fury. Rage.

Hunger.

His stomach ached for something meaty. Raw and bloody. He sniffed the air, his keen sense homing in on the nook where the girl was hidden. Beyond the scent of animal furs, Father Jacques inhaled the salty aroma of blood pumping through a heart.

Eat the girl! growled a voice inside the Jesuit's head. *Eat the lamb's sweet meat.*

"No. No. No." He slammed the cross-dagger into a post. "I am a

8

disciple of God. He gives me strength! Lead me not into temptation, oh Lord." The wave of hunger passed. He chanted faster.

Shrieks echoed from beyond the cellar door. Feet stomped down the stairs. The doorknob rattled. Nails scraped the door, clawing to get in.

Father Jacques backed away, praying the barricade would hold. Even if it did, without food and water they couldn't last another day in the cellar. *We have to escape.*

He went to the back wall, climbed up a stack of crates. With a crowbar, he tore planks off a tiny window. Snow blew inward, stinging his face. The mist had cleared. He could see the stables and the open front gate. The square portal was too small for Father Jacques, but not the girl. Tears welled in the priest's eyes as he realized his last hope had come down to the fate of a nine-year-old girl. "Come, child, now!"

She climbed out from her hiding place, hugging the doll to her chest.

The priest kneeled, taking Zoé's hands. "There's still a horse in the stables. I need you to ride out to Fort Pendleton." He pulled a small diary from his coat pocket. "Give this to Brother Andre." He stuffed the journal into a trapper's fur-skinned pack along with her doll.

"No, I'm not leaving..." She started to cry.

"You must, Zoé! We won't survive down here another day." He pulled the pack onto her back, fastening the straps around her waist.

"But what about you, *Père*?"

"You'll have to go on your own."

From the bed Wenonah rasped, "Zoé, wait..." Her wrist stretched one of the ropes. "Come here, my child."

"Mama."

"No, Zoé!" Father Jacques grabbed the girl just short of her mother's gnarled fingernails. "Don't touch her." He carried Zoé to the back wall. She sobbed and jerked in his arms, reaching for her mother.

He stood her on a crate and shook her. "Listen, child! We need you to be strong. Go now, or you'll never see your mother again."

"But I'm afraid to go out there."

"Remember the story about the lost children who came upon an angel?"

She nodded, sniffling.

"There are angels in the woods, and they will protect you, but they are leaving now, so you must hurry."

The beasts wailed inside the cellar's stairwell. An axe blade chopped through the door, cracking it.

The girl screamed and ran up the crates.

Father Jacques helped her out the window. She dropped down to the snowy ground.

"Hurry, Zoé!" He watched her run across the snowfield.

The axe blade smashed through the door. Dozens of white fingers tore at the hole. The priest held up a cross. "God is my savior!"

Another growl issued, this one from *inside* the cellar. He circled, searching the shadows until he spotted broken ropes at Wenonah's bed. She now moved in the darkness just beyond the lantern glow. Her bones made popping sounds. The last stage of the change.

The priest stepped toward the row of beds. He barely made out the woman's spindly shape hunched over, feeding off the flesh of a dead man. The crunching and tearing sickened Father Jacques and at the same time beckoned him to join Wenonah in the feast.

No, stay righteous! The Jesuit coughed. He stumbled to his altar and opened his holy book. The words blurred. His vision spiraled. Inside his stomach, the hunger grew, cold and burning, clinging his flesh to bone, filling him with a hollow emptiness, then turning—*Yes!*—spreading through him with a sweet rapture known only to saints and angels. "I am a shepherd of death..."

The cellar door crashed open.

Father Jacques raised his arms and smiled as he turned to face the ravenous horde.

2

Ontario Wilderness

The oncoming blizzard roared like a phantom bear. A boreal wind whipped through the forest, shaking the pine branches. Searchers in fur parkas steered three dogsleds through the white squall. Huskies barked at the cracking whips. The search party fanned out between the trees, sleds racing one another.

Riding in the lead sled, Inspector Tom Hatcher clamped his black lawman's hat against his head. Frosty wind raked his face. Snow blinded his vision. He leaned inward as pine branches brushed the right side of his body. The British detective felt out of place in his two-piece suit, necktie, and gray overcoat. While the hunters carried rifles, Tom gripped his trusty pistol.

If Father could see me now, Tom thought, *out in the Canadian wilderness dogsledding with a brigade of fur traders. And if that isn't crazy enough, I'm following the guidance of a native woman.*

Jostling and jerking in his rickety seat, Tom watched the Ojibwa tracker's long, billowing black hair as she deftly drove the sled through the trees. Anika Moonblood was like no woman Tom had ever met. She only stood about chest-high to him, but she was feisty, and the way she moved through the wilderness was downright preternatural. Her light brown face, with high cheekbones and sparkling green eyes, reminded Tom of a wildcat. Like a puma or lynx. He might have found Anika pretty if it weren't for the hardness of her face. He had yet to see her smile.

Anika pulled the reins on the dogs. The huskies yelped as the sled skidded to a stop in the deep snow. She hopped off and crouched at the crest of a hill, her deerskin clothes almost blending with the trees.

Tom scanned the woods and saw what the tracker had found. Footprints. The inspector snapped on his snowshoes and climbed upward, raising his knees, awkwardly plowing through the drift. He stepped up beside the tracker. "Any sign of Sakari?"

Anika pulled strands of black hair off a branch. "She was taken upstream."

Tom scanned the frozen landscape. A legion of snow devils spiraled across the pure white dunes, spinning upward and catching the fierce crosswinds. Endless snow froze against his cheeks. Vision diminished to twenty feet. A familiar parasite of foreboding gnawed at his stomach as the afternoon sun was swallowed by gray clouds.

"The blizzard will soon be upon us," Anika said.

The inspector spoke over the wind, "Let's push a little further."

"We go the rest of the way on foot." The tracker trudged forward, her slender frame fading into the white mist.

The other sleds caught up. Tom glanced back at the pale faces of the searchers, a mixture of British soldiers in red greatcoats and Scotch laborers bundled in hooded fur coats. The lower halves of their faces were covered with scarves, and their eyes were shielded by goggles made of caribou bone with two tiny round holes. The native goggles made the white men look like Indian fur trappers. Even though Tom couldn't see their eyes, he sensed their fear. They had been searching for the missing woman for over an hour now, and the blizzard only seemed to be getting closer. It wouldn't be long before the snow completely covered the trail.

Tom briefly looked at Percy Kennicot, offering the clerk a gleam of hope. Ice crystallized on the man's mustache. He and his Cree Indian wife, Sakari, had ventured out into the woods on horseback, headed toward Manitou Outpost. The horses had gotten spooked. They separated briefly. Kennicot heard his wife scream, followed by an animal growl. Percy had searched the evergreen forest but found only Sakari's fallen horse, its throat slashed. The killer had carried off

Percy's wife into the woods.

Tom had told his men to be wary of a rogue trapper in the area or possibly a band of cutthroat Indians. None of the searchers seemed to like that he was in charge. To the soldiers and fur traders, Tom was the newcomer. The man from the city. But they were all scared ever since colonists from Fort Pendleton had started to go missing in the woods. A few weeks ago, a French Canadian hunter had been found disemboweled. Whether the colonists liked Inspector Hatcher or not, he had been hired to track down their killer.

As Tom snowshoed through the woods, he wondered if leaving behind his city comforts had been the right decision. Montréal had been cold, but the interior of Ontario was constantly below zero. The blizzard's endless breath seeped into his bones. White wisps puffed out of his chapped mouth. His cheeks and nose were numb, and he feared frost bite might eat away his face.

How long can we survive out in this godforsaken weather?

The rest of the search party, all colonists who spent their lives enduring such brutal winters, seemed to handle the cold just fine. He now envied their heavy fur parkas and otter skin boots. *Just keep your body moving, Tom.*

The inspector led the search party forward, doing his best to keep Anika in his sights as the swift tracker crept like a wraith in the fog. She stopped and waved them over.

Tom quickened his pace to catch up. She showed him a faint blood trail. There were more tracks, too. Deep impressions in the snow. They followed the tracks until they reached the frozen stream of Beaver Creek. They halted.

"Great Scott!" Tom said.

Suspended in the ice was the butchered body of Sakari Kennicot. But only the upper torso, it seemed. She had been disemboweled. Several ribs were exposed. And one arm had been completely severed at the shoulder.

Percy Kennicot ran ahead of the pack, brushing past Tom. The dead woman's husband fell to his knees and wailed like an animal.

Seeing the remains of Sakari Kennicot, Tom's mind flashed to images from his last case in Montréal: butchered bodies of women being dragged up from the harbor. Nothing but skeletons strung together by grey sinews. It was the grisly work of the most formidable killer Inspector Hatcher had ever tracked.

The Cannery Cannibal.

Just two years ago, Inspector Hatcher had worked in Montréal alongside British and French Canadian detectives to solve the case of the century. For over a year, the Cannery Cannibal had terrorized the harbor city, abducting dockside prostitutes who sold their bodies near the cannery district. The twisted things the killer had done to those girls. The way he butchered them, carving the flesh from their bones. The hair and skin on their heads had been left, as if the Cannery Cannibal couldn't bring himself to cut up their faces. He left that meat to the fishes when he dumped the women's skeletons into the water. Inspector Hatcher had found traces of white powder caked in the eye sockets.

While trying to think like a killer, Tom had spent numerous nights imagining the cannibal carving up these women like a butcher flaying meat off an animal, leaving behind a skeleton with the woman's head intact. It was only later, after he found the killer's dockside lair, and final victim, that Tom discovered the beast made up the women's faces like the powdery visages of Renaissance queens.

Now Tom gripped a tree, trying to erase the memory. The wind shook clumps of snow off the nearby branches. He sensed he was being watched. Catching his breath, he scanned the forest to see if the Cannery Cannibal had somehow followed him to the backwoods of Ontario. But that was impossible, because the notorious murderer was rotting away in prison, awaiting his eventual hanging, if not already dangling from the gallows.

3

Montréal, Quebec

The Laroque Asylum loomed like a fortress for the damned. Its stone walls were powder gray with chinks and cracks from years of brutal winters and internal suffering. Built in 1790, the asylum had been designed to separate the insane from the civilized. A private kingdom for the mentally ill.

Father Xavier Goddard stepped out of his stagecoach onto the cobblestone driveway. Snow flurries swirled around his black robes. He endured the biting wind as he covered his bald head with a black fur cap. Wearing the Russian mink furrowed the brows of his fellow priests, who wore the typical cleric's hat. But the fur cap was an heirloom from his Uncle Remy, who'd sailed the high seas with the French Navy and brought the expensive cap back from Siberia. Despite its contrary image to the priestly vow of poverty, the mink hat was a daily reminder of his cherished uncle, while keeping Father Xavier's bald head warm during Quebec's harsh winters.

The Jesuit turned to his apprentice, Brother Francois, who

climbed out of the coach, gazing up at the towering asylum. The young man was wearing a black cassock buttoned to the throat and a black soup-plate hat, while Father Xavier wore the black cassock and white collar of an ordained priest. Each Jesuit carried a small case, much like a house doctor's medical kit.

Father Xavier gave his apprentice a fatherly look. "Francois, did you pack everything I asked?"

The layman patted his duffle bag, and his eyes brightened. *"Oui,* I'm ready to see how you work."

The young ones are always eager at first, Father Xavier thought. He scrutinized the man's delicate features and innocent eyes. *Maybe Francois will be different than his predecessors.*

"Let's get started." Father Xavier ascended the steps.

Francois followed. "How long will the ritual take?"

"Hours or days. Depends on the willingness of our subject to cooperate."

The asylum's enormous front door opened with a heavy grate. A short, stocky man hobbled out using a cane. "Top of the mornin', Father, thanks for comin' so quickly," he said in a thick Irish accent. With his smudged cheeks and crooked teeth, the warden of Laroque looked like some Cretan who had spent years on a pirate's ship. He had stringy red hair and scraggly mutton chops. A grubby hand jutted out. "Me name's Warden Paddock."

Avoiding the hand, Father Xavier stared at the doorway. He got a cold feeling from more than just the gale that swept along the St. Lawrence River. A coven of ravens landed on the rooftop, squawking. "He knows we're here."

The warden's eyebrows knitted together. "I beg your pardon?"

Father Xavier said, "Never mind. Take us to Gustave Meraux."

"Aye, aye, right this way." Warden Paddock and Francois entered the white stone fortress. As Father Xavier was about to cross the threshold, something shrieked from behind him. He turned around. Down the hill, a steamboat cut through the cracking ice that covered the St. Lawrence River. Across the river stood Mount Royal, the three-crested hill from which Montréal got its name. The sky above the harbor city had turned pink with streaks of orange.

Feeling adrenaline coursing through his veins, Father Xavier smiled. "A beautiful day to face the Devil."

The two Jesuits followed Warden Paddock through the main corridor. They passed a set of red-coated soldiers standing guard with rifles. The warden unlatched an iron door then led Father Xavier and his apprentice down a set of winding stairs.

"We currently have one hundred and seventy inhabitants," Paddock said. "There have been so many crazies coming in lately, that we've had to build additional cells down in the undercroft."

"Warden, I am only interested in the one you sent me for," said Father Xavier.

"Aye, Gustave Meraux arrived two weeks ago, and ever since, has wreaked nothing but havoc among the inmates."

At the bottom of the stairs, the undercroft tunneled beneath the old fortress.

Torches illuminated an arched ceiling and metal bars. In between the cells, water dribbled down moss-covered walls. Father Xavier's shoes splashed through puddles. He winced at the foul smells of urine and defecation. Francois covered his mouth with a handkerchief.

"We're still working on the sanitation," the warden said with embarrassment. "We are understaffed at the moment. Several workers quit since Gustave arrived."

Moaning issued from many of the cells they passed. Most were shrouded by the sepulchral darkness. Inside one half-lit chamber, a fat man with a massive head emerged from a corner. "Feed time! Feed time!" He pressed his cheek against the bars, his bulbous tongue licking the air.

Father Xavier reeled at the prisoner's brown teeth and atrocious breath.

"Not yet, Mortimer. Six-thirty is feed time. Six-thirty!" Paddock banged his cane against the bars and the fat man retreated. The warden shook his head. "My apology, Father, but they have to learn routine or the whole place becomes a madhouse." He laughed at his own joke.

From somewhere down the tunnel echoed a cackling scream.

"That's Gustave," the warden said. "The craziest of them all."

The high-pitched laughter made Father Xavier shudder. As a boy, he had once seen a group of gypsies at a carnival. One of the performers, a fire breather wearing clown makeup, spewed out long tongues of fire then cackled at the crowd. The ominous laughter had made young Xavier sprout gooseflesh. The priest's fist tightened around his duffle bag. He quickened his steps. "Tell me what you know about Gustave Meraux."

The warden, hobbling on the cane, did his best to keep up. "I'm sure you two have heard of the Cannery Cannibal."

Father Xavier nodded. The past two years had been a time of darkness for Montréal. The Cannery Cannibal had haunted the harbor, killing thirteen women, most of them prostitutes.

15

Warden Paddock said, "Gustave earned the name Cannery Cannibal, because he took the women back to the cannery where he worked, cut them up, cooked their meat and innards, and stored them in little tins. He's a bloody sicko, that one."

As they reached a barred door separating this chamber from the next, Father Xavier took a deep breath. "Your report stated that Gustave has given you reason to believe he is possessed by the Devil."

Paddock's keys jingled as he searched through a large key ring. "Upon his capture, Gustave has been the source of many bizarre occurrences. The prisoners on either side of his cell were found dead. One gouged his own eyes out. The other rammed himself into a wall until he bludgeoned himself to death. And our rat population has doubled. They seem to be drawn to Gustave's cell like he's the bloody Pied Piper."

Francois said, "So the cannibal has become a man with ungodly abilities?"

"A man?" Warden Paddock gave a nervous laugh as he tried different keys in the door. "I don't think any of us comprehend what he's become."

Father Xavier said, "But you are sure he embodies a demon?"

"I come from the moors of Ireland, Father. I know the Devil when I sees him." He slipped in a key that fit. "Ah, here we go." The barred door creaked open to an even narrower passage. From the darkness echoed the cackle of damnation.

4

In the Ontario woods, Tom Hatcher examined the woman's body half-submerged in the ice. Sakari Kennicot's butchering was different than the cannibal murders he'd seen in Montréal. Those women had been carved with a knife. Judging by the slashes and torn muscles, Sakari appeared to have been mauled by an animal. She lay face down, her black hair fanned out over white ice. There was enough current flowing beneath to bob her up and down, but the top layer of ice kept the dead woman's half-eaten carcass from floating downstream.

"Did wolves do this?" asked a blunt-faced soldier named Sergeant Cox.

Tom crouched at one of the deep impressions, trying to remember all the tracking skills he'd read in a book on his journey to Fort Pendleton. "The tracks are too big. The killer walked on two feet. I'm guessing one of the trappers wearing large fur boots." That meant any number of suspects, from the neighboring Indians to lone trappers who passed through to deliver pelts to the fort.

Anika shook her head and pointed upward. "No man stands that high."

Tom turned, craning his neck, gazing up at the tall pines, not seeing anything at first. He stepped back a few feet. Snow fell from the darkening sky and dusted his lashes. Eight feet up were broken branches and white slashes in the bark.

"Bloody hell," said Sgt. Cox. "That must be from Silvertip." Fear spread across the faces of every man in the search party. They began chattering, swinging their rifles toward the trees.

Tom watched the expressions of his soldiers. "What is Silvertip?"

Sgt. Cox said, "The biggest grizzly ever to walk these woods."

"A grizzly?" Tom looked to Anika.

Not answering, the tracker walked to the edge of the tree line, staring out at the surrounding pines. Tom followed her through whirling snow. Anika showed him broken branches. There were other trees marked by the same scratches. All around them, the snowstorm made the evergreen branches dance.

Anika's eyes flitted like a rabbit wary of a predator. "We are in its hunting territory. We should go."

Tom wished he had a high-caliber rifle as he scanned the mist-enshrouded forest. "I thought bears were in hibernation."

"It's not a bear. Something worse." Anika dipped a hand into her pouch and sprinkled some kind of rank-smelling herbs along the banks of the stream.

Tom didn't ask what she meant by "something worse." Like many of the Ojibwa Tom had met, Anika Moonblood was prone to superstition. She was an excellent tracker, but as far as providing solid facts for his case, she was of little help.

Inspector Hatcher walked back to the panicked group. "Everybody, just calm down. Sergeant, set your soldiers up along the perimeter and watch for the bear." He nudged one of the soldiers, a young private named Wickliff. "Come with me."

They hustled back to the dogsleds. Wickliff's face looked pale from more than just the freezing wind. "Jesus, I never saw nobody dead before. I'm sure you seen plenty, Inspector. I heard you found the killer who murdered all those women. That true, sir?"

Tom's fists tightened on the rope he was holding. He glared at the soldier.

Wickliff took a step back. "Uh... that's just what the sergeant was informing us, sir. I meant no disrespect."

"Just do as I say. We've got to work fast." Tom loaded up the soldier with a grappling hook, sleeping bag, and some rope, then headed back to the stream. Tom called over two men who were just standing around. "Give us a hand here." He handed each of them ice picks. "You two, chip the ice. We need to pull out the body and strap it down before nightfall." To Wickliff, he said, "Hand me that grappling hook." As Tom gave orders to the three men, speaking in the cold, matter-of-fact tone of a detective, he noticed Percy Kennicot staring at him with bloodshot eyes. The British clerk rose to his feet. He pumped his fists.

Inspector Hatcher put a hand on Kennicot's arm. "Sorry, Percy, I know how this feels..."

Kennicot slung off Tom's hand. "Don't touch me." Wiping a fur-sleeve across his red nose, Kennicot marched toward the dogsleds.

Tom turned back to the woman's mutilated body and began the grisly task that was his duty. A half-hour later, he and his helpers wrapped up the remains of the dead Cree woman with blankets and strapped her down to the dogsled.

The huskies began barking and yelping. Anika came running out of the whirling fog. Her eyes looked frightened. She jumped on the sled and grabbed the reins of her dogs. "Something's coming through the woods. We must go now."

5

Montréal, Quebec

At Laroque Asylum, Father Xavier stepped through the gate and entered the narrow passage, wary of the cells to his left and keeping close to the moss-covered walls to his right. The arched ceiling hung low above their heads. There were fewer torches, separated by longer stretches of darkness. Father Xavier observed several oak doors with barred windows.

"Solitary confinement," Paddock said. "We call it 'The Crypt.' Most inmates will do anything not to stay down here. A few days in The Crypt and they're ready to behave. But not Gustave Meraux. He seems to thrive in this pit."

"Why didn't they hang him?" Francois asked.

"The fur trading forts claimed they were having problems with cannibalism out in the wilderness during winter. A sort of lunacy that was not only affecting isolated fur traders, but also the surrounding Indian reservations. So the courts decided to donate Gustave to medicine. Alive, no less. See if we could find a cure to this epidemic. Problem is, the doctors are afraid to go near him."

They reached the final cell. It was sealed by a thick plank door with a small, barred window. Huffing sounds reverberated off the stone walls—heavy breathing and whispering voices. The prisoner was speaking in tongues.

"This is as far as I go." Warden Paddock backed away. "God be with you both." Turning, the Irishman hurried back down the corridor, his feet splashing through puddles of urine.

Father Xavier cringed at the foul water that soaked the bottom lining of his cassock. He hated working in such dreadful places. But he went wherever God's work was needed, which was generally in the shadowy world of the savage and unclean. He stopped ten paces from the door. A draft blew against his face, as if a window were open. But there were no windows in the tunnels beneath the asylum. He turned to his apprentice. "Let's begin."

Francois drew a line across the floor with a piece of chalk, whispering, *"Ad Maiorem De Gloriam."* He drew another at the threshold of the door. Wind rustled the young man's hair. He yelped and backed away.

"He just whispered my name."

"Keep your thoughts pure, Francois. Remember my instructions." Father Xavier pulled out a glass container of holy water and splashed the walls.

"Sorry, sir." The apprentice's lips quivered as he returned to his chanting.

The prisoner, still lurking somewhere in the dark cell, roared like a caged tiger.

Torch flames danced.

Father Xavier walked over to a table and opened his case. He retrieved a black book with a red cross painted on the cover. He put a violet sash around his neck. Then, unraveling a cloth bundle, he rolled out a set of silver crosses. The center cross had a daggered tip. He hoped it wouldn't come to using that one. He raised one of the blunt-edged crosses, kissed it then gesticulated. "In the name of the Father, the Son, and the Holy Ghost, I claim this chamber as a sanctuary of God." He nailed a crucifix to the oak door. "I cast out the demon that possesses this body."

Gustave spoke in Aramaic, "I will send a legion of rats to strip flesh from your bones." Long, white fingers wrapped around the bars of the door's window. "You will suffer an eternity of pain."

"Who are you, Gustave?"

A cadaver-white face with solid black eyes peered from the cell. He

19

had a thick, black and silver beard and tousled hair that hung to his shoulders. Multiple voices spoke, "I am the Dark Shepherd. The collector of lost lambs."

"What is thy name, demon?"

"I am *Legion*. Like the wind, I am everywhere." His voice grew deeper as he chanted, *"Ego agnosco ostium damno tui animus, ellebarim, ellebarim, ellebarim."*

The possessed man's intense gaze mesmerized Father Xavier. He felt tentacles of temptation pulling him toward the darkness. His collar tightened around his neck. The priest held up a silver cross to the door. "You won't have me, disciple of Lucifer. I am a warrior of God. You will cast yourself out of this man. You will free Gustave Meraux."

Gustave growled and retreated to the back of the cell. "I smell your weakness, eunuchs..." He chanted a different phrase.

Francois screamed and slammed against the wall, slapping at his face and chest.

Father Xavier hurried to his apprentice. "What is it?"

"Spiders. Get them off me." He thrashed his body against the wall like a man on fire.

"They're just an illusion." Father Xavier kept his cross aimed at the cell door while his other hand gripped his apprentice by the collar. "Ignore the sensation. There are no spiders. The demon is playing a trick on you. Look into my eyes, Francois. Speak your prayers and the spiders will disappear."

But the young brother's eyes rolled back to whites. "They're in my head!" He wailed, clawing red streaks across his face. "Get them out!" Francois shoved Father Xavier to a corner and then bolted into the darkness. His screams faded into the chorus of insanity that echoed from every cell.

Left alone in the dank underbelly of Laroque Asylum, Father Xavier turned to his unholy adversary. Gustave's face twisted into a victorious grimace.

6

The wrathful snowstorm closed in around the search party as the dogsleds raced back to Fort Pendleton. Tom pulled his collar tight around his neck. His only sense of direction was the creek that remained just past the branches to his left. Beyond a few meters of visibility, the world tapered off into a whirling white maelstrom. He rode in the lead dogsled. The huskies yelped as Anika drove between the spruce and pines.

With each passing second, the blizzard turned angrier. The shadowy trees looked like giant stick figures charging toward them, lashing out with long, spiky arms.

Snapping branches echoed up ahead.

Anika yanked on the reins of her dogs. The three-sled caravan halted. The huskies barked, backing into one another.

"What is it?" Tom's heart beat wildly.

"Shhh. "Anika gripped his arm.

The sound of something moving through the trees was coming from downwind. It occurred to Tom they were now dragging the grizzly's food with them on the dogsled. The woman's bundled carcass was right behind his back.

"Silvertip can smell us," Sgt. Cox called out over the wind.

They were completely exposed. Tom pulled out his pistol. Anika nocked an arrow into her bow. The other men raised their rifles, spacing out between the trees.

Up ahead came thundering footfalls. Cracking branches.

Tom hopped out and hid behind a pine. Beyond a thick clumping of spruce, he spotted a large animal charging towards them. His heartbeat quickened.

What started out looking like a monstrous beast formed into a galloping horse silhouetted against the snow and fog. A rider slumped across its back. As the brown horse came within shooting range, Tom saw the rider was a small person wearing a hooded parka.

"Nobody shoot!" he yelled. "It's a child."

7

With only a single torch to hold back the darkness of the tunnel, Father Xavier recited Latin passages from his exorcism book. His eyes were growing weary. His throat was parched, and his stomach groaned with hunger.

Gustave Meraux peered out the door's barred window, his black eyes gleaming. "You are nothing but a scared little boy, eunuch. A lost lamb like all the others. Join my flock. I will guide you through the shadows of the Valley of Death." The voice moved inside Father Xavier's head. *I will take you to where the children play forever.*

The priest's chest tightened at the familiar phrase. He raised the cross. "I am a warrior of God. I cast out this demon in the name of—"

Gustave chanted, "*Ego agnosco ostium damno tui animus, ellebarim, ellebarim... Ego agnosco ostium damno tui animus, ellebarim, ellebarim, ellebarim...*" Then he opened his mouth wide and cackled.

Father Xavier's ears ached as the laughter from his boyhood memories returned. The gypsies circling the crowd. The fire-breathing clown spitting flames, cackling maniacally at a small boy crying into his mother's arm. As Father Xavier shook the memory from his head, he heard skittering sounds. A horde of rats sniffed along the chalk line on the floor. Father Xavier reeled, praying the boundary would hold them at bay.

"God is my savior. He blesses me."

"*I* am the only god down here!" Gustave yelled with a blast of fury. "Devote yourself to me, priest. Join my flock and I shall grant your every wish."

"Never!"

"Then my horde shall feast upon your flesh."

The rats squeaked in unison. A gust of arctic wind blew against Father Xavier's face, making him shiver. Rats crawled beneath his robe, running up his legs. He kicked out. Felt the urge to collapse, to curl up into a tight ball, to drown out that maddening laughter with his own screams. A voice inside his head shouted, *"Run, run, run!"* But Father Xavier willed himself to remain at his altar. *Illusions. They aren't real!* The sensation of rats running up his legs vanished. He leaned toward the wind, the fetid breath of damnation. He sought that refuge where the Divine lived. The sanctuary he had created in his mind as a boy. The Golden Orchard. It gave him power. He remembered the reason he had become a priest, the pact he'd made with the Virgin Mary. His childhood fears dissipated. His body filled with faith. He squared his shoulders to the door.

"I am a warrior of God. With His will I am strong." Father Xavier stepped to the barred window and locked eyes with the cannibal that had butchered thirteen women. "You are no match for me, duke of Satan. And you are no match for God's divine will."

The exorcist splashed holy water in Gustave's face. The prisoner hissed and retreated into the darkness of the cell.

Father Xavier held his holy book, and glaring into the door's dark window, chanted the scriptures. "In the name of God, I cast out this demon."

Gustave screamed like a man on fire and ran face-first into the door. Bones cracked. He rammed the door again and again, his nose smashing against the metal bars. Blood sprayed Father Xavier's face.

Gustave Meraux dropped to the floor.

8

The dogsleds crossed the icy planks of Beaver Creek Bridge. As Anika drove, Tom kept a blanket bundled up around the little girl they'd found in the woods. She was shivering. He tightened his arms around her and did his best to rub circulation back into her stiffening limbs. The girl coughed vehemently.

"Is she going to be okay?" Anika shouted over the storm.

Tom said, "I'm doing my best to keep her warm. Just hurry."

On the other side of the creek, the curtains of snow thinned enough to see Fort Pendleton nestled among the aspens, spruce, and hemlock. The caravan of dogsleds reached the twelve-foot-high stockade wall. The top of the spike-tipped fence looked like a row of jagged teeth. Rifle barrels jutted out the slits of the three front watchtowers. The huskies barked.

"It's just us!" Tom shouted over the wind. "Let us in, quick!"

The barrels retreated back into the square cutouts of the towers. At the gate's door, a slat opened and a set of dark gray eyes peered out. "Did you find Sakari?" asked Lieutenant Hysmith.

"She's dead, sir," Sergeant Cox answered. "We have the body."

"What killed her?"

"We believe it was Silvertip, sir."

"Where's Percy?" Lt. Hysmith asked.

"Passed out, sir," answered the sergeant. "We gave him some rum."

Tom yelled, "Let us in, Lieutenant! We have an emergency on our hands." He held a lantern to the small Indian girl's pale face. Her teeth were chattering. "We need to get her to Doc Riley."

Lt. Hysmith shouted, "If she's Indian, take her to the medicine woman across the creek."

Anika said, "No, this is Master Lamothe's daughter, Zoé."

Hysmith frowned. "What's *she* doing this far from her outpost?"

Nestled in Tom's arms, Zoé coughed, hacking up spittle and blood. Tom yelled, "For Christ's sake, Hysmith, open the damn gate!"

The lieutenant hesitated a moment. "All right, in you go."

The double doors opened inward. The three dogsleds entered the fort.

9

Father Xavier climbed up from the undercroft of Laroque Asylum, exhausted and hungry. As Warden Paddock approached, Father Xavier said, "Gustave Meraux won't be disturbing your inmates any longer. I did my best to save the man, but I'm afraid he is dead."

The warden's jaw dropped.

"What happened?" It was Brother Francois who asked the question. His face was bandaged where he'd clawed his own cheeks. Francois was holding a teacup and a half-eaten biscuit with marmalade. He had crumbs on his cheek.

Father Xavier directed his report to Warden Paddock. "Gustave Meraux was indeed possessed by a demon. He tried to play games with my head, but finally realized that as long as I live, I was not going to give in to his chicanery. So the demon rammed Gustave's body into the cell's door. I heard bones in his face breaking against the bars. Then he dropped and was silent."

Paddock grinned. "Bloody good riddance, I say."

"You'll send a doctor down to confirm the death?"

"Of course."

The stagecoach arrived, and Father Xavier and Francois walked across the cobble driveway. As Father Xavier was about to climb into the coach, the warden grabbed his arm. "Is that *thing* that possessed him gone?"

The exorcist looked up at the white-walled asylum. The ravens were gone. "From Laroque, *oui.*"

Paddock's eyes turned glossy. "Thank you, Father." His grubby hand shook Father Xavier's.

"Good day." The Jesuit priest climbed into his stagecoach and sat across from Francois. The novice hung his head, avoiding eye contact.

The carriage rode off, making its journey to the twin-towered cathedral that loomed at the heart of the city.

Father Xavier removed his gloves, glaring at the apprentice sitting across from him. "You abandoned me in there."

Brother Francois kept his head lowered. "Sorry, Father. I have shamed you."

Father Xavier sighed. "No need to feel shame, Francois. Very few Jesuits have what it takes to battle the Devil's legion."

"I promise to be more prepared next time. I'll train harder."

"Exorcising demons is dangerous work." Father Xavier gazed out the window at the city lights. In the Montréal harbor, fishing vessels and sailboats were tied down for another frosty December night. "I've seen many an apprentice lose his faith when the Devil mirrors his own darkness. This work is not for you, Francois. I suggest you return to your mission work with the nuns in Beaupré."

The young man nodded. *"Oui,* sir."

The carriage returned to the Notre-Dame Basilica.

As Father Xavier headed for his room in hopes of falling asleep, he was intercepted by a clergyman. "Father, the Archbishop wishes to speak with you."

He met with Bishop Rousseau in the sacristy. The archbishop was a rotund man in his seventies. His plump face looked eternally agitated.

Father Xavier gave a full report of the exorcism and the releasing of his apprentice.

"Are you certain the demon left Laroque?" asked Bishop Rousseau. "There are plenty of other feeble minds there for it to possess."

"I'm certain, your holiness. After Gustave died, I exorcised the entire asylum. I felt the presence of evil leave."

"But your work is not done."

"It never is."

The bishop sighed. "Then rest up, Father. I am certain it won't be long before I need your services again."

10

Laroque Asylum

Warden Paddock marched down the basement tunnel with two burly orderlies and two guards carrying rifles mounted with bayonets. The five men relit the torches, bringing light back to the asylum's dark underground cells. The Crypt was unusually silent.

The warden smiled, happy that the Cannery Cannibal was finally dead.

Gustave's in bloody hell where he belongs.

They reached the oak door with the black iron bars. It glistened with blood. There were a few teeth scattered about the floor.

Paddock kept a good distance as the orderlies pounded on the door. "Gustave?"

Silence.

"Can you hear him breathing?" the warden asked.

The orderly pressed his ear to the bars for a tense moment. "Nothing, sir."

"Open it."

The two guards aimed their rifles. One orderly held up a pole with a metal noose, while the other unlocked the door and pushed it open.

Gustave Meraux lay face down in a pool of his own red muck. A rat scurried over his protruding backbone.

"Let's be quick about this." Paddock tapped his foot, checking his pocket watch. In an hour, he had an appointment with his favorite prostitute. He couldn't wait to get between her thighs. After all the stress the day had brought on, the warden was ready to fuck it all away.

The orderly entered, easing the wire garotte over the dead man's head. Gustave lay stiff, a bloody pile of meat and jutting bones, looking like some kind of strange fish that had washed up on shore. The stink of the sea was heavy in the air. The orderly stretched out the long pole and pulled the noose tight. A pale hand lurched upward, snatched the pole.

Paddock gasped.

At the tunnel entrance, torches began to extinguish. One by one, each section went black, as the darkness moved towards them like a rolling river of ink. Paddock turned back to the cell. In the flickering flame light, the pale-skinned ghoul leaped to his feet. The pole stabbed through the orderly's back.

The final torch burned out.

Pitch darkness.

Laughter reverberated inside the cell.

Men screamed. Shots fired. Barrel flames lit up a ravenous face biting into an orderly's throat.

Darkness again.

Paddock pissed his pants. Backed into a cell. Turned. Ran. Stumbled through the tunnel. Past the Crypt's gate. Tried to lock it. Dropped his keys. Yelped and continued running through the darkness.

Prisoners howled in their cells.

The warden fell against the bars. Hands grabbed his arms, pinning him against cold iron. A prisoner mumbled into his ear. "Feed time. Feed time."

Paddock fought to break loose.

The rancid stench of fish guts stung his nose.

"No, please, no!"

A slimy hand gripped his cheeks. The Cannery Cannibal cackled. Inches from his face. Warden Paddock screamed as teeth sank into his jugular.

Part Two

The Messenger

11

Fort Pendleton
Ontario, Canada
The storm's howl heightened into a maddening shriek, rattling the window panes of Noble House, causing Master Avery Pendleton to wonder if it was more than just the wind.

"The Beast of Winter has arrived," Walter Thain chortled, chomping a mouthful with an annoying smack of his lips.

Pendleton's gaze went from his glass of brandy to the rotund officer sitting across the table. Red grease stained Walter's multi-chinned jaw as he stuffed his engorged cheeks with blood sausages. The glutton was eating right out of a silver tin like some mongrel off the street.

Pendleton scowled at his officer. "Percy's wife was murdered, and all you can bloody do is eat?"

"You know what bad news does to me stomach," said Walter, peeling back another metal lid and pulling a sardine out by the tail.

"Well, ration your food. We have a long winter yet." Pendleton tossed a napkin at Walter. "And for Christ's sake, wipe your chin."

Pendleton went to a window, where snowflakes clung to the glass, as if fleeing from a terror that lurked in the storm. The ice crystals gathered around the edges of the window, forming a frost border. Beyond were the night and the angry storm.

The Beast of Winter had indeed arrived.

Feeling an ulcer burning his stomach, Master Pendleton snapped his fingers. A Cree Indian butler named Charles brought over a tumbler of brandy on a silver tray. Pendleton sipped his liqueur and peered out the fourth-story window. He had a bird's eye view of the fort village below.

His village. Pendleton had purchased this fort along with Manitou Outpost two years ago. Hudson's Bay Company had offered the two forts and surrounding territory up for sale so cheap that Pendleton and his Montréal partners took the deal and formed Pendleton Fur Trading Company. It was only after moving into Fort Pendleton and setting up trappers at Manitou Outpost that the officers understood the reason the HBC governor was so eager to relinquish this territory. The forts were cursed.

Falling snow powdered the rooftops of a dozen cabins. Windows were aglow with candlelight. Inside the cabins, dark shapes moved about as the colonists went through their suppertime routines, no doubt praying over their meals for salvation from the Beast.

Another bloody death, Pendleton thought. The latest victim had been Percy Kennicot's wife, Sakari. Percy was one of the officers who lived here in Noble House. He was also a friend and colleague of many years. Avery Pendleton had dined with the Kennicots on many occasions and was saddened by Sakari's loss, even if she had been just a homely native woman. She had left behind three children.

How many more must die before this beast is brought down?

As if to mock Pendleton, the snowstorm formed into a monstrous face. Pendleton blinked and it was gone. How many glasses of brandy had he drunk?

Behind him, Walter Thain continued to smack and slurp down sardines like a walrus.

Another migraine tightened around Pendleton's skull like a vise. He grabbed the edge of the windowsill.

"You all right, Master Pendleton?" the butler asked.

Pendleton pinched the bridge of his nose. "Charles, get me some aspirin and fetch Willow for me."

"Lady Pendleton left, sir."

"What do you mean she left? When?"

"A few moments ago."

Pendleton looked back out the window. A woman in a white fur coat and cap was hurrying across the courtyard. The blizzard shrouded her. Pendleton's face tightened when he lost sight of his wife.

12

Willow Pendleton pulled the collar of her snow fox coat tight around her neck. "Damn this horrid place." She crossed the fort's courtyard through the snowstorm. "And damn Avery for bringing me here." Her words and sighs puffed out in angry vapors. Her shoes sank in a foot of snow, soaking the ankles of her stockings. Her body trembled from more than just the skin-prickling, teeth-chattering cold.

"God, please release me from this hell. I deserve better than this!"

She had spoken the prayer daily and now wondered if anyone in heaven was listening. Raised as a proper Catholic, Willow had worshipped the Madonna like she was her own mother. Willow had believed that God and His angels were watching over her. Guiding her to the happy life she deserved. *Deserved!* But now her faith was dying out.

There's still hope, spoke her encouraging voice. *There's always the Spring.*

Spring! Ha! challenged a little-girl voice. Spring is ages away. You could die of boredom before then. You could go to sleep one night and never wake up.

It was ten days till Christmas. The holiday would give Willow a brief reprieve, but then the festivities would pass, and she would have to endure four more months of winter and isolation.

And Avery Pendleton's long spells of silence.

A whirling snowstorm engulfed the fort and tossed Willow from side to side. All the colonists were inside their homes, their doors latched after hearing the news of another death. There was only once place Willow felt truly safe.

She reached the chapel, a log house that looked like all the others. Its only distinguishing feature was a cross on the roof. Willow entered the house of worship eager to speak to the only man she could trust.

13

"Forgive me, Father, for I have sinned," spoke the young English lady.

Brother Andre's chest swelled with guilty pleasure whenever Willow Pendleton addressed him as "Father." Even though the young missionary was only twenty-five and not yet an ordained priest, Brother Andre accepted the title. It wasn't as if he were being a charlatan. Andre was the only representative of the Catholic Church living inside Fort Pendleton. Sitting in the darkness of his cramped booth, Andre leaned toward the screened window. Willow was breathing heavily. The scent of her perfume made the booth smell like a rose garden.

Is she wearing it for me? Oh, stop such boyish nonsense, Andre chided himself. He knew from Willow's previous confessions that her vanity was to rouse the other men. It was a wicked game she played. A flirtatious gaze or swivel of her hips to get the fur traders and soldiers to look at her with hungry eyes. She did this to spite her husband, Avery Pendleton. But Willow never cheated, though she could have any man in the fort.

"Tell me what's on your mind, Madam."

Willow spoke with a shortness of breath, "I have been having impure dreams these past few nights. Certainly blasphemous."

Brother Andre's loins tingled with anticipation. "Describe the dreams to me."

"They happened much like before. I'm in my boudoir, seated at my beauty table. I'm wearing nothing but my corset and knickers. I hear my door open. In the mirror I see a man who is not my husband. I feel butterflies in my stomach and...stirrings in places I dare not mention. The man puts his hands on my bare shoulders. I lean into him. His hands untie my corset..."

Andre's heartbeat quickened. "Go on..."

Willow let out a soft moan. "I close my eyes. The stranger slowly undresses me, taunting me with soft kisses upon my neck. As I surrender fully, near to fainting, he carries me to the bed and ravishes me like a wild heathen. And then I open my eyes..."

Andre released his breath. Willow had described this recurring dream several times this month. Each time the imaginary affair had been with a different man. Sometimes he had no face, just various shades of skin color, often reddish brown like the tribal savages. A few of the fantasies had been of Lt. Hysmith, although she swore the two had never done more than exchange proper words. But the last few confessions stirred Brother Andre's own impure thoughts, for the mysterious lover in Willow's dreams had been *him.*

He said, "You open your eyes, and..."

"The man making love to me is Inspector Hatcher."

Brother Andre's smile dropped.

"Ever since the inspector arrived..." Willow paused, breathless. "...my night dreams have turned into daydreams. When Avery's not around, I lie in bed and imagine Tom is there with me. We are lying beneath the quilts, behaving like curious new lovers." She gasped. "I know I shouldn't have these dreams, Father, but they torture me."

Andre leaned his head back against the booth's wall. His hand squeezed into a fist around his rosary. "God is listening, Willow. Keep sharing."

"Lately, on the nights Avery visits my bed," she continued, sobbing now, "and I feel his cold hand touch me, I want nothing to do with him. I don't understand why I can surrender to a stranger but not my own husband. I've been feigning headaches. I don't know what to do."

"God hears you and forgives you. As well you should forgive yourself, for these dreams are caused not by you, but the Devil."

"Yes, Father."

"Only Satan would tempt you to sin against your husband." Brother Andre rolled the rosary between his fingers. "I suggest you light a votive at the altar and pray to the Virgin. Ask Her to fill you with restraint and release you from the Devil's grip."

"Yes, Father, thank you and God bless you."

The door to her booth slid open and her footsteps echoed toward the altar.

Remaining inside his booth, Brother Andre leaned his head against the screen, whispering his own confession. Once again, the English lady had stirred up the celibate man's loins. He touched himself, reliving Willow's fantasy of him ravishing her in bed, his face between her bare bosoms, kissing the pink rose petals of her areolas...

The front door opened, and a hollow wind roared into the chapel like God's fury. Brother Andre jerked his hand away. "Oh, dear God, please forgive me." He stepped out of the confessional closet, both relieved and disappointed that Willow had left. Once again thoughts of her roused Andre with a heat that spread across his loins. He went into his bedchamber and sat on his bed. "I vow to be chaste! I vow to be chaste!" As he chanted, he grabbed a rubber cudgel and flogged his thighs.

14

At Hospital House, Tom Hatcher soaked his frost-bitten hands in warm water.

Myrna Riley, the gray-haired wife of the fort's doctor, brought a tray with a porcelain teapot and cups into the patient's room. "Here you go, gentlemen. Black tea with milk and sugar. I've got vegetable soup cooking for the little one when she's awake."

"Thanks, love." Doc Riley dipped a rag into a basin and wiped Zoé Lamothe's forehead.

Tom was grateful to be drinking something to warm his body.

Myrna paused on her way out of the room. "Oh, Inspector, Lieutenant Hysmith's in the front room. He insists that you speak to him."

Tom stepped out into a waiting area.

Lieutenant Zachary Hysmith stood by the front door, unraveling a snow-frosted scarf. He wore a long greatcoat over his red uniform and a lieutenant's hat, which he removed. He had cropped silver hair and a sharp widow's peak. "Tom, upon your arrival, did Master Pendleton not orient you on the protocols of fort security?"

"Of course," Tom said. "Why, is something ailing you, Hysmith?"

The lieutenant had a burning look in his eyes. "The way you spoke to me in front of the garrison was disrespectful and absolutely unacceptable." He removed his gloves, and Tom wondered if the uptight soldier was going to slap his cheeks with them.

"I was concerned about the girl." Tom squared up to him. "You were being a horse's arse and wasting precious time. Doc thinks she might have pneumonia."

Hysmith hesitated briefly, considering this. "Well, you broke protocol bringing her here. I have the fort's security to think about. We don't let just any heathen inside our walls."

"I had a life or death crisis. When that happens, bugger protocol."

Hysmith's face turned red. "Inspector, you may have done as you bloody wished back in Montréal, but as long as you reside at this fort, you will adhere to my orders!"

"The only authority I answer to is that of Master Pendleton. If you have an issue, Hysmith, go discuss it with him. Now, if you'll excuse me, I have a sick girl to tend to." Tom stepped back into Zoé's room. Hysmith followed.

Tom said, "Doc, tell us some good news."

The old man pressed a stethoscope to the child's bleach-white chest. "Wish I could, gentlemen. But she's got a bad case of pneumonia." Doc Riley pulled down the flesh beneath Zoé's dilated eyes. "Symptoms of scurvy and frostbite, too. And by the looks of her ribs, she hasn't eaten in days. Maybe a week." Doc scratched his white sideburns.

"How far could she have ridden in that blizzard?" Tom asked.

Doc said, "It's twenty miles between here and Manitou Outpost."

"All that way to deliver a diary?" Tom asked.

Hysmith's brow furrowed. "What diary?"

Tom picked up a small, leather-bound book off the table. "Zoé was carrying this with her. We think she was trying to deliver a message."

Hysmith examined the diary. "What kind of language is this?"

"Looks Persian." Tom held up a folded parchment. "I found this letter inside written in French." Tom began reading. "'I pray this diary reaches Father Xavier Goddard at the Notre-Dame de Montréal

Basilica. It is of dire importance. The Jesuits are the only ones who can stop the madness that has befallen Manitou Outpost.' It's signed by a Father Jacques Baptiste." Tom shook his head. "I can't make any sense of the diary itself."

Hysmith said, "The priest is from Quebec. Why not write in French?"

"I don't know," Tom said. "Do either of you have any idea what 'madness' Father Jacques is referring to?"

Doc shrugged. "I haven't the foggiest."

"Let me take the diary," said Hysmith. "Master Pendleton and I can decide what to do with it."

Tom kept the journal. "First I'm taking it to the chapel. Brother Andre might have some answers." He looked down at the Métis girl lying in bed. Zoé coughed, her lips stained with red speckles.

Doc said, "She seems alert now."

The girl hugged her chest, shivering.

Tom spoke in French, asking the girl why she was out riding in the woods alone.

The girl's jaw quivered as her head rolled from side to side across the pillow. She gasped and mumbled something.

"She's hungry," Tom said. "Tell Myrna to bring the soup."

Doc Riley said, "Wait, there's something else you should see." He rolled back the quilts to show her left leg. He turned it. Zoé's calf was black and blue with several scratches. "Looks as if she was attacked by some kind of animal," Riley said. "The area around the lacerations is infected. I'm not sure what's causing the infection--the pneumonia or the scratches. Take a look at her epidermis." He rolled up her shirt. The girl's belly caved inward, the bones of her ribs pressing up against thin skin, which had somehow turned translucent, exposing branches of blue veins beneath.

"She's so cold."

Tom placed his hand on her forehead. It was like touching the skin of a cadaver.

Doc leaned over the girl's mouth. "Her breath has a chill to it." Zoé moaned. The old man jerked then stood abruptly. Wiped his cheek. "She just licked me." Doc shook his head, chuckling. "Okay, lass, I guess it's time we feed you." He shouted to his wife, "Myrna, bring in the soup—"

There came an odd growl, as if a vicious dog had entered the room. With a rabid snarl, Zoé sat up and bit down on Doc Riley's hand. The old man buckled over, crying out. Tom grabbed the girl. Her jaw clamped down tighter on the old man's hand. She growled and wrenched.

Tom pried open the girl's mouth. Doc Riley slipped free, his hand dripping blood across the quilt.

Zoé flopped on the bed, convulsing, eyes rolling back.

Tom shouted to Hysmith, "Your scarf!"

While Hysmith held the girl down, Tom strapped her wrists to the bedposts with the scarf and his belt. Zoé arched her back. Her bloodstained teeth chomped the air.

"Okay, let her go." The three men backed away. The girl fought against the bindings. Staring at them with feral eyes, Zoé licked the blood around her lips.

15

Tom entered the chapel, the cold wind howling at his back. The nave was dark except for a table with glowing candles. As he walked down the center aisle between the pews, Brother Andre approached. The French Canadian missionary wore a black cassock and soup-plate hat. He was a young man. His shoulder-length brown hair and blue eyes made him appear like a clean-shaven Jesus. "*Bonjour* Inspector, what brings you to church on an evening like this?"

Tom pulled out the diary and letter and explained that it had been sent by Father Jacques from Manitou Outpost. "I heard you traveled here with him from Quebec."

"Yes, Father Jacques is my mentor." He read the letter. His eyes filled with concern. "Has something happened to him?"

"I don't know," Tom answered. "Can you translate the diary?"

"No, I can't read Aramaic."

"Why would your priest write in a language you can't read?"

"The journal is for Father Xavier. The priests often send coded messages to one another. The handwriting appears rushed."

Tom took back the journal. In the last pages, the elegant handwriting worsened. There were smears of ink and rips in the paper where the priest had written with too much pressure.

Tom said, "In the letter Father Jacques says, 'The Jesuits are the only ones who can stop this madness.' What does he mean?"

"I don't know." Andre's eyes looked deep in thought. "Over a month has passed since we last met."

"Do you know this Father Xavier?" Tom asked.

"No, I only know of him. He was Father Jacques' former

apprentice. They used to do mission work for the archbishop."

"Is that why you're here?"

"Father Jacques and I came to do mission work with the Ojibwa, but the savages weren't interested in being saved. So we concentrated our efforts on converting the fur traders and set up chapels at both forts."

Tom said, "I'd like us to go to Manitou Outpost as soon as the blizzard passes. We have to get word to them that we have Zoé."

Andre said, "We'll have to get permission from Master Pendleton."

Tom checked his pocket watch. "He'll be having supper about now. Let's meet with him at Noble House at eight o'clock sharp."

As Tom left the chapel, Lt. Hysmith approached with an agitated expression. "Inspector! Inspector!"

Tom sighed, "What is it, Lieutenant?"

"Have a word with your son about obeying curfew."

"What do you mean?" Tom asked, wondering what his teenage son had done this time. "Chris is at our cabin."

"On the contrary," Lt. Hysmith said. "He was last seen hanging among Bélanger's crew. The soldiers reported that your son rode out with the *voyageurs*, but he didn't return with them. I don't know what kind of boy you're raising, but if you don't discipline him, then I will."

16

Tom marched across the snow-covered fort grounds, pumping his fists. He didn't know whose neck he wanted to wring more, Lt. Hysmith's or his son's.

Why the hell was Chris venturing outside the fort? And in this storm! The blizzard was hitting Fort Pendleton with all its might. Tom headed toward the far corner. The French Canadian *voyageurs* and laborers were the men who built the cabins and paddled and portaged the canoes on long journeys. They had their own village within the fort.

Tom walked between the huts. Huskies barked from a pen, some growling at his intrusion. Smoke that smelled like cooking venison billowed from the rooftops. He knocked on Michel Bélanger's ramshackle of a cabin. A pock-faced native woman opened the door.

"I'm looking for a blond-headed boy about this high." He marked the height at his chest.

She pointed to a rectangular cabin in the center of the village. "Skinning Hut."

He marched through a storage area made up of log poles and cross beams. Flapping in the wind were tools, jaw traps, and a wide variety of fur skins: skunk, rabbit, muskrat, beaver, and deer. Tom ducked his head in several places, pushing aside pelts. The French Canadian laborers also did a little trapping, trading furs to Fort Pendleton in exchange for clothing, tools, food, and rum. The trappers only posed a danger when their drinking got out of hand, which could happen on any given night. Tom knew from experience that a drunk trapper was nothing but trouble.

A week ago he'd found his teenage son here drinking rum with Bélanger and his crew. Chris was so drunk he had stumbled all the way back to the cabin. Remembering the incident intensified Tom's anger. He approached the elongated hut. From it came the stink of blood and offal. He entered. Lanterns hung from the ceiling. At a long table, a dozen fur-clad Frenchmen and Indians were butchering animal carcasses. In the center of the table, antlers jutted out of a crate of severed deer heads.

Tom stopped at the threshold. "Excuse me, men." The *voyageurs* all shot glares in his direction. Tom recognized several he had arrested for brawling at the saloon. A large wolfhound with a humped back snarled.

"Quiet, Makwa!" yelled Michel Bélanger, a stout man who stood well over six feet.

The shaggy-haired beast lay back down, issuing a low growl.

Bélanger approached, his enormous hands dripping red. He had long blond hair and a thick beard. "What can I do for you, Inspector?"

"I'm looking for my son." He scanned the rugged bunch standing around the table, but they were all men with weathered faces and angry scowls.

Bélanger said, "Your boy is not with us."

Tom felt his blood pulse. "I know Chris left the fort with you earlier. He's back at the Indian village, isn't he?"

The Frenchman narrowed his eyes. "Why should I help you? You've done nothing but spit on our people."

The other laborers, still gripping their bloodstained knives, gathered behind Bélanger.

"Because my son's outside the fort during a goddamned blizzard," Tom said, resting his hand on his pistol. "If anything happens to Chris—"

Bélanger raised his palm. "No need to blow your lid, Inspector. He's in good company. We left him with Chief Mokoman."

"Then take me to him."

17

Snow swarmed like white mosquitoes, biting Tom's face, as he rode on Bélanger's dogsled to the Ojibwa village. They crossed the bridge over Beaver Creek. The pines towered high above like ancient sentries. Shadow shapes hovered within the spiky branches, clotting out the moonlight. *Beware the woods after dark*, the soldiers had warned, *or the manitous might make ye their next meal.*

Christopher Hatcher knew of the dangers of being outside the fort, yet he continued to ignore them.

The sled rode past a tree decorated with animal skulls. The top one had moose antlers. The snowstorm whirled around Tom with relentless fury. If his son was truly at the Indian village, then he was with the last people Tom wanted around his boy.

Bélanger's sled reached the Indian village. Along the border, several skinned deer carcasses hung from the trees, spinning in the wind. Beneath them were snow-dusted blankets covered with rocks, fetishes made from bones and feathers, and bowls of frozen blood.

Tom shook his head. "Damned savages."

The Indians believed the beast that had been stalking the woods was not a grizzly but some kind of evil spirit.

Passing the deer carcasses, Bélanger pulled the dogsled to a stop in the center of the village. It was made up of a dozen or more birch bark huts. Among the smaller homes stretched long wood structures with domed roofs called wigwams. The village normally bustled with Indians, but tonight none were outside. Perhaps waiting for Silvertip to collect its offering of meat and blood and move on.

"Take me to him," Tom said.

"How about asking politely?"

Tom glared at the big Frenchman. Bélanger waved his arm. "All right, this way."

Tom followed him to a wigwam that was illuminated from within. It resonated with the sounds of beating drums and chanting. Through the stretched-hide walls, shadows danced.

Bélanger stopped outside the entrance. "The natives are in ceremony. We wait."

"Bugger that." Tom lifted the flap and stepped into the wigwam.

A dozen natives were sitting in a circle, beating drums and singing in their Ojibwa language. Several elders dressed in ceremonial costumes were dancing backwards around a fire. Past all the movement of feathers and flames, Tom glimpsed a teenage boy with blond hair and blue eyes. Chris Hatcher was sitting cross-legged in the circle and wearing a deerskin parka. His face was painted white with red stripes. He accepted a pipe from Grandmother Spotted Owl, an elderly woman with silver braids. Chris puffed on the pipe a few seconds and then coughed.

"Christopher Orson Hatcher!" Tom yelled.

The drumming and chanting stopped. The elders ceased dancing.

Chris' eyes widened at the sight of his father.

Tom stepped around the fire. "What do you think you're doing?"

"I—"

"It's past curfew."

"But you were gone, so I—"

"Come with me this instant!"

Chris looked around at the Indians. "But we're not finished with the ceremony."

Tom pointed toward the entrance. "Now, Chris!"

The boy handed the peace pipe back to Grandmother Spotted Owl.

"Best listen to your father," she said.

Nodding, Chris stood, glared hatefully toward his father, and stormed out of the wigwam.

As Tom started to exit, Bélanger grabbed his arm. "You interrupted his rite of passage."

Tom glared at the tall *voyageur*. "This village is off limits to my son. Don't ever bring him here again."

18

Tom stood at the stove in his kitchen. As he stirred pork stew boiling in a cast-iron pot, he noticed his hand shaking. He squeezed it into a fist. The stress from today's events still had a grip on him. First Sakari Kennicot was found dead, mauled by some kind of rogue bear. Then a child rode in on horseback from Manitou Outpost, delivering a cryptic journal from a priest. Zoé was deathly ill and might not survive the night. And now Tom's throat burned from yelling at his son for the last hour. All the stress compounded at the center of Tom's skull. He drank from a glass of whiskey. The fiery drink was the only thing that seemed to settle his nerves.

He sat down at the table. He stabbed a hawk feather into an inkwell and logged the events of the day in his journal.

December 15: Strange dreams have tormented the colonists lately, myself included. Many have complained about recurring nightmares of a bogeyman in the woods. Some claim to have even seen ghosts walking the courtyard, scratching at the windows. Others hear voices. I believe the sounds are only the storm winds. And the nightmares are nothing more than mass hysteria caused by too many campfire tales and Indian legends. The wilderness people are a superstitious lot.

According to the logs from the previous chief factors, there has been a long history of bloodshed in these woods ever since Fort Pendleton and Manitou Outpost were built by the Northwest Company in 1802. Back then the two forts had been run by Scottish fur traders and mostly occupied by French Canadian voyageurs, who man the canoe brigades along the rivers between here and Montréal.

The chief factor of 1802, Commander Wallace, wrote that an Ojibwa medicine man cursed the Nor'esters for building on sacred land. Soon after, the fur traders were discovered skinned and hanging from the ceiling. The bloody work of Iroquois Indians? That was the belief of the winterers the following year, according to a Commander Magnus McDonnell. The Scotsman later went mad and cannibalized his men.

The twin outposts remained abandoned until 1821, when Hudson's Bay Company took over this territory. They fortified each of the forts with watchtowers and twelve-foot stockade walls. A Master Covington wrote the next series of journals. He also complained of nightmares. The Hudson's Bay crew eventually abandoned the forts after Master Covington reported, "These forts are making my men crazy and causing bouts of cannibalism."

Two years ago, Avery Pendleton, presiding partner of the Pendleton Fur Trading Company, settled a colony here of approximately fifty people. A few British officers live among a majority of French Canadian laborers who all have native wives and half-breed children. The fort is protected by a small garrison of a dozen soldiers under the command of Lieutenant Zachary Hysmith. Master Pendleton brought me in to investigate a series of murders and bring about peace to a fear-stricken colony. Is Fort Pendleton being stalked by a bogeyman? A legendary beast of winter?

I think not. But the threat of a killer is a very real one as he (it?) has claimed four victims now. Last week our sentries reported a tall figure roaming the woods, watching our fort. The killer has yet to be fully seen, because it moves within the snowstorms.

Today Percy Kennicot's wife was slaughtered. I originally thought our stalker was a disgruntled trapper, but evidence suggests something the size of a bear, which is impossible, as the grizzlies should be in hibernation. If not a bear, then what kind of predator? Anika believes it is some form of manitou. This, of course, is rubbish. Then how do I explain the visions? Isolation, especially during long winters, can cause ill effects upon the mind, which would explain colonists having strange visions. And the beast that slaughtered Sakari Kennicot, there is a logical explanation for that, as well.

Tom heard a door open and looked up from his journal. Chris came out of his bedroom dressed for bed and wearing a towel around his neck. His hair was damp, his face finally clean of the red and white mask the Indians had painted. Now he looked like the embittered teen Tom was accustomed to seeing.

Chris pulled out his chair with a hard scrape and slumped at the dinner table.

Tom spooned stew into two bowls and set one in front of Chris. "Eat and then it's off to bed with you."

Chris pushed his bowl away. "I'm not hungry."

"I'm not going to tell you twice." Tom sat at the opposite end of the table. He stared at his son until the boy finally pulled his bowl back and dug a spoon into it. Chris kept his head down as he ate, the locks of his hair falling over his eyes.

Tom sipped his whiskey, his gaze fixed on his son. "Are you going to explain why you were at the Indian village again?"

Chris muttered something.

"What was that?"

"Nothing."

Tom sighed. "What's it going to take, Chris? Am I going to have to throw you in jail next?"

"You'd like that, wouldn't you?"

The boy's defiance stoked the fire burning beneath Tom's skin. "Did you ever stop to think how your actions reflect upon me? My own son keeps breaking the laws I've been hired to enforce."

His son only shrugged.

"We stay inside the fort for a reason. The woods are too dangerous, especially at night. And no one goes to the Indian village. It's forbidden."

"I wasn't trying to disobey you, Father. I just..." Chris looked up with pained blue eyes. "I just wanted to know more about where we come from."

"We come from Montréal. Now finish your stew."

After dinner, as Tom was washing dishes, Chris came into the kitchen. "If you won't let me go to the Ojibwa village, will you at least tell me about my grandmother?"

"There's nothing to tell."

"But you keep this drawing of her." He set a flap of buffalo hide on the table. Illustrated in black ink was a portrait of Captain Orson Hatcher, Tom's father, dressed in his uniform and sitting in his chair. Behind him stood an Indian woman. The sight of the drawing filled Tom with revulsion. "What were you doing in my room?"

Chris said, "I found it when we were unpacking. How come you never talk about your mother?"

Tom tensed, holding his breath in with clamped lips. He knew the day would come that his son would question his heritage. "I barely knew the woman."

"How did Grandfather meet her?"

Tom remembered asking his own father such questions, but rarely got a response. Only once, after much pestering, did his father give Tom an answer. *All Indians are heathens who live a Godless life of pain and suffering. They are drunkards and savages never to be trusted. Your mother, pretty as she was, had the savagery in her blood.*

"Your grandfather was a soldier back then, patrolling the frontier. He said that even though Indians weren't worth a lick of salt, sometimes the isolation of the wilderness can wear down a man's sensibilities. During one terrible winter when he was suffering from pneumonia, he accepted a squaw as a gift from the chief. She nursed my father back to health and kept him warm during cold nights. The following August, she gave birth to me. When my father's mission was completed, he brought me to Montréal. I was still just a toddler."

"How come he didn't bring your mother?"

"You see how savage they live. She never would have adapted to city living."

"So...if you're half-Ojibwa, what does that make me?"

"Just look at your skin. You're about as white as it gets. Consider that a blessing."

Tom was thankful Chris had gotten the blond hair and Welsh blue eyes from his mother's side. The freckle-faced boy was growing into a young man way too fast. In a couple years he would reach six feet like his father.

Chris gazed at his grandmother's drawing, his eyes bright. "Do you wish you had grown up with your tribe?"

"Enough questions. Now, off to bed."

"Okay..." Chris grumbled and headed toward his bedroom. "Goodnight, Father."

"Straight to bed, I mean it." Tom stared down at the drawing of his father and the Indian woman. Orson Hatcher's voice echoed inside Tom's head. *Your mother was the biggest mistake I ever made. You were the only good that came out of it. Be thankful I brought you back to Quebec and raised you to be a civilized Christian.*

19

Tom trekked across the square of snow-covered ground in the center of the village. During the day, the courtyard was bustling with Indian trappers bringing furs to exchange for guns, powder, supplies, and rum. At night, the fort was locked down, and only the families of the employees who worked for Pendleton Fur Trading Company were allowed to stay inside. Tonight, with the fierce snowstorm thrashing the log cabins, Tom was the only colonist who dared to venture outside. Holding his hat against his head, he forged through the whipping wind, feeling pinpricks on his exposed skin. Last he checked, the temperature had fallen to twenty below.

At the rear of the fort stood Noble House, Fort Pendleton's center of commerce. The massive, four-story log structure, modeled after Fort Edmonton's Rowand House, loomed like an English manor over the other single-story cabins. Each of Noble House's four levels had eight windows spaced evenly apart. Some windows glowed with amber light. The fourth level, where Avery and Willow Pendleton lived, had a balcony and six dormer windows.

Tom climbed the dozen steps and knocked on the main door at the second level. A Cree woman in a servant's dress answered. Her round, reddish-brown face scowled.

Tom tipped his hat. "Good evening. I'm here to see Master Pendleton."

The squaw's frown remained. "He in meeting."

"Can you tell him Inspector Hatcher needs to speak with him?"

She let him in then wandered up the stairs without another word.

The second floor was a large fur-trading room with stalls for stacking pelts. They were empty now, for the furs were locked away in the cellar. A long table and chairs sat in the middle of the room. That was where the clerks sat and figured how much each pelt was worth.

Remaining at the doorway, Tom removed his black hat and glanced into an oval mirror on the wall. He wet his fingers and matted down a stubborn cowlick. The brown hair on the side of his head was starting to grow over his ears.

I'm past due for a cut.

Someone tapped on the front door. Tom opened it. Brother Andre stood on the porch, hugging his chest and shivering.

"Good, Andre, you're right on time."

The Jesuit missionary stepped inside, dusting snow off his overcoat. "This is our worst blizzard this year. It was a miracle I made it here."

A woman's voice said, "Well, my lucky stars, look who the storm blew in."

Tom and Andre both turned, speechless, as Lady Willow Pendleton entered the foyer. She wore a red velvet gown that formed her narrow waist and torso into a voluptuous V. As usual, she was showing off plenty of cleavage. Most of the women of the fort colony wore drab cotton dresses and bonnets. Each time Tom had seen Lady Pendleton about the village, she wore a colorful dress, fur coat, and makeup. From afar she had been easy on the eyes. Up close, Tom felt like he was staring into the sun. Her sparkling blue eyes made him want to look anywhere but into them.

What was it about this woman that caused him to shift in his boots? She wasn't just an ordinary woman. God had molded Lady Pendleton after an angel and blessed her with the life of high society. Even though Tom stood head and shoulders above her, he felt small in her presence. Ordinary. He could feel his cowlick rising again and wished he had run a comb through it.

"What brings you two to Noble House?" she asked.

Tom blinked. How long had he been staring? "Uh yes, Mrs. Pendleton, Brother Andre and I are here to meet with your husband. I assume you heard about the lost girl we found in the woods."

"Ha! Avery doesn't tell me anything." Willow touched Tom's wrist. "But I heard the whole story from the servants. The news has created quite a stir. She's Pierre Lamothe's half-breed daughter, Zoé, am I right?"

Tom nodded. "Do you know her parents?"

"Of course. Pierre and Wenonah. He's French and she's Ojibwa. They also have a teenage daughter, Margaux."

Tom pulled out a small pocket journal and jotted down the information. "What can you tell us about Pierre?"

"He used to be the fort's chief factor working for Hudson's Bay. When my husband bought the forts, Pierre was moved to Manitou Outpost. Any news on his whereabouts?"

"We only came across the girl." Tom returned the journal to his coat pocket. "But I'm assuming Pierre is looking for her. Andre and I need to speak with Master Pendleton as soon as possible."

"Sorry, but all the officers are still in their meeting." Willow touched Tom's arm again, making him feel uncomfortable. "The rule here at Noble House is when the men are behind closed doors, they are not to be disturbed." She offered them her arms. "We can wait in the ballroom."

Andre immediately took one of her arms. "It would be my pleasure, Lady Pendleton."

Tom hesitated, wondering if it was proper to escort the chief factor's wife.

"Oh, don't be bashful." Willow slipped her arm around his. "It could be midnight before the officers adjourn."

She led Tom and Andre into a large, open ballroom where native women were hanging greenery and red fabric over the windows and fireplace. Other servants trimmed a tall Christmas tree with hand-carved wooden ornaments.

"We're a week away from the annual Christmas ball," Willow said with enthusiasm. "We invite all the local Indians and trappers over to celebrate the holidays. All the chiefs come. It will be a marvelous occasion. You both will be coming, too, won't you?"

"I wouldn't miss the party, Willow," Andre said, his tone a bit too zealous. If Tom didn't know better, he might have thought the Jesuit brother was smitten. Then again, what man wasn't under Willow's spell?

Tom merely nodded. As the fort's appointed peacekeeper, he and the twelve soldiers under his command would be on duty the night of the Christmas party, making sure the heavy drinkers didn't demolish the place. Upon Tom's arrival, he had been informed about the annual Christmas ball. The party would be a mix of Ojibwa trappers and French Canadian *voyageurs*, English and Scottish fur traders, and countless native women. The men and women drank rum and danced all night. Acts of lust would surely follow, as many of the men chose their wives at the annual ball. The Indians were known to sell off their teenage daughters for the low price of a keg of rum or even something as small as a coat or a top hat they fancied. Just about every man Tom had met out here had an Indian wife. The British officers had married the daughters of the Ojibwa and Cree chiefs. The only exceptions were Master Avery Pendleton, who transported Willow from Montréal, and Doc Riley, who brought his wife, Myrna, all the way from Ireland.

One of the garlands fell from a window.

"Oh, dear," Willow said. "Pardon me, gentlemen."

Tom and Andre watched Lady Pendleton move about the grand room, showing the servants exactly how she wanted the decorations hung. Despite her petite frame, Willow commanded orders like a British Navy captain.

"I hope my wife is not holding you two hostage." Avery Pendleton's deep voice echoed off the wood floor. The chief factor was coming down the stairs with Lt. Hysmith and Walter Thain in tow. They entered the ballroom and gathered behind Master Pendleton. The wealthy tycoon from Montréal stood like a regal statue with his hands gripping the lapels of his tailored suit. At age forty-five, he had dark hair with silver at the temples. The company officers all looked a bit haggard, as if ready to turn in for the night. Lt. Hysmith seemed peeved that Tom wanted to talk with the chief factor.

Tom said, "Gentlemen, I know it's late, but Brother Andre and I need to meet with you about the matter of Zoé Lamothe."

20

As the tower guards were changing shifts, Chris Hatcher sneaked between two cabins. The wind had died down. Snow continued to fall but he could see, thanks to the light of a full moon. His shadow stretched long across the white dunes in front of him. The shin-deep snow thwarted his efforts to get out of sight quickly.

A sentry up in the watchtower whistled down. "'Ey, kid, what are you doing outside past curfew?"

Oh, bugger! "I have to deliver a message for my father." That sounded believable enough. "Be back before you know it."

"Did Lieutenant Hysmith approve this outing?"

Chris sighed. He couldn't go anywhere around here without getting approval from the fort's head of security. Fort Pendleton was like living in a bloody prison, and Hysmith walked the grounds like he was some high and mighty warden. "He's in a meeting with my father," Chris said. "With all the commotion about Sakari going missing, it's been topsy-turvy around here, eh mate?"

"You ain't shittin', kid." The guard above the gate spat tobacco. "I'm not even supposed to be on duty tonight. Goddamned clerk should have known better than to venture off with his missus."

"Ain't life a bloody tosser," Chris said, repeating an expression he'd heard among the soldiers.

"Sure enough, mate. Ey, better get back soon. If Hysmith sees you out, he's gonna have your arse." He laughed hoarsely.

Chris ran past a cemetery. Several crosses were made from canoe paddles. They were painted with French names. It seemed the *voyageurs* and laborers died in greater number than the British clerks and officers. Beside the graveyard was a shanty. From around back came a familiar sound of flute music. Tonight it carried a melancholy tone. Dogs barked as Chris rounded the shack's corner.

The music stopped. Inside the dog pen, Anika Moonblood was seated on the ground among her huskies. She silenced her dogs with a command. "Who's out there?"

"It's just me."

"Your father know you're out this late?"

"He doesn't mind. Can I come in? I brought you something."

Anika opened the wire-mesh door. Chris sat beside her in their usual spot in the hay. Recognizing the familiar visitor, the dogs settled into their protective circle. A small fire pit with crackling birch wood kept them warm.

Anika was dressed in deerskin pants and a frayed coat with a fox-fur collar. Her long, black hair hung across her shoulders. Her green eyes looked especially sad tonight.

Chris offered her a bundle wrapped in rabbit fur. "I made you something."

Anika loosened the binding and opened the pelt. Inside was a block of wood with smooth edges. She flipped it over and her eyes turned glossy. Chris beamed. He had whittled eight dog faces, one for each husky that she owned.

"Your whittling skills are improving."

"Do you like it?"

Anika held it to her chest. "Very much."

As they sat there, petting the dogs, Chris asked for a drink from her rum flask.

"Will your father mind?"

"Nah, he won't care. I'm fourteen now."

She handed him the horn flask. He gulped it down too fast and coughed. Anika smiled. She continued playing her flute. The high-pitched notes fluttered upward, like birds taking flight, a happier tune. But it wasn't long before the low notes seemed to sink into the earth with an eternal sadness. Chris sat back against the wall feeling the melodies connecting him to Father Sky and Mother Earth. Anika's flute music was the only thing in the past two years that eased his grief.

21

In Master Pendleton's study, a fire crackled and popped in a stone hearth. Above the fireplace hung a drab gray painting of an upper class family—a bearded man in a dark suit, fur coat, and Wellington top hat standing beside a woman in a ball gown with a fox stole around her neck. The gentleman's hands rested on the shoulders of young Avery Pendleton, who was holding a red violin. A shelf behind a large oak desk displayed a collection of violins and fiddles.

Master Pendleton lit his pipe as he stood at the study's window, facing out at the falling snow. "This is a bloody awful mess."

"It's a matter we need to deal with quickly, sir. Zoé is near death." Tom glanced around the long conference table at Brother Andre, Lieutenant Hysmith, and Walter Thain. They all seemed to wait for Master Pendleton's response. He took his time, puffing on his pipe.

The study smelled of tobacco and leather, and, not surprisingly, fur. A menagerie of mounted animal heads adorned the walls: bucks, antelope, mountain goats, and wild boar. Tom sat next to a stuffed wolverine. The ferocious beast was the emblem on the company flag. There were also numerous pelts draped on the walls. On the floor was a tiger-skin rug that looked out of place with the rest of Pendleton's collection.

Puffing his pipe, the chief factor sat down at the end of the table. "With Pierre Lamothe's sick daughter in our possession, we clearly have a problem on our hands."

"Doc thinks he can save her." Tom accepted a tumbler of brandy from a red-skinned man wearing a butler's uniform. "But Father Jacques' letter suggests something may have happened to the other colonists."

Hysmith said, "You discerned this from a brief address to a Montréal priest?"

"The letter suggests urgency," said Brother Andre. "I'm afraid Father Jacques and the others are in need of our help."

Tom added, "Why else would he send a young girl twenty miles to deliver the diary?"

Pendleton picked up the book and flipped through the pages. "What are you proposing, Inspector?"

"That Brother Andre and I and a few soldiers ride out to Manitou Outpost tomorrow. Explore the matter and inform Pierre we have Zoé."

Hysmith shook his head. "No, it's too risky with these frequent storms and that killer out there. Let Lamothe come to us."

"What if he doesn't know we have Zoé?" Tom asked. "He could be searching the woods for her. Notifying Master Lamothe seems the noble thing to do."

Pendleton leaned back in his chair, smoking his pipe. His deep-set eyes gazed at the painting above the fireplace. "Inspector, I'll approve the mission under one condition. You deliver the message to Master Lamothe that he needs to come retrieve his daughter, then head straight back before nightfall."

22

Willow Pendleton paid a late-night visit to Hospital House. Doc Riley was still awake, tending to the needs of Zoé Lamothe. The sick girl was sleeping. Her malnourished body, so thin she looked skeletal, was a dreadful sight. Both wrists were bound to the bed, now more securely by rope. Willow hated seeing a little girl tied down, but Doc Riley said she was prone to violent outbursts.

"Never seen such animal behavior before..." Doc listened to Zoé's heartbeat. "Must be the heathen in her. And take a look at this." He lifted up one of her eyelids. Zoé's iris was covered in a gray membrane that looked like cataracts. "She may have gone blind from the blizzard. I won't know till she wakes up. I gave her enough laudanum to keep her down till morning." The old man sighed and looked across at Willow. "So, you've been having trouble sleeping?"

She nodded, doing her best not to burst into tears. "Each night I toss and turn and wake up perspiring from a fever." She didn't mention her dreams about Tom Hatcher.

Doc felt her forehead. "You don't have a fever now. Worrying too much about the upcoming Christmas ball, lassie?"

"I suppose." She touched his wrist. "Doc, I was hoping you could fix me up with another cocktail. Something to give me sweet dreams."

The Irish doctor smiled. "I reckon I got something in me cabinet to bring peace to such a lovely lady." As he left the room, Willow noticed a small doll sitting on a chair. It was a sad little thing—torn Indian dress, face covered in soot, half bald with a single tuft of black hair. Willow picked up the doll. Its reddish brown skin was made of leather so smooth it felt like human skin. The only remarkable quality was the doll's single fiery green eye, like a cat's. Willow cradled it. Dolls had a way of calming her nerves. Humming, she worked a knot out of the hair. She felt a strange sensation and realized Zoe's pale eyes were half-open and staring blankly in her direction.

"Zoé, are you awake?"

The girl gave a slow nod.

"It's me, Willow. We met at the rendezvous party last summer, remember?"

"I remember your perfume," she said in a French accent. "You're the lady who kissed my father."

"I beg your pardon?" Willow thought back to that night in July. Pierre Lamothe had pulled Willow into an empty bedchamber. The intoxicated French commander had been all hands and lips. Had the girl witnessed this?

48

"You're holding my doll, aren't you?"

Willow waved a hand in front of Zoé's gaze. "Can you see me?"

"No, but I know what you're up to."

"I was just straightening her hair. She's very pretty. What's her name?"

"Noël."

"That's a lovely name. It's the French word for 'Christmas'", isn't it?"

Zoé nodded. Those dull eyes staring through slits gave Willow the shivers. "You know, Zoé, I have a whole collection of dolls in my boudoir. Maybe after you get better, you can come over and see them."

"I've already seen them. Your favorite doll is named Maggie."

"How did you know that?"

"I have a friend who talks to me when I dream. He calls me, 'The Secret Keeper.'" The girl smiled. "He told me all your sinful little secrets."

Willow's heart skipped. "What in heaven's name are you talking about?"

"The wicked thing you did last summer. The man you dream about. Don't worry, Willow, you'll be with him soon."

Feeling goose bumps sprout up her arms, Willow backed out of the room and bumped into Doc Riley.

"Whoa, hold up there, lassie. Everything okay?"

"I need to get home."

"Don't forget this." Riley held up a vial of liquid. "I mixed you up a special concoction I give Myrna. Sends her right into dreamland."

She grabbed the vial. "Thank you, Doc." She kissed his cheek.

He blushed. "Now, don't go letting Myrna see you do that. She'll think we're up to something." He winked then looked into Zoé's room. "I heard you talking. Did the girl wake up?" Her eyes were fully closed. Her bony wrists hung limp in the ropes that bound her to the bed.

"No, that was just me talking to her doll." As Willow left Hospital House, once again embraced by the bitter cold, she felt tormented by what Zoé said.

Maggie talks to me when I sleep. She tells me your sinful little secrets.

Willow wondered how the girl could possibly know about the face-changing man who visited Willow in her dreams.

23

Shortly after midnight, Chris sat at Anika's kitchen table, his head warm and fuzzy with rum. He refilled his glass from her canteen.

She sat next to him, whittling a stick into a raccoon face. Chris liked that she let him drink. Unlike his father, she treated Chris like an adult. As she worked her blade into the wood, he studied her face. Of all the Indian women he had seen, Anika was by far the prettiest. Especially when her face softened and she smiled, which was rare. Her face remained hard and taut most of the time. She could be silent for long stretches.

Chris picked up his unfinished flute and knife and started shaving off the wood. Whittling helped take his mind off missing his mum. He worked at the holes, hollowing out the flute. He blew splinters out the end, making a funny sound.

Anika glanced at him sideways and smiled.

Chris held up the flute. "What do you think?"

"You're learning much faster than I did."

He put the flute down. "This one takes too long. Show me how to whittle something else, like a bear."

Anika picked up the instrument. "Whittling a flute takes time and patience. It's more than just about carving out the wood with a blade. You are merging with spirits of the tree that made the branch. They are teaching you wisdom about yourself. When the flute is finished, you and Great Spirit can make sweet music together."

As she handed him back the flute, someone knocked at her door. When she answered, Chris' father entered, his eyes tense with anger. "Christopher Orson Hatcher, you're supposed to be home in bed!"

Chris stiffened. "I-I couldn't sleep."

"That's no excuse to disobey me. Now, get on home. Anika and I have an early ride tomorrow."

"Where are we going?" Anika asked.

"Manitou Outpost."

Her eyes sparked with fire. "Whose foolish idea was this?"

"Mine," Tom said. "Zoé's sick and her family will be looking for her."

"I'm not taking my dogs," Anika said. "I'll only go if we take horses."

"That's a matter between you and Master Pendleton." Tom pointed out the doorway. "Chris, let's go."

Chris stood. "Let me go with you tomorrow."

"Absolutely not."

"Please, Father. I can shoot a gun now. I'm ready. Please, let me help."

"I said, 'no.' Now go on home."

Chris seethed. He hated being scolded in front of Anika. He started to argue back, but his father had that crazy look in his eyes. "Goodnight, Anika." Chris hugged the native woman, wishing she could stay back at the fort with him tomorrow.

"'Night, Chris. Thanks again for the gift."

He grabbed his flute and whittling tools. Then, without looking at his father, Chris started the walk back to their cabin.

24

Tom remained behind with Anika, furious that the native woman was constantly spending time with Chris. She packed her tracking gear, tossing her snowshoes, stuffing arrows into a quill. "You're too hard on him, Tom."

"It's none of your concern how I handle my son. And I don't want you giving him any more rum. He's too young to be drinking."

"He's trying to become a man. You treat him like a child."

"He just turned fourteen."

"Ha! At that age the men around here are married and voyaging in a fur brigade."

"Well, he comes from a different world than yours."

Anika gripped a tomahawk and shoved it into her pack. "You think we're all savages here, don't you?"

"I'm not in the mood to argue." He opened the door and stepped out onto her porch. "I'll be knocking on your door before sunrise. I need you to be alert tomorrow, so go get some sleep."

"I'm a grown woman, Inspector. I'll sleep when I'm damned well ready." She slammed the door in his face.

25

Tom's cabin was dark when he arrived. The door to his son's bedchamber was closed.

I'll deal with him in the morning. Tom lit an oil lamp on the dining table. He felt an itch at the back of his throat. His hands were shaking, and he was now too riled up to sleep. With insomnia threatening to keep him up another night, there was only one course of action to take.

Tom grabbed a crowbar and opened the lid to a large crate. It was full of brown bottles of whiskey. Pulling out a bottle, he popped the cork, filled a glass, and downed the drink in two gulps. He squinted as the hot alcohol sent fire to the back of his eyes. He pressed the glass to his forehead and sighed. As he walked toward his bedroom, he thought he saw shadow shapes moving outside the windows. Mere tricks of the eyes, he decided. His imagination running wild again. An image of the mutilated woman half-submerged in the ice flashed in his mind. Shredded face, severed torso, exposed ribcage, disemboweled. That vision stirred the murky waters as skeletons of a dozen other slain women bubbled up from the dark recesses of his mind. Then came the whispering voices.

His waking nightmare was interrupted by a single light emanating from the crack beneath his son's door.

Tom entered the room. "I said, 'lights out.'"

"I can't sleep." Chris was sitting on his bed, slicing bark off a foot-long stick. His face was red and damp. He sniffled.

"Son, your constant disobedience has got to end. You say you want to be treated like a man. Well, you've first got to stop behaving like a child. When I say do something, you do it. A man abides by his father's rules, and he doesn't break curfew."

Chris rolled his eyes as he cut at the stick with hard strokes. His cheeks, covered with patches of blond whiskers, turned a deep red. Tom hated this awkward stage. As a parent he struggled between letting Chris think for himself and disciplining him. If his son would only make better decisions. Part of Tom was ready to teach him to be a detective like Orson Hatcher had taught Tom. But another part wished he'd sent Chris off to prep school in England, where he wouldn't be influenced by the unruly wilderness people and their backwoods thinking.

Every day Tom worried about what Chris might do next. If the rift between them widened, he might run away with some Indian girl. Tom pictured his son living like a savage among a tribe of Indians, and it sickened him. *If I let Chris follow the Indian way, he'll never be respected in the white man's world.*

He watched Chris etching his blade into the stick. "What's that you're whittling?"

"It's a flute." Chris blew at the mouthpiece, and an awkward, high-pitched shrill sounded from it. "Holes ain't quite right yet."

"*Aren't* quite right. We don't say 'ain't' in this family."

"It's hard to remember when the villagers say 'ain't' all the time."

"Well, none of them finished their schooling. That's why they have such hard lives. You keep reading your books, and one day you can become an inspector like me, or maybe a police chief."

"I'd rather be a fur trapper. They go on lots of adventures."

Tom smirked. "Your grandfather would roll over in his grave. Hatcher men are born to be lawmen. You come from three generations..."

Chris rolled his eyes again. Tom tightened his fist, containing his temper. "May I see your flute?" Tom spun the whittled instrument between his fingers. Across the shaft were carvings of a buffalo locking horns with the antlers of an elk. "This is fine work. How did you come up with the design?"

The boy beamed. "Great Spirit showed me. See, the wood has a spirit inside it. So does the knife." He held up a blade with an antler handle. "I just ask for the totems inside the wood to reveal themselves, and Great Spirit guides my hand with the blade."

Tom's face tightened. "Who taught you such rubbish?"

"Uh...Anika."

"Chris, I don't like you spending time with her. Rumor is she practices witchcraft."

"People are wrong about her. They just don't like her because she doesn't go to church."

"Well, from now on stay away from her. She's nothing but a crazy drunkard."

"She doesn't get drunk any more than you do."

Tom backhanded him.

Chris gave his father a stunned look and dumped his whittling supplies on the floor. Tom stood at the edge of the bed, his arms shaking. "As soon as I get back tomorrow night, you and I are going to discuss how Hatcher men behave, and your disrespecting me will end once and for all. Now get to sleep." Tom blew out the oil lamp.

As he closed the door, his son yelled, "I hate being a Hatcher! And I hate *you!*"

Tom aimed a fist at the door, tempted to punch his hand through it. Ever since Chris' mother died, the boy was always walking his own line. Since they had arrived at Fort Pendleton, he had taken an interest in everything Tom was against. His arms wouldn't stop shaking. The back of his hand still stung from striking his son's face. Tom looked into an oval mirror hanging on the wall. His haggard face was mostly hidden by shadow.

What kind of father am I becoming?

In the reflection flashed the face of a madman.

Tom refilled his glass to the rim. Whiskey seemed to be the only remedy to dilute the memories that haunted his mind. Now, as he downed another glass, the visions of slain women returned. If he didn't drink himself to sleep, his dreams would be haunted by the maniacal face of Gustave Meraux.

26

Montréal

Nightfall draped a purple veil over the harbor. Fishing boats tied down in their shadowy slips rocked with the tide and knocked against the barnacled docks. A full moon shimmered in the river's black water that smelled of dead fish and the backwash of sewage.

Gustave Meraux's bleeding body stumbled along the dock. Although he felt no pain, he suffered from hunger and loss of blood. His ribs were exposed, his stomach caving inward. If he didn't feed soon, his body would die on him.

He whispered to the dark waters, "I need food, Master."

His prayer was answered as a horde of rats scurried along the ropes that railed the pier. Gustave snatched one wet-haired rodent and bit off its head. He squirted the blood down his throat. Devoured the meat, bones, and fur in seconds, slurping up the ropy tail like a noodle. The meal barely sated his appetite. The rats now crawled around his feet. He scooped up two more.

As Gustave ate, his pale, half-naked body hobbled between the fishing boats. He thought about that priest who had come to visit his cell. Father Xavier had been a worthy adversary, but Gustave got the better of him and Warden Paddock, pretending to be dead. After devouring the warden's innards, the cannibal had managed to escape the asylum, but at the cost of his body. Gunshots and stab wounds from the guards' bayonets had riddled his chest, arms, and belly. A shot ball lodged into his thigh caused him to walk with an awkward gait. A normal man would have already fallen dead. But Gustave was destined to be immortal.

He hobbled along the dock. The rats followed. At the end of the pier stood the hulks of several gray buildings. A sign in broad curvy script read MERAUX CANNERY. Gustave entered an abandoned warehouse. The room had high ceilings like a cathedral. Only the Cannery Cannibal's house of worship had paid homage to a different god. He could hear the echoes of screams as his fingers played along chains that dangled from the rafters. Blood still stained the stone floor. The rats scampered past him, searching for morsels in the empty tins that were scattered about.

Gustave limped across the warehouse, almost collapsed, but caught hold of a post to keep from falling. The bleeding wounds were draining him. He righted himself then pulled his gimp leg a few more feet until he reached an altar. The women's jewelry that had adorned the bench was missing. He lifted the floorboards beneath and felt down in the black hole covered in spider webs. The faded pink box was still there, evidently overlooked by the police who had raided his lair. Gustave set it on the bench. He twisted a key, winding it up. In a crevice on the front, the figurines of a gentleman waltzing with a woman in a ball gown began spinning. The box played warped music.

The music box had a divide in the top's center, which opened out like two wings on the left and right side of the box, revealing three compartments. In the center lay a flaying knife and several dusty black candles. The two winged compartments housed tins of powdery makeup and lipstick. Gustave swayed to the music as he pulled out the candles and placed five in a circle at the altar where a spiral was etched into the wood. He lit each candle. Shimmering light danced along the wall, revealing a mural of a dark-skinned figure. It stood as high as the ceiling, its massive black head hidden in the shadows.

Gustave kneeled and raised his bloodstained hands. "I have returned, Master."

Part Three

Manitou Outpost

27

As dawn filtered through the trees with golden fingers, Kunetay Timberwolf rode his dogsled through the forest. The snowstorm had passed, leaving behind a quiet world covered in sparkling white. The blizzard had also left behind an unseen presence that made the fur trapper's arms sprout chicken skin.

Kunetay stopped his dogsled alongside the bank of Beaver Creek. The four huskies backed against one another, barking at the places where the wind was whirling up the snow. He didn't like the rotten stink that filled his nostrils. The branches above clacked together like the sound of two sparring bucks' antlers.

Bad medicine.

Kunetay pulled down his hood. His black braids were decorated with colored bands and feathers. Fetishes to protect him from evil spirits. When some of the trappers from his tribe began disappearing in the woods, Kunetay went to the medicine woman, Grandmother Spotted Owl, and asked for protection. His three-fingered hand clutched the prayer bundle necklace he wore around his neck. *Keep me safe, Manitou of Hawks.* According to the legends of his people, many spirits inhabited these woods.

Manitous.

They took many animal forms. Some spirits were good, leading man to the best hunting and trapping grounds. But other manitous were tricksters who disoriented the mind like too much rum and caused hunters to become lost. Never to be found.

Kunetay remembered Grandmother Spotted Owl's warning. Stay clear of the woods near Makade Lake. That is the where the wiitigos hunt for food.

The old medicine woman was right. There were no good spirits here. But the fear of tricksters was not enough to make Kunetay turn his dogsled around. To turn back now meant he would have nothing to trade with the white settlers for food for his family and rum for himself.

He cracked his whip at the huskies and continued downstream. The forest opened to a clearing that surrounded Makade Lake. The dark waters were frozen over. Halfway across were several tree-covered islands. According to legend, evil spirits lived on those islands and came out each winter to feed. It was an old campfire tale the Indians used to scare the white trappers and to keep the native children close to camp.

The dogsled reached the edge of the lake where the beavers had built a village of mud huts. There were no active beavers today. And the huts had been demolished, the logs strewn across the icy banks. Had the storm winds been so strong to level an entire beaver village?

Leaving his sled, Kunetay climbed over a stack of logs. He quickened his step when he saw his traps scattered across the snow. Every one of them had sprung, the iron-jaw teeth clamped around severed legs and paws. The beaver and coon they had snared should have been his. Kunetay kicked a pile of bones.

While three of his huskies hovered together, his lead dog sniffed splatters of fresh blood on the snow. There were numerous tracks. Gray holes in the slush longer than his boots. The footprints were made by predators that walked with a two-legged gait and, judging by the spaces between each step, stood much taller than Kunetay. A cage that he had built had been ripped open, leaving behind tufts of fur.

He howled at the lake, his voice echoing.

As if to mimic his rage, something howled back.

Kunetay spun around.

Ahead, where the tracks led into a thicket of briars, the wind swirled up a funnel of snow. Thorny branches clawed the air.

The rotten stink returned. Kunetay's eyes watered as the odor brought back a memory from last summer. His hunting party had come upon a dead grizzly. They tried to salvage the meat, but when Kunetay cut into the bear's swollen belly, it released horrid gases and poured out offal swarming with maggots. Here at the edge of Makade Lake, the stench of rotting carcass once again struck his senses.

Something besides the trees moved inside that twister of snow and sticks. White shapes. They were there and then they weren't, as a spinning wall of snow moved around them.

Kunetay shook his head. The forest was playing tricks on his eyes. It was just the wind and nothing more.

Then what had torn into the traps and eaten all the animals?

For a terrifying second, the trapper saw the white shapes again, rising up from the ground. A small spruce uprooted, got sucked up into the white twister, and then shot out like a spear and splashed off the shore near Kunetay. He leaped back onto his sled. Grabbed the reins. The huskies yelped and moaned, their tails tucked between their legs.

Kunetay shouted and slapped the reins. The dogs raced back up the trail along Beaver Creek. The raging tempest followed, ripping through the trees, tossing limbs. The Indian ducked as a log flew past his head. Smaller branches and pinecones struck his back and legs. He lay flat on the sled. The dogs dashed so fast between the trees Kunetay had to hang on tight.

Falling behind, the things inside the twister released guttural shrieks that made his chest clench.

"Kunetayyyyyy."

The trapper wailed at the sounds of the *wiitigos* calling his name.

28

Just before dawn, Chris lay in bed, listening to the murmur of people talking outside his window. His father, Anika, and several soldiers were loading up their horses. Chris ached inside, as if his father's rage had whittled him hollow. His jaw still hurt from being backhanded last night. But the greater pain was being left behind. It wasn't fair. Chris rarely got to leave the fort. He felt like a prisoner, trapped between boyhood and manhood, and his father refused to let him prove he could be a grownup.

His father knocked and opened the bedroom door. "You awake?"

Chris rolled over.

His father sat on his bed. "I came to apologize about last night. It was wrong of me to hit you. Hatcher men don't hit one another. And I...just wanted you to know it's not something I'm proud of."

Chris remained silent. He wanted his father to feel guilt for what he had done.

"It seems like yesterday you were just a small boy bouncing on my knee. I guess you're growing up faster than I'm ready for."

Chris rolled over. "You promised to teach me police work. How am ever going to become a detective like you and Grandpa if you don't let me help?"

His father gazed out the window, deep in thought. After a moment, he said, "All right, get dressed. I'll saddle up another horse."

29

Tom led a patrol of ten horse riders through the snow-dusted forest. It wasn't long before Anika galloped past him on her Appaloosa. Her stern face gave him a quick nod, as if to say she would be guiding the way. The native woman wasn't one to take orders, so Tom let her have the lead. He wished he didn't have to bring her along, but the tracker knew the fastest route across the forest and creeks to reach Manitou Outpost. She was also their translator if they came across any Indians. Riding at Tom's flanks were his son and Brother Andre. Behind them rode Lt. Hysmith and five soldiers.

Tom weaved his horse through the pines, wary that the grizzly that killed Sakari yesterday might still be in the area. So far they hadn't spotted any tracks. Nor did they see so much as a rabbit or deer. Tom scanned the forest on either side of the trail. The blue spruce were thick, pressing right up against them. He felt vulnerable then, wary that at any moment a giant paw could tear through the foliage and rip one of them off their horse. Feeling a sudden need to protect his son, Tom rode up alongside Chris, shielding him from the dense evergreen branches that now brushed against Tom's shoulders. He nodded. Chris returned a nod, his eyes full of confidence. For the first time, Tom saw in his son a new air of maturity.

Tom remembered back when he himself had been a teen working alongside his father. Inspector Orson Hatcher had been a renowned detective and was well sought after for his keen intellect. He was a superb sleuth, but a difficult father, always lecturing, always correcting his son's mistakes. Orson had pushed Tom to grow up faster than he had wanted to, involving him in numerous cases and exposing him to images no child should witness. When Tom was twelve, he visited a morgue and saw his first corpse, a female cadaver lying on the table. It was the first time he'd seen a woman without any clothing. Her killer had stabbed her with an ice pick thirty times.

By age thirteen, Tom was learning to shoot a pistol and piece together evidence to solve a crime. His teen years were a blur, as he and his father were always moving. Orson and Tom Hatcher had earned a reputation for solving mysteries that stretched beyond Montréal. They worked in London, Paris, Rome, Munich, Prague, and Budapest. Tom had gained plenty of knowledge from working alongside his father. But Orson had cheated Tom of his childhood, his innocence, and for that he resented his father. Tom had vowed to himself not to involve Chris in his work until the boy was mature enough to handle it. That day had finally come.

30

For Chris, this journey was the adventure of a lifetime. It was only his second time to ride a horse, and he was still getting used to his stubborn palomino, who jostled and jerked and tried to wander off on his own sometimes. Chris was in awe at the vast landscape of the Canadian wilderness, the forest-covered hills that surrounded the many lakes and open fields. He loved the smell of pine needles. His whole life he'd only known the city of Montréal. It was noisy there, bustling with people and horse buggies on the streets and boats trundling along the rivers. Here in Ontario, when the wind stopped, there was deep quiet and stillness. Now that Chris had finally gotten to leave the fort and see all the beauty of the wilderness, he was feeling better about moving here.

The ten horse riders reached an open valley that carved between the hills. Their pace was slowed by an uneven terrain of granite rocks. Chris looked over at his father, who was deep in thought. He had been silent most of the journey.

"Father? Why did we move so far away from Montréal?"

Tom narrowed his eyes. "It's complicated."

"Is it because of what happened to Mum?"

His father faced him, and Chris saw his eyes were full of grief. Chris was familiar with that pain. Over the last two years, he had cried many times over the loss of his mother. For most of that time he had blamed his father. If it weren't for him trying to track down the Cannery Cannibal, Chris' mother would still be alive. But with the recent move, the pain and sadness had finally numbed, and he was ready to talk to his father about it. "Please tell me why we moved. I'm old enough to understand."

His father sighed. "Gustave Meraux was a member of a very rich and powerful family. They felt he was being framed by the British and that I was a part of some conspiracy to bring down the Meraux Cannery. During Gustave's trial, I received some death threats. I had no choice but to move us out of Quebec as fast as possible."

Just last month, Chris had been attending a boarding school. His father had shown up, frantic, and told Chris to pack his things. It was the middle of the semester. They left so abruptly Chris didn't even get to say goodbye to his mates. That day he and his father boarded a steamboat and journeyed down the Ottawa River. Chris had been so angry he didn't speak to his father the entire journey. Tom passed out drunk each night. Each day Chris walked the upper decks, watching his world change with each bend of the river. In Ottawa, they switched to canoes. A brigade of French Canadian *voyageurs* took them deep into the woods. Chris remembered how strange he felt when the canoes pulled up to the docks. Up the hill stood a massive fort.

Chris asked, "But why Fort Pendleton? We're out in the middle of nowhere."

His father looked back at the soldiers and lowered his voice, "I had to make a fast decision. After Gustave was sentenced, I was approached by Master Pendleton. He told me he was having some bizarre happenings at his fort. People going missing. Trappers fearful of a killer stalking them. A man's body had been found in his cabin, half-eaten. Cannibalism has been a growing concern during winter. Since I caught the Cannery Cannibal, Pendleton felt I was the man for the job. I was intrigued by the case and figured Ontario would be a good place to start a new life."

Chris stared off at the surrounding pines. "Are we going to live here forever?"

"I don't know. We're here for the winter. Come spring I might make a different decision. Until then I need you to accept that this is our home. Can you do that for me?"

Chris nodded.

They reached the end of the rocky field, where a wall of tall pines stood. At the edge of the forest, they waited with Anika and Brother Andre until the soldiers caught up.

Chris spotted a cropping of rocks etched with monstrous looking figures. One looked like a man with deer antlers. "What are those?"

"Petraglyphs," Anika said. "We are entering the forest of the manitous."

Chris had heard stories about Indian spirits that roamed the woods. According to Anika, there were both good spirits and evil spirits.

Tom climbed off his horse and examined the petraglyphs. "What do these etchings mean?"

Anika said, "It's an Ojibwa warning not to hunt these woods. This land is sacred hunting ground for the manitous."

"That's nothing but bloody superstition," said Lt. Hysmith. "We've crossed through these woods many a journey and never came across the likes of a manitou."

"Sometimes they take the form of an animal, like a deer or wolf," said Anika. "Sometimes they move through the woods unseen like the wind."

As a cold gale blew against his face, Chris felt the hairs on his neck rise. He scanned the surrounding woods. The trees were gray and leafless with spiky branches that intertwined. His palomino backed up and tried to turn around, but Anika grabbed its reins.

As the ten riders followed a winding trail through the thicket, no one spoke. Chris held his breath until the trees finally opened up into a clearing. The patrol stopped their horses at the shore of a lake that was frozen over. It made constant cracking sounds as the wind moved the plates of ice.

"Makade Lake," Anika whispered.

Chris stared across at a dozen small islands covered with pine trees and rocky cliffs.

Anika pointed. "That's Manitou Outpost." At the lake's edge stood a small fort with a few structures that rose above a spiked fence.

Brother Andre said, "Strange. There's no smoke coming from the chimneys."

"Trappers should be moving about," said Anika.

"Let's keep going." Tom steered his horse.

The horse riders rounded the lake toward the fort. A three-story log house loomed higher than the stockade. A Pendleton flag with a wolverine emblem flapped at the top of the spiked fence. Manitou Outpost was surrounded by towering trees and a backdrop of snow-peaked hills. The fort grounds were much smaller than Fort Pendleton, enough to house three or four families.

As the patrol reached the stockade, the first thing that concerned Chris was the open front gate. The second thing was what lay just outside the entrance.

31

The ten riders reached Manitou Outpost's open gate. Tom surveyed the area. In the center of the fort stood a three-story log house. All its windows were dark and frosted over.

Lieutenant Hysmith pulled his horse up alongside Tom. "Something's not right. Post seems deserted."

"That's the feeling I'm getting. What do you make of this?"

In the clearing just before the gate was a red patch of snow clotted with ropy entrails covered in frost.

"Some fool gutted a deer here," Lt. Hysmith said.

"No," Anika said. "Innards are too big. A horse is more like it."

"Where's the carcass?" Hysmith asked.

"Over here, Lieutenant," yelled one of the soldiers. The group on horseback rode over to where some soldiers gathered at a clumping of trees. Half buried in the snow was the carcass of a horse, the bones picked clean. Blood smeared the trail. Footprints went in two directions. One set led toward the forest, the other to the front porch. Tiny hairs littered the trails. Anika hopped off and examined the tracks. "These were made by fur boots."

"Silvertip must have attacked one of their horses," Hysmith suggested. "Some of the trappers went into the woods to hunt for it."

Tom nodded. It was as good a theory as any.

Something disturbed the tree branches with a clacking sound. The nervous horsemen jerked their rifles toward the woods. Above the wind came a screech. Tom located the golden eyes of a hawk perched in the branches. A white rabbit quivered in its talons.

"Bad omen," Anika said.

"I don't believe in omens." Tom turned his attention back to the fort.

Anika pointed upward. "Look at the sky."

Clouds the color of coal swirled over the tree line. A gust blew against Tom's face. Fresh snow began to sprinkle around them.

"Another bloody blizzard's coming," said Hysmith.

"That's all we need." Tom hopped off his horse and walked it toward the gate. "Let's make this visit quick as possible."

Hysmith barked orders at his men. "Private Pembrook, come with us, rest of you keep your rifles on the woods."

Four of the soldiers remained outside the compound in case any of the hunters returned. Inside the gate Tom, Chris, Anika, Brother Andre, Lt. Hysmith and Private Pembrook tethered their horses and waded through the knee-deep drifts. Sleet-heavy wind raked across Tom's cheeks. His skin burned and tingled. Surrounding the lodge house were four single-story log structures, all weathered and dilapidated. Two appeared to be additional cabins. One building was a combination horse stable and work area for a blacksmith. The stalls in the stable were empty.

"No horses, no livestock," Hysmith said.

"No colonists," Brother Andre added.

The fifth building was a small shack with a cross on the roof. Beside the chapel, a dozen crosses formed the boundary of a snow-covered cemetery.

"Let's check the lodge first." Tom looked at the missionary. "Andre, since they're familiar with you, you do the talking."

"Fort's been abandoned." Anika motioned to the open front door.

Tom had the same suspicion. "Well, let's assume they might still be here and go in with caution. Hopefully, we'll find everyone's sleeping and the door just blew open." Even as he spoke, Tom found his theory hard to believe. He spotted Chris venturing off toward the stables. "Son, stick with me."

Tom climbed up the steps to the front porch, gun barrel pointed at the ground. He found it strange how all the windows were boarded up. Chains hung above the entrance, jingling as iron-jaw traps knocked together in the wind. The front door rapped repeatedly against a wall inside. It swung toward them, and Tom caught it with his boot. He noticed a raccoon pelt nailed to the door.

"What does this mean?" Tom asked.

"A welcome sign to trappers," answered Andre. "Master Lamothe opens his post to trappers who are just passing through."

Tom pushed open the door. "Stay alert and be ready for anything. Nobody shoots unless I say."

The Jesuit called out, "*Bonjour*, Master Lamothe, Wenonah. It's Brother Andre."

Tom entered next. A stench like rotten carrion assaulted him. Stopping just inside the doorway, he waited till his eyes adjusted to the gloom. The gray light filtered between the slats that covered the windows and lit up only part of a large, open room. Most of the front den was hidden by heavy shadows. "*Bonjour*, anybody up?" Tom frowned at the sight of a shotgun lying on the floor. Several shells had been expended. "Son, fetch a couple lanterns."

Chris hustled back to the horses then returned quickly. Within moments, Tom lit two lanterns, giving one to the Jesuit. Tom ventured inside, Chris hovering close to his heels. They broke off into pairs, spreading about the expansive room. Flame light from their lanterns rippled over pine furniture and a rock fireplace with a mounted moose head. The ashes in the hearth were cold. The room had an unnerving chill that seeped right through Tom's coat and trousers.

"Hello?" Andre called again.

Tom expected to hear footsteps running down the stairs, but the lodge remained silent. Reaching a staircase, he shone his light upward. A pine banister led up to the second floor.

"How many people live here?"

"Between fifteen and twenty," Andre said. "Sometimes more if they have visitors."

Tom nodded. "See if you can rouse them."

Andre called up the stairs, speaking French. This time his voice was plenty loud enough to wake up anyone sleeping. Tom, Anika, and Hysmith exchanged glances.

Tom said, "Looks like they abandoned the place."

Andre shook his head. "No, Father Jacques would have come straight to our fort."

"Maybe that's what the message was about," Tom said. "Why they were leaving this place and where they were headed."

"But if the message were to me, he would've written that in French." Andre's eyes filled with hope. "Maybe they all headed to our fort after all, but took a different route."

"Or maybe they were attacked by that bear," Chris said. "And only the little girl got away."

"The boy's got a point," Hysmith said. "I suggest we head back now so we're home before nightfall."

"We have some time," Tom said. "I want to explore a little further."

"I'd like to visit the chapel, if I may," Andre said. "See if Father Jacques left behind another message."

"Good idea," Tom said. "Chris, Pembrook, stay down here and keep watch. Lieutenant, Anika, let's check upstairs."

Hysmith nodded and held up his shotgun. Anika drew a buck knife. Tom gripped his pistol and ascended the stairs, holding out the lantern. The old wood creaked under their boots. The railing wrapped around the entire second story. Beyond stood several doors, some open, some closed. At the top, a hallway stretched into a curtain of blackness.

Tom shone his light into one of the rooms. An empty bed. On a nightstand stood a framed portrait of a white man, a native woman, and two girls. One he recognized as Zoé. She was holding her doll. The other was a teen girl with long, brown hair.

"So this is Zoé's parents and sister." Tom showed the picture to Anika.

"Pierre and Wenonah Lamothe, and her sister, Margaux," she said.

Master Pierre Lamothe, wearing a three-piece suit and Wellington hat, looked more sophisticated than Tom expected, like a gentlemen raised in the upper class. The Frenchman had short brown hair and a thick mustache. His keen eyes indicated he was an intelligent man. The Ojibwa woman beside him, Wenonah, was dark brown and homely with her black hair up in a bun. She wore a dress with a lacy collar. Zoé and her teenage sister, who were Métis like Tom, had lighter skin.

Tom said, "I sensed from Pendleton that there might be some bad blood between him and Lamothe."

Hysmith said, "Pierre wanted the chief trader's position at Fort Pendleton. He had worked his way up the company ranks, but Master Pendleton decided to do the job himself. Pierre was not happy being sent to manage the trappers here at Manitou Outpost. Not an easy task since the French trappers live like heathens."

Tom set the frame back on the table and moved between the bed and dresser. The lantern flame reflected across an oval mirror. "What is this?" He stopped, seeing his fragmented reflection as he leaned inward. Someone had smashed the mirror. Beside it, scratches were etched into the wall—four lines then a slash, four lines then a slash—like someone had been keeping score in a card game. They added up to twenty-eight.

He looked at Hysmith. "What's significant about these?"

"Trappers often etch lines in a tree to count off the days."

The wind rattled the panes in the windows. Anika looked out at the approaching storm. "This valley has been hit by blizzards for over a month."

"You think they were snowed in for twenty-eight days?" Tom asked.

Anika nodded. "If they ran out of food, they'd go out hunting. There are a few small cabins scattered out in the forest for hunting or a place of refuge if trappers get caught in a storm. They may have migrated south to one of those cabins."

"How far?"

"A full day's ride."

"We'd never make that in this storm," Hysmith said.

"I wasn't suggesting we do," said Tom. "I'd rather just get home before nightfall."

Hysmith said, "Then you're satisfied, I hope."

"Not quite." Tom left the room. "Let's check the other bedchambers first." They pressed farther down the hall. Each time Tom passed a window, he opened the curtains. The gray light outside pushed back the gloom, but not by much. He found more empty rooms, but no signs of the inhabitants.

32

Andre approached Father Jacques' chapel near the back of the compound. It was a small, leaning shack. The paltry cross on the thatched roof looked as if it had been assembled with some scrap lumber and baling wire. The simple, rustic design seemed to fit Father Jacques Baptiste. A man from the impoverished side of Montréal, he had never been one for lavish décor.

Andre pushed open the door, entering the small nave. He half expected to find the missing colonists sitting in the three rows of pews. But they were empty. One of the side windows was broken, letting in the snow, which frosted the pews.

As he walked down the center aisle, a raven landed on the sill of the open window. Andre stopped. The black bird hopped onto the edge of a pew, cawing. Two more ravens flew in. They squawked as he passed. He shooed them. He hated those black-feathered scavengers. They watched him with beady eyes, opening their beaks. "I have nothing for you. Go away."

At the altar Andre lit the votive candles. The fire offered some warmth and light to the cold, gray nave. Stepping up to the altar, he saw that the crucifix on the back wall was hanging upside down. He righted it and crossed himself. He entered a narrow room where Father Jacques worked when mass was not in service.

Andre went through his mentor's cabinets.

Where is his case?

Even though Andre had been his apprentice going on three years now, Father Jacques was a secretive man and never shared what he wrote in his journals. His reports went directly to the Notre-Dame Basilica in Montréal. The archbishop read the diaries then forwarded them to the Vatican, where supposedly the Pope himself read them. Father Jacques also carried a mysterious case that had always made Andre curious.

He slammed the last door. Aside from the curio cabinet, a chair and writing table were the only furniture in the room.

He must have taken the case with him.

The sound of flapping wings and cawing grew louder, startling Andre. He stepped back into the nave. Sitting on the edge of the pews, like a congregation of dark angels, were twenty ravens. A draft blew in through the shattered window, so cold it seized Andre's breath. Behind him came the sound of wood knocking against wood. On the back wall, the crucifix was hanging upside down again.

33

At the bottom of the stairs, Chris jerked with his lantern. "What was that?"

Private Pembrook whispered, "Probably a rat."

"It sounds bigger." Chris cocked his pistol, aiming at the doorway to the next room. There it was again, the faint sound of a branch scraping a window. Or maybe it was claws dragging across metal.

"Bugger, I don't like it." Private Pembrook climbed halfway up the staircase and tried to see past the railing. "Lieutenant? Inspector?" No one responded.

"They must be at the far end of the lodge." Chris took a few steps into the darkness beyond the staircase.

Pembrook hustled down to the foot of the stairs. "Wait, we shouldn't leave our post."

"Then stay."

"Don't leave me in the dark." Pembrook followed Chris into the next chamber. The lantern light offered a few feet of visibility, but each time he turned, black nothingness filled in the void around them. Chris passed several columns that had been notched by hunting knives. He and Pembrook stepped into another room half-lit by pale daylight coming through a window. Foul odors burned Chris' nostrils. His eyes watered. He held his breath just long enough to adjust to the stench.

"A 'skinning room,'" Chris whispered. It was where dead animals were gutted, skinned, and butchered. He weaved between racks of beaver pelts stretched out for tanning. His hand grazed the soft fur. "Why would the trappers leave behind all these pelts? Aren't they worth a lot of money?"

"There's enough here to buy a year's worth of rum. They must have left in some kind of hurry."

Chris rounded a corner and explored a back room. The walls were lined with pens made of chicken wire. A kennel like the one Anika had. Most of the cage doors stood open. Tufts of fur covered the meshwork and surrounding walls.

Something crunched beneath his boots.

Bones.

Pembrook whispered, "Blimey."

Piles and piles of dog skeletons littered the floor. Fur-covered skulls stared up at them. From the darkness, an animal growled. Turning with his lantern, Chris spotted two glowing eyes. The beast exposed its fangs.

"Shit!" Pembrook bolted.

34

On the third floor, Tom paused when he heard a crashing sound from downstairs. A strange howl echoed throughout the lodge. Tom hurried back down the stairs. "Chris?"

Private Pembrook entered the lantern's halo, his eyes wide. "There's a wolf in the lodge!"

Chris was missing. Panic shot through Tom as he followed the sounds of snarling at the other end of the lodge. "Son!"

Tom, Anika, and Hysmith stepped into a kennel. Their boots crunched over animal bones. "Chris!"

"Over here."

Tom found his son hovering in a corner behind a sled. At the far wall barked a dog. Tom shone his light into the pen. The door was still closed. A tail brushed against the mesh. Growling inside the cage was a hairless husky that was all bones. It screeched and leaped at the latched door.

Everyone stepped back. The dog's front teeth chomped at the metal. Its eyes gleamed solid white. As the dog snarled, strings of gray saliva dripped off its fangs.

Anika yelled, "It's got rabies."

"Everybody stand back." Hysmith pressed the barrel of his shotgun against the cage and fired, splattering the dog's head across the wall. The wound didn't kill it though, because the headless beast continued to ram the cage door, smearing red across the chicken wire. With each attack, the mesh bulged, snapping the wood frame. Tom and Hysmith fired several more shots into the husky's chest and ribs until the white flesh was riddled with red holes. The slain dog flopped on the ground with its legs still kicking. Hysmith reloaded and continued to shoot it until all the life finally shuddered out of the writhing mass.

Tom helped his son to his feet. "You all right?"

"Yes, sir. Just spooked."

"Next time I tell you to stand post, you stay there."

"Yes, sir."

Tom knelt beside Anika, examining all the dog carcasses that covered the kennel floor. They had been eaten, many of them torn apart.

"Could the killer bear have gotten in here somehow?"

Anika shook her head. "Doorway's too small for a grizzly. There's no scat or bear paw prints."

"Then what in hell attacked the sled dogs? And don't tell me it was a manitou."

"I'll tell you what happened," said Hysmith. "The huskies caught rabies and turned on each other."

Tom stood and reloaded his pistol. "Well, there could be more in the lodge, so everybody stay alert."

Hysmith checked his watch. "It's time to head back."

Tom said, "We still don't know why the trappers abandoned their post. I'd like to keep exploring."

"No way in bloody hell!" Hysmith pointed to a window. "You hear that wind out there? There's another storm rolling in."

As if to emphasize the lieutenant's insistence, the wind howled and sleet began to hit the windows.

Anika said, "If we don't leave soon, we'll have to stay the night here."

Tom said, "Fine, we go then."

The four of them returned to the front den. The door opened, and Sgt. Cox entered with a gust of frosty air. He approached his lieutenant. "Sir, snowstorm's gettin' worse."

"Tell the men to saddle up. We're leaving." Hysmith looked around. "Where's Pembrook?"

Anika said, "He stayed behind at the stairs."

"Did he go outside?" Hysmith asked.

The sergeant shook his head. "No, sir, we haven't seen him."

From the back part of the lodge a door slammed.

Lt. Hysmith called out, "Pembrook, get your arse back to the front!" When the soldier didn't come, he said, "We have to find him."

Tom felt a gnawing in his gut. He turned to the soldier. "Sergeant, bring in two more men. Chris, get your horse and wait outside the gate with the soldiers. Anika, go with him."

"Come with us," she pleaded. "Let the soldiers find Pembrook."

"Don't worry about me," Tom said. "Just have the horses ready when we come out."

Chris and Anika exited the lodge house as three more soldiers entered.

Tom and four gunmen searched the second floor, crossing back through the skinning room ,past the kennel and into a dining hall. Still no sign of Private Pembrook. The last room was a kitchen. The storm blew sleet in through several shattered windows.

Tom aimed at a silhouette with long hair who was standing in a corner. "Who's there?"

"Don't shoot, it's just me," spoke a man with a familiar French accent.

Tom raised his lantern to the Jesuit's face. "Andre, what are you doing here in the dark?"

"I came in through the back door. The wind blew out my lantern."

Tom said, "Have you seen Pembrook?"

"No, no one."

One of the soldiers yelled, "Sir, I found blood."

They all gathered at a door. There was a marking on it. Blood had been smeared on the door in the shape of a handprint. Tom touched it. "It's dry, so this couldn't be Pembrook's."

Tom pulled the door open and was knocked back by a rotten stench. Bloody steps led down into a dark cellar. He listened for a moment, but all he heard was the wind rattling the windowpanes.

Tom descended the stairs first, holding his lantern and pistol. One by one, the soldiers followed. At the bottom was a splintered door. It had been chopped open. Tom crossed the threshold into the cold, dark undercroft. The earth floor was covered in black puddles. Barrels and stacked crates lined the walls. Windows were boarded over. The soldiers fanned out. The depths of the cellar seemed endless.

Tom bumped into a twin bed. There was a row of them, with bloodstained mattresses. At the closest bed, a rosary hung from the shadows. Tom raised his lantern. Mounted on the bedpost was a severed head.

35

Outside Manitou Outpost, a gray tempest spiraled above the lodge house. Thunder rumbled. Snow fell in heavy sheets, pounding Chris Hatcher as he walked his horse outside the gate. Under a cropping of trees, Anika and one of the soldiers were readying the horses for the ride home. The boy mounted his skittish palomino and waited.

Anika climbed onto the saddle of her horse. "Don't worry, they'll be out soon."

Chris tried to hide his fear, but his hands were trembling. He was still shaken by the sight of that rabid husky. His clothes were smeared red where he'd fallen onto the pile of dog carcasses. The beast in the cage had been so diseased that it took several shots to kill it. There could be more dogs inside the fort, hunting for food. He watched the gate, wishing his father and the soldiers would come out. Chris imagined them inside the lodge, fighting off a pack of rabid dogs with white eyes.

"Anika, what happened in there?"

The native tracker stared at the lodge house. "The post is haunted with dark spirits. I sensed it when we arrived." She reached into a furry pouch and sprinkled tobacco and feathers on the ground, whispered some phrase in her Ojibwa tongue. When she was done, she looked toward the woods. "This whole forest is a bad place. We are not wanted here."

Chris stared at the surrounding pine trees. Snowflakes swirled among the shaking branches. The forest was alive with eerie sounds: howling winds, snapping wood, the constant cracking of the ice that covered Makade Lake, and underneath it all strange, distant moans.

"Do you really believe there's a spirit world?"

The native woman nodded. "It's all around us."

A hawk flew over them, screeching. Something fell between Chris and Anika, landing in a snow dune. The tracker hopped off her horse, reached into the deep impression, and pulled out a dead rabbit by its feet. The head was missing. Blood spattered the snow.

"Hawk Manitou is warning us," she said. "We should go get them."

"No," barked Private Wallace. The red-coated soldier was the only sentry who had remained outside. "Orders are to stay put until they return."

"But they might need our help." Chris rode his horse toward the open gate.

Wallace, who was on foot, marched after him. "Kid, get back here!"

"I'm not..." Chris froze. He spotted a white form moving through the woods behind Anika. Inside a spinning wall of snow and branches, a blurry shape was charging right towards her.

36

Tom swung his light around him, then back to the bedpost where the head stared with hollow eye sockets. Long white hair hung around the dead man's ghoulish face. His cheeks and lips had been eaten away, leaving behind a skeletal grimace.

"Oh dear God!" Brother Andre gasped. His knees buckled and he looked away, leaning against a pillar.

Tom gazed at the rosary that hung from the bedpost. "Is that Father Jacques?"

Lt. Hysmith nodded, in shock.

"Here's another one." Tom set his lantern on the dirt floor beside a human skeleton that had been gnawed to the bone. A skull was still attached to the neck, suggesting that it was a second victim. He couldn't discern if it had been a man or woman.

Lt. Hysmith said, "The dogs must have broken through the door and eaten them."

Tom shook his head. "Dogs didn't mount a head on a post. The priest wrote in his letter that the colonists had suffered some kind of 'madness.' If the trappers were isolated here for over a month, I'm guessing their food ran out, and they resorted to cannibalism."

"Then the killer could still be here," Hysmith said.

Tom scanned the surrounding darkness. Something glinted. A silver cross jutted from a post. He pulled it out. The cross' bottom half had been sharpened into a dagger. The blade was well-crafted, the work of a sword maker. Engraved into the metal was a fiery sun, the emblem for the Jesuits.

He showed it to Brother Andre. "Do you recognize this?"

The young missionary was a blubbering mess. He shook his head.

"Why would a priest carry such a weapon?"

Again, Andre had no explanation. Was he lying, or was his mentor a man of many secrets? The cryptic diary Father Jacques wrote in Aramaic suggested the latter. Along one of the walls Tom came across a desk with blood-speckled parchment and an inkwell. There were several holy articles laid out on the desk: silver crosses, a bottle of holy water, and a black book with a red cross on the cover. The priest had been performing some kind of ceremony. Perhaps offering a final Mass to the survivors before they were overtaken. Tom sensed something in the gloom above him. He raised the lantern to a large circle of blood smeared on the stone wall. Stepping back, he realized it formed a pattern. A red spiral.

"What do you make of this, Lieutenant?"

"Some kind of totem. Probably to ward off evil spirits. The French trappers are a superstitious lot."

"But this looks as if it's part of the priest's altar."

What had Father Jacques been doing down here? The barricaded door and empty food tins suggested he had been hiding down in the cellar. Zoé must have been with him. Had they been hiding from one of the others? Between fifteen and twenty people had lived at Manitou Outpost. Thus far only two had been found, both dead. Zoé made three. That left too many inhabitants unaccounted for. But where were they?

A cry from the darkness seized his breath. Across the cellar there was a commotion among the soldiers. "Oh, Jesus!" One of them vomited. Another soldier came running with a lantern. "Lieutenant! Inspector!" The soldier's face had turned bleached white. "Pembrook's dead!"

37

Outside, the thing in the white squall howled, its hellish shriek startling Chris Hatcher's heart. He pointed. "Anika!"

The shape charged behind her. The native woman spun just as her horse whinnied and reared up on its hind legs. One of the hooves struck Anika in the head, and she went down. The snowstorm engulfed her and whirled toward the fort.

Beyond the wall of snow, the charging thing roared. The horses bumped one another, running in circles.

Private Wallace raised his rifle and fired into the mist as it swallowed him. There was a loud scream. The soldier flew out and smashed against the stockade.

The white shape turned, lumbering toward Chris just beyond the storm's veil. He tried to gain control of his horse, but it galloped frantically into the woods. Branches scraped his face and shoulders. He ducked, wrapping his arms around the palomino's throat for dear life.

His horse turned too quickly. Chris slid off. Smacked the ground, landing on his side. His pistol flew into a mound.

"Jesus!" He plunged his hands into the freezing snow, digging.

Endless sleet turned the world into a blinding white hell. Grabbing the pistol, he crawled into a thicket.

Something roared like an enraged bear.

Chris wailed a cry of panic. He rubbed his eyes with frozen fingers, trying to get his vision back. Above the raging wind echoed the crunching footsteps of a predator circling him. The ground shook with each approaching step.

Chris held the pistol, hyperventilating.

Somebody please come help me!

Chris felt like a ten-year old boy again, afraid of the boogeyman. He wished his father were here to chase it away. Tell him such evils didn't exist. But this time the beast of Chris' childhood nightmares was real. And now as his vision came back into sharp focus, he saw a horrific face peering through the branches. And it was grinning.

38

Gun barrels aimed, Tom, Lt. Hysmith, and three soldiers walked side by side across the cellar. Gray light poured in through shattered windows, casting a legion of shadows among the barrels and crates. Storm winds whistled through the portals. Tom's gut burned with regret. They had stayed here too long. Private Pembrook had been found dead. But only his severed legs had been discovered. The rest of the soldier had been dragged off.

The basement stretched half the length of the lodge. At the midway point lay a trail of blood. Ropy intestines disappeared into a gleaming red hole in a log wall. Scattered across the ground were piles of bones from both animals and humans.

What kind of beast...

Tom said, "Let's leave quick."

"The hell we are," Lt. Hysmith said. "Whoever killed my soldier is still here."

The soldiers exchanged nervous glances then stared back at the hole. A sound issued from it that Tom wasn't expecting. A woman sobbing.

Lt. Hysmith stuck his light inside the portal. In the next chamber, a woman hovered in a corner. She was naked, all the bones of her spine and ribs pressing outward against blue-veined skin.

"Ma'am, are you okay?"

The woman whirled, remaining crouched. Long, black hair hung over her face. Shriveled breasts flopped on her frail chest. Her bloated stomach sagged against grossly protruding pelvic bones. Tom had seen hunger victims before, but none this skeletal.

Hysmith said, "Dear God that's Wenonah..." The lieutenant froze,, as feral eyes gleamed in the lantern glow, reflecting like a nocturnal animal. Her face was greased with red muck. She gnawed on a severed arm.

One of the soldiers yelled.

The woman loped towards the opening, half-crouched, and released a guttural snarl that reverberated around the cellar.

Tom raised his pistol. "Back away, everyone."

Before the men could raise their rifles, Wenonah lurched out of the hole with the speed of a wolf and pinned a screaming soldier to the ground. She wrenched her head, ripping out the private's throat. His screaming ended with a wet, gurgling gasp. Tom, Hysmith, and the other soldiers fired, knocking her back. As they quickly reloaded, the white ghoul rose, standing a head taller than all of them. Her stick-like limbs were too long for her body. A hunk of red flesh dangled from her lips. Her face remained in the shadows between the halos of light from two lanterns.

Lt. Hysmith fired his shotgun, blowing off her lower jaw. Wenonah screamed like a banshee, her bloody tongue dangling from the roof of her mouth. She lunged at the lieutenant, daggered nails slashing down, gripping his rifle. He and Tom blasted holes into her chest point blank. The Ojibwa woman flew backward, rolling across the floor and landing in a twisted heap against the back wall.

Cursing, the soldiers fired at her skull until there was nothing left of her head. Her decapitated skeleton kept moving. They fired again and again until her clawing hands finally went limp.

Tom's arms trembled. *We just killed Zoé's mother.*

The cellar began spinning. Tom grabbed hold of a post to keep from collapsing.

More gunshots fired. This time from outside. Everyone turned toward the windows. Some kind of beast roared, and a boy screamed.

Tom's blood ran cold.

39

"Chris!" Tom stumbled out the front door.

His heart hammered. He waded through the snow.

Sleet blurred his vision.

Outside the gate, he slipped through the entrails of a gutted horse. "No."

At the fence lay a soldier who was bloody and broken, his head twisted in the wrong direction. Anika lay facedown in the snow. Lt. Hysmith rolled her over. "She's alive."

Chris was nowhere in sight.

"Son!" Tom followed bloody tracks along the stockade.

His throat clenched. He struggled to breathe.

He raced into the woods. Branches clawing. Trees spinning. Bloody footprints everywhere. "Chris!"

The trail ended at a snow mound with red blotches.

Tom fell to his knees, digging.

He dug up a hand, an arm, a shoulder, blond hair. So much blood. When he uncovered what was left of his son's face, Tom fell back against a tree and wailed.

Part Four

Outbreak

40

The patrol of six riders returned to Fort Pendleton that evening. In the cemetery, the soldiers dug graves as a crowd of mournful villagers watched. Avery Pendleton stood among them in utter shock. Four bodies lay bundled in blankets on the snowy ground. Their boots were the only part exposed.

The mission to Manitou Outpost had brought about horrifying news and more deaths. The French Canadian fur trappers he had employed were all gone. They apparently ran out of food and cannibalized one another for survival. Pendleton had heard of such atrocities happening during the long winters, usually among the Indians. He never imagined cannibalism would happen among his own workers. The chief factor, Master Pierre Lamothe, was never found. His daughter Zoé seemed to be the only survivor. The sick girl was still tied to her bed at Hospital House, recovering from pneumonia.

The news that stabbed into Pendleton's heart like a knife was the loss of Chris Hatcher. Pendleton had encouraged Tom to move his son out to the fort, a refuge far away from Montréal where they could start a new life. Now, two weeks later, Tom Hatcher's boy was dead.

As the soldiers began digging four graves, the inspector and Brother Andre watched with solemn faces. The Jesuit missionary had his bible open and mouthed a silent prayer. Tom just stood there, his eyes bloodshot.

Pendleton offered a sympathetic look, but Tom kept his gaze on his son's covered body.

The soldiers rammed their shovels against the ground. After they removed the two-foot layer of snow, the black earth underneath was hard as slate. They were making very little progress. One of the soldiers rested on his shovel.

"Keep digging," Lt. Hysmith ordered.

"Ground's frozen solid, sir."

"Put some more muscle into it!"

The soldiers continued to chip at the ground. After a few more strikes of the spades without so much as an inch of depth, Sgt. Cox turned to his lieutenant. "Sir, looks like we gotta store the bodies till next thaw."

Lt. Hysmith nodded. "All right, get some sheets."

"No." Inspector Hatcher grabbed a shovel and started hacking at the frozen soil. He grunted as he struggled to dig his son's grave. The shovel handle snapped. He cursed and hurled the broken pieces. He fell to his knees, his hands shaking.

Pendleton put a hand on the inspector's shoulder. "Tom, I'm sorry. We're going to have to store them for now. We'll give him a proper burial at first thaw. Andre, see to it he gets home."

As the Jesuit escorted Tom away, Pendleton gazed down at the four bodies that were wrapped like mummies. He nodded toward the soldiers. "Okay, men, store them in the Dead House."

41

Tom slammed open the door of his cabin and went straight for a bottle of whiskey. He unplugged the cork and drank from the bottle. Coughing, he took a seat at the table and swigged again.

Andre stood inside the den. "Maybe you shouldn't drink so much."

Tom didn't answer, just kept gulping and coughing.

Andre sat down at the table and motioned toward the bottle. Tom slid it across the table into Andre's hand. Together the two men drank, sinking deeper into their own misery.

42

Ojibwa Village
Midnight

> *Kunetayyyyyyy.*

Kunetay Timberwolf awoke to the calling of his name. With a violent jerk, he sat up in his bedding, the buffalo hide bunched around his legs. Sweat drenched his face. Fever burned beneath his skin, but far deeper, at the center of his chest, ached a painful coldness, as if his heart had turned to ice.

Bad dreams.

The Indian rubbed his damp face and got his bearings. The small hut was filled with the soft sounds of his wife and children sleeping at the far end. He could smell their skin, their hair, the moon time blood of his wife. Kunetay's belly ached with hunger. He crawled out of bed and crouched in the orange glow from the cooking pit. He rummaged through the food, gnawing on a piece of deer jerky. He devoured all the salted venison, but it wasn't enough. Outside, there came a distant howling. Kunetay jerked his head. The wind raked its nails across the birch bark walls. *"Kunetayyyyyyy."*

The *wiitigos* had tracked him.

Somehow the trapper did not feel fear. At the doorway, the deerskin flap flew upward. The freezing gale entered his home. It whirled around him in a frosty embrace, merged with the cold in his chest. It spread to his loins, causing his member to grow stiff. He had visions of mutilated bodies. Blood on the walls. Blood on him. Voices whispered inside Kunetay's head. He grabbed a knife and approached the bed.

His wife sat up. Mumbled something about the cold.

He threw more wood on the fire. His wife buried herself beneath the fur blankets. He stood over her. One of the children got up and stared at his father with sleepy eyes.

Kunetay froze. "Go back to sleep, Little Elk." The small boy climbed back in bed with his mother.

Kunetay glared at the knife in his hand. What was he about to do?

The voices returned, whispering in his head.

"No, not them," he said.

Fully naked, the Indian stepped out into the night. He welcomed the frosty air. His bare feet stepped through the snow. His dogs barked. He opened the pen, and they backed to the corner, showing their fangs. He grabbed the closest dog by the nape and dragged it out. Behind the hut, the trees swayed, the branches clacking. The night shape-shifted into many animal forms. One towered above all the others. Kunetay craned his neck, staring upward. The full moon outlined a head with broad antlers, a long snout. The beast's fangs glistened with frozen drool as it released a breath that smelled like carrion. The thing growled. Kunetay felt his own cravings for meat as he crouched behind his dog and dragged the knife across its throat.

43

The entire fort colony—over forty men, women, and children—gathered inside the chapel for the funeral service. Wearing a black mink coat and matching hat, Willow Pendleton cried. They all hung their heads as Brother Andre gave his eulogy.

"Dear God in heaven, we are gathered here today to pay respects to those we've lost." The Jesuit lit candles at an altar that displayed oval photos of Chris Hatcher and Sakari Kennicot, as well as trinkets belonging to the victims who had died within the past three months. A flask, a comb, and a few uniform buttons represented the three soldiers who had been slain yesterday. Also on the altar was Father Jacques' rosary and bible.

The congregation stood in the nave and sang hymns. Willow stared numbly at Tom Hatcher, sitting in the front pew, stoic beside a teary-eyed Percy Kennicot. Tom's red eyes gazed at his son's photo. Willow wished she could take away Tom's pain. Seeing him lose his only child made her heart ache.

Sniffling, Willow pressed a handkerchief to her nose. Her husband Avery gripped her other hand. She searched the faces of the crowd. Lt. Hysmith stood in his red uniform along with his soldiers. Behind the garrison stood Anika Moonblood. She wasn't singing. A bandage covered part of her forehead. Willow glowered at the Ojibwa woman. Rumor was she was supposed to be protecting Chris yesterday. She probably wanted the boy to die like the others.

You put a curse on our fort, didn't you, witch?

Anika looked up. Feeling pierced by the witch's gaze, Willow glanced away.

44

One by one, the colonists approached the altar and paid their respects. When Anika got her turn, she opened a rabbit pelt, taking one last look at the object inside. The antler carving of a white buffalo was her most treasured gift from her uncle Swiftbear.

Anika held back any tears, withdrawing the sorrow into her tight face. She set the tiny buffalo on the altar beside Chris' photo. *May this guide you safely to the land of White Buffalo.*

Tom stepped beside her, whispering his own prayer. His eyes were full of pain and rage. Anika felt she needed to say something.

Apologize. But there were no words.

Brother Andre and the mourners sang more hymns. The native woman walked back up the center aisle, feeling a dozen angry eyes upon her, accusing her. A man mouthed the word "Witch," then returned to his singing. She walked back to her pew feeling as if a clawed hand were wrapped around her heart, squeezing tighter and tighter.

The chapel went quiet. Everyone bowed their heads.

Brother Andre held open his bible. "'Ashes to ashes and dust to dust...'"

When the service was over, Anika remained seated as the mourners left the chapel. Avery Pendleton tugged at his wife's arm, but she shrugged it off. He walked up the aisle, buttoning his black fur coat. He grimaced and tipped his hat at Anika, then exited the chapel.

As Brother Andre went to his chambers, Anika found herself inside the nave with only Tom Hatcher and Willow Pendleton. The chief factor's wife sat in the second row pew, sniffling. Why had she remained behind?

Anika approached the altar. Candlelight outlined the silhouette of Tom's head. She set a hand onto the inspector's shoulder. He tensed, but let her keep it there. Pulling out his son's whittled flute, Tom blew into it, whistling a shrill sound that had no melody.

45

Brother Andre tapped on the open door to Master Pendleton's office. "Sir, I was wondering if I could speak with you about a matter?"

The chief factor was sitting at his desk, writing notes in his log. Without looking up, he said, "I'll be with you in a moment. Have a seat."

Andre sat down in one of the plush leather chairs that faced the enormous cherry-wood desk. He surveyed all the mounted antlers and stuffed animals, including a marble-eyed wolverine that seemed to bare its fangs at the corner of the chief factor's desk.

Pendleton stabbed his quill into an inkwell. "All right, so what is this matter?"

Andre fidgeted with his hands. "It's regarding Father Jacques' diary, sir. His request was that it reach Father Xavier at the Notre Dame basilica in Montréal. The message seems urgent and, after all that's happened—"

"With Father Jacques dead, the diary serves no purpose now."

"But maybe if Father Xavier translated it, we could learn more about what happened at Manitou Outpost."

"We've assessed what happened. The bloody trappers turned cannibal on each other. It occurs out here during winter, especially at the more remote posts. Sorry, Andre, but your priest chose the wrong fort to do his mission work."

His heart ached for the loss of his mentor. "But Father Jacques stressed how important the diary is to the Church. He risked the life of a little girl to deliver it to us."

Pendleton sighed, "What are you proposing? That I send my couriers to Montréal in the middle of winter?"

"Actually, sir" --Andre sat forward-- "I wish to deliver it personally. The bishop needs to be informed that Father Jacques was killed."

"And how do you propose to get there?"

"I was hoping your *voyageurs* could take me in one of the canoes. I just need to get to Ottawa. From there I could catch the ferry—"

"Out of the question. No one leaves the fort until spring."

"But it would only take a few days—"

"My decision is final, Andre! End of discussion."

Andre huffed, his upper lip shaking. "Then may I at least have his diary back?"

"No, it's staying with me." Pendleton returned to writing in his log. "Now, if you'll kindly see yourself out, I have more urgent matters to deal with."

Andre glowered at the chief factor. He had disliked Avery Pendleton since the day the Jesuit missionaries had first left Quebec and journeyed to Fort Pendleton. Now, with the denial to carry out his mentor's holy mission, Andre wanted to dump the inkwell on Pendleton's stubborn head. But Andre had endured enough Catholic discipline to refrain from acting out his hostile emotions. And he had plenty of self-inflicted bruises to remind himself of his devotion to the Church.

As Andre rose to leave, Lt. Hysmith knocked at the open door. "Beg your pardon, Master Pendleton, but we got an Indian messenger outside the gate. There's been more killings at their village."

46

A patrol of soldiers on horseback followed an Indian messenger across the creek to the Ojibwa village. Tom and Anika rode among them, gripping rifles. Tom's head ached from a hangover. Vengeance burned in his blood.

As the horse riders rode into the village, Tom saw several red patches in the snow. Anika made a sobbing sound and put a hand to her mouth. According to the Indian messenger, Kunetay Timberwolf had gone on a murderous rampage in the middle of the night. At least ten men, women, and even a few children were missing. One trapper's body was lying facedown. His head was split with an axe, the weapon left jutting from the back of his skull. The killer's bloody tracks crisscrossed into numerous trails. As Tom and Anika dismounted their horses, Chief Mokomaan approached with three Indian warriors. They all carried bows nocked with arrows.

"What happened?" Tom asked.

The old chief shook his head as he gazed at the carnage all around them.

Tom searched the village for the killer. "Where is Kunetay?"

"Gone," Chief Mokomaan said, his voice filled with pain. "Into the woods."

Tom said to Lt. Hysmith, "Spread out the men and find Kunetay." With the lieutenant relaying orders, the dozen soldiers charged off on a manhunt.

Anika said, "Is Grandmother Spotted Owl alive?"

"She's with the tribe." Mokomaan pointed to a large wigwam where two warriors guarded the entrance. Anika hurried to the wigwam and stepped inside. Tom felt a stabbing in his chest, as he remembered the night Chris had been sitting among the elders and smoking a ceremonial pipe. He suppressed the pain, doing his best to concentrate on the crime scene. Tom turned to the chief. "Where is Kunetay's hut?"

Mokomaan led him to a birch bark hut that was set off from the others, bordering the tree line. The air reeked of offal. The gate to a dog pen stood open. There were no huskies inside, but the snow was saturated with blood and tufts of fur. At the hut's entrance, Tom saw something on the outside wall that stopped him in his tracks.

Red spirals. A dozen of them were marked around the entrance.

Tom turned to the chief. "What do these symbols mean?"

Mokomaan kept his distance from the hut. "Warnings of evil spirits."

Tom stepped inside Kunetay's hut. Butchered limbs and ropy entrails hung from the rafters. Boiling in a stewpot was a woman's head and heart. Tom covered his nose with a handkerchief and explored the rest of the hut. In the dark corner lay two small bodies. What the trapper had done to his own children turned Tom's stomach. He stepped back outside as Anika was approaching.

Tom marched past her. "We have another cannibal on the loose." He cocked his Winchester rifle, heading toward the woods. "Let's find the son of a bitch."

47

Fort Pendleton

Hospital House

Willow sat in a rocking chair, cradling an Indian doll. Zoé Lamothe was still sleeping, her thin arms tied to the bedposts. She hadn't woken in over a day, and Doc Riley had said she might have gone into a coma. The girl was unaware that her mother was dead and her father missing. Zoé was the only known survivor who had escaped the massacre at Manitou Outpost. The thought that Pierre Lamothe might well be dead troubled Willow. She had first met the French Canadian officer back in Montréal last summer. She was attending a company banquet with Avery. Pierre, a handsome gentleman in his thirties, had sat next to her. As Avery gave one of his typical speeches about the upcoming fur-trading season, Willow had felt a hand caress her thigh. Her heart rising in her chest, she glanced toward Pierre. He gazed at her with a mischievous look in his eyes.

A wheezing sound snapped Willow out of her reverie. Once again, Zoé's eyelids were half-open, the pale white irises gazing blankly.

Willow shivered. She left the girl's room and sat down at the kitchen table with Doc and Myrna Riley. The elderly couple were playing cards.

Doc asked, "Did Zoé wake up yet?"

"Not so much as a stir. Her forehead is ice cold."

"I don't know how that lass keeps hanging on. She should be dead." Doc coughed into a handkerchief. His skin had a sick pallor to it, as if he were coming down with a cold.

"Take some more castor oil," Myrna said.

"I just had some." He winked at Willow. "Sometimes she forgets who the doctor is in this house."

Myrna dealt the cards. "He forgets I worked in a hospital in Dublin for fifteen years before he dragged me out to this godforsaken land."

"You love Canada and you know it."

Willow smiled as the old couple quarreled. The three drank tea and played a hand of Reverse, her favorite card game.

"Christ, this pain," Doc Riley grumbled when it was his turn to deal. He peeled back the bandage on his hand. The bite had turned the skin a purplish-black. Vile yellow pus oozed from Zoé's teeth marks. Three fingers had swollen to the size of sausages.

Myrna shook her head. "Quit fussing with it."

"It burns like the Devil's tits." Doc pressed a knife to the engorged skin and lanced out more of the mucus. "Get me some more morphine, will you, love?"

"You're getting poison all over my clean floor," Myrna said. "Come with me. I'll redress it for you."

The Rileys went down the hall to the apothecary room, leaving Willow alone at the table. She heard a cough coming from the dark bedroom where Zoé slept. The door stood partially ajar. *I should probably go in there and check on her again. Maybe feed her another spoonful of castor oil.* But Willow didn't budge from her seat. The girl's strange, white-membraned eyes gave her gooseflesh.

Willow dealt herself a hand of Solitaire. Her fingers trembled.

There was another reason she was feeling a bit unsettled today. Inspector Hatcher, the man who had sparked life back into her heart, had left this morning on another dangerous mission. She prayed that Tom and the other men returned safely.

A strange groan sent a chill up Willow's spine. She turned toward the bedroom, listening. There it was again, a raspy moan from the darkness beyond the doorway. *Zoé must have woken up.* The door slowly swung open, the hinges creaking. Had the girl gotten out of bed? Impossible. She was tied down. The candlelight in the main room illuminated the foot of the bed. It was too dark to see if Zoé was still in it.

Willow grabbed a candle and approached the open door to the bedroom, trying to make out the lump buried beneath the covers. "Zoé, everything all right?"

The girl growled like some kind of animal. In the murky room, her shadow moved on all fours. Willow reeled. The shape of the girl's head looked all wrong, twisted at an impossible angle. Zoé hissed. A draft blew out the candle in Willow's hand. Pitch darkness blinded her. Before she reached the door, it slammed shut. "Hey!" Willow twisted the knob, but it wouldn't open.

"What's the matter?" Myrna Riley asked from the end of the hall. Her candle parted the darkness, illuminated the closed door to Zoé's room.

"That little hellion's holding the knob." Willow put her weight into it, but the door felt like it was nailed shut.

"Here, lass, step aside." Myrna pounded. "Child, open the door now, you hear?"

There was a sound of nails scraping down the door. The two women yelped.

Behind the door echoed more growls, as if a feral dog were on the other side. Feet scampered across the wood floor.

Inside the bedroom, glass shattered. The door opened on its own, swinging inward. A cold draft blew Willow's hair. She and Myrna rushed into the room. The bed was empty, the frayed ropes lying loose across the blanket.

Willow ran to the broken window. Outside, bloody footprints trailed off across the snowfield behind Hospital House.

48

The forest behind Kunetay's hut was thick with brambles. The hunting party of soldiers spread out through the pines. Every man was quiet except for the sounds of his boots crunching the snow and branches scraping against coats and rifles. Tom, hell-bent on getting the first shot at the cannibal, led the manhunt.

From behind, Anika called, "Tom, slow down. You're going to get yourself killed."

"We can't let him get away." Tom charged forward at an unrelenting pace. He stepped over pools of blood and splintered bones. With each tree he rounded, he anticipated a crazed Indian leaping out.

The blood trail led into a clearing surrounded by tall spruce. Scattered about were carcasses of dogs and humans who had been torn apart, gnawed upon, and then discarded.

The soldiers gathered, speechless.

Among the red footprints were dozens of larger tracks, like the ones they'd found near Sakari Kennicot's body two days ago.

Anika crouched beside the bear-sized tracks.

"Are these from Silvertip?" Tom asked.

"*Maji-manidoog.*" Chief Mokomaan said, shaking his head. "*Wiitigo.*"

Lt. Hysmith and his soldiers all glanced at one another suspiciously.

The chief continued speaking in his native tongue, pointing toward the woods surrounding the clearing.

Tom looked at Anika. "What's he saying?"

She stood, dusting snow off her hands. "The *wiitigo* is an evil spirit that roams the woods in winter. It comes from the islands of Makade

Lake and feeds on every animal and man in its path."

"Rubbish," Tom said. "It was Kunetay who murdered all those people last night. I saw what he did to his own family. He turned cannibal."

Chief Mokomaan spouted off words in an angry tone, his fierce gaze now fixed on Tom.

Anika interpreted, "He says it was the *wiitigo* that turned Kunetay cannibal. He was feeding the others."

"What others?" Tom asked.

She gestured to the many footprints in the snow. "There are more *wiitigos* out there hunting in a pack." Anika put a hand on Tom's shoulder. "We must go, before they return to feed again."

49

Fort Pendleton

Avery Pendleton trudged across the snowfield, following the small bloody footprints. *Damn that heathen child.* He glanced over his shoulder at Willow and Doc. "What the hell was Zoé thinking?"

"I don't know." Willow sloughed through the snow, holding up the hem of her dress. "She just turned wild and escaped out the window."

"She may have dementia." Doc coughed into his handkerchief.

"You shouldn't be out here," Willow said. "Let Avery and I find her."

Doc carried his medical kit. "The girl needs immediate attention. With her running barefoot in this mess, I might have to amputate a few toes."

"That girl is nothing but trouble," Avery said. "We never should have allowed her into the fort."

His wife scoffed. "That's Pierre's daughter you're talking about. You would have just left her in the woods to die?"

"She was already deathly ill," Avery said. "If she had died out there, it would have been the priest's fault for sending her. Now she's become my responsibility. If she dies while in our possession..."

"We'll find her," Willow said.

The trail showed disturbing signs that the girl had fallen a couple times in the knee-deep snow. Red patches and streaks indicated that her hands were equally as shredded as her feet. The failure of Pendleton's company suddenly flashed before his eyes. The Montréal partners were going to have his neck in a noose if this incident led to any kind of feud among the wintering partners.

Avery followed the continuation of bloody footprints, wondering if the frozen corpse he was sure to find at the end of this trail would also mean the downfall of Pendleton Fur Trading Company. Master Lamothe had the power to bring down this company if he felt Avery was at fault for his daughter's death.

A gunshot blasted, echoing across the fort.

Avery hurried between two cabins. Twenty yards away, the animal caretaker, Farlan McDuff, was gripping a shotgun outside the barn.

Avery screamed, "Goddamnit, McDuff! What are you shooting for?"

"I saw some animal attacking me goats." The Scotsman pointed to the thatch-roofed pen next to the barn. The mewling goats were bumping against one another.

"You fool, that was a child, not an animal." Avery grabbed McDuff's shotgun.

"It didn't look like no..."

The herd cleared to reveal a slain baby goat, its throat ripped out. Next to it was a severed human foot. The girl's blood trail ended at the barn's open double doors. From inside came the sound of a child wailing.

"God damn it, McDuff!" Avery tossed the shotgun. He looked across the fort to see if anyone had come running in response to the gunshot. No one did. Fortunately today all the soldiers were out in the woods. The watchtowers were empty.

Doc examined the severed foot. "We need to do something." The physician started for the barn, but Avery grabbed his arm. "Not yet, Doc."

"But Zoé could be bleeding to death."

"Well it's her damned fault for leaving the hospital," Avery said.

Inside the barn, the girl's wailing changed to a sputtering, croaking sound and then went silent.

"Dear God, she's dead," Willow cried. "You fools killed her!"

Avery put his hands on his wife's shoulders. "Woman, calm yourself! I'll handle this matter." The chief factor paced. He saw himself sitting before his board members, trying to explain how he could have let such an atrocious incident happen under his command. His partners could never know this happened. After a moment of thinking, a solution began to form. Avery rubbed his palms together. "Doc, McDuff, listen up."

The doctor and stubble-faced caretaker gathered with the fort chief and his wife. Avery pointed down at the severed foot. "This never happened. If we find her dead, we must dispose of her before anyone knows how she died."

Willow said, "You can't be serious."

"I'm dead serious. If word of this gets back to my partners, you and I could lose everything." She glared at him with hateful eyes, but he knew how much she loved her fancy dresses and furs and servants and all the accoutrements that went along with being his wife. She would keep quiet. Avery could see the other two men were thinking it over. "Doc, the girl was your responsibility. Do you want her death tainting your record?"

The old man shook his head.

"And McDuff, you stupid fool. You blew off a little girl's foot. I'm willing to overlook this, if you'll keep hush about it."

McDuff nodded. "Whatever you say, Master Pendleton."

"Good. Then we'll go in there together. Retrieve her body. McDuff, you take her outside the fort and bury her in the woods."

"Ground's too frozen."

"Then take her far off and leave her for the wolves."

"Avery, how can you be so heartless?" said Willow. "Maybe there's hope. She still could be alive."

"Doubtful," Doc said. "She's lost too much blood."

"But what if she is?"

Avery glared at his wife, wishing she were anywhere else. The woman was too damned emotional. He thought of asking McDuff to go in there and finish off the heathen in case she was still hanging on to a thread of life.

"If she's still alive, then there's a chance I can stop the bleeding," Doc Riley said. "I could do surgery on her leg to make it look like I amputated the foot due to frostbite, which she is certain to have by now. Then the blame falls back on the priest for sending her out into the storm."

Avery liked the plan. "Do you have a tranquilizer in that kit of yours?"

The old man pulled out a syringe. "This will put her out till Christmas."

"Good, then let's go in assuming she's still alive. Willow, stay outside and let us know if anyone is coming." Avery grabbed a lantern that hung near the door and lit it.

"McDuff, when we find the girl, you wrap her up in one of those horse blankets while Doc sticks her." Raising the lantern, Avery stepped through the entrance, his boots padding across dry earth and hay. The musty barn had no windows. Gray light filtered in through cracks and holes in the timber walls. The space beyond the haystacks was as pitch dark as a coal mine. The dirt floor was littered with bloody feathers. The sight of this brought a moan from Farlan McDuff. "Ah, me chickens."

Crimson puddles led to a large chicken coop at the far corner.

"Zoé?" Avery eased toward the open wire-mesh door. A shadow shape moved on all fours, retreating away from the light.

"Oh *shite*, she's still alive," said the doctor.

"Be careful, sir," McDuff said, holding up the horse blanket.

"Doc, ready with your needle?"

"Ready."

"I'll flush her out." Avery peered into the coop, his lantern lighting up a dozen mutilated chickens. Zoé was crouched in the back corner. Her face and chest were covered with blood and feathers. Strings of entrails dangled from her mouth. The girl looked so thin and frail. Avery opened the door farther. "Come on out, Zoé."

The girl craned her head, drawing back her lips like a dog, exposing gray gums and gnarled teeth. Growling, she scampered across the dirt floor.

Avery kicked the door closed and dropped down the latch just as the girl rammed against the cage.

Bony fingers, pale as alabaster, clawed through the wire mesh.

50

At half past midnight, Farlan McDuff climbed out of bed cursing the moon. He could hear his goats outside at the barn, bleating and running back and forth, their hooves pounding the frozen ground.

"Ah hell," McDuff pulled on his clothes and fur parka, grabbed his double-barrel shotgun, and stepped out the back door.

The two-story barn's silhouette stood roughly fifty paces behind McDuff's cabin. The dark shapes of the herd were running around inside their pen. "Something's definitely got 'em spooked."

The livestock caretaker knew his twenty goats like they were his own kin. He could tell all of them apart and had given each a name.

As McDuff made the cold hike toward the barn, he searched around for the mongrel causing the disturbance. He hoped it was just a dog. Anika Moonblood, who lived in a cabin across the cemetery from McDuff, had a wolf-dog named Makade. It was a real nuisance, always sniffing around the barn and unsettling the goats and chickens. He'd like to kill the bastard, but the last thing McDuff wanted to do was start a feud with an Indian witch.

Earlier today he had thought he was shooting at the wolf-dog, when instead he had shot the girl. What a mess that was. He had aimed at the ground behind her and didn't mean to hit her. But the damage was done, her foot blown off at the ankle. McDuff felt sore about the whole experience, but a bit relieved, too, once he saw that she had caught some form of rabies. She had killed his youngest goat, Little Micmac, which broke McDuff's heart.

The thought that Zoé was still locked up inside the chicken coop didn't make him sleep any easier. McDuff didn't know why the fort chief wanted to keep her alive. She had clearly changed into something that was no longer a little girl. Then a thought struck McDuff. What if Zoé broke out of her cage? Impossible. He had built that cage strong enough to hold wild hogs.

He reached the pen. The goats were gathered in the far corner, climbing on top of one another as if trying to escape over the fence. Everything was moving shadows against a white ground. It was darker than usual tonight. The moonlight shining through the clouds offered just enough illumination to see a couple mounds that McDuff knew by the knot in his gut were dead goats.

"Ah, ballocks." He grabbed the lantern he kept hanging at the barn's entrance and lit it. He stepped into the pen and held the light over the two mounds. Sure enough, some predator had gotten into the pen and torn two of the goats to pieces. "What a bloody mess. Zoé!"

McDuff searched around to see if that damn girl might have broken out after all. The last time he saw Zoé, she seemed to have grown, her spine and limbs long and bony. She had paced her cage on all fours, hobbling like a wounded jackal. Had she grown strong enough to bust loose?

"Child, are you out there?" A disturbing mewl from the darkness made McDuff's scrotum tighten. He approached the frightened herd. "Easy there, I'm here now." He could hear teeth crunching. He held up the lantern. The goats split off into two herds running along the fence in opposite directions. Only one remained—the billy goat named Haggis. He had a large head with thick, curled horns. Haggis' snout was dripping with red muck. The ram's teeth moved side to side as he chomped on raw meat. On the ground was another dead goat.

Haggis looked up at McDuff. The caretaker gasped. The horned goat's eyes had turned solid white. The fur on its face and body hung in patches like it had some form of mange. The billy goat ambled toward him, bleating and shaking its head.

McDuff backed toward the center of the pen. "No, Haggis." He set the lantern down and aimed the shotgun, his arms shaking. As McDuff was about to pull the trigger, something bumped his legs from behind. He fell hard on his rump. The shotgun flew out of his hands. McDuff searched around, confused. At the edge of the lantern glow stood the other goats, surrounding him in a perfect circle.

Every goat had poached-white eyes. They mewled together.

McDuff crawled for the shotgun.

The curled-horned goat roared. The herd charged toward the old man in the center of the circle. As Haggis bit into his throat, McDuff feared he was going straight to hell, because his last image was the goat-eyed face of the devil.

51

The next morning, the soldiers found Farlan McDuff's bones in a red pile, his hair-covered skull sitting atop the stack. The goats were gathered in the far corner of the pen, pale white eyes watching Tom, Lt. Hysmith, and the other soldiers. The herd appeared to have the same disease as Zoé. Several mounds of fur and gore lay strewn about the pen, victims of the hungry herd. The lead billy goat, with its red-stained face and curvy horns, charged the fence. Tom and his gunmen fired shots into the pen, ripping the ram to pieces. They turned their rifle barrels toward the herd and dropped every last goat.

The soldiers made a bonfire and burned the infected bodies. Under Master Pendleton's orders, they threw McDuff's bones onto the flaming heap for safe measure. The stench of cooking meat and burning fur made Tom's eyes water. Some of the dead goats spasmed, their legs kicking and heads jerking as the fire consumed their bodies.

The soldiers looked in shock at the loss of the animal caretaker. Tom had only known Farlan McDuff a couple weeks. Chris had taken a shine to the old Scotsman and helped him feed the animals in the evenings. McDuff had been one of the few villagers whom Tom had felt comfortable allowing them to spend time with his son. Seeing the man's bones pop like logs in the fire filled Tom's stomach with acid. As he and the soldiers silently watched the fire, Willow ran toward them, screaming about Doc Riley.

52

Tom and the soldiers marched to Hospital House. All the front windows were broken. Doc Riley was making a hell of a lot of racket inside. The garrison aimed their rifles at the two-story white house.

Tom shouted, "Doc, why don't you make this easy and come on out?"

A shriek sent nervous looks among the soldiers.

Hysmith said, "He has the sickness."

Tom looked back at Master Pendleton, who stood at a distance. "What do you want us to do?"

Pendleton said, "We all know what has to be done."

Tom said, "Men, stay out here. If Doc comes outside, don't let him touch you. Lieutenant, follow me." He and Hysmith kicked open the front door.

Blood stains covered the den's wood floor. In the dining room, a pile of human bones lay in a clotted puddle on the table. In the kitchen, they found what looked to be Myrna Riley's skull and neck bone, her gray hair fanning out across the floor.

Rifles aimed, Tom and Hysmith walked shoulder to shoulder down a hallway. A door marked with a red spiral stood partway open. At the sight of the marking, Tom's stomach turned. Inside Riley's bedroom, a shadow moved across the wall. The floor creaked. They entered the room, barrels pointed at the ghoulish thing smearing red spirals on the wall with his hands. Doc Riley had changed so completely, the only recognizable feature was his bald forehead and bushy sideburns. His body had withered away to something skeletal with blanched white skin. He was taller, too, now towering over Tom and Hysmith by at least a foot. Doc's arms bent at impossible angles. Moaning, he opened his mouth, webs of sticky drool clinging to his teeth.

As Doc Riley lurched, Tom and Hysmith pulled their triggers.

53

Pendleton led the garrison to the barn.

The gunmen set their lanterns on the haystacks. Pendleton watched Inspector Hatcher's eyes as he got a clear look at the pale-skinned creature crouched inside the chicken coop. *Creature* was definitely the proper word for it. What had days ago been a little girl now looked nothing like the Métis child Avery had seen sitting on Pierre Lamothe's lap. Now she had an elongated head. Her eyes were white and devoid of pupils. Thin skin stretched over stick-like bones that made popping sounds as Zoé paced. When the gunmen got closer, the girl's bloodstained teeth gnawed at the wire mesh.

"That thing brought the disease in here," Pendleton said. "It must be put to death."

Among the executioners, Inspector Hatcher stared with a stone cold face. "Let's bloody get on with it."

Lt. Hysmith raised his arm. "Aim." The six gunmen raised their rifles. "Fire!"

Part Five

Desperation

54

That night, Avery entered Willow's private boudoir and climbed into bed with her. The fort master felt riled up from the events of the day. He needed a release. Willow was lying on her side, turned away from him. He put a hand on her shoulder. She shrugged it off.

He sighed. "For the last time, it had to be done, Willow."

She clung to the Indian doll that had belonged to Zoé.

"Oh, *bugger*," Avery said. "I've been doing all I can."

"You wanted that child dead from the beginning." She knew how to twist the daggers that cut at his pride.

"I'm *concerned* about the welfare of the colonists. We have a crisis on our hands, and all you can think to do is decorate for a Christmas ball."

She sniffled into her pillow. "I'm trying to raise people's spirits."

"Well, you can forget about this year's ball. I cancelled it."

"How could you?" She cried into her pillow.

Avery stroked her arm. "Willow, be sensible."

"Don't touch me." She pulled away and ran into her powder room.

"Ah, to bloody hell with you!" Avery tossed one of her pillows and walked out of the room, slamming the door.

55

Anika carried a lantern into the enclosed dog pen behind her cabin. The huskies were restless this evening. She tossed scraps of meat into their bowls in case they were hungry. None of them ate. She put her hands on her hips. "What is it?"

The eight huskies looked up at her with sad eyes and moaned. She looked out at the stockade that separated the cabins from the forest. "Is there something out there?"

Did they sense the *wiitigos* that attacked the Ojibwa village? Or maybe they felt her own emptiness. It had been a tough year, and tonight was weighing heavy on her heart. She drank from her leather flask. The rum burned down easy, warming her stomach.

Anika sat down against the wall inside the pen. The dogs gathered around her, licking her hands and cheeks. She giggled, surprised to hear herself laugh. She petted their bushy fur, and the dogs settled, lying around her. Only one dog remained sitting on its haunches. Makade, the lead male. His pointed ears were perked. He stared at Anika with bright blue eyes, his head slightly cocked. As always, she sensed her late husband's spirit watching her through Makade's eyes. The black dog, a mix of husky and wolf, had been her husband's favorite.

She promised herself she wouldn't think of Ben tonight, but how could she not? This time two winters ago she and her husband had been taking their dogs for a walk outside the fort like they did each afternoon. Makade, who was the most adventurous, set off into the forest. Ben went searching for him alone. Anika had no idea that day would be his last. *I should have searched with him.* She knew these woods better than he had, how to avoid their dangers.

She took another swig of rum.

At once, all eight dogs lifted their heads and turned toward the pen's gate. Footsteps crunched over the snow. The huskies stood, barking.

"Who's out there?" she asked.

No one approached. Finally, the dogs settled.

Anika said goodnight to each of them and returned to her ramshackle of a cabin. As she climbed her porch steps, a heavy feeling burdened her chest. It would be another night of sleeping in an empty bed. While most of the trappers ogled her and patted her rear end, they would never choose her as a mate. At age thirty, Anika was well past ripe. Most white men wanted a squaw who was between twelve and fourteen. A fresh bloom to deflower. Anika was left to wither on her own. She feared dying a lonely widow.

She opened her door and paused at the threshold. The air inside reeked of foul tobacco. A figure sat in a rocking chair in the corner. An orange glow from a pipe lit up Avery Pendleton's face. He raised a tumbler of liquor. "Where have you been?"

She tensed her shoulders and closed the door.

He stood, his dark frame rising above her. "Answer me."

"I couldn't sleep, so I checked on the dogs." Anika's throat tightened until she could barely breathe. She circled Pendleton in a wide arc and stepped to the nook of her kitchen. She guzzled the last of her rum and set the flask on the table. She kept her eyes on the wall. "Shouldn't you be with your wife?"

"I'll be with whoever I damn well please."

"Then I'm sure there's a servant girl who would welcome your charms."

"You have a sharp tongue for a heathen woman."

She flinched at the sound of a match striking wood. The room illuminated with the flickering of an oil lamp. Pendleton's crooked shadow moved along the wall toward Anika's. She retreated inward, seeking the strength to stand up to him. "My grandmother taught me to say what is my womanly right to say."

"Your grandmother was banished for being a witch," Pendleton said. "Perhaps you should be reminded that living here is a privilege. The other native women must be married to live inside the fort." He was behind her now, breathing close to her neck. "There's a reason I take special care of you." His hand touched her shoulder, gripped a knot of her long hair. "I am your master." He bent her over the table. Anika clenched her eyes shut, hearing the familiar chink of his buckle and the drop of his trousers. "And you have a womanly duty."

56

An hour later, feeling less tense, Avery Pendleton sat in his study smoking his pipe, trying to ignore Willow's sobbing coming from down the hall. He should have known better than to bring a refined city woman out to the wilderness.

He poured himself a tumbler of brandy and pulled his favorite violin off the shelf. The instrument, painted bright red, gleamed in the glow of his kerosene lamp. The violin had been hand-crafted by his grandfather, Sir William Pendleton, who owned an instrument shop in London when Avery was a boy. His chest swelled as he remembered the summers spent assisting his grandfather, sweeping out the wood shavings and bringing in supplies. The shop always smelled of fresh spruce and maple. The walls down in the cellar were covered with shells of violins, violas, cellos, and fiddles waiting to be caressed by the master's hands. Avery had spent hours watching Sir William deftly shaping the wood with his knives, chisels, and gouges. He'd paint and varnish the instruments and string them with steady fingers. His styles modeled Amati, Guarneri, and Stradivari, the famed violin makers from Cremona, Italy. In the evenings, Sir William taught Avery how to play everything from Mozart on a violin to an Irish jig on a fiddle. "Every instrument has its own soul," his grandfather had said. "When you pluck the strings and drag your bow across like this" --he closed his eyes and dragged the bow up and down across the middle strings with a melody that vibrated in Avery's chest-- "you channel that soul for everyone to hear. You become one with the music."

The red violin Avery now held was a Stradivari. He cherished it most, because it was the first instrument Sir William had allowed him to stain. The color red symbolized the power Avery had felt as he was changing from a boy into a man. He placed his chin on the violin's chinrest and gripped the neck. He gently set his fingertips on the fingerboard. He plucked a few strings to make sure they were in tune. Satisfied, he closed his eyes and played a serenade by Mozart called Eine Kleine Nachtmusik. He escaped into the music, allowing his mind to relax and float with the vibration of the melody. His fingers massaged the strings like a lover. He played for over an hour, smiling the entire time, and when he finally stopped, he wiped his damp eyes with a handkerchief. If only Sir William were still alive to hear his pupil play. After his grandfather's death, when Avery turned twelve, he began to play like a master violinist, as if Sir William's ghost were channeling through him. Avery had wanted to play in an orchestra, but his father abhorred the idea and steered Avery into becoming a fur trader with Hudson's Bay Company.

He set the violin back on the shelf and sipped his brandy. He noticed that Willow's room had gone silent. Whenever she got upset, he could always soothe her with his music.

Avery's mind now at ease, he concentrated on the problems at hand. The colony had narrowly missed being wiped out like Manitou Outpost by some strange form of rabies. Inspector Hatcher had described a dog there as having the same condition as the goats. The Ojibwa believed that people and animals could be haunted by evil spirits. Last night one of the trappers went on a rampage and slaughtered over a dozen people. Kunetay Timberwolf was now missing, as were Pierre Lamothe and several trappers. Pendleton thought of Zoé and Doc Riley. The infected had become savage animals reduced to predator instincts. Their bodies looked as if they had been eating themselves from within. After the doctor was bitten, it had taken him two days to turn.

After the executions, Pendleton had assembled every man, woman, and child inside the chapel. Thirty colonists altogether. With the help of Brother Andre, who had once worked in a hospital, they checked everyone for signs of white scabs, exposed blue veins, or symptoms of pneumonia or dementia. Fortunately no one had been around the doctor in the past couple days except Avery, Willow, Farlan McDuff, and Tom Hatcher. Everyone was clear. The disease was contained and destroyed with the bodies they burned outside the fort.

But with a hungry pack of cannibals stalking the woods, Pendleton feared his problems were far from over. "I have to get more help." He opened a drawer to his desk, pulled out Father Jacques' diary, and read the enclosed letter.

I pray this diary reaches Father Xavier Goddard at the Notre-Dame Basilica in Montréal. It is of dire importance. The Jesuits are the only ones who can stop the madness that has befallen our village.

The journal was written in Aramaic. Pendleton leaned back in his chair. What had the priest written in the coded portion?

57

Brother Andre awoke to someone knocking at his door. It was still dark outside. He checked his pocketwatch. 2:00 a.m. He rubbed his eyes.

More pounding knocks. "Andre, wake up." Pendleton's voice.

Andre climbed out of his single bed and opened the door.

The company owner entered. "Pack your things. You're leaving tomorrow morning for Montréal."

Andre smiled. "Bless you, sir."

"I will be going with you. I need to take care of some business there. You will hand-deliver this diary to Father Xavier. Find out if the Jesuits know how to stop this bloody disease."

58

Next morning, Anika felt a fiery pain between her thighs as she and her dog Makade exited the fort's gate. The sentry up in the watchtower whistled down to her. "Ey, pretty bird, you be careful out there in them woods. The beasts might smell your lovely red meat and *eatcha.*" He laughed hoarsely and spat tobacco.

Anika flicked her hand at him and kept walking. She had no fear of Kunetay Timberwolf. She wanted to put an arrow through each of his eyes. Carrying her bow with an arrow nocked, she and her favorite husky crossed the bridge over Beaver Creek and followed the meandering trail through the forest. Makade woofed. Noises were coming from ahead—axes cutting wood, people shouting, horses whinnying. Beyond the trees she could see the twenty birch bark huts that made up the Ojibwa village. She entered, shocked to see every tribe member was out and packing up their horses and sleds. Women and children were being guided into canoes that were loaded down with bundles of supplies.

Anika spotted Pendleton and Hysmith speaking with the chief and several warriors. They appeared to be in a heated debate. Anika ducked behind a hut. She stopped a young scout and spoke her native language. "Why is everyone packing?"

"We're leaving today," he said. "Migrating to Otter Island."

No! Anika thought as she left the boy and hurried through the bustling crowd. Her heart pounded against her breastbone as she made her way to a hut covered in buffalo hides. Her uncle Swiftbear was out front, strapping his huskies into a dogsled. He looked older today, with more silver hair interwoven with the black. The dogs yipped at the sight of Makade, one of their cousins.

"Swiftbear?"

The stout man turned around. "What are you doing here, Little Pup?"

She hugged him. "I heard the village is migrating."

"We must." He nodded toward the trees. "The *wiitigos* are hunting in our territory again. I wanted to hunt Kunetay down and kill him for what he done." He sighed. "But Chief says we must go."

Anika knew about the beasts of the Ojibwa legends. The natives believed the *wiitigos* were immortal creatures that blew in with the blizzards and took animal forms. Anika had learned about evil spirits through her uncle's campfire tales. When she was a little girl, she swore she heard a *wiitigo* once, snapping branches in the forest, making guttural huffing noises. Every few winters Ojibwa trappers were found half-eaten in the woods. When this happened, the tribe would pack up and migrate down river.

Swiftbear said, "The Mediwiwin are gathering at Otter Island."

The Mediwiwin were a circle of medicine men and women from the various tribes. Swiftbear and Grandmother Spotted Owl were both members.

Anika gripped her uncle's forearm. "Take me with you."

"I wish I could, Little Pup, but you belong to the white traders. Chief will make you return, then take away my rum. I need my rum."

Anika teared up. She knew Chief Mokomaan would never let her go. When her husband Ben died, she became Master Pendleton's property. She had wanted to return to her tribe, but Avery gave the chief a fancy fur coat and tophat in exchange for Anika. At first, she was told she would be working as the fort's field guide and translator. It wasn't long before Anika learned that Master Pendleton had other uses for her. Now, even if she did manage to sneak herself and her dogs out with her uncle, at some point on her journey, one of the tribe members would tell the chief. Anika would be left behind or returned to the fort, where brutal punishment would await. Avery Pendleton would kill one of her dogs, just like he did to Minagwi the day Anika spat in Avery's face and refused him sex. She had to stay behind. Leaving would only bring suffering to everyone she loved.

She hugged her uncle. "I'm going to miss you, Swiftbear."

"Keep safe, Little Pup. We return in spring."

She nodded, wiping her eyes. She hugged each of the dogs, who barked and licked her face. Then she entered a wigwam. "Grandmother?"

The interior was dark except for the glowing embers of a central fire pit. Coon tails and strings of bones and feathers dangled from the ceiling. As her eyes adjusted, Anika saw the form of an old woman sitting in the black shadows. On the ground in front of her were several bowls containing sage, dried flowers, roots, twigs, crow feathers, and threads of human hair.

She waved Anika in and spoke Ojibwa. "Over here, child. Sit."

Anika sat cross-legged on the white buffalo skin like she had as a young girl, hanging onto every word her grandmother said. Grandmother Spotted Owl was a small woman, under five feet. She was frail and wore her long silvery-white hair in braids. Her face was taut around sharp bones with only a few small wrinkles. She claimed the herbs kept her looking younger than her sixty years.

Anika sat speechless, trying hard not to let her tears fall. The thought of separating from her grandmother tore at her heart.

"Ah, child, don't cry," Grandmother said in a soothing voice. "I won't be far away. Keep your eyes to the trees and your ear to the wind."

Anika remembered the hawk at Manitou Outpost. "You were watching over me the other day."

Grandmother nodded with a twinkle in her eye. "You are beginning to see. Nature offers its own magic."

"Grandmother, I'm afraid to stay here."

The old woman frowned. "The beast you fear is inside the fort."

"I need your help." Anika picked up the bowl of crow feathers. "Teach me to conjure a spirit. A mean one. I want Master Pendleton to suffer for what he does to me."

Grandmother said, "We do not use our magic for evil."

"Please, if I don't fight him with magic, he will never stop."

Her grandmother gazed up at the hole in the hut's roof. "When you conjure a trickster for a favor, the day will come when the trickster demands a favor from you."

Anika nodded, tears running down her cheeks in streams. "I wish I could be strong like you."

"Strength comes from facing that which scares us," Grandmother said. "As women, we hold our own power inside." She picked up a dove's feather from a bowl and added it to a small pile on a round piece of leather. "I have faced my own beasts in my youth. And I sit here before you alive, while the bones of my enemies rot in their graves." She pulled the leather up into a small, tight ball containing an assortment of feathers, roots, and animal teeth. She held it up with two leather chords. A prayer bundle necklace.

Anika smiled with falling tears. *She knew I was coming today.*

"Wear this, child, and you will be protected from bad spirits. Both outside and in." She tied the necklace around Anika's neck. The bundle filled her heart with warmth. Grandmother Spotted Owl sat back and smiled. "When you are alone in your cabin, always remember...there is no separation between us."

59

Tom hiked alone through the pines outside Fort Pendleton. He had a relentless hunger to avenge his son's death. He wasn't afraid to come across Kunetay Timberwolf or any other cannibal. Tom carried a high-caliber rifle, one strong enough to bring down a bear. He welcomed a chance to use it.

He heard a noise in the distance that sounded like a lone bird singing. He followed it, stepping through thick brambles. As he got closer, he recognized the hollow sound. A native flute. The forest opened up to an Indian burial ground. Several small structures covered the graves. At the edge of the cemetery sat Anika, playing a flute.

Tom sat down on the log next to her. Her intense green eyes remained fixed on the graves. She continued to play her melancholy song. The music penetrated Tom, pulling down his anger into a deep reservoir of sadness he wasn't ready to feel. His face muscles tightened.

Anika pulled down the flute. "You shouldn't be out here."

"Neither should you."

They both sat in silence for a spell, listening to the wind, watching snow drift across the burial ground. "What are those structures?" Tom asked. Covering each plot were small, birch bark huts with holes in the front. They looked like elongated birdhouses.

"Spirit houses. My people believe the holes allow the spirits to leave the bodies."

"Where do they go?" Tom asked.

"Most of them journey to *giizhig-oon* where they fly among the eagles." She pointed to the sky to describe the Ojibwa afterworld.

"*Giizhig-oon*," Tom said. "Sounds like our version of heaven." He looked at all the spirit houses that covered the hillside. "What did you mean by 'most of them journey?'"

"Not all spirits find their way. Many get lost in the forest and become manitous." Anika held up her instrument, showing him the ornate animal totems on the shaft. "The sacred flute guides their spirits up to the sky."

As she returned to playing the melancholy music, Tom thought of Chris and wondered if his spirit had found its way to heaven.

60

"Good riddance to this backwoods prison." Willow stomped outside the fort's open gate with her butler carrying her two suitcases. She stumbled through shin-deep snow.

Brother Andre ran to her aid. "Lady Pendleton, let me give you a hand."

"Thank you." She gripped his elbow, and the Jesuit guided her toward the river.

"I didn't know you would be journeying with us," he said.

"Well, Avery's not leaving me here. That's for sure."

At the river dock, the *voyageurs* were loading up two canoes with crates and bundles of furs. Her husband Avery, dressed in his typical black wolverine coat and top hat, was gathered with the other officers. When they saw Lady Pendleton charging across the dock, the men disbanded.

Avery looked absolutely livid when he noticed the butler toting his wife's baggage. "Willow, what are you doing outside the fort?"

"I'm going with you."

"The hell you are." To the Cree butler he said, "Charles, take her things back inside this instance."

"Yes, master." The servant turned and headed back up the hill.

"No, wait," Willow insisted. "Avery, take me with you to Montréal."

"I'll do no such thing. You belong inside Noble House."

"You can't just abandon me out here in the wilds."

"Lt. Hysmith will look after you."

"But what about those beasts? Aren't you concerned they may attack again?"

Avery nodded toward the group of soldiers who continually watched the woods. "Until we return, the fort gate will remained locked. No one will enter or leave. Trust me, darling, you'll be safer here. A canoe ride in winter is no journey for a lady."

Willow pouted. "But we'll be apart for Christmas and New Year's." She hoped the idea of missing their first holiday together might change his mind.

Avery kissed her forehead. "Don't you fret, darling, we'll celebrate when I return. I'll buy you something special."

"How long will you be gone?"

"Three to four weeks. Now be a good wife and get inside before you catch cold." He waved the lieutenant over. "Escort Lady Pendleton back to Noble House."

"Right away, sir."

Before Lt. Hysmith could take her arm, Willow walked over to Andre and threw her arms around his neck. "You be careful." In his ear she whispered, "I'm going to miss our daily confession."

He blushed, his angelic blue eyes beaming. "As will I, Lady Pendleton." He climbed into one of the canoes along with several *voyageurs*, eight French Canadian and Scotch men per canoe, gripping paddles.

Tears crystallized on Willow's cheeks as she walked with Lt. Hysmith back up the hill toward the fort. At the gate she stopped and turned. The two canoes paddled away from the dock and down the river. Avery sat in the center of the lead canoe, looking prominent with his top hat. He stared forward, not even bothering to wave goodbye as his canoe disappeared around the bend.

Willow stepped back inside her winter prison. She shuddered as the gate's double doors clacked shut behind her.

Part Six

The Jesuits

61

A horse carriage dropped off Brother Andre at the Notre-Dame Basilica. He felt small and humbled standing before this grand cathedral. The twin towers seemed to stretch toward the heavens. The setting sun cast a bright orange glow on the statues.

Andre inhaled a deep breath. *It's been a long time,* he thought. Three winters had passed since Andre last stepped foot inside the cathedral. Grabbing his suitcase, he entered the front door. As he was heading down a massive hallway toward the sacristy, a member of the clergy approached. *"Bonjour,* may I help you?"

"Oui, I have an urgent message to deliver to Father Xavier."

"Give it to me. I must first take it to Bishop Rousseau."

Andre said, "I would prefer to speak with the bishop face to face. I have other news to report."

The clergyman, who was tall and crane-thin, scowled down at Andre like he was some beggar off the street. "The bishop is very busy."

"This is of dire importance," Andre insisted. "Can you tell him that Father Jacques' messenger has arrived to offer a full report about the mission work at Manitou Outpost?" He handed over the letter, but secretly kept the diary.

"Wait in the nave."

Minutes later the clergyman returned. "The archbishop will speak with you."

Andre entered a room that was wall-to-wall books. Interspersed between the bookcases were paintings of angels and saints. Bishop Rousseau stood at a window, watching the snow falling in a courtyard. He was a heavyset man with gray hair. He wore a shimmering white robe and around his neck hung a pallium, a white band with six black crosses that signified his authority. A violet skullcap called a zucchetto covered his head.

As the archbishop turned, Andre was suddenly overcome by shortness of breath. Bishop Rousseau had intimidating blue eyes set in a plump face. He held Father Jacques' letter in his hand. "I appreciate you making the journey to deliver this message."

Andre bowed. "*Merci*, it is an honor to meet you, sir."

"Have a seat." The bishop pointed to two plush, winged-back chairs.

They sat across from one another. "So you have his diary for me?"

Andre handed it over.

The bishop scanned the pages, reading. His eyebrows knitted, as if he understood the coded passages. "You have additional news to share?"

"*Oui.*" Andre told him about the massacre at Manitou Outpost and the unfortunate demise of Father Jacques. How a disease that turned people into violent cannibals had reached Fort Pendleton and the neighboring Ojibwa village. A pack of killers, who might be carrying this disease, were still roaming the woods.

Andre took this opportunity to share his progress as a missionary. "I have successfully converted all the residents at Fort Pendleton, as well as a few of their Ojibwa neighbors." Andre felt his cheek twitch as he remembered he'd failed to get Anika Moonblood to accept Jesus Christ as her savior. "I want to show them that God is on their side. I am devoted to doing whatever is needed to serve the Church's divine mission."

Bishop Rousseau nodded, his eyes deep in thought. "You wish to become a priest one day?"

"*Oui*, your holiness, very much."

"I might be willing to ordain you sooner."

Andre's heart lunged.

Bishop Rousseau leaned forward over his desk. "But first, I have a mission for you. Father Xavier could use a new apprentice."

62

Grief struck Father Xavier's chest like a dagger when he heard that his mentor, Father Jacques Baptiste, had been brutally murdered.

Translating the Aramaic, Father Xavier had read the entire journal in a few hours and then returned to Bishop Rousseau's office. Behind his desk on the back wall hung a painting of Saint Ignatius of Loyola. The Christian Soldier. The founder of the Jesuits.

Father Xavier gazed down at the diary. He remembered Father Jacques' final passages.

I have explored the Savages' legend in the name of the Holy Church in hopes of disproving it. But my mission has failed on that account, for I have beheld the gaze of the Devil and, suffering from the most formidable temptations, feasted upon the Beast's sacrament.

So much insanity has plagued us. It was Margaux Lamothe, Pierre's eldest daughter, who caught the disease first. And then our people. I tried to exorcise the possessed. But there were too many. Out of fifteen colonists, there are only four of us left, Pierre, myself, Wenonah, and a nine-year-old girl. By God's grace, Zoé hasn't shown any signs of the infection. As for me, it won't be long before I succumb to the savagery like all the others. This Evil must be stopped before the hunger spreads.

Father Xavier looked up at Bishop Rousseau who was sitting behind his desk. "The outbreak is happening again."

"Worse than before." The archbishop clasped his ring-covered fingers. "I need you to travel to Ontario. Stopping the Devil's Plague is of highest importance to the Vatican."

Father Xavier took a deep breath, considering the dangerous mission. He would be traveling to the deep interior of Canada. Indian country. He had read Father Jacques' previous reports from the past three years. The woods around Manitou Outpost were haunted by evil spirits. In the end, they had infected a colony with madness and killed his mentor. "This battle cannot be won by one priest. We need an army of exorcists."

Bishop Rousseau said, "You are the only one I have in Quebec."

"Then we must request more from the Vatican. From Paris and London, as well."

"There's no time, Father. The plague is spreading. This matter needs to be dealt with immediately. And I have complete faith that you are the best exorcist for the mission." He motioned to the painting on the wall. "Not since St. Ignatius have the Jesuits had a finer warrior than you."

Father Xavier sensed the bishop was merely stroking his ego, but the comparison to his hero did boost his spirit. "I will need a new apprentice. Someone I can count on, preferably a priest."

Bishop Rousseau nodded. "I have already selected a man for you. Brother Andre is not ordained yet, but he has three years' experience working with Father Jacques."

"As an exorcist?" Father Xavier asked.

"As a missionary." The bishop tossed a pouch of coins onto the desk. "I'm relying on you to train him to become an exorcist."

63

Brother Andre had spent an hour of training with Father Xavier and was already feeling annoyed. The exorcist was domineering and barked orders like an army general. He was in his mid fifties. He stood over six feet and, with his broad shoulders and high forehead, he had a strong, overbearing presence. What unsettled Andre the most were the priest's piercing blue eyes. They could appear warm and mirthful one moment and icy the next. He imagined Father Xavier could stare down the Devil.

"You will do everything I tell you," the exorcist said, as the two walked down a hallway. "The tasks we perform will test every ounce of faith you have. If you don't think you can handle working with an exorcist, then speak now, and I will find another apprentice."

Andre stiffened his shoulders. "I just spent three years on the frontier living among the Savages. You will find none as dedicated as I, Father."

"Very well." He smiled and put a hand on Andre's shoulder. "Let's get started."

The priest led him down a flight of stairs to a tunnel beneath the cathedral. The undercroft. Feeling a sense of adventure, Andre followed his new mentor along a torch-lit passage. A guard was down here, sitting at a table. Father Xavier signed a book. He took an oil lamp from the table then led Andre into a stone chamber with an arched ceiling. Their footsteps echoed off the walls. Andre's jaw dropped at the sight of all the relics: statues, swords, goblets, tapestries, and tables covered in silver crosses.

In the center of the chamber were eight chairs sitting around a circular stone table.

Father Xavier said, "This is where the monks bless our holy weapons."

On the back wall hung a large painting of a Christian soldier fighting off a horde of demons with a sword.

Andre said, "St. Ignatius Loyola."

"Yes, the founder of the Jesuits." Father Xavier looked down at Andre. "Do you believe in demons?"

"I believe what the Bible says about them," Andre said, feeling nervous under his mentor's suspicious glare. "But honestly, I've never seen anyone possessed by one."

"Have you ever seen an insane person?"

"Of course, sir."

"Then you've seen a possession. Our duty as exorcists is to banish demons who possess people's bodies and guide the victims to the light of God." Father Xavier pulled two cases off a shelf and began filling them with silver crosses. The cases reminded Andre of medical kits. "Father Jacques had a case like this. Was he sent to Manitou Outpost to perform an exorcism?"

"Yes. Three years ago we were informed that a demon had possessed an Ojibwa man who was the chief's son." The priest gathered a few plum-shaped vials and filled them with holy water. "Father Jacques was sent there to release the possessed man from his demon. That mission was successful."

"Why didn't he tell me that was his true mission?"

"Your mentor was under strict orders to keep his mission secret and document his findings. That's why he left you behind at Fort Pendleton. We generally wait for our apprentices to become priests before we invite them to join the exorcists. Bishop Rousseau is making an exception for you." Father Xavier continued down a passage and entered a library filled with volumes upon volumes of books.

"The Basilica's archives," Father Xavier said. "Every book you see has been duplicated and stored at the Vatican." The priest meandered through the labyrinth of bookshelves, the flame of his oil lamp flickering across dusty spines. He pulled a black book off the shelf. It had a bold red cross on the cover. "*The Roman Ritual of Exorcism.*" He handed it to Andre. "Read it and memorize the protocols for the ceremony and all the prayers, word for word. You have two weeks."

Andre flipped through the pages, feeling overwhelmed by the daunting task.

"Come, I have one more thing to show you."

The priest led him into another chamber that had a life force unlike anything Andre had ever felt. Father Xavier lit a torch. Giant silver crosses were embedded into the four walls. In the center of the room sat a long, stone sarcophagus. On the lid was a relief of St. Ignatius holding a cross-shaped dagger to his chest.

Father Xavier stepped around the stone coffin. "Andre, what I am about to show you is of highest secrecy. There are very few Jesuits who know of it. You must swear to the Christ, our Lord, to never speak of what I am about to show you. Not to anyone."

"I swear, Father." Andre crossed himself.

Father Xavier grabbed an iron rod that had a key on the end of it.

He twisted the lock, and the lid grated as it slowly opened.

Andre gasped.

Inside the stone coffin lay a mummified creature. Dry, flaky skin shriveled around the thing's twisted form. It had the body of a man and the face of a beast with sharp teeth. The bony arms, legs, and torso were incredibly long.

Father Xavier said, "In the 1600s, this mummy was found frozen in a bog in northern Quebec."

"What..." Andre looked up at his mentor. "What kind of animal walks like a man?"

"It's neither animal or man." Father Xavier gazed with those piercing blue eyes. "What you are looking at, Andre, is physical proof that demons walk the earth."

64

Tom Hatcher sat alone at his table, drinking one whiskey after the other, trying to piece together the events that had caused his life to spin out of control.

Two years ago, when he had been working as an inspector in Montréal, he nearly went insane investigating the case of the Cannery Cannibal. Over the span of two years, twelve women, all prostitutes from the harbor docks, were butchered and dumped into the river. After the last victim, several months passed. The case almost went cold until Tom and his partner staked out the docks, watching the riverboat that worked as a brothel. A man tried to abduct one of the prostitutes. Tom and his partner intervened, rescuing the girl, but the man got away.

The next day Tom received a strange gift at his home. A music box that played baroque music. When he opened the box, two ballroom dancers spun in a circle. Inside was a rolled scroll and a sardine tin. Written in elegant handwriting was a message.

Dearest Inspector,

You cannot stop the Shepherd of Death from saving the lost lambs. Like the wind, I am everywhere. If you do not stop, I will come after your family and eat your wife and son's livers while you watch.

The Cannery Cannibal

The sardine tin was filled with bloated fingers lined up like blood sausages.

Tom had been so enraged that he had moved his family to Lachine.

He then returned to Montréal and led a relentless manhunt. He studied the music box, the scroll, and tin for clues. The stationery was from expensive parchment and had a fancy emblem on it of an M. The silver tin was from the Meraux Cannery. They canned everything from turtle soup and oysters to mincemeat and clam chowder. One of their clerks reported missing tins each month. Tom suspected Gustave Meraux, the cannery owner's eccentric son and heir to the Meraux fortune.

Inspector Hatcher and his squad raided Gustave Meraux's mansion. In his study was a collection of music boxes. Gustave was nowhere to be found.

The Montréal police shut down the Meraux Cannery and seized every dockside warehouse and boat. Tom found the killer's lair in a dock house near the fishing boats and made a shocking discovery. The cannibal had been cooking up the dead women in soups in a large vat and storing their meat in tins.

65

The Montréal harbor was empty except for a young woman walking along the pier. She wore a shabby coat and peasant dress. Gustave Meraux sized her up as one of the prostitutes who worked the docks offering their wares to the fishermen and sailors. Many of the whores lived in a large houseboat that acted as a brothel. That was where the wench appeared to be headed.

Gustave crouched behind a sailboat that knocked against the docks. As the young woman's silhouette passed, he grabbed her from behind, clamping his hand around her mouth. Her frail body bucked in his arms. She let out a muffled scream. "Hush, hush, little lamb," he whispered and pinched her nostrils. She kicked out and clawed the air, then finally went limp. "That's a good girl."

The cannibal threw her body over his shoulder and carried her back to the cannery warehouse. A dozen rats looked up as Gustave entered his lair. He tore off the woman's dress and undergarments. Naked flesh no longer aroused his libido, only his hunger. He wrapped her in chains and raised her body till her feet dangled a foot above the ground. He placed his cheek to her warm belly. The smell of her sweet meat stirred up hunger pangs in Gustave's stomach.

"I'll be back for you."

He limped over to his altar and opened his music box. Warped music played his favorite baroque melody. The figurines of a dancing couple spun in endless circles. Gustave lit the five black candles on the altar. The mural of the black-skinned beast stared down at him.

Gustave bowed. "I have brought you a gift, Master."

The mural spoke to Gustave through the music box's warbled tune. The ballroom dancers spun round and round.

"Yes, Master."

Humming the melody, spinning like a gentleman dancing with a lady, Gustave peered into a shard of mirror that still hung on a nearby post. Blood covered his face and stained his thick, black and silver beard. Using the knife, he shaved off most of the whiskers, leaving only a few patches. He grimaced, showing off his red teeth and gray gums. His long, greasy hair was disheveled. He cut his hair, as well, preferring it short. There was a time he could seduce any woman with this face. His libertine days were over. Reaching into his music box, he pulled out a tin and dabbed white powder onto his cheeks. As he prepared himself for one last ceremony, he heard the flapping of wings. A flock of ravens flew down from a hole in the roof. Gustave stepped around the birds and rats. He went to the girl and powdered her face, as well, till she was as beautiful as a Victorian doll. With the flaying knife, he carved a red spiral on her forehead. She woke up screaming. She kicked out. Her twisting body rattled the chains.

Her flopping breasts made Gustave salivate. He wanted so desperately to cut off a piece of her and have a nibble. But this girl, the final sacrificial lamb, was not for him. He returned to the glowing altar. Above the burning candles, the mural appeared to whirl like a funnel. "She's ready for you, Master."

Black smoke floated out of the wall, the mural evaporating. The warehouse echoed with cackles and squeaks. The girl screamed louder, drowning out the music box. Gustave turned around. Standing in the center of the room was a giant black shape whose head and body were formed by flapping ravens and squirming rats.

Gustave limped toward his master. The thing towered over him. The rats and ravens writhed within its mass. Hundreds of beady eyes stared at the Cannery Cannibal.

The music box began playing the melody backwards. He heard the command of his muse. "Yes, Master."

Gustave slashed the woman's wailing throat. She dangled from the chains, red liquid streaming over her breasts. He then backed away, allowing the spiraling, dark mass to swallow her whole.

Gustave heard crunching and gnawing and the chittering of creatures in a feeding frenzy. In seconds, they reshaped into the giant, black form. At the chains, a red skeleton dangled. The dark beast lumbered toward the doorway.

"Please, Master, take me with you."

The music box played the tune Gustave wanted to hear. A song that promised vengeance and eternal suffering to his enemies. Smiling, he slashed his wrist, dripping his blood in a clockwise spiral on the stone floor. He kneeled on the symbol and sliced open a dozen red wounds along his ribs and belly. As he bled like a disciple on the cross, he raised his arms to the dark lord.

The mass exploded outward, swarming around Gustave's body. The rats and ravens fed, pecking and gnawing, releasing the Cannery Cannibal from his mortal prison until there was nothing left but tatters and bones.

Part Seven

Dark Night of the Soul

66

Screams echoed throughout the forest.

Running, running, running...

Tom stumbled through a thicket of trees. Branches swatted his face.

Clawing, clawing, clawing...

A snow mound up ahead. Blood spread across the white dune, forming a red spiral.

He fell to his knees.

Digging, digging, digging...

Uncovered the face of the Cannery Cannibal.

A bloody mouth opened.

Cackling, cackling, cackling...

Tom jerked awake, feeling as if an axe were splitting his skull. The room spun, adding vertigo to his pain and nausea to his roiling stomach. His mouth tasted like talcum powder. The cannibal's cackling faded.

He blinked his eyes. The room came into focus. *Another nightmare.*

Twilight shone through the windows. Was it dawn or dusk? Did it even matter? Tom rubbed his face, trying to remember the last time he was sober. He remembered being seated here at the dining table, gulping down one glass of whiskey after the next.

Now an empty bottle lay sideways on the table next to the glass. He spotted a picture frame facedown on the table. He turned it over to the side that displayed a black and white photo. A younger version of himself was dressed in his suit and black lawman hat, standing proud between his wife and son. The portrait had been taken three years ago in Montréal. Beth had her blonde hair pinned up and was a timeless beauty in her Sunday dress. Chris Hatcher, wearing his suit, was age eleven in the photo. His hair had a cowlick that never combed down properly. He had his father's high cheekbones and mother's blue eyes.

Feeling the pressure build again, Tom pinched the bridge of his nose. His head was in such a haze he couldn't remember why he'd pulled out the photo. Maybe to torture himself. The image of his family just made him want to open another bottle and sink back into a mindless slumber. Before he could succumb to the whiskey devil, Tom growled and upturned the table. The bottle and glass hit the wall and shattered. He kicked his chair, knocking it over.

Tom stumbled into the den, fists clenched, arms shaking.

Something scraped wood in the shadowy corner. Tom turned, wobbling, still half-drunk. "Stop it!"

At the back corner of the den the crate that looked like a coffin took up half the wall. Something inside was scratching to get out. Tom grabbed the crowbar and smacked the top of the crate. "Shut up already!"

The scrapes, like claws dragging across wood, continued relentlessly.

"Blast you!" Tom jammed the crowbar into the edge of the lid. He pried, jacking up the nails at each corner. He removed the top, tossing it to the floor with a thundering crash. Inside the crate was a wooden grid housing brown bottles. He grabbed one by the neck and pulled out the cork. He guzzled the whiskey. A river of fire scorched his throat, flowing down into his belly. Tears glazing his eyes, he fell back against the wall and slid down onto his rump.

Christ, I can't take any more of this.

Two weeks had passed with him wasting away inside this cabin. He had spent both Christmas and New Year's so bloody pissed the holidays were nothing but foggy memories. He smelled a foul odor from something rotting in the kitchen. Or was it coming from him?

Tom took another swig. *I've got to get out of this cabin.*

The walls felt like they were pressing in. As the twilight in the windows faded, and the room grew darker, Tom began to see tiny fireflies floating out in front of him.

He blinked, focusing his eyes, seeing them more clearly.

Glowing red spirals.

He swatted at them. The spirals spun upward like dust, then drifted back down in front of his face.

He blinked again, and they were gone.

I've gone completely mad.

Then realization hit him like a punch to the gut. He stood, remembering his dream. The red spiral spreading across the snow dune, digging up the face of Gustave Meraux.

Heart racing, Tom paced. Outside, nightfall was quickly claiming the last of the twilight. *I have to know.* He put on his coat and lawman hat and lit a lantern. Grabbing the crowbar, he headed out the door.

The red fireflies returned, leading the way.

67

Tom crossed the fort grounds to the back side of Hospital House. After removing Doc and Myrna Riley's dead bodies, the soldiers had boarded up the doors and windows of the two-story white building to keep the children out. Climbing the steps to the back porch, he clumsily worked the crowbar, prying at the boards covering the door. He removed three of them, creating a gap. It was as dark as a copper mine inside.

He leaned in with the lantern. The smell of decay smacked his senses. Blood still stained the floor and kitchen counters. The building had been quarantined out of fear that it was contaminated. Tom wasn't worried about catching the disease. He knew very little about viruses but was almost certain one couldn't survive below-zero temperatures.

He ducked in through the gap. As he stood upright inside the kitchen, he felt disoriented. The effects of the whiskey doubled his vision. He leaned against a wall for a moment, allowing his equilibrium to stabilize. Wind blew in through the boarded windows. Most were shattered. Shards of glass covering the floor reflected the lantern light like crystals. Tom twisted, pushing away the darkness at each side of the kitchen. Three passageways led off into different parts of the house.

Which way to the master bedroom?

He took the hall on his right. The wood floor creaked beneath his boots. Up ahead, the blood-streaked door stood ajar. Pushing it open, he held up the lantern, lighting up the red-spattered bed. Tom pictured the ghoulish thing Doc Riley had become, with arms jutting out at impossible angles. On the wall above the bed was the macabre pattern he had been painting with his bloody hands.

Red spirals.

A memory from the Cannery Cannibal's lair flashed through Tom's mind. He suddenly felt sick to his stomach and vomited. The red spiral had been Gustave Meraux's signature, carved into the foreheads of the thirteen women he butchered. In the two years Tom spent tracking the killer, he never understood what the symbol meant. Now it was showing up again, first at Manitou Outpost, painted above Father

Jacques' altar. Then around the entrance to Kunetay's hut. And here it was again by the hands of Doc Riley, who had contracted the disease from Zoé. The only connection between them and Gustave Meraux was cannibalism. *What do the spirals mean?*

Lights suddenly filtered in through the cracks between the boards. *Oh shit.* He wasn't supposed to be in here.

"Hello, anybody in there?" a man called from the kitchen.

Several sets of boots entered and clumped down the hallway.

"It's Inspector Hatcher," Tom yelled. "In the master bedroom."

Lt. Hysmith entered with two of his soldiers. They lowered their weapons. "What in God's name are you doing in here at this hour?"

"Trying to make sense of those symbols."

"What?" Hysmith looked at the wall and scowled. "I don't see nothing but a sickening mess."

"No, look how the strokes make a pattern of spirals. I saw this back in Montréal. I think it's some kind of message."

Hysmith frowned. "Inspector, you're drunk and it's late."

"I'm fine. I need to work."

"Not tonight you don't." Hysmith waved him over. "Come with us, Inspector."

They escorted him back to his cabin. Tom had difficulty walking straight. The moon seemed to sway in the sky. The earth went topsy-turvy as he fell to the snowy ground. He was embarrassed that the soldiers had to help him to his feet.

At the cabin doorstep, Hysmith said, "If I may offer some advice, please take a bath. You're about as approachable as a dead skunk."

68

Tom soaked in a tub in the corner of his bedroom. The water, which he had boiled, had quickly turned from warm to bone-numbing cold. He couldn't stop shaking. Even the whiskey failed to warm him. He was so drunk again that he had already forgotten about why he had ventured out to Hospital House. It didn't really matter anyway. Once Master Pendleton got word of Tom's drunken behavior, he was probably going to lose his position.

Nothing much mattered anymore. His pistol sat on a bench beside him. He picked it up, rubbing the Hatcher family crest engraved in pewter on the gun's handle. He remembered the day his father gave him the gun. Tom had just been promoted to inspector at the police station in Montréal.

Orson Hatcher brought Tom into his study and pulled out a wooden box that encased the pistol. His father smiled. "Son, by becoming a detective, you have made me very proud. Your grandfather gave me this the day I made inspector, and now I'm passing it down to you. One day you will pass this along to your own son. Hatcher men were born to solve crimes."

Now the gun weighed heavy in his hand. A pull of the trigger and Tom could escape this miserable life. He ached to be with Beth and Chris again. Would they be there waiting for him in the afterlife? Or would a darker hell await him? He imagined his father frowning down from heaven. *Don't do it, son. If you quit on yourself, you quit on everyone. I never raised you to be a quitter. You are a Hatcher, and no matter how tough life gets, a Hatcher man never gives up. So somehow you've got to find a way to turn things around.*

But I'm only half a Hatcher, Tom wanted to argue. *A bloody half-breed.* His whole life he suffered the shame of being Métis—half-white, half-red—coming from two separate worlds and belonging to neither. He could feel the savagery in his blood from the half of him that was Ojibwa. Like the red people, he had a weakness for alcohol, an untamed heart. He lacked the white man's restraint. Shivering in the freezing tub, Tom cried until there were no more tears left.

I'm of no use to anybody if I'm dead.

He set the pistol back on the bench.

As he was climbing into his red long johns, he heard a knock at the front door.

Who was visiting at this hour?

He was surprised to see Anika, holding her flask of rum. Her green eyes were glossy. "I thought maybe you could use some company."

"I'm fine on my own." He started to shut the door.

"Tom, wait." She placed her hand on the door.

He pulled it back open. "What?"

"I... I'm sorry about Chris..." Her eyes were filled with pain. "I was supposed to watch over him..." Tears dribbled down her cheeks.

Tom wanted to blame Anika for Chris' death. To channel all his hate toward this wretched woman. But seeing her tears softened his anger. "It wasn't your fault. I never should have let Chris leave my side. I..." The overwhelming pain returned, and Tom hurried to the kitchen and poured himself another whiskey. Gulped it down.

Anika entered his den and shut the door.

Tom stared at the native woman for a long moment and then went to the cupboard and pulled out a second glass.

69

Tom woke, feeling dizzy.

The sun shone through the windows of his bedroom, causing him to squint. He rubbed his eyes. Another morning, another headache. He remembered soaking in the bathtub, gulping down one glass of whiskey after the next. Then Anika visited him, and he couldn't recall anything that followed.

Warm skin brushed his back.

Tom jerked back the covers. Anika was nuzzling up against him. Her hair covered her face. The small woman had tan skin and a slender, lean-muscled body. The sight of her small breasts with brown nipples stirred Tom's arousal.

"Oh, Jesus." He touched her bare shoulder. "Anika."

"Mmmm." She rolled over, pulling the covers over her head. She started snoozing again.

"Christ, what have I done?" Tom dressed quickly, throwing on his long johns and trousers. He went to his kitchen. An empty bottle stood on the table between two glasses. He paced. *Why did I let her in?*

The whiskey demons scratched at the crate, tempting him to open another bottle. "Bugger off!"

His drinking was getting him into constant trouble. Now he had Avery Pendleton's mistress in his bed.

Tom looked out his back window. It was the brightest morning he'd seen in over a month. A large snow owl flew down and perched on a post. Its golden eyes stared at Tom. The Ojibwa believed seeing animals was a sign. Tom just didn't know if this predator bird was a good omen or a bad one.

Someone knocked at the front door. The owl flew off.

"You have a visitor." Anika ambled out of the bedroom with a blanket wrapped around her. Her bare feet padded across the wood floor. Her hair was disheveled. She held a hand against her forehead, the look of a hangover on her face.

The pounding at the door echoed in Tom's head. "Who is it!"

"It's me." Willow Pendleton.

Shit, if she sees me with Anika, the news will go straight back to Master Pendleton. Tom held a finger to his lips, signaling Anika to keep quiet. He spoke through the door. "Can you come back later? Now's not the best time."

Willow said, "Please, Tom, I need to see that you're okay. I'm worried about you."

"Okay, give me a moment." To Anika he whispered, "Keep quiet," and shooed her back into the bedroom and closed the door. He looked into an oval mirror on the wall. A face with bloodshot eyes reflected back. His beard had grown thick and unruly. *I'm a bloody wreck.* He dipped his hands into the washbasin and splashed icy water onto his face. Once he looked halfway presentable, he opened the door. What appeared to be an angel stood before him, a vision in pure white in her long, snow-fox coat. Her blonde hair was tucked beneath her furry white hat. Her porcelain-doll face was pink from the cold. "Good morning, Tom."

"Morning," he said, scratching his beard.

Her perfume struck his senses. The fragrances of lilac and orange blossom. For a brief moment, while his eyesight was still hazy, Tom had the illusion that his wife Beth had returned, as if miraculously sent down from heaven. Then his haziness cleared, and he stared at Lady Willow Pendleton. She held up a dish covered with a towel. "I brought you a shepherd's pie. It has roast lamb in it."

His favorite. Just like Beth used to make. "Where on earth did you find lamb?"

"In the storehouse where we keep the canned foods. I have to confess, it was my cook who baked the pie. But I had her make it especially for you."

He accepted the warm dish. "Thanks, but you didn't have to—"

"I wanted to..." She smiled then, blushing, looked down at the porch. "I just wanted to make sure you were eating okay."

"I'm fine." Tom didn't quite know what to make of the gesture. Her behavior seemed peculiar for a married woman. It took a moment for his dull senses to catch the twinkle in her eye. *Dear God, she fancies me.* The idea of it made his chest tingle.

Willow looked over his shoulder. "Um, would you like to invite me in? I could make you a pot of tea."

"No, not now." He blocked the threshold. "I mean... perhaps another time."

"Oh, okay." She backed away. "I'm sorry, Tom, I didn't mean to bother you."

She hurried down the steps.

"Willow, wait."

At the bottom step she turned back around, gazing up at him with those bright blue eyes. Her full lips were pouting.

"I mean no disrespect, Willow. It's just..." He stared off at the surrounding cabins, squinting at the glare from their snow-covered rooftops. "I'm not in the right frame of mind to be good company.

Another day, perhaps."

"Okay, that would be nice. Take care of yourself, Tom. And know that others care about you, as well." She sauntered across the courtyard, white fur blending with the bright snow. Tom stood in the doorway, awestruck. He shut the door. *Damn, that was close.* He walked back into his bedroom. Anika, who was fully nude, peered out the window. "I think she fancies you."

"Never mind her, what the hell were you doing in my bed?"

Anika turned toward him. The sight of her nakedness added arousal to his anger. Her hair hung wild over her shoulders. "I thought I was pleasing you."

"Please, cover yourself." Tom lost his train of thought as Anika pulled the dress up her legs. Her tan breasts jiggled with the movement of her hips. He had vague memories of kissing those brown nipples. A wave of emotions flooded over Tom, as his mind relived the sensations of their bodies moving together beneath the blankets. Last night his head had been dizzy from alcohol, while his body engaged in an act of pleasure he had not experienced in well over two years. The musk of their sex still lingered in the bedroom. She was dressing herself way too slowly. Tom's animal urges made him want to throw her down on the bed and ravish her again. But that was a very bad idea. Everyone in the fort knew that Anika was Master Pendleton's mistress. A mistake made once can easily be forgiven. If he made the same mistake twice, it would only complicate his life.

When she finally got her dress over her shoulders, Tom breathed easier. Anika sat on the bed and tied the leather tassels of her moccasin boots. "You don't remember last night, do you?"

Tom buttoned up his shirt. "I remember that you came over, and we were drinking a lot. After that, everything's a bit foggy. If I took advantage of you, I'm sorry."

Anika giggled as she pulled on her parka. Her face was much softer as she smiled.

"What's so funny?" he asked.

"You're not like other men."

"Oh, how am I different?"

"Most men don't care how I feel. I feel in my chest that you do." There was a new spark in her green eyes.

Tom felt guilty for scolding her. She was probably just a lonely widow who needed some winter comfort. Last night he had ventured down a path he shouldn't have and now feared the Ojibwa tracker might want something more. "Listen, Anika...this has been a very confusing time for me. If Master Pendleton learns you and I slept together..."

Her face hardened. "You don't have to tell me to stay hush. No one will know." She exited the room, wrapping her mane up in a ponytail. "I won't bother you again." By the tone of her voice, she was clearly upset.

"Anika, I didn't mean it to sound—"

The back door slammed shut.

"Fine, woman, then bloody bugger off!" Tom pushed one of his chairs.

70

That afternoon, Tom paid a visit to the empty chapel. He lit a votive and kneeled before the Madonna's altar. The statue of the Virgin Mary gazed down at him. He gesticulated and inwardly recited the poem that he had been reading all morning.

On a dark night, Kindled in love with yearnings, oh, happy chance! I went forth without being observed, My house being now at rest.

Then he walked down the aisle to where a second altar had been set up to remember the six who had passed away. The nave was nearly pitch black at this end. The shimmering light of the single candle barely illuminated the wall and pews. The framed photos—ovals and squares—were all mere shapes in the gloom. He started to light a votive candle, then stopped, remaining in the darkness. He couldn't bear to look at his son's photo yet. And believing that spirits watch from above, he couldn't bear for his son to see his father in this wretched state.

In darkness and secure, By the secret ladder, disguised oh, happy chance! In darkness and in concealment, My house being now at rest.

The last two weeks of heavy drinking had been Tom's "Dark Night of the Soul." He had suffered much like Saint John of the Cross, the Spanish poet and mystic who wrote the famous Catholic poem about loneliness and desolation. Tom had sunken into the deepest despair of his life. Each day and night passed slow and torturous. He kept to himself as a hermit, staying locked away inside his cabin. Each night he had tossed and turned in bed, shaking, mouth as dry as cotton. He heard noises in the den, as if the bottles of whiskey stashed inside their crate had somehow turned into living things that clawed at the wood, tempting him to get out of bed and pour himself another fiery throat scratcher.

We can make you forget, the voices chanted. *Escape from your misery is just a gulp away.*

Even now, Tom felt the thirst itching at the back of his throat. He swallowed. He drew strength from thinking about his visit from the angel. First she came to him as a snow owl, then as a woman who resembled his wife. Down to the very scent of her.

I remained, lost in oblivion; My face I reclined on the Beloved. All ceased and I abandoned myself, Leaving my cares forgotten among the lilies.

Tom took a deep breath. It was time to face his son and accept that Chris was gone. Tom struck a match and lit a votive candle. The wick sparked. Flame light reflected in the glass frames. He stared at the ovals and squares, a memorial of the dead. Six faces stared back at him. In the center was a portrait of Chris wearing his prep school uniform.

Tom clasped his hands. "Son...I tried to be a good father... I tried so hard to protect you, and I failed." He swallowed hard. "I know my drinking was hard on you, and I said some hurtful things... I'm sorry. When I lost your mother..." Tom wiped a forearm across his eyes and sniffled. Thinking of Beth's death was the hardest memory to pull up. His mind would never relieve him of the image of her body, found inside the cannery warehouse. "Chris, if you only knew the monster I faced...you might understand. The whiskey helped me sleep. And some days it allowed me to forget." He felt as if a heavy weight were lifting from his chest, opening up feelings that he could only describe as hope. "But I realize now I cannot go on this way. As much as I would like to die and join you and Beth, something won't let me take my own life. Maybe I still have a purpose here." He picked up his son's flute. He could only see the outline of it, but he could feel the holes and intricate carvings. "It's a mighty fine piece. I wish I could have appreciated your talent more." Sighing, he slipped the flute into his coat pocket. "Please forgive me, son, for the mistakes I made. From this day forward, I promise to stay sober."

Part Eight

Masquerade

71

Montréal

Horse hooves *clip-clopped* as the carriage carried the Jesuits along Rue St.-Paul through the Bourgeois Centre of the port city. Father Xavier rode with gloved hands in his lap. As he watched each familiar building and street go by, he felt a bit of sadness. The bishop had assigned him on this mission with such short notice that Father Xavier was still adjusting to the idea that tomorrow he would be leaving his favorite city in Quebec.

Sunlight passed over the face of his young apprentice, who sat in the opposite seat. Andre had gray circles under his eyes.

"Have you been up late reading again?" Father Xavier asked.

"*Oui*, I'm trying to memorize the rituals."

"Good, you will need to know them by heart. Did you pack your holy water?"

Andre nodded. "As well as my crosses, robes, and sash."

Father Xavier was hoping the young brother could follow the strict disciplines. He would play a supporting role of reading scriptures, while Father Xavier dealt directly with the demon that possessed its host. Battling the Devil's Plague was a beast much greater than one man could handle, so Father Xavier was teaching Andre everything he knew. By the end of the training, the young man would be ready for priesthood. He was certainly dedicated and showed promise. But Father Xavier had been performing exorcisms for twenty years, and he had yet to find a novice who had the strong-willed spirit necessary to fight the forces of evil. Time would tell if Andre's faith matched his devotion.

The carriage pulled up to the curb.

"Ah, *Hôtel de Rasco*." Father Xavier smiled, stepping out. "The most luxurious lodging in all of Montréal."

Andre looked up at the flat façade of the five-story stone building. "Father, shouldn't we be staying at a nearby church to honor our vow of poverty?"

The old priest waved a hand at the notion. "Nonsense, your fort master invited us to spend our last evening at his hotel. I don't think the Church would mind if we indulged for one night on our journey."

The carriage driver pulled off their luggage.

Father Xavier grabbed his two bags. "Come, Andre, let's get out of this cold. I believe this hotel has a café that is famous for its hot cocoa and *crème brûlée*."

72

Avery Pendleton walked *Hôtel de Rasco's* main corridor with a teenage mistress on his arm and a high step in his gate. His reunion with Celeste Douglas, the redheaded debutant he had met here last summer, was a much-needed reprieve from his problems at Fort Pendleton. Celeste was an heiress to a fortune, and at age seventeen, already quite the tart in bed. If Willow didn't start behaving like an obedient wife, Pendleton thought Celeste would make a fine replacement.

The lovers reached the hotel's grand lobby, and Pendleton's nose was greeted with the floral scent of dried roses. The décor of *Hôtel de Rasco* was an elegant display of European nobility. The walls were adorned with paintings of British colonial ships, Parisian cityscapes, and Italian vineyards. The first level offered seating in several parlors with plush velvet chairs. One parlor had a man in a brown derby hat playing a piano. With a silly grin on his face, he danced his fingers along the keyboard and bowed his head at the guests walking past.

A polished staircase wound upward to five stories of rooms. The stairs and lobby were busy with the hustle and bustle of guests, many of them dressed in aristocratic attire. Two men in black overcoats stood out among the others.

"Andre, welcome back." Pendleton patted the young missionary on the shoulder. He studied the second man, a tall priest in his mid-fifties who looked Russian at first glance due to his black mink hat. When he spoke, he was undeniably French Canadian. "*Bonjour, messier*." The priest tipped his hat, revealing a bald crown with trimmed, white hair above the ears.

Andre introduced them. "Master Pendleton, meet Father Xavier."

He shook the older man's hand, feeling a strong grip. "I appreciate you making the journey, Father."

"I'm happy to go where God calls me."

Pendleton noticed Brother Andre was eyeing the young redhead on his arm. "Yes, and this lovely woman is Lady Celeste. Her great grandfather is a shareholder. I was just escorting her."

"It is a pleasure, Mademoiselle." The priest bowed to the young lady.

Celeste said, "How about we all go into the parlor for some tea?"

"Perhaps later," Pendleton said. "I'm sure these gentlemen would like to get to their rooms."

Celeste said, "Okay, darling, then take me to my boudoir. This dress is absolutely suffocating."

"Why don't you run along without me? I have business to attend to." He ushered her to the stairs.

She whispered, "Don't make me wait too long, lover," then sacheted up the stairs.

When Pendleton returned, he caught Andre whispering something to the priest. The younger Jesuit had a cold look in his eyes. "Andre, there will be no mentioning of Lady Celeste to Willow or anyone else for that matter. Do we have an understanding?"

The young man nodded. "*Oui*, Master Pendleton."

"Splendid." Pendleton slapped his hands together. "I'm sure you two are exhausted. Let me get some help for your luggage." He snapped his fingers, and two bellhops came over.

Andre looked up at a crystal chandelier and marble staircase. "This hotel is the most elegant place I have ever visited."

Pendleton said, "It was designed by an Italian named Francisco Rasco back in 1832. He wanted to provide the most luxurious lodging for the *haut-monde* class. You two may find it interesting that Charles Dickens once stayed here with his wife. He was directing three plays for the British garrison at the Royal Theater across the street."

"Is that so?" said Father Xavier. "*Oliver Twist* is one of my favorite books."

"Tonight, meals and accommodations are on me." Pendleton handed the Jesuits their keys. "You each get your own rooms. I suggest you get some rest this afternoon then rendezvous upstairs at the Grand Ballroom at six o'clock. I have a surprise in store for this evening's venue."

When the Jesuits were situated with their bellhops, Pendleton hurried up the stairs with a spring in his step. He had developed a fresh hunger for his young quarry, who was getting out of her dress in

126

his hotel room.

73

Retreating to his room, Andre set down his luggage. He touched the plush mattress of the four-poster bed. He would sleep well tonight. Above the bed hung a painting of a woman standing on the docks, holding the hand of a boy. The two were waving goodbye to men canoeing down the river. It reminded Andre of his youth, when he and his mother waved farewell to his father. Only he was going off to fight a war. He never returned.

So long ago, Andre thought as he pulled off the painting and hung his crucifix on the nail. A bowl and pitcher sat on a bedside table. He filled the bowl with water, blessed it, and then rinsed his face.

Still a bit on edge, Andre sat on his bed and did his afternoon meditation. He prayed for Willow. Poor Lady Pendleton was married to an adulterous letch who didn't appreciate his beautiful wife. Andre first begged God for forgiveness for having evil thoughts about Master Pendleton, wishing him to catch syphilis. Willow deserved so much better. *If I weren't destined to be a priest...*

Gripping his rosary, Andre chanted several Hail Marys then asked to be forgiven for lying to Father Xavier. Andre had not been getting much sleep these past few nights because he was experiencing horrible nightmares. In his dreams, he was haunted by two women cloaked in fur. They had alluring, cat-like eyes and seductive voices and smelled of orange blossoms. Just like Willow. Andre had heard her confessions so many times that he was now reliving her dreams, only in his version she showed up as twins who ravished *him*. Each night, Andre had woken in a wet release from his lower regions. An overwhelming sense of guilt followed. No matter how much he willed to keep his vow of chastity, his body betrayed him.

Deep down, he knew that confessing to Father Xavier was the right thing to do. But Andre feared his mentor would shame him for being weak. Perhaps abandon him and report to the Bishop that Andre was not fit to be a priest.

He pulled out his diary and wrote:

My lifelong dream of becoming a priest is coming to fruition. But working with Father Xavier has been more challenging than I expected. He constantly disciplines me. I feel like I'm in Catholic school again with the nuns so ready to smack my hands for not answering questions fast enough. I read all day just to keep up. When I speak to Father Xavier, I never know how he's going to respond. One moment he's jovial, the next chastising me. I feel so weak-minded around him. He expects me to know every verse of The Roman Ritual of Exorcism before we return to the fort.

What did I learn today? The main parts of the Ritual are performed by the exorcist. I, as the assistant, am to join him in reading the Psalms and Gospels. The priest must have piety, prudence, and personal integrity. He must perform exorcisms with humility and courage, not relying on his own strength, but on the power of God. Even though I am not yet a priest, Father Xavier expects me to be equally as courageous and full of faith.

Andre stared up at the ceiling. "Am I strong enough, Lord? Do I have enough Holy spirit within me to face those possessed by evil?"

He heard pecking at his windows. He opened his eyes. Shadows moved behind the sheer curtains. He pulled them open. Several ravens walked on the edge. More black birds cawed as they flew down to perch, causing others to flap upward. Beaks tapped the windows.

There was a double knock at the door.

He shut the curtains and approached the door, holding out his crucifix. He opened the door and was relieved to see Father Xavier. The priest grinned. "Are you in the mood for some hot cocoa and crème brûlée?"

"Merci, Father, but I think I'll stay here and do my excamen."

"A fine way to spend the afternoon." The priest seemed to be in a cheerful spirit. "By the way, Avery Pendleton requested that we be ready for dinner promptly at six o'clock. Tonight we can allow ourselves a bit of fun." Father Xavier placed a white theater mask over his face. "We've been invited to a masquerade party."

74

At six o'clock that evening, the Jesuits ascended the staircase to a ballroom on the second level. A string quartet played baroque music. The musicians wore Renaissance costumes complete with white wigs and powdered makeup. Several high society couples gathered at a masquerade party. The men were in suits and top hats and the women in long gowns and fur stoles. All the attendees wore masks of various shapes and colors like a Venetian Carnival.

Father Xavier and Andre wore white drama masks and their religious robes. They passed one lady who had a stole of silver fur around her neck that still had a fox's head attached. The priest shook his head at Andre and whispered, "Why would anyone wear such an atrocious thing?"

A waiter carrying a tray passed by. Father Xavier stopped him. "Excuse me, *Serveur*, but who are all these people?"

"Members of a private club. They meet here every month." He offered the Jesuits a tray with champagne and wine glasses.

Andre's voice grew excited. "Can we? I've never had champagne."

"Not tonight. *Merci, Serveur*." Father Xavier removed his mask and set it on a table. Andre did, as well, and the two Jesuits walked side by side.

"Andre, we must keep our wits about us. Drinking only dilutes your spiritual awareness and clouds judgment." He could see his apprentice was not enjoying his strict discipline. "Have you been reading from *The Roman Ritual of Exorcism*?"

"*Oui*, Father."

"Then tell me the purpose of an exorcism."

Andre said, "To follow the command and example of Jesus to 'drive out the devils' of those who become possessed."

"What are the versions of the Rite?"

"There are two. One focuses on exorcising people, while the other focuses on exorcising places."

"And what are the two main elements necessary to perform an exorcism?"

"Authorization from the Church authorities and faith of the exorcist."

"You must have unyielding faith. Without a complete belief that God is working through you, no priest stands a chance against the forces of evil."

"My faith is unbreakable."

Father Xavier smiled. "Good, Andre, you're learning fast."

A man in a top hat and a black wolverine mask approached, escorting a redhead with a fox face. Master Pendleton pushed up his mask. "I see you two have decided to forgo the masks I sent up."

"No offence," Father Xavier said, "But they didn't seem befitting of our robes."

"None taken." Pendleton turned to a stocky man who wore the mask of a wild boar with spectacles. "I'd like you both to meet Dr. Andrew Coombs. He will be joining us on our journey tomorrow."

Dr. Coombs pushed his glasses up the snout of his boar face. "I'm looking forward to returning to the wilds. That's where I'm happy as a hog on a teat." He laughed at his own joke.

Andre asked, "You heard about what happened to our last doctor?"

"Yes, a bloody shame. Catching disease is a risk all good doctors take, I'm afraid. Especially out in the field." Dr. Coombs scratched thick beard whiskers that protruded the bottom of his mask. "But I assure you, I have experience working with epidemics. I just finished a mission in Lower Montréal where I battled a nasty case of cholera."

Andre said, "The effects of the Fort Pendleton's outbreak are much more dangerous."

"Let's not bring that up," Pendleton said, raising a champagne glass. "There's plenty of time to talk on the boat. Tonight we enjoy ourselves."

Lady Celeste stroked the black fur of Master Pendleton's coat. "Oh, Avery, you tell them the story of how you encountered the wolverine."

"Yes, do tell us," Dr. Coombs said, his face still concealed behind the hog's head. "I find the wolverine to be a quite fascinating predator. Sharp fangs and razor-like claws. A highly cunning beast."

"I'm certainly intrigued," Father Xavier said.

Pendleton smiled. "Very well, then, since you're all so inclined. Three years ago I was hunting turkey in northern Ontario with my Labrador. It was early autumn and the trees had just turned the most magnificent shades of red and orange. I was creeping through the woods, blowing into my turkey caller, when out of nowhere a black wolverine leaped from a tree and clamped its fangs into the nape of my lab. I tried to beat the varmint senseless, but damned if it wouldn't let go. The poor dog ran in circles yelping until it collapsed and bled to death."

Celeste gasped. "Oh, no."

Pendleton continued, "Well, I was furious, as you can understand. I aimed my shotgun..." He demonstrated this with his arms, taking a rifleman's stance. "...and shot at the snarling beast. It kept racing around the lab's body, dodging buckshot. The wolverine stole bites out of the dead dog as if to mock me. Despite my blasting, the stubborn creature wasn't about to leave its meal. I ran out of shots and stopped to reload. For a hair-raising moment it charged toward my boots. Just as the wolverine leaped for my thigh, I swung my shotgun like a cricket paddle. I smacked the beast square in the snout, and it sailed through the air until it landed paws up." He elbowed Dr. Coombs. "I showed the furry little devil what happens when you mess with Avery Pendleton."

The group clapped. Pendleton bowed, his face beaming.

"A splendid tale," Dr. Coombs said. "You know, the wolverine is the largest land-dwelling species of the weasel family."

Pendleton nodded. "While it killed my treasured Labrador, I respected the predator's tenacity. Ever since then, I have worn only coats made from wolverine pelts."

Father Xavier said, "Some say you are defined by what you wear."

Pendleton narrowed his eyes. "Then shall I call you 'Father Mink'?"

The priest smiled. "Touché."

Pendleton put his arm around Celeste. "Now, if you'll excuse us, Gentlemen, this little fox and I need to mingle. You may enjoy the ball until ten, and then I'm afraid you'll need to excuse yourselves."

"What happens after ten?" Father Xavier asked. "Everyone turns into pumpkins?"

"No," said Pendleton. "The party is open to members only. Until then, drink and eat as much as wish."

A crowd gathered around Pendleton. A man with thick, gray sideburns and a mask of a rat held up a fiddle. "Avery, we were wondering if you would play us an old Irish jig."

"Well, I'd be delighted." Pendleton placed the fiddle on his shoulder and played a fast-tempo tune. He danced through the crowd like a gypsy, grinning and twirling and kicking out his feet. The masqueraders cheered and danced around him.

75

Noble House

Willow sat at her beauty table powdering her cheeks. She kept looking in the mirror at the doorway, wondering when the man in her dreams was going to finally enter her boudoir and ravish her. She ran a brush through her hair, humming. There was a time in her life when her husband had been that man, three years ago, when Willow was eighteen and still living in Montréal. Avery Pendleton had started out so romantic, courting her for months, bringing her flowers and chocolates and escorting her to balls like a noble gentleman. He took her on carriage rides and picnics in the park. He doted on her. She had felt so in love then. He proposed to her on a bridge overlooking the St. Lawrence River. As her wedding present, he gave her a long, white fur coat and matching hat made from the finest snow fox. "You can wear all the furs your heart desires," he had promised.

Her dream life changed when Avery decided to return to Ontario to run the fur-trading fort. "Darling, you will love Ontario," he had said on their river voyage. "The wilderness is vastly more beautiful than the city. There are lush forests teeming with wildlife. Every furry animal you can imagine. And the moon and stars are brighter in the clearest skies you've ever seen." His enthusiasm for fort life had been infectious. She had indeed loved the harbor city of Montréal, but when

131

she arrived at the fort, Willow was immediately let down. Most of the colonists were foul-smelling, rum-swilling barbarians who had Indian wives and mixed-blood heathen children. The educated officers were either pompous womanizers or the quiet types and dreadfully boring. With Myrna Riley gone, Willow was the only white woman. She feared she would die of boredom. When his workers began disappearing, Avery's work became more demanding, and he began to spend more time with his officers. They spent every evening in the study sipping brandy and discussing God knew what. Over the past year, Avery grew more and more distant, having very little to say over dinner. Willow had grown so lonely and depressed. Then not long ago she discovered Doc Riley's little magic curio cabinet.

Willow pulled a glass tube out of her table drawer and removed the cork. She sprinkled white powder into her long pinky nail and snorted. She wiped her red nostril. When the rush hit like fireworks inside her head, she continued humming and drew eyeliner beneath her big blue eyes.

76

Hôtel de Rasco
Montréal

After Pendleton finished entertaining the crowd, a quartet started up another classical piece, and several masquerading couples flowed into a waltz.

Father Xavier watched as Dr. Coombs tried to sip his champagne through his hog mask. "This is too queer for me, if you know what I mean. I could go for something a little more stout, like an Irish beer and a thick-legged woman." Chuckling, he clapped both Jesuits hard on the shoulders. "See you on the boat, my good chaps."

Andre shook his head. "I still haven't a clue what the doctor looks like."

"I'm sure we'll have no trouble recognizing him," Father Xavier said. "I don't know about you, but I'm famished. Let's make our way to the buffet. I think we've earned the right to indulge in some fine cuisine."

Two slender debutants wearing mink coats and gold-sequined masks sauntered over. They were identical in height and appeared to be sisters, with the same pinned up dark hair and long, graceful necks. Each lady took one of Andre's arms and rubbed fingers through his thick hair.

"Ooh, *bel homme*, you are so delicious," said one.

"Such deep blue eyes," said the other.

"How about a dance?"

"No, I saw him first."

The twins played tug of war with Andre. Father Xavier shook his head as the brother looked like a mouse caught between two cats. "Sorry, ladies." He pried Andre from their clutches. "You'll have to find somebody else to fight over. This young man is training to be a priest."

"Oh, such a shame," they said in unison and then sauntered off toward their next victim.

The young Jesuit rubbed a hand through his mussed hair. "So many aggressive women in this hotel."

Father Xavier frowned at his pupil. "God is always testing us. You have to stand your ground and be quick to deflect offerings that might tempt you away from your vows."

They reached a quiet corner, where a lavish buffet offered delicacies of herring, mackerel, and Father Xavier's favorite. "Ah, Russian caviar." He spooned some on a cracker. "Now, if I were allowed only one sin..." He tossed the cracker into his mouth, savoring the salty flavors of the imported fish eggs. "Absolutely divine." He filled up another cracker. "Care for some?"

Andre shook his head, staring down at the floor. "Father, I have a confession..."

"Let me guess, you have a craving for chocolate covered strawberries."

"No, no, it's not the food. I...I lied about why I haven't slept much lately. I was afraid to tell you the truth."

Father Xavier raised an eyebrow. "You should always tell me the truth, no matter what. In our line of work, trust between an exorcist and his assistants is equally as important as faith."

"I'm sorry."

"Forgiven. Now what is your confession?"

The young apprentice took a long deep breath. "Being grabbed by those twins stirred up my body in impure ways."

"Really..." Father Xavier smiled. "Well, you're a man at the prime of his youth."

"That's not all. For several nights in a row I have dreamt of performing carnal acts with two ladies."

"Every man's fantasy. Such dreams are quite normal." He walked along the buffet, filling his plate.

"But, Father, these dreams are so vivid, that when I awaken I feel tempted to act upon them." Andre looked up from the floor. "I want so much to become a priest, but I'm having difficulty upholding my vow of chastity."

Father Xavier raised an eyebrow. "Have you remained chaste?"

"With women, yes, but when I'm alone..."

"I understand your conflict. Okay, listen to me, Andre. Thirty years ago, when I was about your age, I struggled with these very same feelings. Women are certainly tempting creatures. They stir up all sorts of wild desires. You must remember that while there is pleasure in satiating your lower desires, it taints the mind and steers you from a spiritual path."

"But how do you have so much restraint?"

"The key is devotion to God above all. Instead of looking at all the things that tempt my lower desires, I concentrate on my mission. When you devote yourself to fulfilling your higher desires, the lower ones go away. To do this, you must perform meditations twice daily to reflect on your growth. I can't stress enough the importance of keeping up with your daily excamen."

The novice inflated his cheeks with a heavy breath then exhaled. "Becoming a priest takes so much discipline and sacrifice."

The twins passed by again, fluttering their fingers, and the young Jesuit's gaze followed them.

Father Xavier tapped him on the crown. "Concentrate on God, Andre."

"This party is making me dizzy. If it's all right with you, I think I'll return to my room and meditate."

"That better be all that you do."

Andre blushed and descended the staircase.

Shaking his head, Father Xavier snacked at the buffet. Chastity had never been an issue for the ordained priest. Once he committed to being a man of the cloth, he no longer looked at women as a source of gratification. He had found his joy in doing the work of God so much greater. But taking a vow of poverty...that had been a greater challenge for a man who had been raised by the upper class. *God, forgive me for my sins.* He indulged in one more cracker of caviar.

77

Tom climbed the porch steps of a ramshackle cabin that sat off on its own next to the cemetery. A dream catcher with bones and feathers hung above the door, spinning in the wind. *I can't believe I'm coming here.* He started to knock then stopped just short of rapping the door. *No, this is a mistake.* He turned to walk back down the steps then paused, gripping a post. *No, right now I need to go anywhere but home.* He went back to the door and knocked. Anika answered with a look of shock.

"Hi," Tom said, feeling nervous, despite the fact that he was six feet tall and the native woman was no higher than his chest. "I...was wondering if we could talk."

She was wearing her usual deerskin dress and moccasin boots. Anika stared up at him a moment with those wildcat eyes, considering his request, then, without a word, she opened the door wider. Tom removed his hat and stepped into the tracker's private den.

He was immediately greeted by two huskies, one solid black and the other gray and white. While the other dogs stayed in their pen behind the house, these two must have gotten special privileges. As the friendly dogs sniffed Tom, he scratched each behind the ears.

"Makade, Ozaawi," Anika said in a commanding voice. "Leave him be."

The dogs curled up on a blanket near the stove fire. Her den smelled of sweet grass and apple cider and something delicious cooking in her tiny kitchen.

"I was just about to have a bowl of stew," she said. "You're welcome to some."

"That would be great."

While she went to her kitchen, Tom did a quick scan of her den. It was illuminated by several candles. Her furniture was sparse—two rocking chairs, a crude dining table with two chairs, a bookshelf stuffed with weathered hardback books. He read some of the spines. French titles like *Candide* and *Zadig* by Voltaire, *Le Paysan perverti* by Nicolas-Edme Rétif, and *le Diable amoureux* by Jacques Cazotte. Among the French novels were a few British encyclopedias, a dictionary, a book of Gaelic tales, and novels by Charles Dickens, Jonathan Swift, and a large collection of Jane Austen's: *Pride and Prejudice, Sense and Sensibility, Mansfield Park,* and *Emma.*

Tom looked at Anika as if seeing her for the first time. "Have you read all these?"

"Many times. I mostly read during winter."

"How did you get books out here?"

She spooned stew into two bowls. "My husband brought them from Montréal. He taught me to read."

Tom shook his head. *To believe I've slept with this woman, yet know so little about her.* Full-blooded Ojibwa, a native tracker, practicing witch, and reader of Jane Austen—Anika Moonblood was an

135

enigma. Tom felt his guard around her softening but he still wasn't sure if he could fully trust her.

We come from such different worlds.

There was still a lot of savage in her. Her bow leaned in a corner beside a workbench with knives and flint arrowheads that she carved to make her own arrows. A few times Tom had seen her out back with her bow, shooting a target. She was an impeccable archer.

Above the bench was a shelf covered with wood carvings—animal figurines, pipes, and musical instruments. He picked up a flute with an ornate pattern on it that looked like a totem pole. It reminded him of the last argument that he and Chris had the night before they journeyed to Manitou Outpost. Chris had been whittling a flute. Tom had chastised him for spending time with Anika and taking on her Indian ways. His son's passion for whittling had filled Tom with a fear that the Indians were going to change Chris into a heathen.

"Stew's ready," Anika said.

Tom placed the flute back on the shelf.

They ate rabbit stew at her table. Tom found himself not only enjoying the meal, but also her company. Her face softened, and for the first time Tom saw her exotic features as pretty. He remembered seeing her naked in his bedroom. Her smooth, reddish brown skin, small breasts, dark nipples. This stirred up primal urges. She gave him a look that told him she was feeling something, too. *She's Avery Pendleton's mistress*, Tom reminded himself. Thoughts of explaining himself to Pendleton brought Tom to his better judgment.

After supper, Anika pulled out two glasses and a flask of rum.

Tom held up his hands. "None for me."

"Just one drink."

"No, I've quit drinking."

As she poured a glass of rum for herself, Tom told her about his battle with whiskey and his recent decision to sober up. He felt relieved to get some burdens off his chest.

She brought a fur pouch to the table and offered it to him.

"What is this?" he asked.

"A medicine totem bag. Reach in and draw one."

He put his hand into the pouch. It was full of flat stones. He pulled out a white stone that was carved with a buffalo.

Anika cocked her head, narrowing her eyes at Tom.

"What?" he asked.

"You drew White Buffalo, the most sacred of all totems. It is your guardian, and you can call on its medicine for strength."

Tom looked at his watch. It was getting late, but for some reason he didn't want to leave. He felt a bond developing with this native woman, perhaps even a friendship.

78

At the masquerade party, Father Xavier walked in step to the baroque music. He spotted Avery Pendleton walking arm in arm with Lady Celeste. Another woman joined them, taking Avery's other arm. He kissed her neck and then the two women kissed. They stepped between a red velvet curtain and disappeared into the next chamber.

Curious, Father Xavier followed. He parted the curtain. Beyond was a dark lounge with plush furniture and dozens of moving shadows. The sparse candles provided barely enough light to see what was happening. People were moaning. A woman's curvy shape moved into the candlelight. Father Xavier gasped at the sight of her bare breasts.

He felt fingers dancing up his back. "Are you going into the Forbidden Chamber, Father?"

He turned to see the sisters wearing twin masks. "No, I was just leaving."

The sisters moaned in disappointment then stepped between the velvet curtains.

Feeling flustered, Father Xavier exited the ballroom. He walked along the hallway outside the ballroom. Small groups were scattered about, smoking cigarettes and laughing. Who were these people? He had heard that the wealthy elite were rumored to throw orgies, but he never imagined he'd witness one. No wonder Andre was so shaken. Perhaps he could sense they were surrounded by sinners. Father Xavier wondered about Avery Pendleton, their escort to Ontario. He was certainly a scoundrel. The man seemed to relish in sinning. *I must keep Andre as far away from that letch as possible.*

The priest went to a window overlooking the snowy streets. A horse buggy traversed down Rue St. Paul. Across the street stood the Royal Theater. In the far distance stretched the harbor, the boats all docked for the night.

Tomorrow he and Andre would begin their river journey to Ontario, first by steamboat, then by canoe. How long the journey would take was uncertain. Father Xavier had never been to a wilderness fort and was curious about the rustic life that his former mentor had. He was also eager to investigate the strange disease that had wiped out Manitou Outpost. Andre had spoken of a detective who was investigating the attacks, Inspector Hatcher. He was last seen grieving the loss of his son. Father Xavier felt compassion, for he had also lost people dear to him.

A childhood memory surfaced from the dark vault of his mind. He saw an image of himself as a young boy dressed in a Catholic school sweater, knickers, and a tweed cap. He came home from school one day to the sound of screaming from the far end of the family mansion. Young Xavier hurried up the winding marble staircase, passing statues and paintings of French royalty. At the top of the stairs, he ran down the wide corridor, past his father's library, an exotic room filled with books and stuffed hunting trophies. The screaming escalated from a room at the end of the hall, where a door was slamming open and closed.

Father Xavier snapped out of his reverie, his gaze returning to the flowing river. *Now why did that memory come up all of the sudden?*

Behind him a group of men chuckled and one of them said, "*Ego agnosco ostium,* Father."

The priest whirled around. The men in top hats had their backs to him and were laughing. He tapped one on the shoulder. "Excuse me, but did one of you just say something in Latin?"

"No." The man laughed with his friends, as if the priest were some kind of street beggar.

"My apologies." Father Xavier looked down the hallway. Several masqueraders were crowded outside the ballroom's front door. From somewhere in the crowd, a man cackled, giving Father Xavier goose bumps. Despite the festive evening, he suddenly felt like something was off. Maybe the caviar wasn't agreeing with him.

The man's deep voice spoke again, like a whisper in his inner ear. "*Ego agnosco ostium damno tui animus, Xavier, ellebarim, ellebarim, ellebarim.*"

Feeling the hairs on his neck bristle, the priest moved toward the gathering of socialites. Through the crowd of masked men and women, he spotted one man who stood at the far wall, facing him. He wore a black cape and top hat. His face was hidden behind a white tribal mask with red outlining the eyes and mouth. He lifted a gloved hand and twirled his finger in a circle. The whispering voice returned to the priest's ear.

"*Ego agnosco ostium damno tui animus, ellebarim, ellebarim, ellebarim.*"

The Jesuit pulled out a cross. *Is that you, Gustave?* A week after the exorcism, Father Xavier had learned that Gustave Meraux had killed the warden and escaped from the asylum. The demon had tricked him, playing dead. The Cannery Cannibal was once again on the loose.

138

The man in the tribal mask descended the staircase. Father Xavier followed, but several people crisscrossed in front of him. He leaned over the railing, peering down into the lobby. The man in top hat and cape knocked a bellhop aside and hurried out the front door.

Father Xavier dashed down the stairs and outside. A horse carriage sped by as he looked in both directions of the dark street. The mysterious man had vanished.

Did I just imagine that was Gustave? The priest stood there, suddenly feeling sick to his stomach. *That settles it. No more indulging for the rest of the journey.* As Father Xavier turned to head back into the hotel, a strange marking caught his eye. On a window covered in frost, the mysterious man had scratched a word—*ellebarim.*

79

Tom and Anika sat in rocking chairs, looking out the window at the cemetery. A thought occurred to him that Anika's husband was buried out there. "If I may ask, how long ago did your husband pass?"

She kept her gaze on a stick of wood she was whittling. Bark and woodchips flew to the floor. After a long silence, Tom said, "Sorry, I shouldn't have asked."

"It's been two winters," she said. "Only he's not buried here. He's out there." She pointed over her shoulder with the knife, indicating the forest. Tom waited for more, but there was no story that followed. He didn't pry. He couldn't imagine what her life had been like till now, growing up in the Ontario wilderness, marrying a man who worked for Fort Pendleton as a clerk. Now she was a widow living alone in a remote fort village where the men were either barbarian trappers or high society rakes like Avery Pendleton. Tom wondered if Anika's affair with the fort master was her choice. Again, he didn't pry. He watched her whittle, the deftness of her small hands as the antler-handled knife shaved flakes off the wood.

"Who taught you to whittle?"

"My uncle Swiftbear." Anika's face seemed to light up. "He said that whittling is a way to get the bad spirits out. They go into the wood, shape-shift, and become manitous. Protective spirits."

"I saw the ones you did on the shelf. You must have a lot of protective spirits."

"Not near enough." The blade dug in, carving notches and smooth curves to form wings. With each feather she etched, the animal seemed to take on life. Tom became mesmerized by her craft and could see why

139

Chris had taken an interest in it. The end of the stick quickly shaped into an owl head. She held it up to him.

"That's a mighty fine piece," Tom said.

"Here." She reached into her bag and pulled out a second knife and a stick. "Try your hand at it."

"No, I couldn't."

"What else are you going to spend your time doing?" She smiled.

"Okay, I'll give it a go." He accepted the knife and stick and started slicing off the bark.

"Wait." She grabbed his wrist. "First ask yourself what you would like to give away so that it no longer burdens you. Then ask the wood what spirit it would like to become."

Tom thought a moment and immediately felt a heavy pain in his chest. "My grief for my son."

Anika's eyes glazed over. "Then give it to the wood. The spirits will do the rest."

He started whittling with long, angry strokes. It felt good. Damn good. Like lightning was shooting out of his hands. A very crude spirit began to take form in the wood. And it looked like nothing from the animal kingdom.

80

Later that night, Andre tossed and turned in his bed. Women were haunting his dreams again. This time they rose from the floor around his bed like ghosts, one after the other, caressing him with phantom fingers. He woke in a knot of damp sheets. His skin was clammy. He climbed out of bed and washed his face with cold water from the bowl. Wide awake now, he put on his robe, and reached for his journal on the nightstand. He wrote at a ferocious pace.

Forgive me, oh Lord, for I am a horrible sinner, not fit to be a priest. I can't control the evil between my legs. No matter how much I flagellate myself, nothing seems to stop my desires. At tonight's party, my loins burned for those high society ladies. I had lustful thoughts and animal urges. Am I no better than the red-skinned heathens? Is there nothing that can tame the beast within me? I beg for mercy and strength to remain chaste, oh Lord.

Andre's constant tingling had been the main reason he left the party early. The whole night every woman excited him to no end. So many bare shoulders and low-cut dresses exposing cleavage. A visual feast of feminine flesh. The air was filled with such intoxicating perfume, Andre felt as if he had stumbled into the Garden of Eden, and Eve was there in many forms offering forbidden fruits. Against Father Xavier's warnings, Andre had returned to his room and relieved himself in sin. Afterward, he flogged his thighs, crying out in shame, "I am not fit to be a priest!"

Now, sitting on his bed with his back against the headboard, he drew on the lessons of his mentor for strength. Andre wrote more calmly in his journal:

Father Xavier said that once the Devil knows your weaknesses, he uses them to lure you to the valley of darkness. It is those who venture too far away from God that open themselves for possession. Daily meditation and prayers are the pathways of the righteous. To remain on the side of the Light, it is an exorcist's spiritual duty to meditate twice daily and constantly pray for forgiveness and strength.

Andre put his journal back on the nightstand. Remembering the meditation Father Xavier taught him, Andre sat cross-legged on his bed and closed his eyes. *Just silence the voices.* He envisioned himself on a grassy bank beside a lake. The waters were choppy, the wind blowing. He imagined the bright sun calming the wind until the lake went placid. *Concentrate on the stillness. Allow yourself to sink deeper and deeper into the water.*

There was a soft tap at the door. Andre opened his eyes and listened.

There it was again. The faintest tapping. He pressed his ear to the door. "Father Xavier, is that you?"

A French woman's voice whispered, "Andre... it's me, *mon amour.*"

"And me," giggled a second woman.

He peered through the keyhole, but the hallway was pitch dark. He inhaled the scent of floral perfume.

Fingernails clicked on the door. "Let us in, *amour.* We want to see you."

"*Oui, oui.*"

Andre closed his eyes. *Please, don't.*

Through the door, he heard giggles. Together they said, "You know you want to."

His nether regions stirred with an insatiable desire. His hand, as if having a will of its own, put the key back into the hole and unlocked it. He turned the knob, opened the door an inch, and then backed quickly toward his bed.

The door opened slowly. In the hallway stood two young women in fur coats. Twins. Andre remembered the two belles who wore identical gold masks at the party and fought over him for a dance. Now he gazed into the faces of two goddesses with smooth skin and cat-like amber eyes.

"Dear Lord, help me." He stepped back.

The two women stepped across the threshold. The door closed behind them.

"Mon homme..." The twins smiled as they sauntered toward Andre.

"We never got that dance."

81

Evil hides behind many faces.

The phrase came to Father Xavier in his sleep. The words echoed through his head in a raspy, whispering voice, waking him in a clammy sweat. Lying in the darkness of his room, he thought maybe he'd heard the voice again, echoing from the hallway.

Ego agnosco ostium damno tui animus, ellebarim, ellebarim, ellebarim...

It was the same mantra Gustave had chanted during his exorcism.

Father Xavier climbed out of bed. Carrying a candle in one hand and crucifix in the other, he padded barefoot across the room and listened at the door. The man's voice whispered, *Damno tui animus ellebarimmmmmmmmmm...*

Father Xavier opened the door, but no one was there. He stepped out into the dark hallway. One end was lit by moonlight that shone through a window. The opposite end tapered off into a void that seemed as deep and as dark as the tunnels beneath Laroque Asylum. He sensed a presence hiding there in that chasm, watching him with a malevolence so cold it sprouted gooseflesh up the priest's arms. He thought he saw the outline of a white and red mask press against the moonlight. If the shape had been there at all, it had retreated quickly, merging back with the darkness.

The wood creaked. A cold breeze blew through the hall, snuffing out his candle. Father Xavier stepped back into his room. If Gustave's demon had made its way into the hotel, then a dark hallway was not the proper battleground. He locked the door and doused it with holy water. He then grabbed a piece of chalk and drew a fresh line at the base of the threshold. He whispered a prayer and gesticulated. He sat on his bed and took a much-needed deep breath.

"You can't let the Beast scare you," he told himself.

After the episode earlier that night with the man in the red-and-white African mask, Father Xavier couldn't help feeling the dark forces now had an edge on him. He thought about the exorcism he'd performed on Gustave. Father Xavier had felt the Beast probing his brain, seeking some kind of weakness. The Jesuit had learned in his exorcist training to lock up his mind like a vault. Normally he was a master at it. But there was a moment during Gustave's ritual that Father Xavier became unhinged. In that moment of weakness had the Beast penetrated the vault?

Ego agnosco ostium damno tui animus, ellebarim, ellebarim, ellebarim.

Why did that mantra agitate him like an over-starched priest's collar, constricting his throat?

And what did it mean?

Using the chalk, he wrote the phrase on the wall beside his bed.

Recognizing the words in Latin, he read them out loud, "I know the doorway to condemn your soul, *ellebarim, ellebarim, ellebarim.*"

The last word, *ellebarim*, was neither Latin nor French nor Aramaic. Nothing that he'd ever seen in studying demonology. Father Xavier chalked it on the wall again, this time by itself.

Think, think, what does ellebarim *mean?*

The doorway to condemn my soul. What doorway did the dark forces find?

He studied the word closely, but his mind couldn't get a handle on it. Then he turned around and saw the word reflecting in the dresser mirror. His flesh went cold.

"Mirabelle."

82

Inside Andre's room, the oil lamps flickered. All but one extinguished, casting the two fur-cloaked women in silhouette. They petted one another's coats, purring. "You like what you see, Andre?"

"Very much so," he whispered. He was too enchanted to care how they knew his name. As they approached, each rounding one side of the bed, Andre's heart beat so wildly he feared it would burst. "I-I vowed to remain chaste."

The sister to his left pursed her pouty lips. "Ah, *mon amour*, why would you deny us?"

"When we both want you so badly," said the twin on his right. She stroked his ankle with feathery fingers.

Andre swallowed.

They danced together at the foot of his bed. The curves of their breasts protruded as the gaps of their coats widened. Fur slid down smooth skin, baring luscious shoulders. The coats fell to the floor. The twin sisters stood before him, curvaceous and supple, the dark doorways between their legs beckoning him to enter. Moaning, one woman ventured her hand downward, long fingers sifting through the dark nest. Her twin turned her back to him, dancing slow and sensual, hands reaching into the bun of her pinned-up hair and pulling it loose. Her long hair cascaded down her back. Above her buttocks was an odd marking. A tattoo of a red spiral seemed to spin.

Andre's body filled with so much lust he feared he might burst. Never in his life had he felt so much fire beneath his skin, so much craving to devour a woman's body, to sink so fully into her flesh. And here he had two identical beauties, offering themselves like fine delicacies.

"Are you ready for us?"

"*Oui*," he breathed, lying back on the bed. "I am ready for you."

No, fight it, Andre, begged the voice that was his. *Remember your vows.*

At the end of the bed, they crawled toward him like stalking jaguars. Their hands pawed up his legs, rubbing the bulge in his robe.

Don't let them.

Their amber eyes glowed brighter, as if catching the light of the moon. Their strokes intensified.

Dear God, help me.

One sister climbed onto his pelvis, pressing her weight down on his aching member. Her moisture soaked the fabric of his robe. She began to rock.

Angels in heaven...

As she arched her back, moaning, her sister opened Andre's robe and kissed his chest.

Fill me with Spirit.

He felt his chest swell with power. He chanted, "I am a man of God. I vow to remain chaste. Lead me not into temptation. Deliver me from—"

"You have already sinned, *mon amour*," said a voice from his past. The faces of the twin sisters shifted into his cousins, eighteen-year-old girls who had become dockside prostitutes. Their amber eyes glowed with yellow fire. "You gave up your chastity long ago."

"No, you stole it!" He reached up and grabbed the crucifix off the wall. "God release me of all past sins." He pressed the cross to the chest of the nearest sister. The flesh above her breasts smoked, and she burst into flame. Her sister screamed. Her eyes rolled back white. Her hair flapped wildly.

"Get out! Get out!" he yelled.

Pounding at the door. "Andre, open the door!" called Father Xavier.

Andre snapped his eyes open. The twins were gone. He was sitting cross-legged on his bed, wearing his robe. Three oil lamps were still burning. He released a breath of relief. Another dream.

The knocking continued.

"I'm coming." He checked his watch. Midnight. After pulling his robe closed and tying it into a knot, he opened the door. Father Xavier was standing in the hall fully dressed in his cassocks and holding his black case. "I heard you screaming."

"I had a nightmare," he said, breathing heavily. "The twins tried to seduce me again. I know who they are now." Andre shared a story of when he was twelve. He had entered the houseboat where his twin cousins lived. It was a brothel full of women sitting on the laps of sailors and dockworkers. The twins took him back to their room and molested him. He felt so ashamed. "Tonight, in my dream, they turned into demons."

Father Xavier began flicking holy water on the door and walls. "Get dressed and prepare for a long night of ritual. As I've suspected, Andre, you are being stalked by a pair of succubae."

Part Nine

Illusions

83

Another week passed without an outbreak of the cannibal disease. Since the canoe brigade left for Montréal, Fort Pendleton had remained locked down like a prison. No one had left the confines of the fort, nor was anyone let in. The Ojibwa had migrated to the south end of their reservation. The snowstorms had stopped. The woods remained quiet. The pack of hungry beasts seemed to have moved on to other feeding grounds.

Relieved of his detective duties, Tom had passed the time holed up in his cabin. The hermit life had become a quiet haven for healing and staying out of trouble. He played countless hands of Solitaire, ate, slept, and whittled. He already had his own collection of odd-shaped figurines. None of the animal totems looked as finely crafted as Anika's, or even like animals for that matter, but Tom was still developing his skills. "Whittling takes patience," she had told him. "Let the spirits teach you, and you will get better." He didn't believe Anika's talk of woodland spirits and manitous, but he did like the way whittling occupied his mind, and especially the way he felt after finishing a piece.

He returned to the rocking chair that had become his whittling chair. He sat facing out his back window at the spiked fence that surrounded the fort. The twilight, made pink by the setting sun, was fading into another night. For the first time in three years, Tom wasn't afraid to face the night sober. Something had changed in him since he started whittling. His mind was clearer. His willpower was the strongest it had been in years. He was physically stronger too from chopping logs daily, even though he had enough wood to whittle for months to come.

Holding his knife, he wondered what animal he could whittle next.

He did as Anika had suggested last week, *First ask yourself what you would like to give away so that it no longer burdens you. Then ask the wood what spirit it would like to become.*

He contemplated what burdens he wanted to give away. He felt into the pain inside his chest. It didn't take long to connect with the sadness. He missed his wife. Even though she had been gone for over three years, her ghost was still with him. "I wish to release the pain of missing Beth." Announcing the intention flooded Tom with emotions. Part of him didn't want to let her go. He searched a crate of sticks for the right piece of wood, but none seemed to call to him. Then he felt a sudden urge to go into his son's room. The feeling was similar to the hunches he experienced when doing detective work. He entered Chris' room. At the back wall was a shelf displaying animal totems that the boy had whittled. All of them were finely crafted. Chris really had a gift. Tom wished he could have appreciated it when his son was alive.

Why am I in here?

And then he saw it. The flute that Chris had been whittling the night they got into a fight. Tom picked up the flute. Several holes were unfinished. Half of the shaft was intricately carved with a buffalo locking horns with an elk. The rest of the hollowed out stick was blank. Tom felt a familiar tingling in his hands. This was the stick.

He sat back in his rocking chair, clutching the flute to his chest. "I wish to release the pain of missing Beth. What spirit would like to appear in this wood?"

As he said this, he heard a hooting sound. He looked out the window. The snow owl that he'd seen a week ago landed atop the stockade wall. Tom laughed. "I guess I'm supposed to whittle an owl."

With his knife, he began shaving off small splinters along the shaft. He tried not to think, to just let the blade guide him. He hollowed out two more holes and blew out the shavings. The flute made a sound that was much prettier than before. Smiling, he turned the instrument over to the end opposite to the sparring buffalo and elk. He began carving a pattern into the blank wood. All of Tom's sadness rose to the surface. Tears welled in his eyes as he saw what the blade was carving. It was a woman's face. Beth's face.

84

Tom awoke the next morning to the sound of an angel singing.

Am I still dreaming?

He rubbed his face. Gray light filtered in through the bedroom windows. He felt lighter, peaceful. Last night he had whittled well past midnight. He had cried for hours as he carved his wife's visage into the flute. He had spoken to her ghost, as if Beth were there in the room with him. He reminisced about their happy times together. Then something amazing happened. His cravings to drink went away. He slept straight through the night.

Today was a fresh new day. As he stretched in bed he heard the angel singing again, along with the sound of pots banging in the kitchen.

Tom sat up. Someone was inside his cabin! Was Anika back? If he had been stone-cold drunk, he might have made the mistake of sleeping with her again. But last night he had gone to bed alone.

He climbed out of bed and pulled on his trousers over his red long johns. The floor was cold, so he slipped into his boots. He opened his bedroom door to the smell of frying bacon. He froze. There in his kitchen, cooking at the stove, stood his long-dead wife.

85

Propelled by a paddlewheel, the steamboat rightly named *Persistence* trudged up the Ottawa River. Father Xavier walked along the upper decks. Snow flurries speckled his heavy coat and Russian mink hat. He kept his hands warm in his pockets. His fists clutched around a metal cross and flask of holy water that he now carried with him everywhere.

After leaving Montréal a week ago, the vessel had crossed over from French Quebec into British Ontario. They might have reached Ottawa sooner were it not for the sheets of ice that floated over the surface of the river. There was only a narrow channel of open water, and oftentimes the ice raked against the sides of the boat. The steamer had gotten stuck once, but the ice chippers jumped into their dinghy and broke it up.

Today there was a crowd of onlookers up on deck. At the corner rail, a couple was feeding bread to some seagulls. The passengers were a mixture of Brits, Scotch, French, Irish, Danes, Americans, and even a Chinaman. It seemed the farther west they traveled, the more Canada was becoming as culturally diverse as Europe.

Father Xavier spotted Andre at the bow, leaning over the rail. He wore his flat-brimmed hat and a heavy, gray coat over his cassock.

"*Bonjour*, Andre. How did you sleep last night?"

"Peaceful, Father. I haven't dreamed of the twins since the hotel."

Andre had a healthier complexion to his face. Father Xavier almost lost another apprentice to the dark forces. Last week at the hotel, Andre had faced the demons of his past and summoned up enough faith to fight them. Father Xavier spent that entire night performing a ritual to keep the succubae at bay.

"You should feel great confidence in yourself, Andre. Female demons can be the most challenging for a man to conquer."

"Looking back on it, it was a relief to finally face what happened with my cousins. Their abuse when I was a boy tormented me for years. I feel different now. More awake."

"Splendid." Father Xavier grinned. "Then tell me what you've learned in your reading."

Andre paused to reflect. "Hmm, an exorcist must not easily believe that a person is possessed by an evil spirit. He should be able to distinguish a possessed person from someone merely suffering from a physical illness."

"And what are the signs of a possessed person?"

"He speaks or understands unknown languages, like Aramaic. And he can show physical strength beyond what's normal for his age and build." Andre scrunched his eyebrows together. "Father, how do you know if an exorcism is successful?"

The boat dipped with the rapids, and Father Xavier gripped a rail. "That is often hard to tell. Sometimes the evil spirit goes into hiding and appears to have left the body. An exorcist must always be wary that the demon may be tricking him. You must follow up with the recovering person to see if they show any more signs. You must learn what words agitate the demon out of hiding. Only time can tell if the person is free and clear of the evil spirit."

They paused to take in the beauty as the forest landscape transformed into the wood structures of an approaching river town. Along the shore stood a mill where logs floated. Lumbermen worked along the shores, guiding the logs. Steamboats, York boats, dinghies, and canoes all competed for space in the icy harbor.

"We're finally reaching Ottawa," Andre said. "I'm ready to stand on still land again."

"It would be a delight if we could find a place to have breakfast." Father Xavier looked down the starboard side. The steamer was paddling toward a dock. Seagulls flew by, cawing toward a dinghy where fishermen were carrying buckets filled with this morning's catch. Several wood buildings lined the pier. "Ah, I see a tavern up ahead. Perhaps they'll have some coffee and eggs."

The steamboat's captain yelled at the crew as the vessel bumped against the docks.

"We're halfway through our journey, Father. But the river ride only gets harder." Andre pointed toward a group of voyagers packing two long canoes.

86

Tom stood mesmerized by the miracle he was seeing.

He was somehow back inside his Montréal house. In the kitchen, Beth Hatcher hummed as her powdery hands prepared breakfast. She was wearing an apron over a long, green gown with buttons that went up the front to a lacy collar. It was the dress she often wore when they went to mass. She turned away from him, pulling a tray of biscuits from the oven. The side of Beth's face seemed to glow in the morning light. Her blonde hair, not yet fastened into a bun, dangled over her shoulders.

If he were still dreaming, Tom didn't want to wake up.

He entered the kitchen, his legs shaking. Warm feelings sparked the core of his heart, reigniting an old flame. The angel hummed a beautiful tune, the melody of a woman in love. She scraped eggs off the iron skillet.

He stood directly behind her now, breathing slow and deep, inhaling her perfume. Lilacs and orange blossom. The scent took him back to a time when the love between two young newlyweds was in full bloom. Tom and Beth had married in France, where Tom was working at the time. On their honeymoon, they traveled the countryside visiting several small villages. As they were riding an open carriage on a sunny day, the air became filled with the aroma of citrus. The landscape changed from vineyards to orchards of orange trees blooming with white blossoms. Entering a Provence called Grasse, they passed a sign that read, *Manufacture de Parfum.*

Beth's blue eyes had lit up. "Oh, Tom, can we stop there?"

He checked his pocket watch. "We need to keep on schedule to make our train."

In truth they had hours to spare before they needed to leave for Paris, but Tom had no interest in touring a perfume factory. Beth pleaded him, winning him over with her infectious enthusiasm. She had used this tactic to talk him into visiting art museums, old cathedrals, a chocolate factory, and a dreadfully boring night at the opera. Once again Tom acquiesced and instructed their horse buggy driver to turn down the dirt road that wound through the orange trees. The tour of the perfume factory turned out to be the highlight of their trip. The stone buildings, set in the center of the orchard, had once been a monastery. The factory workers who brought in baskets of fresh-picked flowers were smiling and laughing. The perfume makers were an elderly French couple who bickered in a playful way. The man had tufts of white hair spiking from his cheeks, and the woman was tall and slender with a youthful gleam in her eye. The older couple took the newlyweds on a private tour. In an open-air room where flower petals were poured into glass vats of boiling oils, they described the process of making the perfect fragrance.

At one point, while the ladies sniffed scented gloves, the old man escorted Tom off to one side where they had a view of the purple fields of lilac. "*Messier*, I must say, you have selected a beautiful blossom."

Tom nodded and looked across at Beth. She made eye contact, smiling as she held a white glove to her nose and listened to the talkative woman ramble about rose petals. Tom's chest swelled. "I feel like I'm the luckiest man."

The old man waggled his finger. "You know, the secret to making the perfect perfume is mixing just the right ingredients. Some say the rose is the scent of love, but I say the pathway between two hearts is lilac." He went to another sun-kissed window that had no glass, but was merely a square portal bordered with honeysuckle. Beyond stretched the orchard of orange trees. The old perfume maker inhaled deeply then released a long, drawn-out breath. "The citrus scent of the orange blossom adds a touch of sweetness." He picked up a purple bottle off a shelf. "This is a fragrance I call *Embrasser de Paradis*. The Kiss of heaven. I made it for my wife when we were young and I was just learning how the power of a woman's love can enrich a man's life." He handed the bottle over to Tom and winked. "A wedding gift. May your marriage always smell as sweet as mine."

Now Tom stood in the kitchen, intoxicated by the scent of lilac and orange blossoms. Beth stood right here in front of him. Her ghost was so real and so close he could almost touch her. He desired to pull her into him and kiss her. He feared if he touched the angel, she would disappear.

Beth turned around, her eyes widening. "Oh, Tom." She placed a hand against her chest. "I didn't hear you wake up." Her voice was different. Tom saw double, as a ghostly face overlaid his wife's. Beth shifted into Willow.

Tom leaned back against the table, blinking. "What..." He touched her arm to make sure she wasn't just a mirage. Willow Pendleton was really standing in his kitchen.

"What are you doing here?"

She laughed. "Making a royal mess of breakfast. I hope you like

151

runny eggs."

Tom looked at the feast of eggs with broken yolks, charred links of bangers, and black, lumpy biscuits. "Yes, of course, it looks delicious."

"You don't have to lie. I can see that it's atrocious." Spots of white flour smudged Willow's cheeks and nose. Her face shifted back into Beth's.

Feeling entranced by her scent, Tom wiped away the flour, caressing her cheek. Her hand touched his, holding it against her face.

"Oh, heavens." She pulled away abruptly, tucking a strand of hair behind her ear and looking out the window. "It's a beautiful morning, isn't it? The sun is finally breaking through the clouds."

Beth turned back into Willow again, then back into Beth. Tom's feelings were so confused he could no longer tell the difference. He touched her shoulder. Beth turned around.

Tom whispered, "God, how I have missed you."

His wife smiled. "You have?"

"I think about you constantly."

"And I, you," she breathed.

Beth placed her palm on his chest. The warmth sent tingles deep into his body. He was overcome by tremors. She gazed up at him with loving eyes, as if she were peering into him. The brightening sunlight made her blonde hair so radiant.

Lilac and orange blossoms. The emotions of their honeymoon all rushed back. Tom felt breathless and dizzy, toppling over the edge, falling down a slippery slope into the silky abyss of new love. He pulled the angel into his arms. He kissed her passionately, desperately, feverishly. The softness of her lips and feel of her touch were as intoxicating as the fragrances that perfumed her skin. She moaned as he unbuttoned her lacy collar, and kissed her neck, venturing his lips downward with each pluck of a button, exploring the valley between her creamy white bosoms.

"Oh, Tom," she breathed, rubbing her fingers through his hair. They stumbled into the den, bumping the rocking chair. The heat of his chest went straight to his loins. Like a wild heathen, Tom pulled her blouse down her shoulders. Her bosoms fell free, cushioning against his chest. She pulled up his shirt and unbuckled his pants. They kissed all the way into his bedroom, knocking against the dresser. They stripped down to their undergarments, tangled again, and fell onto the fur blankets. She moaned sweet whispers into his ear, sending butterfly wings of pleasure flapping through his head. He felt so right in her arms. As he lay on top of her, inhaling the sweet fragrance of lilac and orange blossoms, Tom opened his eyes, seeing the woman he was kissing was not Beth, but the wife of Avery Pendleton.

Tom pulled away. "Oh, God!"

Willow opened her eyes. "What?"

"What are we doing?"

"I don't know," she gasped. "But it's wonderful." Her hair was tousled, her lipstick smeared, and Tom fought back the desire to rip off her undergarments and sink fully into her.

He climbed out of bed. "I'm sorry. I don't know what came over me."

"It's okay." Her lids hanging heavy over her eyes, she reached for him. "Come back to bed."

Tom put on his trousers. His heart raced as he realized the consequences of being intimate with his boss' wife. "We can't go through with this, Willow, you're...you're married, for Christ's sake."

"It's okay, love." She giggled. "Avery and I don't love each other anymore."

"You're still his wife!" He paced the room, fighting with his belt buckle. "Damn it!"

The young woman remained half covered by the disheveled blankets.

"Willow, please, get dressed."

She rose up on her elbow. The blanket fell, exposing one of her breasts. "I'd rather stay right here."

"Just do as I say!" Tom tossed her gown onto the bed.

"Mmm, you're so sexy when you're angry."

"This is no light matter, Willow. If anyone finds us this way..." He pushed aside the curtains and peered out the window. The morning was so damned bright. He had a direct view of one of the watchtowers. And the sentries had a direct view of his front door.

Shit! Why do I keep screwing things up? In a matter of one week, Tom had crossed a dangerous boundary with the two women who belonged to Avery Pendleton. His mistress *and* his wife.

I'm walking on very thin ice.

She finally got back into her gown. Tom took her elbow and guided her to his back door. "No one can know this happened. Willow, promise me you won't tell anyone, or your husband will have my head."

"Promise." She wrapped her arms around his waist. "Mmm, we'll have our own little secret now."

She kissed his lips, and he felt himself succumbing once again. A moment later he pulled away, the ghost of his wife staring up at him. He wanted her to stay, to pretend she was Beth and take her back to bed.

Willow tucked her hair into her white fur hat. "Come dine with me and the officers tonight. I'll have my cook prepare something exquisite."

"No, that's a very bad idea."

"I insist, Tom Hatcher." She kissed him again. "I will tell the officers that you will be joining us for supper." Before Tom could protest, Willow slipped out the back door, humming her way back to Noble House.

87

Willow left Tom Hatcher's cabin feeling as if her feet were floating above the ground. His kiss still lingered on her lips. She couldn't stop smiling. *He adores me.* The idea of it shouldn't have seemed so shocking. Men had chased Willow all her life, telling her how much they desired her, how pretty she was. In Montréal she had fended off many gentlemen suitors. But marriage and three years of fort life had worn down her confidence. And lately, with Avery ignoring her and Tom barely showing interest, Willow had begun to wonder if she'd lost her feminine charm.

Inspector Tom Hatcher actually kissed me.

She giggled to herself, as if she were a Catholic schoolgirl who had just attended the boys' school dance and received her first kiss. She was absolutely giddy thinking about what happened today. For a heart-skipping moment when she was standing in the kitchen, Tom looked at her with so much intensity, and then ravished her just like the wild man in her dreams.

Willow had the recurring dream again last night and woke up before dawn feeling heated and flushed. Every part of her hungered to be caressed, kissed, and fully taken. She had even touched herself in unladylike ways, imagining that Tom was inside her, but that was not enough to satisfy her desires. For months the recurring dreams promised that her lover was coming. The dreams tortured her, especially now that she didn't have Andre to confess them to. This morning Willow decided she could no longer wait for fate. It was time to make something happen.

Now she felt heated and flushed just thinking about having Tom over for dinner. Tonight was the night to live out her fantasy with the man of her dreams. She spun in a circle, as if her lover were waltzing her across the courtyard.

A loud *crack* stopped Willow mid-dance.

Anika Moonblood stood outside her cabin, chopping logs with an axe. She watched Willow pass, giving her the evil eye. Avery's favorite whore wasn't going to spoil this day. Willow smirked, sending Anika a look that said, *I have the better man.*

Out of nowhere, a freezing wind howled between the cabins, nipping at Willow's face. She pulled her white fur collar tight around her throat and hurried across the courtyard toward Noble House, fearful that the Indian witch might curse her.

88

Anika brought down the axe, splitting another log. She was no fool. She had watched Lady Pendleton trying her best to seduce Tom for the past three weeks. This morning after sunrise Willow had visited his cabin. And here she was an hour later coming down his porch steps smiling and dancing.

The axe blade cracked wood.

Willow stopped and stared coldly in her direction. Like a snow fox suddenly startled in the woods. Anika returned a glare that sent the white woman running.

Serves her right.

For the past few nights, Anika had gotten drunk alone in her cabin. She had been tempted to go see Tom, but feared he would only throw her out. Her heart couldn't take that again. The night they slept together, Anika had been aware of everything that happened. Just the touch of his hands made her skin turn warm. The way he had looked at her that night made her feel like she was more than just a white man's whore. There was a depth in Tom's hazel eyes that Anika had never seen in a man before. More than anything she had wanted to go back to him and just get lost in his eyes.

She had thought maybe Tom was being distant with her because he was still grieving. So she stayed away, hoping that in a month or two he would come around and see that she could make him a good wife. Then Anika would express to him that the warmth she felt in her chest was more than drunken lust. But it seemed that Lady Pendleton had swooped in like a fox seizing a wounded rabbit.

Anika noticed something on the ground. Something that Willow had dropped. A white mitten made from fox fur.

89

Brian Moreland
Ottawa, Ontario

As the *voyageurs* loaded the two canoes, lightning bolts crackled the sky over the river harbor. Thunder rumbled. The two Jesuits opened up their umbrellas as they walked side by side along the pier. The wind blew sleet sideways, spraying into Andre's face. "Should we head back to the canoes?" he asked, having to talk over the gale.

"Not just yet." Father Xavier leaned in close. "Have you noticed we're being followed?"

"No. By whom?" Andre looked around at all the fisherman climbing down from boats, carrying buckets filled with fish and black clams that Andre decided were mussels. The Jesuits passed between more men gutting fish and throwing the chum into buckets. Seagulls flew overhead, crying out for scraps of meat. The stink and the crowds and the circling birds were making Andre dizzy. "I don't see anyone..." The crowd of fishermen cleared a view of a woman wearing a fur coat. The hood concealed her head with such deep shadow, it gave the illusion she had no face. It was her familiar saunter and the way her hips moved that made Andre's blood run cold. "No, it can't be."

Father Xavier grabbed his wrist. "Follow me."

They moved beyond the fishy stench and entered a section of the pier where men and women were waiting to board the steamboat back to Montréal.

Father Xavier said, "In your dream, you said you chanted a prayer and burned a cross against the chest of one of the twins...then what happened?"

"She burst into flame." Andre felt his heartbeat thumping his breastbone. "What's happening?"

"My guess is in that in your last nightmare you exorcised her spirit. But what happened to the second sister?"

"She turned into a demon and then I woke up. You think the woman following us is a succubus?"

"Shhh." Father Xavier put a hand to his lips.

The cloaked woman walked past them. Her hood was turned away so Andre couldn't see her face. *Maybe we're just spooked,* he thought. *She's just one of the passengers waiting to board the steamboat. Then why do I feel such a cold feeling?*

And then she turned her head slightly, looking back over her shoulder as she passed. Andre reeled as he saw a crab crawling down her damp, fish-pale cheek.

90

Evil hides behind many faces, Father Xavier thought, remembering the phrase from his dream. He also witnessed the horrid profile when the woman turned. Her gaunt cheek and blue-lipped mouth resembled a cadaver pulled up from the river. She faced forward again and merged into the crowd gathering beneath the covered waiting area beside the steamboat. Many of the women were wearing fur coats, and Father Xavier lost sight of their lady stalker.

On the steamboat's upper deck, a crewman yelled, "All aboard."

The awaiting passengers began to crowd around the ramp.

"Okay, Andre, let's find out if she's really a succubus." Father Xavier pulled out his silver cross and walked along the railing. "Let's each take a side."

Andre nodded and crossed the wide dock to the opposite rail. They walked parallel to one another, searching all the wet and miserable faces of the passengers. Near the rear of the waiting area, where numerous crates were stacked, Father Xavier spotted a fur-cloaked woman standing off by herself.

The priest approached her from behind. Holding his breath, he raised the cross directly behind her neck, and whispered a prayer in Latin. The woman turned and jerked her head back. Her plump face went from shock to a scowl. "I beg your pardon."

"Don't mind me, *Mademoiselle*, I'm just warding off that lightning." He raised the cross to the sky, gesticulating.

"Well, do it somewhere else." She snubbed her nose at him and moved down the railing.

The damsel was something wicked, all right, but not the woman he was looking for. *Where are you, demon?* Father Xavier heard one of the passengers cry out. Turning, he saw Andre across the pier, bumping through the crowd. Ahead of him the hooded figure weaved through the onlookers, heading for the cargo area at the rear of the docks. Father Xavier hurried down the rail. The fur-cloaked woman disappeared into the maze of crates and stacked luggage. Andre followed directly behind her. Father Xavier took a different path, skirting along the water's edge. He reached an aisle where the woman was running in his direction. She stopped and hissed.

Father Xavier held up the cross. "Show yourself, demon. What is thy name?"

A raspy voice said, "My name is *Mirabelle*." She pulled back the hood. Damp stringy hair, like black seaweed, hung over her sickly pale face. The fur coat dropped to the dock. She wore only a soaked nightgown that clung to her skeletal body. The small breasts of an adolescent girl poked the transparent fabric, exposing her nipples. When Mirabelle looked up with her dead gray eyes, Father Xavier froze, staring in awe and terror.

The priest took a step back, feeling dizzy.

The girl craned her neck, walking toward him with raised hands. Blood trickled from two slashed wrists. She whimpered, "Help me, brotherrrrr..."

Andre came bounding up behind the thing that resembled Father Xavier's long-dead sister. Her eyes turned black. Hissing, she fled behind a wall of stacked crates.

"That was *her*," Andre said. "The other twin."

Father Xavier snapped out of his paralysis. "We've got her cornered."

They both ran to the stacked cargo at the far end of the pier, splitting up. As Father Xavier rounded the crates, holding out his cross, he paused to catch his breath. Around that corner was his dead sister.

Evil hides in many skins.

Mustering up more courage, Father Xavier raced around the corner and was thrown back by a burst of flapping feathers. He fell on his rump. A flock of ravens spiraled upward over the harbor. The birds cawed and flew upriver. Andre helped Father Xavier to his feet. They stood at the end of the pier, catching their breath.

"Where did she go?" Andre asked.

Father Xavier just shook his head, ashamed that he was trembling. There was no trace of the girl who looked like Mirabelle. Nothing but a few falling feathers.

91

An hour later, the two canoes carrying sixteen men cut through the rapids. Oars slashed the white-frothed surface as the voyagers paddled up the Ottawa River. A herd of storm clouds pursued them on rumbling hooves. A deafening thunderclap splintered the sky with a dozen bright cracks. The oarsmen ducked, hunching their shoulders as they paddled faster in a race to escape the squall. The attempt was futile, for the icy torrents reached them, and sleet rained down hard. Father Xavier huddled in the middle with a blanket wrapped around his shoulders. The choppy waves added nausea to the priest's misery. Another hot wave surged up his throat, and he vomited over the side.

"First canoe ride, eh, priest?" Dr. Coombs yelled against the wind. The burly physician sat one bench back. His thick arms drove a paddle into the river, splashing cold water onto Father Xavier's back. He glared over his shoulder. Dr. Coombs was actually grinning. "I bet you've spent your entire life in the city, am I right?"

Father Xavier wiped a handkerchief across his mouth. He had thrown up the last of his breakfast and was now just heaving.

Dr. Coombs slapped him on the shoulder. "Don't worry, priest, this is just Mother Nature's way of showing us she's in a foul mood. Kind of like a woman before she gets her monthly curse." He laughed. "It's all part of the adventure."

"Do you have anything...for sea sickness?"

"Sorry, I don't. All my remedies are packed in a crate. I can fish something out once we portage, but until then you'll have to muster up some sea legs."

Father Xavier clung to a rum barrel stored next to him. *If I survive this ride, it will be a miracle.*

He didn't know what was worse, the constant rise and fall of the rapids, or having to listen to Dr. Coombs talking so gleefully about the ride. The Jesuit was thankful Andre was riding up two benches forward with Master Pendleton. Father Xavier would be embarrassed to have his apprentice see his mentor sick as a greenhorn at sea.

He wondered how his Uncle Remy dealt with motion sickness while sailing across the globe with the French Navy.

"Trick is to watch the horizon," Dr. Coombs said, as if reading his thoughts. "And drink plenty of water." He offered his pouch.

"*Merci*, but no." Father Xavier knew if he put anything else in his stomach he'd only wretch it back out. He watched the passing trees that lined the river. It seemed to help, at least with his queasiness. But he was riddled by more than just the upward and downward motion and numbing cold. He couldn't shake the nightmare he had witnessed back at the docks. His dead sister Mirabelle had stood before him in the flesh, her skin as pale and clammy as the last time he saw her.

Somehow the demon that possessed Gustave Meraux had found a way into the vault of the exorcist's mind and unleashed a Pandora's box of dark memories.

92

The Goddard Mansion
Montréal, 1830

When Xavier was ten years old, he lived in a mansion in the elite section of Montréal. His father, a relentless big game hunter, was away on some far-off safari in Africa or India or the Canadian wilderness. Xavier's mother was a busy socialite who made more time for galas and tea parties than her own two children. Xavier's older sister, Mirabelle, was the only family member who ever paid attention to him. She used to read him books and take him on adventures through the garden, where she swore fairies and elves lived. They often flew kites or played hide and seek or sat and fed the ducks at the pond in their back yard. At age thirteen, Mirabelle had been a blooming girl with long, curly hair and freckles covering her nose and cheeks. She was smart and funny and loved to play games. Xavier idolized her.

One day after school, he came home to the sound of screaming from upstairs. He raced up the winding marble staircase. On the second floor he ran down the wide corridor. The screaming escalated from a room at the end of the hall. A door slammed open and closed. His sister's bedroom. As Xavier reached the threshold, the door stopped banging. He stepped inside.

"What is thy name, demon?" Two priests stood at the foot of Mirabelle's bed, chanting and flicking bottles of water. Xavier's mother was in here, too, along with the family doctor. The four adults were all facing his sister's bed. Mirabelle's wrists were tied to the bedposts. Her face was withdrawn, her eyes bulging, her mouth opened into a horrid grimace. She twisted her head at a strange angle, gazing at Xavier with eyes that were rolled back solid white. She snarled, "Brotherrrr..."

The room seemed to shake. Mirabelle's four-poster bed rose off the floor an inch, and then tapped the floorboards. "Xavier, help meeeeee..."

"Mirabelle!" Before Xavier could touch her, his mother yanked him out into the hall. She explained that his sister was under the Devil's spell, and the priests were performing an exorcism.

"Xavierrrrrrrr!" Mirabelle kept screaming his name, pleading for him to help her. He wanted to save her, but the adults wouldn't let him back in the room. So he remained out in the hall, listening to the priests chanting. He brought out his own bible and prayed for his sister. He pleaded for God to send down angels to fight the demon that possessed his sister.

Now, forty years later, Father Xavier floated in a canoe of what could very well be the river Styx, carrying them all to hell. *No, I can't think such thoughts, or the demons have won.* The priest closed his eyes and returned his attention to the deep inner faith that had gotten him through many spiritual storms. *It wasn't Mirabelle back at the docks,* he reminded himself. *It was the forces of evil.*

The demon who had possessed Gustave Meraux, the Cannery Cannibal.

The man at the masquerade party disguised in the red-and-white tribal mask.

The twin succubae in Andre's dreams.

And the skeletal girl with Mirabelle's face...they were all faces of the Beast who calls himself "Legion."

Evil hides behind many faces.

Father Xavier gazed at the faces of the *voyageurs* paddling the canoe parallel to him. On his canoe, Master Pendleton and Brother Andre were facing forward. Father Xavier turned to look at the faces of the men paddling behind him. Dr. Coombs grinned with an odd gleam in his eye. The queasiness returned to Father Xavier's stomach as a dark realization hit him.

No one could be trusted.

93

At dusk, just as the sun was setting behind the fort's spike-tipped walls, and the rising moon cast silvery light along the leafless branches, Tom made the brisk walk across the snowfield that covered the central courtyard. There was no wind, so it was unusually quiet this evening, the only sound being his shoes crunching over hard-packed snow.

Tom felt aristocratic wearing his Sunday best—a brown wool overcoat and three-piece suit. The ensemble was topped off with a D'Orsay hat that had once been his father's. Like the pistol Tom always carried, the one with the Hatcher family crest emblazoned on the handle, the brown top hat held a special meaning. His father had worn it while leading Montréal's police force and hobnobbing with the city's upper crust. Orson Hatcher once said, "A man can rise from middle class to nobility just by wearing the right clothes and mixing in with the right people. Hatcher men have always been able to mix with both worlds." The D'Orsay hat was one of many heirlooms that his father had passed down. While Tom felt more comfortable dressing modestly, he occasionally relished dressing up for formal events. Dining at Noble House was just such an occasion.

"Tom, is that you?" spoke a woman's voice off to his left. Anika was walking with Makade. The black wolf dog woofed. The native tracker was wearing a hooded fur parka. Her bare hand clutched the legs of a dead rabbit that hung by her side. Anika narrowed her eyes at Tom's outfit. "She must have cast a powerful spell on you."

"Who?"

"Lady Pendleton. Isn't that the reason you're wearing that silly hat?"

Tom gripped the lapels of his coat. "I've been invited to supper."

She tilted her head. "Is that all?"

Tom didn't like her tone. "If you have something to say, Anika, then speak it."

She looked away briefly, swallowed, and then once again cut into him with her sharp gaze. "This morning I saw Willow come out of your cabin."

Tom bristled. "She stopped by to check on me."

"She was there for quite a spell."

"It's nothing to be concerned about." His agitation became overpowered by a sudden nervousness. He feared the Indian woman might have peered into the windows and saw him and Willow kissing. "Were you spying on me?"

Anika stepped forward. "Everyone in this damned village knows Willow fancies you. And when you two are alone behind closed doors...word goes 'round is all I'm saying."

Tom's chest burned with a mixed brood of fear and anger. He stared at the surrounding cabins. "And who's spreading such gossip?"

"Never mind that. You should be more worried about having secret liaisons with Master Pendleton's wife. He is not a man to cross."

Tom's anger flared. "Anika, you are certainly not one to speak. Everyone knows you're Avery's whore."

The Indian woman's eyes filled with rage. Grunting like an animal, she turned and stomped off toward her cabin, the dead rabbit in her hand dripping a trail of blood.

94

Inside Noble House, Tom started up the winding staircase. As he climbed the second flight, he heard voices and footsteps coming down. Lt. Hysmith and the heavy-set officer named Walter Thain rounded the banister with one of the native servants, a girl of about fourteen. They stopped at the landing when they saw Tom.

"Good evening, Inspector." Walter Thain nodded. "Good to see you out and about."

"I'm feeling much better, thanks." Tom was grateful he had shaved earlier. He wanted to get on the officers' good graces and return to work.

Lt. Hysmith's face pinched. "What brings you to Noble House?"

"Uh, Lady Pendleton invited me over for supper." Tom furrowed his brow. "It was my understanding you two would be joining us."

"No, not tonight," said Thain. "We have business to attend to." He looked at Hysmith. "Our work seems to never end."

Tom studied the servant girl that stood between the officers. Her eyes never looked up from the floor. "I'm eager to get back to work myself. Perhaps I can assist you. I can tell Lady Pendleton another evening."

"Nonsense," said Thain. "It would be rude to decline a lady's dinner invitation, especially when the cooks have gone to all the trouble." He patted Tom's arm. "Enjoy supper, Inspector, and do behave yourself. Lady Pendleton can cast quite a spell." He winked. Hysmith gave Tom a suspicious look before climbing down the stairs.

Did they know about what happened this morning? He feared one of the watchtower sentries might have spotted Willow leaving his cabin. Or perhaps Anika was the Judas and went straight to the officers. Would she doublecross Tom? If she were scorned, she bloody well might. Hell hath no fury and all that.

No, I'm just on edge, Tom decided. If Hysmith knew the truth then he would have said something. The lieutenant had never been a man to withhold his discontent.

As the officers rounded the lower landing, Thain put his bloated hand on the girl's shoulder. Tom got a creepy feeling. He quietly followed them down the stairs. Thain and Hysmith took the native girl down the bottom stairwell to the cellar.

What was this about?

Tom had never been down to the ground floor. The cellar had no windows. As far as he knew, it was where all the fur pelts were stored, along with the fort's rations of food and rum. Were they doing inventory tonight? If so, why take the girl?

Tom wasn't about to ask why. He was already treading a thin line by what happened today with Lady Pendleton. He returned to the fourth level and reached the door to the Pendleton home. *It's just dinner*, he reminded himself. He knocked. The butler named Charles answered. He was a full-blooded Cree with ruddy cheeks, shortly cropped silver hair, and wore a black three-piece suit with gray vest. A visual clash between heathen and high society. With a gray-gloved hand, he waved Tom inside and took his coat and hat. "Lady Pendleton requests you wait in parlor." The butler hung his coat and hat on a rack then handed him a glass of red wine.

163

"Thanks, Charles, but I'm not drinking." Before he could give back the glass, the butler marched down the hall.

Tom sniffed the fruity wine and winced. Chianti. Thankfully, wine didn't have the same grip on him as Scotch whiskey. He set the glass on a hallway table and entered a formal sitting room with plush Victorian furniture and decorative art. The Pendleton home took up both wings of the third floor. In an adjacent room, three Cree women in servant uniforms placed silverware and plates on a cloth-covered dining table.

Tom checked his pocket watch. *What's keeping Willow?*

He explored the rest of the parlor. A grand fireplace was aglow with a bonfire inside the deep hearth. It put off so much heat he had to keep his distance. Above the mantel hung a large oil painting of Willow. She looked regal, posing in a ruby dress with a ruffled collar that went up to her chin. Her golden hair was pinned up with a lacy hat, allowing just a few ringlets to dangle in back. She was smiling. Even in the painting she resembled Beth. The likeness was uncanny. Willow had the same oval face, dimpled chin, and porcelain skin. Her eyes were a darker shade of blue, but the resemblance was enough to make Tom feel butterflies.

It's just dinner.

"Hello, Tom?" Willow's voice called from some other chamber. "Tom, are you out there in the parlor?"

Confused, he looked around and saw a half-open door at the back of the parlor. It led into a hallway. "Yes, Willow. Just waiting on you to make your appearance."

"Could you be a love and come here a moment?"

He looked back at the dining room. The servants placed a baked ham on the table along with several other side dishes. The aroma of the feast made his mouth water. "I believe dinner is being served."

"It can wait," Willow called back. "I could use your assistance."

"Sure." Sighing, Tom walked down the narrow passage that had, of all things, pink walls with a floral design. He opened a door that led into a closet overstuffed with dresses that reeked of perfume. Coughing, he closed the door. Her private chambers had so many doors, big ones and small ones. "Where are you, Willow? Are you playing hide and seek?"

"Yes." she giggled. "Come find me." Her voice echoed from the doorway at the end of the hall. It was partially ajar. He knocked. "Are you in here?" Tom entered a long, narrow room. Velvet curtains draped the windows. The double doors of a tall wardrobe hung open, displaying more colorful dresses and fur coats of every shade. The woman was not for want of something to wear to a ball. A four-poster bed had a red comforter with two dolls propped against plush pillows. One of the dolls was porcelain with blonde hair. The other was the Indian doll that had belonged to Zoé Lamothe.

Beside the bed sat a beauty table with a circular mirror. An assortment of makeup and brushes was displayed on the table. The room was almost dark, lit by a single glowing candle that was down to the end of its wick. In the far corner he saw several dozen jewel-like eyes reflecting the candle flame. *Great Scott!* He took a step back. There must have been a hundred dolls propped up on shelves.

"I'm in here." Willow giggled.

He rounded a corner to a small nook, hearing the splash of water. Behind a sheer curtain, Willow was soaking in a bathtub. The outline of her head and bare shoulders was a sight to behold. Her breasts floated just above the water.

Tom turned away. "Excuse me, Ma'am. I didn't realize you weren't decent."

He felt flustered. His heartbeat quickened and the excitement in his loins returned. Walking in on Lady Pendleton bathing was the last thing he expected.

"It's okay, Tom." She splashed water at him. "You don't have to be so polite. I've been very naughty."

Damn it, he was aroused now. He looked back at all the porcelain faces. "Uh, this is quite a doll collection."

"I've been collecting my dollies since I was a little girl. They keep me company."

Tom felt as if the pale-faced figurines were all watching him. All of them were girls in various hair colors and dresses. Some had parasols and springtime gowns, while others wore miniature fur coats.

Water splashed as Willow stood. "Could you hand me that towel?"

"Sure." He had to turn toward her to reach for it. Out of the corner of his eye he saw her naked form through the sheer curtain. Soapy water dripped down her body. She stepped onto the rug and toweled herself off.

"I-I'll wait outside." He went back into the pink hall, his heart thumping.

What am I doing? I shouldn't be in here. Entering the boudoir of another man's wife was just as adulterous as sleeping with her. *Christ, that's twice today I've trespassed on dangerous ground.*

If the officers made a surprise visit, how would he explain himself?

"Willow, I should leave."

"No, stay. Come back in. I'm decent now."

Tom had never felt so much lust and confusion. His body and

mind were in constant battle. Which side would win depended on how much willpower he could muster. Taking a deep breath, he opened the door. Lady Pendleton was sitting at her beauty table wearing a silk robe. Her wet hair hung down in long curls around her shoulders. She smiled, gazing at him in the mirror. "I've been waiting a long time for you, Tom." She sprayed perfume on her neck.

He felt himself succumbing to the fragrance of lilac and orange blossom.

95

Anika's blade carved into the rabbit's belly. She ripped out the entrails and put them into a stew pot. Damn the Pendletons. They had done nothing but bring misery to Anika and her people. And damn Tom Hatcher.

As she drank rum, her two dogs stared at her and whimpered.

"Makade, Ozaawi, lie down." She waved them away. "Go on." The dogs curled up by the stove.

Anika set down the disemboweled rabbit. She looked at her fingers, now covered in blood and hair.

I'll never be anything more than a whore and a witch.

The kitchen table was covered with roots, feathers, leaves, and herbs. She sprinkled a pinch of each into the pot. She put it on the stove and set the brood to boil. Then she picked up the object that gave the concoction its most power.

Willow's white fur mitten.

96

Willow looked at her reflection in the mirror and powdered her cheeks. She could barely breathe. Her heart beat wildly, and it was more than just the magic dust coursing through her veins. The man from her dreams now stood in the doorway.

"You can enter now, Tom." With nervous anticipation, Willow closed her eyes. *God, this is finally happening.* She hummed, waiting for her lover to step up behind her and place his hands on her shoulders. She had dreamed this moment for so many nights, she had memorized the sequence. His footsteps approached her from behind, the wood creaking at the weight of his shoes. And then he was directly behind her, breathing, his very presence tingling the back of Willow's neck. Fingers sifted through her wet hair, caressing her scalp, pulling lightly at the roots. His lips pressed against her temple, moving down her cheek to her ear. His heated breath sent ripples of excitement up her chest. As his trail of kisses found their way to her lips, melting into them, his hand slid down into her robe and cupped her breast, squeezing it gently and pinching the nipple. Pleasure and pain. Loving and wicked. He kissed her neck, while both hands fondled her breasts. She leaned back against him, moaning, surrendering fully to his touch. Then he guided her to her feet, so light now she was floating, turning to face him. He slid her robe off her shoulders, admiring the curves and contours of her body as her silk draping brushed down her skin and fell to the floor. She stood before him, baring her naked soul, vulnerable, and never more eager to be taken. Her lover picked her up and carried her to the bed, laid her on her back on the soft velvet spread, her head sinking into the pillows. She pushed Maggie and Noël beneath the pillows, so they wouldn't see what grownups do. In that moment, the man's gentlemanly patience ended, and he proceeded to ravish Willow like a barbarian.

That was how *the dream* went.

When Willow realized Tom hadn't touched her yet, her eyes snapped open. He was no longer in the mirror's reflection. Her heart skipped. "Tom!"

"Over here." He was sitting on her bed, holding the Indian doll in his lap.

"What are you doing way over there, love, when I'm right here?" Willow smiled and let her robe fall slightly, baring her shoulder.

"Willow, I can't go where it appears we are headed."

"Why not?"

"I could give you a number of reasons, but mainly it's just not right to sleep with another man's wife."

"Well, it's a bit too late for that, don't you think?"

"Willow, listen to me. If you were a single lady, the situation might be different. But you are spoken for."

"Avery doesn't care about me. We don't even sleep in the same bed anymore." Willow sat on the bed next to him. "I want *you*, Tom. I have since the day you arrived." She ran her fingers through his hair, tried to kiss him, but Tom turned his head.

"No, don't. If your husband finds out, he will fire me and send me packing."

"I would go with you. Montréal, London, anywhere you want to go." Willow fastened her arms around his waist. "Please, Tom, you must feel the same about me. I could feel it in your kiss today. Tell me you desire

167

me."

"I wish I could say it was you I had feelings for."

She pinched her eyebrows together. "What do you mean?"

"This morning, when I kissed you... I wasn't in the right frame of mind." He took a deep breath. "I've thought about this all day and decided...the only reason I have feelings for you is because you remind me of my late wife."

Willow blinked, suddenly confused. She leaned away from him. "Your wife!"

Tom nodded. "She passed away two years ago. I'm still not over her."

"But wait, you kissed me. You held me in your arms."

"I do feel attraction for you," he said, gazing directly into her eyes now. "But it's just lust, nothing deeper. And I'm not about to risk your marriage or my career to satisfy a physical craving. In the end we would both regret it."

"No, you're bloody wrong, Tom, it was love. I could feel it."

"I'm sorry, Willow. For me, it wasn't."

The room began spinning, the doll faces circling them as if they were on a merry-go-round that was whirling out of control. A rush of fiery anger torched her chest. "Blast you!" She released a deep growl. "How dare you lead me on?" She pounded her fists against Tom's chest. He gripped her wrists, fending off her blows. "Willow, stop."

Tears rimmed her eyes. Her rage turned to sadness as her last chance at happiness was dissipated. He started to rise. She gripped his arm. "Please, Tom, don't go." She opened her robe, placing his hand on her breast. "I can pretend to be your wife if that's what you want. I don't care if it's lust or love. Just take me."

"No." He stood, releasing himself from her clutches. "I'm sorry, Willow. I'm going to pass on dinner."

"Then get out, you blasted fool!" She threw pillows at him. Then she hurled figurines and jewelry boxes from her curio cabinet. In her blind fury, she grabbed the nearest object. Her favorite doll smashed against the threshold, shattering porcelain fragments across the floor.

As the man of her dreams left her boudoir, Willow cried into her pillow. Her chest ached, caving in on itself, crushing her heart. Tom was supposed to be the one to rescue her from this godforsaken prison.

She picked up the Indian doll. "You promised me he would come!"

Then she heard a chorus of whispering voices, just like in her dreams. All her dolls spun around Willow as if her bed were a merry-go-round. Through the Indian doll chanted Zoé's voice, *He's coming, Willow, he's coming, he's coming, he's coming...*

97

Tom left Noble House before anyone could question his early departure. Halfway to his cabin, he stopped at the well house in the courtyard. He leaned against the cold stone wall. He was shaking. His heart beat high up in his throat.

I never should have entered her private chambers.

Tom feared the repercussions of his actions. This far out from civilization, the only laws were the ones made by Avery Pendleton. If Tom disappeared or was found dead out in the woods, who would question how it happened? Who would even notice that Tom was gone? He had no family.

I have to maintain discipline and pray Willow keeps everything secret.

He thought of Anika. Even she had seduced Tom into bed. *I've been such a fool.* He tightened his fist until the shaking ceased. *Remember why you came to Fort Pendleton. To uncover the truth behind all the deaths and disappearances. Don't lose sight of that.* No more whiskey or women. Inspector Hatcher marched toward his cabin with a newfound conviction.

98

Anika tossed the white mitten onto her workbench. She sat down at her table, staring forward. Her hands, covered in blood, twigs, and fur, wouldn't stop shaking.

She had nearly crossed a line that even her grandmother wouldn't cross.

As she was about to summon a trickster to torment Willow, Anika remembered Grandmother Spotted Owl's warning about summoning spirits. "When you conjure a trickster for a favor, the day will come when the trickster demands a favor from you."

Those words stopped Anika from completing the ceremony.

I am not a witch. Nor am I a whore. Just a foolish drunk. She gazed at the flask on the table. Made from a buffalo horn, it had been a gift from her uncle. And a curse for Anika. It carried the rum that made her drunk each night. It made her think evil thoughts and want to do bad things. Made her a slave to the white man, just like it did all her people.

"Firewater is nothing but a trickster," her grandmother had said.

"It will eat you from the inside out if you let it."

Anika admired how Tom had stopped drinking. He had made a promise to Chris. That had made Tom stronger. *Maybe I should make a promise to someone,* thought Anika. She clutched the prayer bundle that hung around her neck.

Always remember, spoke Grandmother Spotted Owl's voice. *There is no separation between us.*

Closing her eyes, Anika connected with the medicine woman's spirit and asked for strength.

99

In the boudoir where the dolls snickered like a hundred little hellions, Willow took Doc's sleeping elixir. She climbed into bed, curling up with the Indian doll that had once belonged to Zoé. The voices of the other dolls finally stopped. Then she heard a girl crying from the corner of the room. That was where Willow had tossed her favorite porcelain doll, Maggie, and shattered its face.

Willow pulled the covers over her head and clamped her eyes shut. The medicine made every part of her feel heavy. As the bed seemed to float like a boat on water, Willow drifted off into a deep slumber. She dreamed of the Métis girl standing in the corner, wearing a blue velvet dress with a lacy collar. Zoé's face was powdered with makeup, and she looked like a larger version of the porcelain doll she was holding.

"Come play with us, Willow. We can be sisters at the grand ball." Behind Zoé, the walls opened up into a ballroom with a black and white checkered floor. Shadow figures danced to music from a string quartet. Zoé waltzed with her doll.

As Willow joined the party, the ballroom went dark and silent. A cone of light shone down on Zoé. Within the velvety blackness behind her formed a figure whose gloved hands gripped the girl by the shoulders. Zoé said, "See, I told you he'd come for you."

Without seeing his face, Willow felt the heat of the man's gaze melting her resistance. A face covered in a red-and-white tribal mask entered the spotlight. A deep voice said, "It's been a long time, Little Lamb."

Willow woke up, gasping.

Part Ten

Dark Welcome

100

Two Days Later

As the two canoes paddled along the river, Father Xavier heard the flutter of wings and pulled down his hood. Ravens flew overhead and landed on a tree upstream. The canoes passed under the branches weighed down by black birds. Father Xavier raised his silver cross and lipped a prayer. The flock cawed in protest, flying up to higher branches.

Father Xavier wondered if Mirabelle's spirit might be one of the dark angels, watching her brother through beady black eyes. He chanted in Latin to ward off such thoughts.

"Birds got you spooked, priest?" Dr. Coombs chuckled. "Ah, the *Corvus corax*. Ravens are the largest species of the genus *Corvus*. Brothers to the crows, jackdaws, and rooks. Their intelligence is similar to wolves."

"Don't you find their behavior peculiar?"

The doctor shrugged. "Overly curious, perhaps. Probably hungry. Here you go, Corvids." He threw one of this morning's fried biscuits onto the icy bank. The birds swarmed down, pecking at it. "Hungry little devils, aren't they?"

Father Xavier said, "For God's sake, don't encourage them."

"Ey, it's nothing to get all bent about."

"There's something sinister about these birds. They've been following us since Ottawa, perhaps even since Montréal."

Another husky laugh. "I highly doubt that."

"Then I'd say, for an educated man, Doctor Coombs, you're not very astute. Every time we've camped, these ravens have slept in nearby trees. And every time we've portaged or canoed up the river, the birds have also flown the same direction. As God as my witness, they are following us."

"Sounds like typical Catholic paranoia to me."

Father Xavier turned in his seat to face the bear-sized man. "What is *that* supposed to mean?"

The bearded doctor paddled the trickling water. "It means, priest, you give way too much meaning to things you cannot see and phenomena that science cannot prove."

"There *are* occurrences that science cannot prove."

"Like what?"

"Miracles. Stigmata. Spiritual possessions. Visions of angels. Science cannot prove them, because they are acts of a spiritual world we may never comprehend. That is why we teach people to have faith in the unknown."

Dr. Coombs snorted. "You're no different than the savage Indians who believe every time the wind blows, a spirit is sending them some kind of message."

"How dare you compare Catholicism to the heathens! The Indians had no religion until our missionaries introduced them to the path of God."

"Ha! Ask any Indian what he thinks of your missionaries, and he will tell you the black robes are a plague that has blighted their way of life. Disease and alcoholism...those were introduced by your missionaries. I've treated too many tribes who died out because of smallpox or the measles. And I've patched up squaws who were battered by their drunk husbands. The Indians may be savages, but at least their beliefs have some basis in the laws of nature."

Father Xavier faced forward, yanking his hood over his head. There was no use arguing with the bull-headed doctor. Father Xavier had debated with men of science before and decided they were a lost cause.

The ravens took flight and disappeared around a bend in the river.

From some unseen part of the forest erupted a macabre opera of birdsong. Much louder than the twenty or so ravens could make. What resounded ahead was a chorus of castrato voices singing an aria for lost souls. The singing was so high-pitched, Father Xavier's ears started ringing. He drew a cross over his heart.

The two canoes rounded the bend.

A tempest of black birds spiraled across the sky, making the gray afternoon look as if nightfall were approaching. A cacophonous *caw-caw-cawing* drowned out the sounds of the paddles chopping into the river. The cloud of flapping black wings swooped down into the trees. Hundreds, perhaps thousands, of dark angels clotted the branches on either side of the river, watching over the voyagers as their canoes completed the last few meters and bumped against a dock that stretched along the riverbank. Up a short hill, nestled in the trees, stood a fort with several watchtowers.

Father Xavier stood, looking down at Dr. Coombs. The large man was mesmerized by the spectacle. "Are you noticing anything peculiar now, Doctor?"

Not waiting for answer, the priest climbed onto the dock. As the voyagers quickly unloaded the cargo, he grabbed his bags and joined Andre and Master Pendleton.

Andre yelled over the noise, "What's happening, Father?"

"An evil spirit has followed us. We have to exorcise it quickly." Father Xavier pulled out his ritual book and handed it to Andre. "Begin chanting." The novice read the verses aloud in Latin. Father Xavier splashed Andre and himself with holy water then flicked it along the dock. The exorcist gazed up at the dark-winged minions and yelled, "I cast out this evil from these—"

A deafening boom startled Father Xavier. The ravens scattered from the trees. The priest turned around. Avery Pendleton was holding a shotgun to his shoulder. He aimed at another bird-infested tree and fired. A black swarm burst into the sky and passed over their heads. For a brief second, Father Xavier swore the birds formed into a demon's face. Then the ravens dispersed with a shriek of fury and flew up upriver.

"There, problem solved." Master Pendleton rested his shotgun on his shoulder.

Dr. Coombs released a husky laugh. "Brilliant thinking, Master Pendleton."

Father Xavier stood speechless, still rattled by the gun's blast.

With a devilish grin, Avery gestured to the fort perched on the hillside. "Gentlemen, welcome to Fort Pendleton."

101

Tom was rocking in a chair, whittling an owl onto his flute, when the quiet afternoon erupted with the cawing of birds followed by gunshots. Gripping his pistol, he stepped out onto his porch. There was a commotion happening outside the fort, as several flocks of ravens flew away.

At the watchtower above the front gate, a soldier yelled, "The brigade has returned!" Soldiers opened the gate's double doors, allowing a parade of voyagers to enter the fort. They dragged sleds full of food crates, supplies, and barrels of gunpowder and rum. The village seemed to come to life as men, women, and children came out to greet the travelers.

Tom joined the gathering at the entrance. Brother Andre was walking with an older man wearing a black Russian fur hat and a heavy coat over his long black robe. The priest stood a head taller than Andre and walked with a powerful gait.

"Andre!" Tom called out as he approached. "Welcome home."

"It's a relief to be back!" the missionary said with a grin. "Inspector, I'd like you to meet my mentor, Father Xavier."

"Welcome, Father." Tom shook the tall priest's hand and felt a firm grip. His vibrant blue eyes were intense and full of conviction. Tom said, "I heard that you've come to investigate the bizarre disease that's infected several people."

The priest nodded. "Yes, we've seen this plague before."

"Well, we could certainly use your insight."

"I'd be happy to meet with you later, Inspector. Right now, I'm exhausted from our journey. Andre, if you'll lead me to my quarters, I would like to put on some tea and get warm." Father Xavier tipped his mink hat. "Pleasure meeting you, Inspector."

The two Jesuits crossed the courtyard toward the chapel.

Tom felt better having a priest in the village. He missed going to Mass each week, feeling like he was part of the colony. Now the chapel could once again become a house of worship.

A hand slapped Tom's shoulder from behind. He turned to see Avery Pendleton standing there in his top hat and a smug weasel grin. "Inspector, how have you been?"

"Good. Back on my feet."

"Glad to hear it," Pendleton said. "You missed the journey of a lifetime. Montréal is spectacular during the holiday season. So, anything happen in my absence that I should know about?"

Tom felt knots in his stomach. Images of adulterous acts with Willow and Anika flashed through his mind. He kept a watchful eye on the crowd, expecting Willow to approach them. But the chief factor's wife was nowhere in sight. "We've stayed inside the fort since the day you left. The guards have kept a watchful eye on the forest, but have not seen any of the predators. It's quite possible the pack has moved on."

"This pack you speak of," came a husky voice. "It sounds like something out of a werewolf tale." A bear-sized man approached. "Perhaps I should have brought my silver bullets." He laughed.

Pendleton chuckled with him, and Tom could see the two men

were quite chums. "Inspector, meet our new physician and disease specialist, Dr. Coombs. He will be taking over Doc Riley's role."

The six-foot-four man was broad in both shoulders and girth. He had an enormous head with a round, flabby jaw and thick, brown beard. "Any more outbreaks among the colony?"

"None thus far," Tom said. "It seems we stopped the virus from spreading."

"You can never be too sure." The physician's arrogant eyes peered over his wire-framed spectacles. "Viruses can go dormant and then sprout up again when you least expect it."

Pendleton nodded. "Inspector, you will be assisting Dr. Coombs in solving this case about the plague."

"I'm ready to get back to work. Anything I can do right away?"

Pendleton looked back at the doctor. "Sure, help Dr. Coombs get moved in. Since we've condemned Hospital House, I'm putting him in Farlan McDuff's old place."

102

Avery stepped into the parlor of his home. "Oh, Willow..."

Holding a Christmas present behind his back, he walked down the floral pink hall. "Guess who's home?"

He had spent the past two weeks traversing with foul-smelling men. Tensions had been high, especially toward the end of the journey. Avery was ready for the pleasurable release that could only come from a sweet-scented woman. And who better to satiate his desires than the fairest of them all?

"Willow, darling..." He knocked on the door to his wife's boudoir. He felt agitation when she didn't swing open the door and throw her arms around him. After being gone four weeks, he expected her to be excited about his return. Surely she wasn't still upset about the way they parted. Then again, she was a woman.

He opened the door. The room was dark. He slid open the curtains, allowing the afternoon light to filter in. Her collection of dolls gazed down at him from shelves that covered every wall. The girlish boudoir was too frilly for Avery's tastes, but if it made his wife happy...

Willow was lying in bed under the covers. So still. Her face looked pale.

She's dead! Avery's heart quickened. He rounded the bed. Touched her arm. She was warm. Her chest rose and she shifted. He released his breath. Then he saw the bottle on her nightstand. Laudanum. An opium-based tincture for producing sleep.

Christ, no wonder she's sleeping in the middle of the day.

An Indian doll was tucked under her arm. Half of its leathery face was worn. It was missing an eye and most of its hair. *Noël, I guess it's finally the end for you.* He unwrapped the present he was holding and pulled out a geisha doll with a silk kimono. He gently lifted Willow's arm and swapped out the dolls. She stirred but didn't awaken. *How much laudanum did she take?*

Avery leaned over her. "Wake up, Sleeping Beauty." He kissed her lips.

She kissed him back, softly at first, brushing the outside of his lips, then her mouth opened, and she kissed with an intensity he'd never felt before from her. A fire erupted between their lips. Even Celeste, his Montréal mistress, didn't kiss this passionately.

"Oh, yes, that's my girl." He pawed her breast, squeezing it.

He yanked down the covers, shoved his hand up her nightgown. She was actually wet. She moaned, squirming beneath him.

Avery had a hard cock that only two weeks without sex could produce. He grabbed Willow's hair with one hand while unbuckling his trousers with the other. She rubbed her eyes. "What's...happening?" she asked in a groggy voice.

"Darling, you're about to give your husband a welcome home present."

Willow's eyes snapped open. She scooted back against the headboard. "Avery?"

"In the flesh." He slid down his pants, letting her see how aroused he was.

"No, I don't want to." She grabbed her doll and hugged it against her chest. The childish display only turned on Avery more.

"Have you been a naughty little girl?"

She averted her eyes and realized she was hugging the geisha doll. "Who's this?"

"Your belated Christmas present." He pushed up her nightgown. "Now how about mine..."

Willow's eyes filled with panic. "Where's Noël?"

"On the floor."

His wife crawled off the bed and searched the floor on hands and knees. "Where is she? Where? *Where?*"

"By your dresser. Jesus, what's wrong with you?"

She scooped up the Indian doll and rocked with it like it was her own damn child.

Meanwhile, his balls were aching. "Damn it, Willow, come back to bed."

She just rocked, her eyes wild.

"Bloody well, then." Avery pulled up his trousers over his erection. "Woman, I don't know what's gotten into you lately, but I will not condone this behavior." He grabbed the bottle of laudanum. "No more sleeping medicine." He slammed her door.

103

"It's okay, it's okay..." Clutching the Indian doll against her chest, Willow stumbled across the room and sat down at her beauty table. She peered into the oval mirror with the trimmed white border.

The doll snickered with Zoé's voice, *Mirror mirror on the wall, who's the most wretched of them all?*

Willow's eyeliner trailed down her cheeks in horrid black tears. She opened her center drawer and retrieved a glass tube with white powder. It was almost empty.

One last magic carpet ride through the clouds, giggled Zoé.

"Just one more." Willow poured the cocaine into her pinky nail and snorted. Her reflection began to stretch.

Did she dream Avery returned?

Her breast and inner thigh hurt. No, he was really back.

Sobbing, she looked at the Indian doll. "He's not who you promised." Willow brushed her hair in hard strokes. "I want the man you promised!"

Zoé snickered, and then the room filled with the sound of a hundred children giggling. *Don't worry,* the dolls whispered in unison. *He's here, he's here, he's here...*

104

Tom carried a crate of medical supplies into the new hospital house. Back to his role as inspector, he was happy to be working again. He spent the afternoon helping Dr. Coombs set up his lab. The disease specialist had brought microscopes, surgery knives, and medicines.

Tom opened the crate full of science books like anatomy, biology, botany, and zoology. Among them were books by Charles Darwin, the scientist who came up with the theory of evolution. His theories of man evolving from apes had outraged the Church, who believed man derived from Adam and Eve. Ever since Darwin's theories were published, the Church and the scientific field constantly battled in a theoretical war.

Tom held up the books. "Where do you want these?"

"On that shelf will do." Dr. Coombs yelped suddenly and stomped the floor, dancing across the room as if he were doing a jig.

Tom laughed. "Something wrong, Doctor?"

"Some kind of critter just ran into the next room."

"Probably a rodent," Tom said. "Every cabin has a few mice and rats. They nest up in the attics during winter. Unfortunately, we don't have any cats out here."

Dr. Coombs looked up at his ceiling. "Well, the little vermin better not come near me."

Tom grinned, seeing the large man get so spooked over a tiny critter. Despite their rough start, Tom discovered the new doctor had a dry wit and good sense of humor. Tom was looking forward to keeping company with a man who could not only speak full sentences, but had a stimulating intellect as well.

More importantly, Inspector Hatcher felt useful again. He had a new mission: Hunt down the Manitou Cannibals and help Dr. Coombs secure this village from any further outbreaks. Then come spring, journey back to Montréal with his son's remains.

After being away from Willow for two weeks, Tom realized he wasn't in love with her. She was strikingly beautiful and resembled Beth, but that was where his attraction to Willow ended. The spoiled little princess belonged to Avery Pendleton, and the rake was much more suited for her childish games.

As Tom returned to the sled for another crate, he spotted a shadowy form with a top hat climbing up the steps of Anika's cabin. Pendleton spoke with her a few seconds, then she let him in.

Tom's jaw went tight. He felt a strange aching in his chest, as he imagined what was happening inside Anika's cabin.

It's none of my damned business. Tom gripped another crate and marched back into the medical lab. He tried to concentrate on work, but for some reason the discomfort in his chest wouldn't go away.

105

Anika backed away from the door as Pendleton removed his hat and fur coat. She knew that hungry look in his eyes. He grinned like a wolverine gazing upon a wounded fawn. "Hello, Anika, did you miss me?"

She looked away. "I cannot be with you tonight."

"And why the hell not?"

She thought of an excuse. "I just started my moon time."

"I don't care." He stepped toward her, unbuckling his belt. "Now, take off your clothes and get into bed."

Anika looked at her bed in the corner and thought of all the nights she had lain with her eyes clamped shut while this beast rammed into her until she was sore. How long was she going to be his whore? She thought of her grandmother and of Tom and knew that she deserved to be treated better. Anika folded her arms and looked into Pendleton's eyes. Her mouth spoke a word she had never had the courage to say to him. "No."

He cocked his head. "What did you just say?"

"No. I... I no longer want to be your mistress."

"You fucking little bitch." He removed his belt and swung it, slapping the side of her face. Anika fell to the floor. Fire burned around her eye.

Pendleton snarled and whipped her shoulder. "No one talks to me in that manner!" The belt lashed down several times, until she felt hot centipedes of stinging pain crawling across her back and shoulders. The beast yanked her up off the floor and threw her onto the bed. "Now take off your fucking clothes!"

Part Eleven

Communion

106

Noble House

Later that evening, Tom gathered with seven other men at the long table in Master Pendleton's study. Among them sat Dr. Coombs, Father Xavier, Andre, and the officers, Lt. Hysmith, Walter Thain, and Percy Kennicot.

From the head of the table, Pendleton said, "I've called you all here tonight first to welcome our new guests. Their knowledge will be a real contribution to our situation." As the chief factor went on, Tom made eye contact with Father Xavier. The bald-headed priest looked strong for a man in his fifties, a man of both physical and spiritual strength. Tom sensed Father Xavier was sizing him up, as well.

The Jesuit's hands rested on a stack of leatherbound books. One was the cryptic diary that Zoé Lamothe had delivered from Manitou Outpost. Father Jacques had written the entire journal in Aramaic. Now the priest for whom the book had been written was here.

Tom said, "Father, can you shed some light on what happened in the final days at Manitou Outpost?"

"Yes, Inspector." Father Xavier leaned forward, clasping his fingers. "Father Jacques was more than just a missionary. He was also an exorcist, documenting accounts of cannibalism happening among the people living on the frontier."

Pendleton's brow furrowed. "Why didn't he tell me this when he first arrived?"

"His true mission was known only to the high tiers of the Catholic Church."

"Meaning the Vatican?" Tom asked.

The priest nodded.

Hysmith said, "So you bloody Catholics planted a spy in our fort!"

Father Xavier said, "The Church has no interest in your business doings. We came to the frontier to save people from a spiritual disease that happens when people live in isolation."

"You claim to know which virus we're dealing with?" said Dr. Coombs, looking over his spectacles. "Are the Jesuits disease specialists now?"

"Not all diseases stem from the human body," the priest defended. "What we're talking about here is an outbreak of demon possession."

This brought chuckles around the table.

Dr. Coombs released a wheezing laugh. "Priest, you think everything is the work of the Devil."

"What else would you expect from a bloody Catholic?" Hysmith chided.

"Enough," Pendleton said. "Father Xavier has traveled all this way. Show him some respect. Father, please tell us what you learned from translating the diary."

Father Xavier said, "I thought it better that you hear it from Father Jacques' own words." He opened the diary and began reading:

"Out here in the wilderness, the dead make sacrifices. Claude and Jean-Luc left with their hunting dogs a week ago and have yet to return. I've lost hope that they ever will. Ever since the blizzards arrived in November, a beast from the woods has been stalking us. Some form of manitou, the trappers claim. Since it killed three hunters, we dare not leave the fort.

"We have been stranded here for weeks, waiting out the storms. Our food stores have run out. I know the madness of hunger. Each passing day, I grow thinner. Each night, I hear the moans of the others as they suffer from ravenous nightmares. The outpost has been fortified to protect us from the savage beast in the woods. What we hadn't counted on was the savagery attacking us from within..."

107

December 10th, 1870
Manitou Outpost

Father Jacques stopped writing at the sound of the fierce wind howling through the lodge house. Down the hall, boots clumped across wood floors as men hustled from room to room, closing shutters that blew open. The native wives of the fur trappers tended to the sick and dying. The inhabitants were hungry. Always hungry. Six days had passed since anyone had eaten. So many mouths to feed. All the livestock was dead, except a few horses. Father Jacques had considered killing the sled dogs for food, but they were all sick, the meat tainted. Getting to Fort Pendleton was the only hope for the Manitou inhabitants. If they didn't figure a way to get to there soon, it was going to be a long winter.

Today, the three-story lodge house creaked and moaned as it always did during heavy storms. Father Jacques' hunger caused the edges of his vision to blur as his mind drifted into dark thoughts. Voices rasped inside his head. Ghosts of the poor souls he could not save. He had a haunting memory of a teenage girl drinking blood from the throat of a dead dog. As Father Jacques and men with rifles approached, the girl looked up, blood dribbling down her chin. She glared with solid white eyes, growling. Several shots fired into her. When the grisly image passed, the priest returned to his journaling.

The first to catch the disease was Master Lamothe's eldest daughter, Margaux. She has since been put to death, an unfortunate but necessary means to our survival. We are now down to fifteen, and time is running out.

Pushing away his journal, Father Jacques stood at a frosted window on the third floor of the main lodge house. His rosary twirled between bony fingers. Outside, the ice covering Makade Lake cracked. The frozen plates pushed together until fissures exploded upward. The crashing booms from the ever-shifting ice was a constant sound that startled Father Jacques during the days and made sleeping fitful during the nights. All around the fort, tree branches clawed violently at the endless wind and snow.

Another week, another storm.

The priest prayed for deliverance from the wintry beast. How much longer could they hold death at bay?

On the ground below, a fox chased a snow hare into a pile of brush. There was a brief frenzy, then the fox emerged with the dead rabbit in its maw. Father Jacques felt an unsettling gurgle in his stomach as the fox tore into the hare's belly. Sacrificial blood stained the snow. *Is this a sign, oh Lord?* The feasting of predator on prey was a fascinating thing to watch. The wrenching jaw. The tearing of meat from bone. The violent display drew other creatures, as two ravens landed on a branch. Their black eyes gazed at the Jesuit priest. The birds cawed, as if they knew the dark thoughts that had been tormenting Father Jacques these past few days.

From the woods echoed a sound of icicles shattering against the ground. The ravens squawked and took flight. The fox dashed off, leaving the snowshoe hare half-eaten. Father Jacques licked his lips, surprised that the sight of the blood and raw meat stirred his hunger.

A part of him wanted to run out into the woods and bury his face in it. He searched the thrashing branches, fearing whatever predator had spooked the animals. From the corner of his eye he caught movement. A flash of white racing between the trees. In the instant it took Father Jacques to shift his eyes, the thing snatched the remains of the dead rabbit and vanished in the blizzard. A white wolf? A polar bear? His rational mind wanted to believe he'd seen an earthly predator. But since the sickness started, Indian superstitions tormented Father Jacques' mind.

Beware the wiitigos... The Ojibwa people believed the forest surrounding Manitou Outpost was haunted by evil spirits. Winter phantoms. Windigos. Over the course of several decades countless men and women had disappeared or died of strange deaths. Their fear of an evil presence was why the Jesuits chose this outpost to do missionary work. In his twenty years as an exorcist, Father Jacques had faced his share of evil. And now, standing at the window, he felt as if someone or something were out there watching him from the woods, hiding behind veils of swirling snow. He could feel its hunger. Or was it his own cravings that tightened the pit of his stomach? The priest caught the reflection of his ghoulish face in the windowpane and turned away.

From down the hall, a sick man cried out. Father Jacques went into the room and blessed him. Anton, a once stout blacksmith, was now a skeleton wrapped in a thin sheet of skin. He coughed, spat up blood.

Master Pierre Lamothe entered the room. "What should we do with him, Father?" The chief factor was gaunt, himself. He hadn't been the same since he burned his daughter's body. That day he'd given over his command to Father Jacques. The priest had become their only hope and salvation.

Father Jacques leaned over the bed and drew a cross over the dying blacksmith's chest. The priest led Master Lamothe into the hallway. "Anton has only a few hours, maybe less. I think there may be a way to save the others."

By that evening, they were down to fourteen people. The priest sat down at a long dining table with a half dozen French Canadian men, their Ojibwa wives, and mixed-blood children. All devout Catholics delivered to God by Father Jacques. The Jesuit's flock gazed at him with desperate eyes, as did Master Lamothe. Beside the chief factor sat his wife Wenonah and their half-breed daughter. Zoé remained stoic while her mother cried.

Father Jacques clasped his hands together. "Anton was a pious man, a devoted husband, a good father. It is his last noble sacrifice that he blesses us with this offering."

Zoé glared at the priest. In time the girl would understand. All the disciples would. *Six days without a meal...and no game to hunt, no livestock to eat.* They were ready to do whatever it took to survive. Sister Claire, the only nun among the colony, set what looked like a piece of fried pork skin on everyone's plate. Father Jacques picked up the crispy meat wafer. "For we have no bread, this symbolizes the Eucharist. And Jesus said, 'This is my flesh.'" The disciples put the communion host into their mouths. There was an immediate brightness in their eyes as they chewed. The priest lifted his cup. "And this is the red elixir, the holy sacrament. And Jesus said, 'This is my blood.'" They drank the blood. "This do in remembrance of me.'"

The wafer and blood filled Father Jacques with a newfound strength. His mouth watered as the nun spooned meaty stew into everyone's bowls.

He smiled at his flock. "Trust in me, disciples. For I am the door. I am the vine. I am the good shepherd. Amen."

"Amen," the men, women, and children repeated.

To the priest's surprise, the others ate their stew greedily. Zoé just stared at her mother and father, who slurped up the broth like half-starved prisoners.

Father Jacques said, "Zoé, best you eat, child, if you want to survive the winter."

The dark-headed girl pushed the bowl away and left the table. Her mother pulled over the bowl the girl had left behind and poured the broth into her own bowl.

Father Jacques pictured Anton's blank eyes and felt a stab of guilt, wondering if he'd made the right decision. *Six days without a meal...* He thought about the fox feasting upon the rabbit. The prey surrendering itself to the predator. The vision eased the priest's mind as he ate the stew of human meat. It was the natural law of survival.

Out here in the wilderness, the dead made sacrifices.

108

Father Xavier watched the bewildered faces of all the officers as he closed the diary.

"He must have written more," Pendleton said.

The priest ran his fingers along the leather spine. There was much more indeed, but much of Father Jacques' documentations were restricted to only the higher tiers of the Jesuits. Father Xavier was ordered to only tell them what they needed to know. "The following passages describe the downfall of Manitou Outpost as their hunger only grew stronger. The trappers eventually were overtaken by the sickness, as were all the dogs."

Inspector Hatcher said, "So the colonists cannibalized one another."

"Not all of them died," Father Xavier said. "Some of the 'Infected' wandered off into the forest. Father Jacques and a few others took refuge in the cellar. The sickness was slowly taking each of them over. They survived for about a week. Once they were out of food and water, they made a plan to escape."

"Then we found Zoé," Inspector Hatcher said.

"And she caused a bloody outbreak," Hysmith said.

"Which we curtailed," said Pendleton. "For now at least, while we're quarantined inside the fort. But there are still a few of the Infected roaming the woods."

Inspector Hatcher said, "They are hunting as a pack. Tomorrow, we should take a patrol out and track them down."

Pendleton shook his head. "No, I'm not risking any more men out there. No one leaves the fort for any reason. We have plenty of food to last us till spring. What we need to do is find a way to make sure this outbreak never happens again."

109

"I'd like to perform autopsies," Dr. Coombs said.

"Autopsies?" Tom thought of his son's body stored in the Dead House.

"Yes," Dr. Coombs said. "I plan to cut up your cadavers right away. See if I can find any traces of the virus."

Tom's blood went hot. "Then I wish to have a say in which bodies."

"All of them are to be examined," Pendleton said. "It's for the common good—"

"No one's dissecting my son." Tom locked gazes with the two men. "I want Chris in one piece when I bury him."

Master Pendleton narrowed his eyes at Tom's outburst. "Okay, Doc, you heard the man. Cut up anyone but the inspector's son."

110

Andre placed a cup of hot tea on Father Xavier's bedside table. "Shall I get you anything else?"

"No, I'm good for now." His mentor looked ten years older. Neither of them had gotten much sleep during the journey by river. They had nearly frozen to death camping in the woods, sleeping beneath canoes circled around an open fire.

"Get a good night's sleep yourself, Andre. Tomorrow we begin ridding this place of evil." Father Xavier smiled and sipped his tea.

"Pleasant dreams." Andre closed the bedroom door. Carrying a single candle, he left their private quarters and stepped into a cold, black void. A familiar sanctuary took form—rows of pews, confession booths, the lectern, the chancel—and sank back into the void as he passed. He stopped at the prayer altar and kneeled. The Virgin Mary stared down with vacant eyes. Andre whispered a prayer as he lit votive candles. The walls around the altar rippled with orange light. Black-winged shadows flapped away, taking roost in the infinite darkness.

Andre heard a hollow sigh. He turned around. He felt a presence, as if someone else were in the nave. A chill seeped along the floor, frosting his ankles with ghostly hands. Holding out the candle, he stepped to the first row of pews. A lone figure sat on the back row.

"Who's there?"

A woman sobbed.

Andre walked up the center aisle, cutting a swath of light through the curtains of darkness. The flickering glow and the woman's shadow cast across the wall. She wore a white fur coat and hat. She was cradling an Indian doll.

"Willow?"

She looked up. Tears and makeup streamed down her cheeks. "Andre..." She rushed into his arms. Hugged him tight. Trembling, sobbing into his chest.

Andre hugged her back, timidly at first, not knowing where to place his hands.

"I need to make a confession," she said.

Feeling suddenly aroused, he pulled away. "Having more dreams about your mysterious lover?"

"Yes, I mean, no..." She grabbed his hand. "I need to tell you about something that happened last summer."

"Oh...would you like to confess in the booth?"

"No, just listen to me." Willow sniffled. "I have committed a horrible sin. When I was in Montréal, I...I had a brief affair with Pierre Lamothe."

The news was like a slap in the face. Andre remembered the leader of Manitou Outpost. Master Lamothe, with his cold, reptilian eyes, had been hated and feared by all the trappers, because he treated his workers like animals. According to Father Jacques, if the trappers disobeyed, Lamothe whipped them with his bullwhip. Every one of the trappers had scars on their backs. The thought that Willow had fornicated with such a sinister snake angered Andre. "How long did this affair last?"

"Two weeks. Avery had gone on a trip with one of his mistresses. I was hurt and angry. Pierre, who was staying in our guesthouse, looked after me. I was seduced by his charms. I fell in love with him and found out I was pregnant." Willow stroked the hair of the Indian doll. "Pierre refused to believe it was his. He broke off the affair, telling me the baby was my problem. He then returned to Manitou Outpost. I felt so abandoned and confused. I could feel the baby growing inside me. I lied and told Avery it was his. He was so proud to become a papa, doting on me, treating me like his little princess. All that changed when I arrived here. I discovered Avery was having an affair with that whore Anika. And Pierre had an Indian wife and two daughters. They came to our Halloween ball, you remember it."

Andre recalled that night. He and Father Jacques had drunk rum and watched with amusement all the villagers and Indians dressed in costume. The officers all wore suits, top hats, and masks. Pierre's mask had been of a jack-o'-lantern. He had danced with his daughters, Zoé and Margaux.

Willow said, "Zoé somehow knew that my baby was Pierre's. She was such an odd little girl. All the men got drunk that night. Avery spent the night with his whore. Pierre pulled me into a room and tried to have his way with me. I slapped him and threatened to tell Avery everything. Pierre threw me to the floor and kicked me hard in the stomach. He told me if I ever spoke a word about their affair or the baby being his, he would kill me." She sobbed. "I was such a fool."

Andre squeezed her hand. "It's okay, Willow. Pierre was an awful man." After a moment of letting her cry, he asked, "Is that why you lost the baby?"

She nodded. "After that Avery wouldn't touch me. Pierre had ruined me. I was so enraged I cursed his name and wished a horrid death would fall upon him." She lowered her head. "I feel like it's my fault that everyone at Manitou Outpost died."

"Willow, look at me." Andre gazed into her glossy blue eyes. "What happened there was not your fault. They were snowed in and ran out food. You can't blame yourself for that."

"But I keep having dreams about Zoé. I fear her ghost is blaming me for all that's happened."

"Father Xavier told me such dreams are nothing but Satan's attempt to lead us astray from God. Let's go to the altar and pray."

"No, just hold me." She threw her arms around him, pressing her head against his chest.

Andre held her for several moments. He stroked her hair. "It's okay, Willow. I'm always here for you."

"I'm so glad you're back. I've been so lost without you."

Her words filled Andre's chest with warmth. He gazed up at the ceiling, closed his eyes. She felt so good in his arms, like a frail little lamb. He needed this comfort as much as she did. Without thinking, he kissed her forehead.

"Oh, Andre..." Willow looked up at him with tear-soaked eyes. "Is it you who's come back for me?" She kissed him on the lips, stirring up butterflies in his chest. The feeling of her soft skin and the scent of her perfume cast him under a spell like a dream so heavenly he didn't want to awaken. In this dream, he was not a celibate monk but a man who surrendered to the fire coursing through his veins.

He kissed Willow back with a hunger he hadn't known he had. As the heat of their lips flared, Andre willed himself to pull away. But instead, his mouth opened and welcomed the moist embrace of her tongue.

111

Tom lay in bed but couldn't sleep. His old friend insomnia was keeping him up again. The wind outside crooned a melancholy chorus, sounding as if the woods were filled with lost souls wandering aimlessly among the trees. Manitous? Windigos? Ghosts of the dead? Tom wondered if Chris' soul walked among them. Tom hated that his son hadn't received a proper burial. The thought of him stored on a shelf in the Dead House made Tom worry that Chris might be suffering in some limbo place.

As a Catholic, Tom believed the spirit went to purgatory: a place of temporary suffering where souls faced their past sins to be fit for heaven. As a husband and a father, Tom had committed sins he wasn't proud of, especially during his days as a detective in Montréal. Thinking of the events of the past three years, Tom wondered if he had already died, and Fort Pendleton was his purgatory.

I was a fool to bring Chris here.

Suddenly Tom was overcome by grief. His face tightened. He closed his eyelids tight to dam off any tears. *Hatcher men don't cry,* came his father's voice. *Stiffen your lip, son. I better not see you cry.*

"All I want to do is sleep," Tom said out loud. "God, just let me sleep."

There's one way you can sleep, came another voice.

He felt the familiar itch at the back of his throat. Before Tom knew it, he was standing in the den, looking down at the long, coffin-sized crate. *Just one drink to make the pain go away.* He pried open the lid with a crowbar and pulled out a brown bottle.

"No I can't."

Sure you can, whispered the whiskey demons. *Just one bottle to get through the night.*

His mouth thirsted for the fiery drink. His hands shook. He thought of the promise he had made to his son. "Not today." Tom put the bottle back into its slot inside the crate. He hammered the lid down tight. He still couldn't bring himself to pour the bottles out. He took comfort knowing they were still available, just in case.

The floor creaked inside Chris' bedroom. Footsteps.

Tom whirled. "Who's in there?"

Silence.

Gripping the crowbar, he pushed open the door. The candlelight from the den spilled into the room, illuminating the collection of whittled animals on his son's dresser. The rest of the room was all slashes of moonlight and pools of shadow. Tom peered around the door at the bed. There was a lump under the covers. For a moment he wanted to believe Chris was still alive, sound asleep. Tom reached into the gloom to pull back the covers. Someone beneath rolled over. A cold hand grabbed Tom's wrist. His mind flooded with visions of a blizzard...clawing branches...a giant human shape with elk horns charging through the trees. A boy's scream filled the room. *"Father..."*

"Son!" Tom yanked back the covers. No one there. An icy draft blew around the room, chilling him. He rubbed his neck, staring down at an empty mattress. "What the hell just happened?" Just the insomnia, he decided, causing him to see things.

Outside, the wind careened with familiar voices calling Tom's name. Two shadows stood at the window. A woman and boy. They put their palms against the glass.

"Beth! Chris!" Tom burst out the back door, running behind the cabin. The woman and boy were gone. There were no signs of any footprints. No trail to follow.

Am I going mad?

When he looked back at the window, Tom saw two handprints on the frosty glass. Seconds later, they faded away.

112

"It's colder than a witch's tit tonight," Private Wickliff said to nobody in particular. He was alone, freezing his bollocks off. He cupped his mittens over his mouth and blew steam into them. The nightshift between midnight and dawn was the most miserable duty for the soldiers. Wickliff was always getting assigned night watch, because at age fifteen, he was the youngest. Carrying his rifle over his shoulder, he walked the perimeter inside the fort's stockade. He didn't need his lantern tonight. The moon was bright, stretching his shadow across the snow. Small flurries fell.

All the cabins were dark. The courtyard empty and quiet. Noble House loomed at the far end like an English manor. As he walked down the fence line, Wickliff began to smell a heavy odor. Like the Grim Reaper's stale breath. He followed the scent across the snow-covered cemetery. Stepped between crosses and tombstones, careful to avoid tramping the graves. He was superstitious about such things. At the far corner of the cemetery, a small storage building stood off by itself.

The Dead House.

The stink constricted his throat as he approached the log structure. It stored a half dozen frozen corpses. Among them were Sakari Kennicot, Chris Hatcher, and Privates Pembrook, Wallace, and McHenry, who were killed during the beast attack at Manitou Outpost. That had been a sad day for the garrison. The dead would rest here all winter until the ground thawed and they could be given proper burials. Wickliff hated that he had been put in charge of the Dead House.

As the moonlight threw his shadow across the closed door, he made sure the padlock was still secure. The lock held. He heard scratching and banging coming from inside. The soldier placed his ear to the frost-covered door. For a moment, he imagined the corpses had unraveled their coverings like awakened mummies, climbed down from their shelves, and were walking around inside there, bumping the canoes and barrels. Then he heard squeaks and chittering and came to a more logical conclusion. *Bloody rats.*

Wickliff continued his march around the fort's perimeter. Maybe it was lunacy caused by the full moon, but he heard more scratching. The stench of death returned. He was too far upwind from the Dead House now. The odor had to be coming from somewhere else. He felt strange all of a sudden. Dizzy.

He heard the noise again, like a blade dragging against wood.

Wickliff whirled with his rifle.

The scraping came from the other side of the stockade's wall. A shadow moved between the small cracks in the twelve-foot timbers. He remembered that the Indian cannibal, Kunetay Timberwolf, had never been found.

With a wall of thick lumber separating Wickliff from the wilderness outside, he felt bold. "Ey, is that you, Kunetay? If so, you stink like rotten shit. I heard you boiled your own squaw's head."

Between the slits in the wall Wickliff saw the shadow rise, higher than a man. It made a huffing sound.

Oh shit, Silvertip's back!

It made a guttural sound.

More shadows came up to the fence, all grunting and whooping.

Shit! Shit! Shit! Wickliff ran along the fence. The shadow-things chased him, raking claws across the logs. He turned, running away from the stockade and jumped behind the well house. His heart beat so fast he feared it might burst.

At the front gate, the giant double doors rattled as something on the other side rammed against them. The doors held.

Wickliff released a nervous laugh. "Bugger."

He looked toward the bunkhouse where the garrison slept. *I should get Serge and the others.* As he thought this, the shadow forms backed away from the wall. Footfalls trailed off, followed by distant snapping branches.

Part Twelve

The Evil Within

113

Next morning, Tom and Pendleton climbed up the ladder to the stockade's landing where Lt. Hysmith and his soldiers were gathered.

"These creatures came right up to the gate," said Private Wickliff. "A whole bunch of them."

"This is just bloody great," Pendleton said, his face red.

Tom peered over the wall. The gate's double doors were scratched all to hell. On the ground below, tracks of every size dotted the snowy hillside. He scanned the perimeter. The forest surrounding the fort was a labyrinth of pines, spruce, and oak. This morning, fog sifted between the trees, cutting visibility down to only a few feet past the tree line.

"Did you get a look at them?" Tom asked Wickliff.

"No, sir. I was walking the grounds. Only saw their shadows. One was tall as a bear, roared like one, too."

Pendleton said, "Why wasn't anyone manning the watchtowers?"

Lt. Hysmith said, "We just have one night guard on duty."

Pendleton said, "Well, I want three men on tower duty for every shift. And tie up some kind of animal out there for bait. If anything comes out of the woods, shoot it."

114

Tom entered the makeshift research lab with Pendleton. The cabin smelled of formaldehyde combined with the stink of things that decompose in morgues. They found Dr. Coombs stooped over a microscope.

"Did you learn anything from the autopsies?" Tom asked.

Dr. Coombs' looked up. "Indeed I did, gentlemen. Found something quite peculiar."

"Then let's have a look," Pendleton said.

Tom followed the physician into a back bedroom. The flame from his oil lamp illuminated a table with scalpels and bone saws and jars of floating organs. On the dissecting tables lay two carved-open bodies. The nearest was Private Wallace, the soldier who had been killed when a beast attacked Manitou Outpost. Wallace's cadaver lay twisted like a broken puppet.

"I found no signs of virus in the male specimen," Dr. Coombs said. "He died from a broken spine."

"He was attacked by a crazed man who turned cannibal," Tom said. "I believe it might have been one of the trappers from Manitou Outpost."

"That's certainly one theory," Dr. Coombs said. "Although I have another theory, gentlemen, that might raise your eyebrows." They gathered around the table that displayed the butchered upper torso of Sakari McCabe. She looked much worse than the day Tom pulled her out of the frozen stream. Her head now lay face-up, mouth wide open, frozen in a primal scream. One eye was as white as a poached fish.

"Does she have the virus?" Pendleton asked.

"Difficult to tell. Too much time has passed since her death." Dr. Coombs walked over to a microscope. "I did find some microbes that might be considered viral, but, like their host, they are also dead."

Tom peered into the microscope. All he saw was a still pattern of gray circles clumped together. "So what can we derive from this?"

Dr. Coombs shrugged. "Not much really, since I'm not even sure if this woman has the strain that infected Zoé Lamothe and Doc Riley. Unfortunately you burned their bodies."

"It was a necessary precaution," Tom said.

Dr. Coombs adjusted his spectacles. "Well, if I'm going to fight this virus, then I need to draw blood from an infected person who is still living."

Pendleton said, "Let's hope we've seen the last of the outbreak."

"You said you found something peculiar," Tom said.

Dr. Coombs' eyes lit up. "Yes, yes." He returned to the table where Sakari Kennicot lay. "What's fascinating about this cadaver are her wounds."

One of the Cree woman's eyes was missing, scraped out of the socket by claws that had ripped the flesh off half her face. Her attacker had taken a vicious bite out of her throat, tearing out the larynx. The arm that was still attached had bloated and turned a purplish-blue.

Dr. Coombs had made incisions in her chest in a Y-pattern, pulling back flaps of skin. Gray organs were exposed.

The doctor grabbed a scalpel and leaned over the carcass. "See these lacerations here?" He pointed to a five-line slash that had sliced across her breasts and torn through skin and muscle. "The claws snapped her breast bone and completely severed her spine."

Sakari's death had perplexed Tom the most, because she looked as if her attacker had been a wild animal. "Would you say a large bear did this?"

"As a doctor, my first inclination would be to say a grizzly attacked this woman and be done with it. But it being the middle of winter, that is highly unlikely. Aside from being a physician, I also have a passion for zoology, and in particular, the study of strange and often unexplained species. Someday I intend to write a book on all the amazing creatures that have been discovered throughout the world."

Tom leaned over the body. "What can you tell us about the beast that killed her?"

"You may not believe me when I tell you." The bearded man opened a cabinet and pulled out a tray of various animal talons and sharp teeth. They were each stored in a separate square marked by name and species—bobcat, cougar, wolverine, as well as numerous bear claws. Dr. Coombs picked up a claw the size of a small blade. "This was from a giant grizzly, the largest known bear ever shot in the world. It stood twelve feet tall, weighed over fourteen hundred pounds, and had paws larger than your head. As predators go, the grizzly is the king of the Canadian wilderness."

Tom held the claw to the light. "So you think we have a giant grizzly roaming the area?"

"Not quite, Inspector. The damage that the creature did to this woman and the depth and power of its claws suggest a larger beast, perhaps fifteen feet tall."

"What out here could be larger than a bear?" Pendleton asked.

"My theory is we have a new species on our hands. A monstrous thing that weighs over two thousand pounds."

Tom said, "Now you sound as crazy as Anika."

"She may not be as crazy as you think, Inspector. The folklore of the Canadian tribes all speak of legendary creatures that roam the wilderness. In northern Wisconsin, Dakota Indians speak of a bipedal creature named *Chiye-tanka.* And on the Pacific Northwest coast, the Athabaskan tribes have their *Wechuge,* and both Indians and Whites have reported seeing a hairy beast called Sasquatch or Bigfoot. These ape-like creatures are like the Abominable Snowmen of the Himalayas."

Tom said, "It all sounds interesting, Doc, but we're looking for real leads, not Indian superstitions."

"Just hear me out. Now as a scientist I'm not one to pay heed to superstitions, but when there's evidence to back it up, I am willing to stretch my mind. Many years back, I had the privilege of voyaging around South America on a surveying ship called the *Beagle*. I apprenticed with a pioneer scientist by the name of Charles Darwin. We collected hundreds of specimens. I've seen new forms of species we never dreamed existed. From plants to animals to microbes to dinosaur fossils. New discoveries are being made every day. The physical world is a fascinating place that is constantly changing, evolving. Darwin shared some interesting theories of how animals evolve through a series of natural selection he calls, 'survival of the fittest.'"

Pendleton asked, "Dr. Coombs, are you proposing our beast is a bear that has evolved into some kind of monster?"

"I've been to the Himalayas in Tibet and witnessed with my own eyes part of a large skull that was believed to come from a Yeti, also known as the Abominable Snowman."

Tom couldn't help but chuckle.

Dr. Coombs remained serious. "Great beasts do exist. Whether we're dealing with another species of bear or a bipedal anomaly, I don't know, but I'd love to have a sample of the claw that could snap a woman in two."

115

Andre, bundled in his gray winter coat and scarf, paced outside an open work shed, partly to keep warm and partly to shake the anxiety he'd been feeling all morning. He couldn't get Willow out of his head. The warmth of her embrace, the softness of her lips were phantom feelings that still haunted his skin.

Andre prayed over and over in his mind, *Forgive me, Jesus, for I have sinned... Forgive me, Jesus, for my fall from Grace... Release me from the temptations of the flesh...* Andre's inner thighs felt bruised from the beating he'd given himself last night. A brisk wind blew against his back, running cold fingers through his long hair, caressing his neck. When Andre pulled up his collar, the angry gale stirred up drifts of snow and clinked metal tools and a chain of horseshoes that hung from the shed's ceiling.

Father Xavier stood inside the shed, giving instructions to the fort's blacksmith. "We need four large crosses made of iron." The priest gave measurements.

"I'll have them for ye by tomorrow." The soot-faced blacksmith picked up a metal rod and went to work, stoking the fire of his kiln.

Father Xavier, who wore his Russian mink hat over his bald head, stepped out of the shed. "Come with me, Andre. We have much work to do."

As the Jesuits walked together, Andre asked, "What are the crosses for?"

"We're going to use them to exorcise the entire fort. We have to be prepared that anyone in the village could be under the demon's spell. We can only trust each other."

The Jesuits strolled silently along the courtyard as they passed a group of laborers pulling a sled covered in barrels. Villagers were out working, chopping wood, mending canoes. Soldiers patrolled the platforms that linked the watchtowers. Fort Pendleton seemed as if it were returning to normal. But Andre felt a change coming on. As if the peacefulness of the morning were all a façade, and the colonists were wearing masks. Or maybe it was him who was hiding behind a mask.

Father Xavier snapped his fingers. "Give me your attention."

"What?"

"I just asked you a question and you didn't answer. You seem distracted by something. Did you dream about the twin demons again?"

"No, not since the hotel."

Father Xavier sighed. "Then what has you so distant?"

"Nothing." Andre had trouble making eye contact with his mentor. Ever since kissing Willow last night, his mind had been in a fog. They had only kissed briefly and then Andre walked her home. *I was just consoling her,* he tried to convince himself.

His mentor said, "You understand that as my apprentice it is highly important you share everything that you're going through. Anything that's distracting you could be the work of the Devil. I need to know you're still working in the light."

"I am, sir." Andre looked up at the sky. It was a gray morning.

I should confess about last night.

But Andre remained silent. He'd come so far in his training. He'd proven his faith and earned his mentor's trust. With such privileged training with an accomplished priest, Andre was well on his way to becoming ordained himself. Confessing to Father Xavier now would only break his trust, and all that Andre had worked toward would be lost.

The kiss was just a momentary fall from grace. It won't happen again.

Even as he thought this, Andre felt the fluttering butterflies sensation in his chest. He stared up at the fourth floor of Noble House. He couldn't help but wonder what Willow was doing.

116

Willow felt as if eels were writhing beneath her skin. Her lips quivered. Her red nostrils itched. She opened and closed her fists as she walked the clearing behind the cabins.

This bloody fort is going right to hell.

Carrying a mink handbag over her shoulder, she hurried past the barn and stables. She had to get away from Noble House. Away from Avery. Another moment up on the third floor, and she might just go raving mad. Last night she barely slept. Laudanum had been the only remedy to make the voices stop, and her blasted husband had emptied her last bottle.

After Avery left, sleeping over at his whore's cabin, Willow had remained alone in her boudoir. The dolls kept speaking in soft whispers, their voices relentless drones, like a hive of bees buzzing around their queen. She had snorted the last of her magic dust. Everything after that was a blur.

This morning she had gone into Avery's study and pulled out one of his pistols. She sat at his desk for a long while, staring down at the gun. She might have ended everything had it not been for Zoé's voice entering her head. *Don't kill yourself, Willow,* the child had said. *I have so many secrets to share.*

I came so close... Willow shivered at the thought of dying in this fort during winter. She had imagined her body wrapped in a blanket and stored away on a shelf in the Dead House with the other corpses. The burial of a commoner would be the final mockery to her tragic life. While sitting at Avery's desk, Willow had laughed hysterically, because it wasn't a desire to live that saved her from pulling the trigger, but her own snobbish pride.

Wind rustled the branches outside the stockade. Rubbing her nostrils and sniffling, she pretended as if she was going to the well house to fetch water. The ruse was unnecessary, though, for there was not a soul at this corner of the fort. The colonists were either working in the square outside Noble House or inside their homes and workshops. She knew the rotations of the watchtower guards. They were at the northeast corner smoking cigarettes. Still wary that someone might be watching, Willow made a mad dash across the clearing.

Hospital House stood off on its own. It was wider than the other cabins. Its timbers were painted white. Ply boards were still nailed across the doors and windows.

Willow hurried around the house to the back door. Boards blocked the entry. Two were loose, each hanging by a single nail. She slid the boards upward and downward, creating a narrow opening. The smell of decay smacked her senses. Dropping the boards, she turned her head and winced. "Oh, God." She covered her mouth. "I can't go in there."

You must, Willow, you promised you would, whispered Zoé's voice.

Willow pulled the Indian doll out of her handbag. "No, Zoé, please don't make me."

The doll's single green eye gazed up at her. *If you want to be a Secret Keeper like me, then you have to find more magic powder.*

As the girl giggled in her head, Willow felt the eels swimming beneath her skin. She stared at the boarded door with the atrocious stink emanating from the cracks. She took a deep breath, then crouched and squeezed her small frame inside. The boards clapped as they fell closed behind her. She yelped, putting a hand on her chest. Her shoes crunched over ice that had blown in and frosted the wood floor of the kitchen. Just weeks ago she had been playing cards here with Doc and Myrna. Zoé had been sleeping in the next bedroom. It was gloomy in here now. The only light came from thin slits between the boarded windows. Breathing heavily, Willow gave herself a moment for her eyes to adjust. Pale gray shapes tapered off into the deep, impenetrable blackness of three passageways. The sound of wings fluttered in one of the other rooms, where a flock of birds must have gotten in to roost.

Inhaling, Willow pressed a hand to her chest, trying to calm the rapid thumping of her heart. The room she needed to get to was through the pitch dark hallway to her left. The corridor seemed to disappear into nothingness. There was no light at the end of the hall, which meant all the doors were closed.

"Blast it, why didn't I bring a candle?"

Oops, we forgot, Zoé snickered.

Willow pulled the doll against her bosom. "This is bloody crazy, Zoé. Let's not do this. Please, can't we just go back?"

What's there to go back to?

Willow remained facing the dark hallway.

I can take you to where children play forever.

Willow sniffled and scratched her itchy nose. Her eyes teared up, and she wiped them before they could crystallize on her cold cheeks.

"Okay," she whispered.

Touching the wall for guidance, she started down the hallway. The blackness swallowed Willow, embracing her with cadaver-cold arms. She passed the patient room where Zoé once slept. Willow imagined that the Métis girl was still in there, tied to the bedposts. Her little head turning on her pillow, solid white eyes staring from the darkness. At this moment Zoé giggled, a sinister sound that raised the hair on Willow's arms.

"Don't do that. You're spooking me."

Sorry, hee hee, I couldn't resist.

Birds squawked, startling Willow. In that dim room, ravens flapped from the dresser to the bed. Feeling a shortness of breath, she quickened her step, reaching blindly out in front of her. Her hand found a closed door at the end of the hall. She turned the cold metal knob and the door creaked open. Shafts of gray light piercing through the boarded windows offered enough luminosity to see the many curio cabinets that made up the apothecary.

We found it!

Willow laughed with tears in her eyes. She set the Indian doll on top of the curio and began rummaging through Doc Riley's medicine drawers. The day she had watched over Zoé, Willow had snuck into this room and stolen some vials of laudanum and magic dust. The drawer marked COCAINE was empty. "No, no, no." She pulled out drawer after drawer. Empty, empty, empty. "Where is it?"

"Looking for this?" rasped a man's voice.

Willow whirled around. A figure stood in the doorway, a shadow against a curtain of blackness. His hand held up a vial of snow-white powder. "Don't worry, Little Lamb. I have plenty of what you seek."

117

"Heave ho, heave ho, heave ho..." Private Wickliff chanted as he and Private Fitch carried the bundled corpse through the cemetery.

Fitch frowned. "Quit saying that, you wanker. Have some respect for the dead."

"Sorry, mate, it keeps me mind off what we're carrying." All morning, the two soldiers had moved bodies back and forth between the Dead House and Dr. Coombs' autopsy room. Their old mate, Private Pembrook, had been dissected and was now being returned to storage. Wickliff hated having the dead soldier's crumpled head resting against his shoulder. Fitch had been lucky to get the feet. At Wickliff's end, the sheets were splotched with pus and smelled like spoiled haggis. The body was heavy and stiff as a pine log. With each step, Wickliff felt like his arms were going to pop out from their sockets.

Heave ho, heave ho, heave ho...

"Just a little farther, mate," Fitch breathed heavily. They weaved between the wood crosses that marked a few dozen graves. They reached the T-shaped shed that had originally been built to store tools, barrels, broken canoes, and dogsleds. A clapboard with painted white lettering hung above the door: THE DEAD HOUSE.

Sgt. Cox was standing just outside the door with his arms crossed. A scarf covered the lower half of his broad, square face. "'Bout time you two nitwits got here," he grumbled. "Follow me." He lit a lantern and guided them into the sepulchral darkness. There were no windows in the shed, just solid log walls with gray mortar. Every time Wickliff came in here, he felt like he was stepping into a mineshaft. He held his breath and winced. And then it hit him. The nose-burning stench that made him gag. His eyes watered. He swallowed hot bile and managed to hold down his breakfast. The Dead House had entombed the foulest of odors as decomposing bodies had been stored in here for many winters. Seemed like every year the beast of winter claimed at least one poor soul. This year the village was already up to half a dozen deaths, and they still had three months until the first thaw.

Up ahead, Sgt. Cox began stomping his boot, dancing around and swinging the lantern light, tossing shadows all about. There was a squeal and a sickening crunch. The sergeant peeled a flattened rat off his boot. "Stupid rodents."

The three soldiers walked single file between two upturned canoes that were stacked on sawhorses for repair. Wickliff felt his end of Pembrook's body slipping and had to stop to pull it back up his chest. "We almost there?"

"Can't rightly tell," Fitch said, his face a faint outline. "I'm the one going backwards."

Wickliff said, "Can we stop, Sarge? My arms are killing me."

"Just a few more paces," Sgt. Cox said.

"This is complete bollocks. I didn't take this job to work in a morgue."

"Quit your moaning."

For some reason the back of the shed was much colder than outside. A chill seeped into Wickliff's red greatcoat, making him shiver. They finally reached the end where the building expanded left and right into a T. The afternoon light from the front door had tapered off at the middle of the building. Wickliff rapped his knee on a crate. "Bugger, why couldn't the builders have put in at least one window back here?"

The back half of the Dead House was so pitch dark, it seemed like nothing existed beyond the circle of Sgt. Cox's lantern. But as they rounded the corner on the right, the sergeant's light revealed that there were things living in this primordial blackness.

Rats.

Dozens of knobby-tailed critters scurried away from the sergeant's stomping boots. At the back wall, he revealed the very thing Wickliff had hoped to never see again. The storage shelf stood six levels high. It had been built for storing barrels and crates. Those had been removed, and now five bodies were tucked away on each shelf like mummies in a catacomb. Pembrook's corpse made number six.

"Fourth shelf," Sgt. Cox barked.

Privates Wickliff and Fitch hefted Pembrook's body over their heads and stacked him next to the inspector's boy. Something wet and furry leaped onto Wickliff's shoulder. "Uhhhhhhh!" He danced around and swatted.

The rat hit the floor, and Sgt. Cox crunched it with his boot. "Damned vermin! This place is infested." The sergeant went to the bodies and peeled back a sheet riddled with holes. "Christ almighty." The corpse was chewed down to the bone.

"That does it," Cox said. "Wickliff, Fitch, your next task is to exterminate these rats. And I don't want to see either of you come out until every last rodent is dead."

"Aye, sir." Private Wickliff looked at all the hairy creatures scampering across the floor, along the walls, and over barrels, and feared he just might bloody well faint.

118

Willow pressed her backbone against the curio cabinet, her body trembling. She peed down her leg like a little girl.

The man cloaked in darkness shook the vial of cocaine.

"No...p-please...d-don't hurt me."

"Just stay calm, Little Lamb. I wouldn't want to flaw that pretty face." He stepped into the gray light. His face was covered by a native mask—white with red outlining the hollow eye sockets, nostrils, and mouth. A band of red dots rounded the forehead.

"You..." Willow gasped. "But how?"

"You dreamed me here. Remember?"

She flinched as his cold hand stroked her hair. "Ah, don't be scared. I'm here to make alllll your dreamssss come trueeeee. Now, just relaxxxxx." The croon of his voice made Willow's eyelids go heavy. A memory surfaced. She was a seventeen-year-old girl walking down a marble staircase, cradling a porcelain doll. At the time, she and Avery were newlyweds and living in the Pendleton mansion in Montréal. Music from a string quartet echoed from the ballroom. Avery was hosting another one of his sordid masquerade parties.

At the bottom floor, Willow passed strangers in the foyer, men and women wearing colorful masks. Hand in hand, they stepped into guest bedrooms. A woman with a cat face and heavy cleavage tugged on Willow's golden ringlets. "Mmm, how precious you are. You must be the Willow I keep hearing about. And what's your doll's name?"

Willow stuck up her nose. "I don't associate with whores."

"Oh." The cat woman rolled back her shoulders. "Well, that's just as bloody well, because I don't associate with snobby girls." She stomped off and entered the toilet.

Willow followed the sound of string music into the ballroom. Couples danced. Most of the gentlemen were dressed in fancy suits, top hats, and masks. The women wore masks, too, but not all of them wore clothes. As usual, Avery, who always wore a wolverine mask, was nowhere in sight.

Willow's eyes widened. A fully naked woman wearing a sheep's mask was sitting in the lap of a hairy-chested man in a white tribal mask. His red-rimmed eyes looked in Willow's direction. His red mouth was frozen in a grimace. "Well, hello there, Little Lamb," spoke a strange man's voice.

Frightened, Willow turned, collided into a butler carrying a tray. A glass of champagne crashed to the floor, splashing her nightgown. In the confusion, she dropped her doll and dashed out of the ballroom, her heart flapping like a bird in a cage. In the foyer, the cat woman grabbed her arm. "You shouldn't run in the house, Miss Priss."

"Let go of me." Willow tore loose from her grip and raced up the marble staircase to her boudoir. It was the only room she felt truly safe. Her own private sanctuary. The walls were pink and lacy and shelved with over a hundred dolls. She dove onto her bed, burying her head in silk pillows, and sobbed. Someone knocked at her door. "Are you in there, Little Lamb?"

Willow leaped off her bed and hid inside her closet.

The door opened, and the man with the tribal mask entered with the sheep woman. He wore pants and shoes, but she wore only a see-through nightgown. Sheep Woman slid her hand across the silk bedspread. "I don't think she's in here, lover."

Willow trembled, afraid she might pee.

"Look at all these dolls." The man set the doll she'd dropped on a shelf with all the others.

Sheep Woman said, "I'm sure Avery's new wife is absolutely spoiled to the core. Look at this darling makeup table." She sat down and leaned toward the mirror. Keeping her sheep mask on, she picked up one of Willow's brushes and began running it through her hair.

Willow gritted her teeth, thought of jumping out and screaming, but was too scared to reveal that she was watching from the closet.

Sheep Woman hummed. The man with thick, black chest hair stood behind her. He pulled the sheer fabric off her shoulders. "Since she's not in here, why don't we carry on with all the dolls watching?"

She turned and laughed. "Oh, tonight I have found such a kinky one. What is your name?"

"Ah, my naughty little lamb, you know the rules," he crooned in that sultry voice. "No names. No faces. Just surrender to your wildest fantasies."

Willow's fear turned into curiosity and arousal as the man cupped the sheep woman's breasts. She moaned and leaned her head back against his stomach. He tore off her sheer nightgown. The woman was curvaceous and beautiful. The man picked her up and carried her to the pink bed. As he lay on top of her, his red and white mask turned toward the closet. "I don't think Willow would mind if we used her bed for awhile."

She felt the dark eyes in those red-rimmed sockets gazing right into her.

The reverie played out in glorious detail, stirring the slippery serpents beneath Willow's skin. She felt flushed and heated. Her eyes fluttered open. Her awareness was back inside the apothecary room with the masked man standing in front of her. She never saw the man's face or knew his name. He was just one of the many men who did sinful deeds at the Avery's masquerade parties. But somehow the first man she had ever lusted for had found her.

We told you he would come for you, Zoé said. *You thought it was Tom or Andre, but nope, it never was.*

Willow shook her head. "No." Her lips quivered. She felt dizzy and feared she might faint. She grabbed the curio cabinet. The mysterious man from her past had to be another hallucination.

"You can't be real."

"I'm as real as you desire me to be." The red circles of the mask appeared hollow, as if he had no eyes, only blackness. Then she saw things writhing in the holes and heard chittering sounds. His knuckles stroked her face with a touch so icy cold it frosted her cheek.

Willow yelped and stumbled to a corner, crouched and hugged

herself. She couldn't stop shaking.

"This will make all your suffering go away." His pale hand jiggled the cocaine vial. "You still want this don't you, Little Lamb?"

Willow nodded and reached out. "Please."

He pulled his hand back. "All you have to do is give me something that's dear to your heart."

"Like what?"

"Leave the doll here with me."

"No. I can't."

"It's just for a spell, while you spend some time in wonderland."

"No, I can't leave Zoé."

"Very well, then." He tipped the vial, sprinkling white powder onto the floor.

"No don't, please," Willow begged.

The hand turned the vial upright. It was still over half full. "So what will it be? Would you rather I touch you until you freeze to the core? In a day or two they'll find you here, shriveled and curled up with your doll. Then they'll store you on a shelf alongside the others in the Dead House, where the rats will chew your flesh to the bone. Is that what you want?"

Eyes streaming tears, Willow shook her head. She looked at the Indian doll sitting on the curio cabinet.

It's okay, Willow, Zoé said. *He's my friend. He'll keep me safe.*

"Hand me the doll."

Willow picked up the doll, hugged it, and then offered it to the masked figure.

Zoé giggled. *Now we can play together forever.*

Feeling hollow and afraid, Willow turned to the masked figure. He pointed to the floor. "Kneel down, Little Lamb."

She dropped to her knees. He held out a long fingernail full of magic dust to her nose. She snorted and immediately plunged into bliss.

119

Deep inside the cavern of the Dead House, a few feet from where the mummies slept, Private Fitch crouched behind a barrel. He waited, staring down at a chunk of cheese on the ground floor. A rat scurried into the lantern glow and began to nibble. Fitch brought down his shovel with the quickness of a guillotine, snapping the varmint's neck with his spade. "Ha, gotcha!"

He picked up the limp rat by its ropy tail and tossed it into a barrel. It flopped on top of a mound of slaughtered rats. Fitch spun in a circle, doing his victory dance, then returned to his crouched stance, gripping the shovel.

"Way to nail 'im, Fitch." Private Wickliff emerged from the dark tunnel, carrying a shovel in one hand and three more dead rats in the other. "I've killed up to thirty-six of these little beasties. How many for you?"

"Forty-two," said Fitch, feeling quite proud. They had made a wager. The one who slew the most rats got a night off from his next watchtower shift. "Guess that makes me Rat King." He did his victory dance. "I'm getting a night off."

"Don't get cocky too quick, mate," said Wickliff. "We ain't done. I can hear a few more lurking in the nooks and crannies. I think they've gotten wise to us."

"Well, it's almost supper time. One of us should go get Sarge, while the other finishes up. I'll stay behind, if you like."

Wickliff spat tobacco. "You just want to lock the win. No way. How about we arm wrestle for it?"

"Bugger that, you're stronger than me." Fitch reached into his pocket and pulled out his lucky silver coin. "Let's flip for it. Winner stays behind to claim the title of Rat King. Loser goes to get the sergeant. I call tails." He tossed the coin in the air. It landed on the dirt floor. "Tails!"

Wickliff grumbled, "Fine, I'm ready to get out of this rat hole anyway."

"Hurry back."

Wickliff offered a sinister grin. "I might just have to hit the crapper first. Happy hunting, Rat King." He turned the corner, leaving Fitch alone at the back T-section. The young soldier grabbed his shovel and lantern and walked between the barrels, searching for any sudden movements.

"Fe, fi, fo, fum...I smell the blood of the rat kingdom."

Being in this dank shed reminded him of growing up at the orphanage back in Lachine, Quebec. He used to play a similar game down in the cellar. Only he chased mice instead of rats. The shortest soldier of the garrison, Fitch had always been the runt of the litter. At the orphanage, all the bigger kids picked on him and made him do the least pleasant chores, like cleaning the cellar. He thought he had escaped that torment when he caught a ferry to Ottawa to work as a security guard for the Pendleton Fur Trading Company. Again, all the other soldiers were bigger and always picked on him and gave him the shittiest jobs. That was his lot in life for being the smallest and weakest. But here among the rats, Fitch felt colossal. He banged the handle of the shovel against the dirt. "I am the mighty Rat King!" He imagined he was a powerful giant, and the rodents were frightened villagers. "Fe, fi, fo, fum…"

The aroma of death must have been affecting his brain, because Fitch suddenly heard a strange chittering echo throughout the Dead House. He raised the lantern over his head. Dozens of black, beady eyes stared down from the rafters.

"Oh, Jesus." One leaped onto his shoulder. He slapped it off, dropping the shovel and lantern. The kerosene lamp rolled into the corner, illuminating the mummified corpses stacked upon the shelves. The bloody sheets began moving and twitching as if the bodies beneath were waking from their post-mortem sleep.

"Oh, bugger this!" Leaving the lantern, Fitch stumbled back toward the middle of the T-section. Rounding the corner, he hurried through the dark toward the open doorway at the front end of the shed. Tiny feet scampered the rafters above. *Squeak, squeak, squeak, squeak.* The horde was following him. His only escape was through fifty feet of darkness. At the end, a portal opened to the snow-white world outside.

A man's silhouette suddenly rose form the floor, blocking the doorway.

Fitch cheered, "Wickliff! Thank God, you're back!"

When his friend didn't answer, Fitch said, "Sarge, is that you?"

The visitor closed the door. The front section of the shed went black.

Fitch bumped into a crate, scuffing his shin. "Hey! Open the door!"

The rats squeaked all around him.

Fitch felt his way between the stacked canoes. "Wickliff, this ain't funny. I can't see anything. Please, mate, *open the damn door!*"

Up ahead in the dark came a throaty, wheezing sound followed by gibbering.

Fitch halted. The entire garrison was probably in on this. He imagined the whole lot of them outside snickering, while Wickliff or one of the others got him to shit his drawers. "Quit trying to scare me."

The wheezing-gibbering voice drew closer. Then a hammering noise, like metal against wood. Something was striking each passing barrel in a slow and steady cadence, moving toward Fitch. "Ey, what the fuck are you doing?"

Trembling, he looked back from where he came. The only light was a faint glow from the T-section. Rats or not, seeing was better than being blind. He retreated. His face cringed with disgust. The floor was an undulating rug of black fur and white, worm-like tails. Shadowy things crawled over his feet, hopped onto his legs. He trudged through the current, slapping rats off his pants. He turned the corner, back into the dim light of his lantern.

No windows. No back door. Trapped.

Wheezing.

Shaking, Fitch whirled around. At the edge of darkness, a figure wearing a fur parka stood hunched over.

"Who the fuck are you?" Fitch shouted.

The man stepped into the lantern glow. His face was hidden in the black pit of his hood. He was one of the *voyageurs*.

"W-What are you doing in here?" Fitch grabbed the shovel. "Answer me."

"Hungry..." The man raised an axe with bony white hands.

Fitch screamed as the blade chopped into his shoulder, snapping his bones. He dropped to the floor.

The hooded man yanked out the axe, wrenching Fitch's body over to one side. Blood pumped out. The rats swarmed the red fountain.

A cold blackness oozed at the edges of his vision. He tasted copper and bile. His eyelids drooped. He didn't die fast enough though, because his last gurgling breaths were spent watching the gibbering man lop off Fitch's arm and sit down to feast among the rats.

120

As Andre and Father Xavier were blessing the cabins, Willow stepped from between two houses. Her white fur coat was soiled. She stumbled aimlessly a few steps then collapsed onto the snowy ground.

"Dear God, Willow!" Andre ran to her aid, skidding to his knees by her side.

"What happened? Willow, speak to me."

Her hair was disheveled. Her eyes rolled back.

Andre pulled her up into a seated position, but she just stared ahead, as catatonic as a doll. "There's something wrong with her."

"She's ill," Father Xavier said. "Get away from her."

But Andre kept holding her. "We need to do something."

Other villagers gathered around.

"You, boy!" Andre said to a teenager. "Run, get the doctor."

The kid scrambled off.

"She's been cursed," said one of the native women.

"By that witch," said another.

"Give us some room," Andre snapped at the onlookers. He rocked Willow. "Everything's going to be all right. We're here now."

Willow stared up with a vacant, heavy-lidded gaze, lips mumbling. As her head lolled back, fear clenched Andre's heart with icy fingers.

121

Tom stepped out of the Dead House with a sick feeling in his stomach. Lieutenant Hysmith came out second, pressing a handkerchief over his nose. Outside, the garrison of eight red-coated soldiers stood around with forlorn expressions. Private Wickliff was seated on the ground, crying. He was the unlucky bloke who found Fitch's butchered body. There wasn't much left of the hapless soldier.

A trail of red footprints zigzagged across the cemetery.

"These were made by a man wearing large fur boots," Tom said. "Let's track him." He followed the bloody boot prints.

Determined to avenge their mate, the soldiers fanned out through the graveyard, gripping their rifles.

Up ahead, Tom spotted a red patch of snow. He kneeled over a severed arm. Most of the muscle along the forearm had been torn off. The hand, which barely clung to the wrist bone, had several large bite marks.

He faced the garrison. "Men, we appear to have another cannibal among us."

The soldiers glanced at one another with paranoia in their eyes.

"It's not any of my men," Hysmith said. "They were with me."

Tom quickly studied their faces for signs of infection, especially Private Wickliff, who was the last to be alone with Fitch. The teen was a blubbering mess. Other than his boots and the cuffs of his trousers, the kid was free of blood. Tom scanned the graveyard and cabins beyond. Whoever murdered Fitch was now loose inside the village.

Tom said, "Lieutenant, have one of them wrap up this arm and take it to Dr. Coombs." He saw that the gnawed flesh was covered in white pus. "Nobody touch it with your bare hand. It may be infected."

Tom marched on and all but one soldier followed. The bloody boot prints ran right past Anika's home, so close Tom could see the two rocking chairs in the window. That unsettled his nerves. He wanted to knock on the door to make sure she was okay, but there was no time. The bright red patches in the snow faded to pink smears then diminished to occasional red droplets. The trail of boot impressions led to the far corner of the fort.

Off by itself stood the boarded-up hospital house.

122

Father Xavier had the sensation of being watched as he stood in Willow Pendleton's bedchamber. The myriad of dolls was packed together on shelves that covered two walls. The priest found their blank gazes unsettling.

The blonde woman who had collapsed earlier was now lying in her bed unconscious. Dr. Coombs lifted her eyelids, exposing blue eyes that stared at nothing.

"Will she be okay?" Master Pendleton asked from the opposite side of her bed. He was on his knee, holding her hand.

"She's snorted a high dose of cocaine." The doctor rose. "We'll need to keep a close watch on her."

"I can stay with her," Andre offered.

"No, I need you to keep with me," Father Xavier said. "We have more training to do."

"But she needs attention—"

"I'll stay with her," Master Pendleton said, his face distraught. "Please, everyone, just leave us be."

123

When the doctor and Jesuits left the room, Avery dropped his wife's hand. He was sickened that she had left Noble House high on cocaine. Now the whole damned fort would be gossiping.

"How could you do this to me?" he asked.

Willow just lay there like Sleeping Beauty waiting for her prince. Avery wasn't about to kiss those pale lips. Her skin was sallow in the half-light. Her face looked older now, with crow's feet around the eyes.

He glanced around the room at her wardrobe of dresses, her velvet curtains, and the damned collection of dolls. He had given Willow everything her heart desired, and she did nothing but embarrass him in return. She always needed to be the center of attention. How many times had he caught her flirting with other men? When Avery first started courting Willow, she was sixteen. A spoiled little debutante. The gorgeous daughter of a wealthy and powerful baron. Avery thought once he married Willow, he could tame her. Make her his obedient wife to show off at business parties and galas. But his marriage was more like a father raising a little girl who refused to grow up.

Kill her, whispered a voice inside his head. *Kill the little slut.*

Avery took one of her lacy pillows and held it a foot over her face. All he had to do was press down, and he would be free of his wife's childish antics.

Behind him came a sound like a porcelain plate smashing against the floor. One of the dolls had fallen off the shelf and shattered into a thousand tiny shards. It was the geisha he had bought his wife for Christmas. On the bed, Willow giggled softly and rolled over onto her side. She slept with a lazy smile, as if having a pleasant dream.

Oh, to hell with this brat. Avery tossed the pillow and left the room.

124

Tom and his soldiers approached Hospital House. Bloody boot prints marked the snow and back porch. The planks had been torn from the doorway. Tom peered into the black maw.

The soldiers lit up a couple of lanterns. Tom, cocking his pistol, eased a lantern across the threshold. Snow spun along the kitchen floor. Beyond the kitchen, hallways split off into three directions. One was a staircase that led to the second story. The wood floor was bloodstained from the day Doc Riley slaughtered his wife. Tom listened. Wind careened through the shattered windows. Then came flapping from some distant room. Birds had gotten in.

Tom glanced over his shoulder at Sgt. Cox and the guards. They all looked like nervous sheep. None of them were trained for police raids. The inspector entered first, signaling the men to cover two of the doorways. He directed Sgt. Cox to take four soldiers upstairs. Then Tom and Hysmith explored the hallway directly left. If memory served him right, it led to the apothecary. He stabbed the light into a room. The bedroom where Zoé had slept. The room was now empty. As Tom crept through the dark corridor, he couldn't help feeling he was back in Montréal, exploring the maze of warehouses at the Meraux Cannery. He heard the sound of chains chinking together, water dripping, and the bubbling of soup boiling inside a giant vat. Tom paused, shaking his head. Since he'd stopped drinking and passed the time whittling out his demons, the flashbacks had ended. But searching for a cannibal inside Hospital House was bringing the horrid visions back.

Aware of his heartbeat, Tom aimed his pistol and continued down the hallway. The corridor opened up into a room with curio cabinets. The lantern light reflected something green. It sparkled like an emerald. On a cabinet sat an Indian doll with a single eye. Zoé's doll. He had last seen it in Willow's room. What was it doing here? There were other objects on the cabinet: a ring, a necklace, a knife, a flask, and a half dozen other trinkets. They were arranged like some sort of altar. On the wall above was another red spiral.

The ceiling creaked. Tom raised the lantern. Above issued a gibbering sound that caught his breath. His mind flashed to the face of the Cannery Cannibal. The gibbering turned to cackling. Then Hospital House erupted with screams and gunshots.

125

As the screams and gunfire faded, Tom and three soldiers charged up the staircase. At the top floor, a long room full of beds stretched the length of Hospital House. Gray light pierced through the clapboards covering two windows. The back half of the room was hidden by deep shadows. The room reeked of gunsmoke and blood. Tom entered and was knocked back by a flutter of air. Black birds flew up from the floor, flapping over his head. Tom reeled at the sight of three mutilated soldiers. Among the dead lay Sgt. Cox. He had claw marks across his face. One soldier was missing.

The ravens flocked together and flew into the shadows. A guttural snarl, like a feral wolf, issued from the far end of the room.

One of Tom's soldiers bolted down the stairs. The other two remained frozen, holding up their rifles with shaking arms.

"Keep with me, men." Tom held up his lantern and eased toward the guttural cawing sounds. He stopped midway when the edge of the lantern glow revealed the body of the missing soldier. Pale hands dug into the dead man's belly and tore out his guts. Tom raised the lantern. The killer, wearing a hooded fur parka, was hunched over, stuffing entrails into his mouth. Flapping birds perched on his back. The parka that cloaked the beast was a squirming mass of living rats with beady eyes and worm-like tales that intertwined.

"Oh, Jesus!" yelled one of the soldiers.

The killer looked up. Nocturnal eyes reflected the light.

At the sight of the face, Tom froze, disbelieving.

Gustave.

The Cannery Cannibal's face split into a red grimace. He rose, a swarm of dark wings flapping around him.

"Shoot him!" Tom screamed at the two soldiers. The gunmen unleashed a frenzy of bullets.

The cannibal charged, loping toward them, closing the distance with incredible speed. Tom hurled the lantern, striking the beast with a burst of flames that rippled across the fur parka. The ravens scattered. The cannibal roared, spinning, a whirling dervish of fire. Tom and the soldiers filled the killer's body with lead until he finally collapsed in a heap of flames.

126

Tom, still shaken from the attack, stood among Pendleton, Hysmith, Dr. Coombs, and the two Jesuits. Firelight reflected in each of their eyes as they watched Hospital House burn like a giant bonfire. The rooftop caved in with a thundering crash of timbers. Black smoke and glowing embers drifted across the fort.

The bodies of the four slain soldiers had been left inside the burning house. Only the corpse of the cannibal creature lay on the snowy ground.

"I've never seen anything quite like this," Dr. Coombs said. "The man's physiology has gone through some kind of metamorphosis." He pointed with a stick, careful not to touch it. "He has claws and look at those teeth." On the charred half of the face, the flesh had burned away, exposing a row of fangs, everyone of them sharp as a canine's. The other half showed the man was not Gustave Meraux, as Tom had feared, but another colonist.

"Who is he?" Tom asked Pendleton.

"Jean Chaurette." The chief factor shook his head. "He was one of the *voyageurs* who just returned from Montréal."

Tom thought of the sixteen men who had recently traveled the rivers by canoe. The last two days of their journey, they had camped in the woods. Four members from that party were standing in this circle now. Tom gazed at Father Xavier, Andre, Dr. Coombs, and then at Pendleton. "Your *voyageurs* must have brought the disease back into the fort."

Master Pendleton scoffed. "No one in my crew showed any sign of the sickness."

Tom said, "Doc Riley didn't show any symptoms right away either, but he eventually began to change into something like this."

Dr. Coombs stabbed a needle into the creature's arm and drew a sample of blood. "Now, I can finally have look at this virus."

Pendleton said, "Find out what you can quickly, Doctor, before another outbreak occurs." To the four remaining soldiers, he said, "Men, throw this body into the fire."

The pallbearers wore heavy coats, scarves, and mittens as they carried the cannibal's corpse and tossed it into the pyre. To be safe, they burned their outer clothing, as well.

"We can't be sure that's the last of it," Tom said. "If one or more of the *voyageurs* brought the disease into the fort..."

The bonfire drew other onlookers, as over forty villagers gathered. Tom looked around at all the men, women, and children who watched the blaze. Any one of them could be carrying the virus within them.

127

Andre stood mesmerized by the bonfire. He'd never seen anything so dazzling as the tall flames that licked the evening sky. Ashes drifted upward like snowfall in reverse. On the ground, the heat melted away the snow in a large radius, uncovering black earth. A group of giggling kids ran past, their boots splashing through mud.

Sweat rolled down Andre's face. He loosened his tunic. He looked around at the crowd of men and women captivated by the glowing spectacle of flames devouring the walls of Hospital House. The children grabbed hands and danced in a circle. Behind them, the towering fire popped and crackled as the timbers disintegrated. A burst of orange embers burst outward, a swarm of fireflies floating over the heads of the children.

Andre called to them, "You shouldn't be so close to the fire."

The kids only snickered, dancing hand in hand like little pagans. They were circling an object that lay on the ground on a flat piece of wood.

Andre looked back at his mentor. Father Xavier was in deep discussion with Master Pendleton and Inspector Hatcher. The gazes of all the parents remained transfixed on the bonfire, as if enchanted by it. Andre approached the children, who were now singing a French nursery rhyme. The object that they danced around had tiny feet and hands. It looked like an infant lying on a sacrificial altar. Andre broke up the circle. "Go find your parents," he said, shooing the kids. They scampered away, giggling.

The heat this close to the fire was sweltering. Kneeling, Andre picked up an Indian doll that had a soot-covered face and singed fur clothing. The leather skin on half its face had melted away, exposing the solid wood beneath. A single green eye stared at Andre, reflecting the light.

A little girl's voice whispered in Andre's mind, *Take me back to Willow.*

Part Thirteen

Hysteria

128

Standing on the chapel's stage beside Master Pendleton, Tom gripped a shotgun. His adrenaline was still pumping from shooting the cannibal at Hospital House. Morale was down. The garrison had lost five more members today. First the cannibal creature killed Private Fitch in the Dead House, and then slaughtered Sgt. Cox and three others on the top floor of Hospital House. Fort security was now down to Lt. Hysmith and four privates, all teenagers.

The lieutenant and his guards appeared anxious, as thirty colonists walked single file into the nave. Dr. Coombs examined them for signs of the infection. Everyone seemed accounted for except Willow, who was sick in bed. Tom had been shocked to hear that she had nearly overdosed on cocaine. He felt pity for the woman, but she was Avery Pendleton's problem to deal with.

Tom had an outbreak to contain.

With the gaze of a hawk, he watched every man, woman, and child standing in line. He prayed none of the children were infected. The thought of having to execute a child in front of his parents...Tom didn't want to think about it. Instead, he focused on the men who gave him the most suspicion: The French Canadian *voyageurs* who had recently returned from their canoe trip.

The latest infected man, Jean Chaurette, had lived among the *voyageurs* in a small cropping of cabins at the front corner of the fort. They were a tight-knit bunch who kept to themselves. When the laborers weren't working, they spent their nights drinking rum and singing French songs that echoed across the fort. Several times Tom had to ask them to stop singing so the rest of the colony could sleep.

Jean Chaurette had been their leader. What was he doing inside Hospital House? Hiding out so no one would see that he was changing into a monster? Tom remembered the altar he'd found—the red spiral, the offerings of trinkets. Were they placed there by Jean or the owners?

The first thought that came to mind was Devil worship. Tom studied the haggard faces of the *voyageurs* who stood in line, awaiting their examination. Among them stood the bearded giant, Michel Bélanger. He glared back at Tom, giving him the evil eye.

Pendleton leaned toward Tom's ear and whispered, "If any of them are infected, you know what has to be done."

129

Father Xavier watched the colonists as they were examined by Dr. Coombs and then took a seat in the pews. The disease specialist studied the throat and eyes of a little boy. After a moment, Dr. Coombs smiled and patted the boy's head. "Pierre, you can go sit with your sister."

Brother Andre checked the boy's name off a list.

Father Xavier released his breath. All the children were free of the disease. Thus far, out of forty people, only two men and one very sick woman had been discovered with symptoms—white scabs, pronounced veins, and fitful coughs. They had been segregated from the others and remained quarantined at the far corner of the nave. Two guards watched over them.

Next in line was a crane-thin man with an unruly gray beard. The grandfather of the previous boy and girl. Father Xavier noticed the old man's hands were trembling. He kept his head down.

"What's your name?" Dr. Coombs asked.

"Jean-Luc Boisvert," he spoke with a raspy voice.

Dr. Coombs held an oil lamp to Boisvert's wrinkled face. He had nasty scabs on his cheeks and forehead. "How long have you had these lesions?"

"Bout a week. It's frostbite." His eyes were bloodshot, the blue-gray irises streaked with white. Like dull marbles. His lips were chapped.

"Open wide and let me see your teeth."

"Why do you need to see my teeth?"

"It's just a procedure."

Boisvert opened his mouth. Half the teeth were missing. His gums were gray and spotted with patches of white foam. Dr. Coombs made some notes. "I'll need you to spend the night in the hospital."

"I ain't infected," Boisvert snarled.

Father Xavier said, "If you are well, then touch this cross and accept the blessings of Jesus Christ." He held up a cross. The old man's marble eyes flared, and he recoiled.

Dr. Coombs snapped his fingers. Two guards took Boisvert by the arms. "Let go of me," he protested. The guards dragged him to the holding area at the far corner of the chapel. Two of the children yelled, "Papa!" Boisvert cursed as he was forced to sit among the other three infected.

Dr. Coombs glared at Father Xavier. "Priest, this is a medical procedure, not an inquisition. Do not disrupt my patients again."

"You are taking much too long," Father Xavier argued. "If they are infected, then they will flee from the cross."

"Oh, rubbish," Dr. Coombs scoffed. "Just stay out of my—"

Andre pointed. "Dear God, look!"

At the prayer altar, candles began to light up as if struck by an invisible match. The flame glow flickered across the statue of the Virgin Mary. Blood tears streamed down her cheeks. Stigmata dripped from her open palms. The miracle caused panic among the congregation in the pews and the people still waiting in line. At the front stage, Master Pendleton and Inspector Hatcher yelled, trying to restore order. Where the infected were quarantined, the sick native woman wailed and began crying blood tears. She bolted, knocking down a guard.

Father Xavier intercepted her, holding up a cross to her blood-streaked face. The native woman hissed, drawing back blue lips. The edges of her mouth split from ear to ear, exposing dozens of sharp fangs covered in white foam. She shrunk away from the cross, releasing an unholy shriek that silenced the crowd.

Father Xavier stepped toward her. "In the name of God, I cast out this demon!"

She climbed over pews. Children squealing in terror dashed out of the way, as the woman grunted and leaped ape-like across the nave.

130

At the front stage, Tom raised his shotgun, but there were too many people in the line of fire. Some fled screaming toward the door, while others froze like confused rabbits. The crazed woman ran low to the floor, a beast on all fours, the hump of her back bouncing upward between the pews. She slashed at the crowd, leaped onto a man's back, knocking him down like a mountain lion topples a deer.

A young boy ran toward the woman, crying, "Mama!"

"No!" Tom rushed down from the stage.

The Indian woman pulled the boy into her bosom and turned toward Tom. Her solid-red face was a macabre nightmare, eyes solid white. Her mouth opened wide, exposing jawbone and rows of shark's teeth speckled with blood and torn flesh.

"Let the boy go!" Tom yelled.

The she-beast released a maniacal cackle and then bit into her son's neck, wrenched out his throat. She dropped the child and charged toward the front of the nave, bounding on hands and feet toward Tom and Pendleton.

"Kill her!" yelled the chief factor as he dashed into a confessional closet.

Tom gripped the barrel of his shotgun and swung, cracking the woman's jaw. She lurched again. He struck her head, hammering down repeatedly, bludgeoning her face. Her nose shattered. Her forehead caved inward, crushing the eye sockets. The white eyes popped. The infected woman clawed blindly at Tom. Her too-wide mouth kept laughing with a maddening, witch's cackle. He moved behind the now-blind woman, pressed the barrel to the back of her head, and pulled the trigger. Her face blew outward. She fell to her knees as if kneeling for communion, her entire face an open, dripping maw. The laughter finally stopped. Tom kicked her back with a boot, and she fell forward against the stage.

131

Tom stumbled back, gravity pulling him down into a seated position on a pew. His bloody hands wouldn't stop shaking. The she-beast lay at his feet, facedown in a crimson puddle that spread around her body. More blood covered the pulpit and back wall. The air was thick with the smell of copper and urine. The screams of the colonists seemed miles away as they fled from the chapel, fading off into the distance.

A hand gripped Tom's shoulder. He flinched. Behind him stood Father Xavier. "Are you all right?"

Tom shook his head.

"It had to be done," said the priest. "You saved the others."

"Not all of them," Tom said. A few rows back lay the dead man and young boy. "She killed her own son."

The confessional closet opened and Pendleton stepped out. He looked down at the slain woman. He made a squeamish sound and put a handkerchief over his mouth.

"That's what the infected become," Tom said.

Father Xavier said, "It's what we'll all become if we don't stop the outbreak."

132

Avery Pendleton put on his top hat and stepped out of the chapel into the chaos of night. Snow fell heavily. Dogs barked. The village was a frenzy of crying children and running shadows. Near the cemetery, a group of French Canadian laborers were in a screaming match with Dr. Coombs and Lt. Hysmith. The soldiers had rifles pointed at the three infected men. The prisoners were bound and sitting on their knees in the snow.

"Release them at once!" yelled a bearded man named Bélanger.

"Back off!" shouted Hysmith, aiming his pistol at the French Canadians. The angry mob roared, waving fists.

Pendleton fired his revolver at the sky, silencing the men. "I will not have mutiny in my fort."

Bélanger said, "They won't release my brother."

The prisoners shivered, teeth chattering. Bélanger's younger brother, René, appeared to be foaming at the mouth.

"He's infected," Pendleton said. "Just like Jean Chaurette and Nadia. You saw what the sickness did to her. She murdered her own son." He looked into the frightened eyes of each man. "Do you want this disease to spread to your wives and children?" As several men shook their heads, Pendleton said, "Take your families back to your cabins. Lock your doors. Anyone out tonight past curfew will be thrown in jail."

The mob disbanded. The men scooped up their children and led their families and barking dogs back to their cabins. The only *voyageur* who stayed was the tall man named Bélanger. He approached his brother.

Hysmith aimed his pistol. "That's close enough."

Bélanger spoke to his brother, a tearful farewell. René just stared forward, a shivering catatonic, spittle frosting around his lips.

Pendleton looked to Hysmith and nodded. The soldiers lined up the three infected laborers along the stockade wall. *Such a bloody shame*, thought Pendleton. They were some of his best workers.

The lieutenant shouted, "Aim!" The four soldiers raised their rifles. "Fire!"

As the three riddled bodies dropped to the ground, Pendleton said to Dr. Coombs, "Is that the last of them?"

"I don't know for certain. But I have plenty of blood samples now to search for the virus."

"Stop this outbreak, Doc," Pendleton said. "And goddamned quick."

133

Tom stepped onto the front porch of Anika's cabin. He hadn't seen her all day. Not even at the chapel. Seeing that her windows were all dark worried him. After killing Jean Chaurette at Hospital House and witnessing the native woman—who turned out to be Jean's wife, Nadia—go on a rampage at the chapel, Tom was now suspicious of every colonist. His mind had a disturbing image of Anika hunched inside the darkness with a dead rabbit in her mouth.

God, let her be all right.

Tom felt a knot in his chest. He didn't know why he was so concerned for the native woman. Her Indian ways represented everything he had been raised to despise, and she was sleeping in sin with Avery Pendleton. But she had also helped Tom through the toughest time of his life. He knocked on her door and then took a step back, gripping his shotgun, afraid of what might come to the door. Dogs barked from inside. Another frightening image came to mind: the dogs had gotten the sickness and killed Anika. When she didn't answer, he knocked again. "Anika, it's Tom. Open up."

Her door opened an inch. Through the narrow gap, he could see her den was gray and gloomy, with only faint moonlight coming in through some unseen window. Her face was a mask of shadow. Behind her, the dogs barked incessantly. She hushed them and then peered back out at Tom. "What do you want?"

"I came to make sure you were all right."

"I'm fine." She remained hidden behind the door.

"You were supposed to come to the chapel for inspection."

"No one told me."

"Are you feeling ill in any way?"

"I'm not infected, if that's what you're asking."

"I need to talk with you. May I come in?"

After a long pause, she opened the door. Tom entered the dark den, wary of Anika's every move and the shadowy approach of her two dogs. Makade and Ozaawi greeted him with wagging tails and warm tongues licking his hands. This put Tom at ease, and he leaned his shotgun against the wall. He hugged each of the dogs in both arms, scratching them behind the ears. He looked up at Anika's silhouette. "Why is every room dark?"

The native woman turned away, her silence peculiar.

He joined her at a window. Outside, the crosses marked the graves of the cemetery. Beyond stood the Dead House, the storage shed where Chris rested until he could be properly buried in the spring. Even after a few weeks, Tom still couldn't believe his son was gone. The knot that was always present in Tom's chest tightened. He looked at Anika. A soft glow from the moonlight illuminated her side profile.

"Are you okay?" Tom asked.

She wouldn't face him. Was she still angry? A week had passed since they'd last spoken. He had been on his way to have supper with Willow. Tom and Anika had gotten into an argument, and she stormed off.

"Anika, I'm sorry if I upset you the other night. I said some awful things—"

"You called me a whore."

"I didn't mean it."

"Maybe that's all I am."

"That's not true."

"People don't even talk behind my back anymore. They just call me names to my face. The women pull their children away and spit at me."

"Well, they're all bloody fools. And so was I." Tom put a hand on her shoulder. "Your teaching me to whittle helped release me from my suffering. I wanted you to know I'm grateful."

Anika released a sobbing sound. Tom brushed back her hair. She turned, and he reeled at the sight of her face. The skin around her left eye was swollen.

"Dear God..." He examined bruises on her cheek and forehead. "What happened?"

"Nothing, just an accident." Her green eyes were a mixture of sadness and shame.

"Don't lie to me. Who beat you? *Pendleton?*"

Tears ran down her cheeks. "I got what was coming to me."

"Rubbish." Tom lifted her chin. "Anika, nobody has a right to hit you. Only a bloody savage would hit a woman." He started for the door. "I'm going to have a word with Pendleton."

221

She grabbed his arm. "No, don't, he'll kill my dogs and do worse to me. Master Pendleton is not a man to cross. Tom, promise you won't say anything."

He pulled Anika into his arms. As Tom held her, stroking her hair, he wondered what kind of monster he was working for.

134

At Noble House, Avery Pendleton clutched a tumbler of brandy and stared out his fourth-story window. At the far side of the fort, Hospital House had been reduced to a giant circle of glowing embers. It looked as if hell had burned a hole into the earth. Pendleton had a vision of the orange-black hole spreading across the village, scorching cabins, setting Noble House aflame. The four stockade walls caught fire, lighting up the five watchtowers like pagan torches. Black demons with orange cracks in their skin climbed up from the hellmouth and dragged screaming villagers down into the expanding chasm.

Pendleton gulped his brandy.

With his fort steadily being eaten away by some strange disease, he worried how this would affect the future of his company. His Montréal partners had invested a lot of money with Pendleton Fur Trading Company and were expecting a large delivery of pelts to their fur factory come spring. Pelts from beaver, muskrat, fox, otter, raccoon, rabbit, and wolf were like gold in Canada. For over a century, a great demand for these had come from the merchants of Montréal, London, and Paris as fur became the fashion. The beaver, one of the most valuable of the pelts, was used to make felt hats. Furs of every animal imaginable were made into coats, hats, boots, purses, and blankets. Despite the decline of the fur trade since the heyday when Pendleton worked for Hudson's Bay Company, there was still a fortune to be made. But the chief factor was already behind on his quota. With Manitou Outpost shut down and the migration of the Ojibwa tribe, there were no trappers left. He would send all his workers out to set traps if it weren't for the pack of cannibals roaming the woods and this goddamned virus infecting his colony.

The sounds of screaming villagers still echoed through Pendleton's mind. He couldn't shake the monstrous face of Nadia Chaurette as she attacked people in the chapel. Another outbreak and twelve more colonists dead.

"What are we going to do, Master Pendleton?" asked Lt. Hysmith. The security officer was seated at the conference table with Walter

Thain and Percy Kennicot. All three officers stared at their chief factor with forlorn eyes.

"We are bloody fucked is what we are," said Walter, always the pessimist.

Percy said, "Maybe we should shut down the fort. Return to Montréal."

Pendleton bristled at the thought of returning with such a paltry amount of furs. His partners would never invest with him again. "We're staying through the winter, and that's the end of it."

"But we could all be dead by then," said Hysmith. "Are you forgetting what happened to the crew at Manitou Outpost? Master Lamothe was in the same predicament as we are, and now he's gone."

"He's right," Walter said. "We can't just stay here waiting for the next outbreak."

"Goddamn it, get a hold of yourselves!" Pendleton stood at the end of the table. "You're supposed to be leaders. The entire colony is already on edge. If the workers see you behaving like this, we're sure to have a mutiny on our hands."

"If that happens, we're doomed," Hysmith said. "I lost five good soldiers today, including Sgt. Cox. I only have four privates left."

Walter and Percy sagged in their seats, brooding over their glasses of brandy.

Pendleton put his hand on the stuffed wolverine that sat on his desk. "Gentlemen, I need you to stay strong for the sake of the village. I am certain there is a way we can stop another outbreak from occurring."

"What do you suggest we do?" asked Hysmith.

"We take measures to make sure the sickness doesn't spread." Pendleton grabbed his black wolverine coat. "Let's find out what Dr. Coombs has learned about the virus."

135

Tom was reluctant to leave Anika alone.

"I'll be all right," she assured him. "Makade and Ozaawi will keep me company." Her face had hardened again, displaying her toughness. Tom hated to see the bruises and welts around her eye and forehead. She had additional markings on her arms and back. The more he had offered to talk with Master Pendleton, the more Anika defended the letch. It wasn't just the threat of losing her dogs that made her endure his abuse. Pendleton had her convinced she deserved the beatings. They were always the result of her disobedience and backtalk. As long as she surrendered to Pendleton's desires, he didn't beat her.

"I don't want to talk about him anymore," she said.

"I have to meet with Dr. Coombs," Tom said, grabbing his shotgun. "Come with me. Doc can give you some medicine."

"I can make my own medicine." She opened the door. "Now stop fretting over me and go."

136

Tom entered Dr. Coombs' medical lab. The disease specialist was peering into his microscope. The cramped room stank of rotting meat. On the center table lay Private Fitch's half-eaten arm. The bite wounds were filled with gray pus. For the first time, Tom noticed dozens of smaller wounds. Rat bites? He still couldn't shake the vision of the cannibal wearing a coat of living rats and flapping ravens. On another table lay Nadia Chaurette, the crazed woman who had run amok in the chapel. Her face was a red gaping hole, the effect of Tom's shotgun blasting buckshot through the back of her skull. At the tip of each of her long fingers were wolf-like claws.

"Quite a spectacle, isn't she, Inspector?" Dr. Coombs said with a grin.

Tom kept his distance, as if the faceless she-beast might suddenly spring to life and lash out with those razor talons. "Why wasn't her body burned with the others?"

"I wanted to do a full autopsy. Don't worry, Inspector, I've taken measures not to touch her." Dr. Coombs placed a glass slide of saliva with the sample of blood under the microscope. He peered into the lenses and made a groaning sound. "This doesn't make any sense."

"What do you see?" Tom asked.

"Normal blood." The physician slumped against a table. "I've studied samples from four people who were infected. There are no viral cells, no mutations, nothing to indicate a physical disease."

"What do you mean there's no virus?" spoke Master Pendleton from the doorway.

Tom felt a rash of anger as the chief factor entered with Lt. Hysmith. Pendleton was dressed in his black fur coat and top hat, which he removed and set on a table. "Something caused Jean and Nadia to turn into beasts."

Dr. Coombs said, "Whatever the catalyst was, it's not showing up in their cells."

"Is it possible we took the samples too late?" Tom asked.

"No, immediately after death there still should have been signs of a strain. I half expected to discover an advanced form of rabies, but even the saliva offers nothing." Dr. Coombs scratched his beard. "Gentlemen, I'm befuddled. There seems to be no scientific explanation for these physical aberrations. Unless..." The doctor went over to his bookshelf and ran his finger along the volumes. He pulled out a book titled *Mysterious Ailments*. "There *have* been cases throughout European history of people turning feral and cannibalistic." He flipped through the pages. "The most recent documented case was of a woman in a village in the Shetland Islands of Scotland. She murdered three people at a farm and mutilated several sheep. A group of hunters found the woman naked and covered in blood. She was described as behaving like a wild animal, with nocturnal eyes that reflected light, territorial, and highly aggressive. It took several shots to finally kill her. The woman's head was removed and her body burned. The local doctor tested her blood, but found no virus to indicate a physical disease."

"Does the book offer any explanations?" Pendleton asked.

"It offers one. However this theory stems more from folklore rather than proven science. In all these documented cases, the wild cannibal was believed to have turned into some kind of lycanthrope."

"And what the bloody hell is that?" Pendleton asked.

Dr. Coombs grinned. "A werewolf."

137

"Werewolves are nothing but creatures of fairy tales," Tom said.

Dr. Coombs said, "I would have agreed with you entirely, Inspector, until I witnessed the cannibals you killed. Now that I've ruled out a virus, I am willing to entertain that our disease is a form of lycanthropy, also known as *melancholia canina*."

Pendleton said, "What do you know about it?"

Dr. Coombs smiled, "I know volumes about the subject, actually. Lycanthropy, which means 'man-wolf,' derives from Greek mythology from Ovid's tale *Metamorphoses*. In one interpretation, Zeus turns a king named Lycoan into a wolf as punishment for killing humans and eating their flesh. In the medical field, lycanthropy is typically diagnosed as a mental illness, where people behave like wolves because they believe themselves to be the animal. They run wild through the woods. They kill livestock. But in reality they are humans who have simply gone insane."

"That I can believe," said Tom. "But how do you explain the cannibal growing claws and canine teeth?"

"All I can do is postulate from previous cases." Dr. Coombs set the *Mysterious Ailments* book on the table and opened it to an illustration titled "Werewolf," created by the artist Lucas Cranach der Ältere back in 1512.

"Since Ovid's Greek myth," Dr. Coombs continued, "werewolf tales have spread throughout Europe, and the man-turned-beast has become a thing of legend. The French call werewolves *'loup-garou.'* In the Shetland Islands of Scotland, the woman I described earlier was called a *'wulver.'* Here in Canada, the Indians believe in shape-shifters. They call them *'wiitigos.'*"

Tom remembered the day he investigated the killings at the Ojibwa village. Kunetay Timberwolf had slaughtered ten people and all his dogs and dragged them into the woods where evidence showed a pack of cannibals had gathered to eat. Chief Swiftbear had called them *wiitigos*.

"I've heard stories about them," said Hysmith. "Mostly campfire tales. The voyageurs call them *windigos*."

Tom said, "Doc, tell us everything you know about these windigos."

"Ah, the windigo legend is a fascinating one," said Dr. Coombs with a gleam in his eyes. "The Indians of the Great Lakes region believe that a shape-shifter roams the forest each winter. They claim it is a spirit that can rise from the ground as a sudden snowstorm. It can shape-shift into animals or walk bipedal like a man, often in the form of a skeletal creature that has long claws and fangs like icicles. In its most monstrous form, the windigo can walk as high as the trees. The beast has a ravenous appetite that can never be satiated. So it devours every animal and man it comes upon. Hunters have claimed that the sound of the windigo's scream can cause a man to get confused, and if the hunter escaped he would become a windigo himself."

Pendleton said, "Doctor, I want answers, not legendary tales."

"But what if the creature the Indians fear exists?" asked the doctor. "Not a spiritual creature, but an anomaly in nature. Some sort of wolf beast that carries the disease. From everything I've seen, I'm willing to entertain the possibility that what we are up against is an ancient form of lycanthropy disease that is causing people to mutate through some kind of metamorphoses. One that causes them to behave like wolves and hunger for human flesh. If so, gentlemen, then perhaps the time has arrived that science and legend have reached a meeting point." Dr. Coombs closed his book and grinned. "This discovery could be a breakthrough in the studies of evolution."

Tom said, "All very good theories, Doc, but none of them tell us how to stop another outbreak."

"To do more studies, I'll need another specimen. Preferably alive."

"Out of the question," Pendleton said. "I didn't bring you here for a science expedition. I just want to stop this disease before it runs rampant."

138

Werewolves and windigos.

As Tom sat alone at his kitchen table and wrote the day's events in his journal, he didn't quite know what to make of Dr. Coombs' outlandish theories. Tom had always thought of man-turned-beasts as nothing more than folklore and myth. But he couldn't deny the evidence. A month ago he had found Percy's wife, Sakari, mauled to death by an animal that had left large bipedal tracks and claw marks high in the trees. Anika had feared a beast more terrifying than a bear, more spirit than animal. A windigo? Did the disease that turned people into ferocious cannibals originate from a spiritual beast?

In his diary, Father Jacques had spoken of a predator that was stalking Manitou Outpost, killing anyone who ventured into the woods. The sickness had spread through the fort, starting with Master Pierre Lamothe's oldest daughter, Margaux. In a matter of a week, the entire fort turned cannibal. Down in the cellar they found the remains of Father Jacques, his head mounted on a post. Wenonah Lamothe attacked the soldiers. According to Lt. Hysmith, she had grown in height by at least a couple of feet. The rest of the Manitou trappers were thought to be roaming the woods as a pack. Zoé, who somehow escaped, had brought the plague to Fort Pendleton. Tom had witnessed the Indian girl and Doc Riley changing into long-boned monstrosities with jackal faces. Tom had seen white-eyed dogs and goats turn on one another. And today, he shot two more colonists who had become infected. Jean and Nadia Chaurette had each grown claws and fangs, every tooth as sharp as a wolf's canines. They had displayed uncanny strength and swiftness.

Had they become werewolves? Tom noted in his journal that not one infected cannibal had grown fur like the werewolves of myth. Nor did it take silver bullets to kill them. If they weren't werewolves then what were they? And what was the source of this disease they carried if not a virus?

Tom wanted to toss out Dr. Coombs' theories as pure rubbish, but there was no denying that people were turning into beasts.

139

Later that evening, Tom returned to Anika's cabin and heard flute music coming from around back. A warm glow emanated from a shed attached to the back side of her cabin. Dogs barked at his approach. He lifted a deerskin flap and peered through the kennel's wire-mesh door. The colorful mix of bushy-tailed huskies and half-wolf dogs recognized Tom. Their barks softened to excited whimpers. Anika was sitting against the back wall. Her green eyes gazed intensely as she played haunting music with her flute.

Tom knocked. "I didn't expect to find you out here."

She pulled down her flute. "You don't have to keep checking on me."

"I'm not. I just have a few questions about the windigo."

She looked at him askance. "I thought you didn't believe in manitous."

"I'm not quite sure what to believe, but I need to explore every possibility. I'd like to hear your theories. May I come in?"

Anika nodded and scooted over. Tom weaved through the exuberant dogs, brushing furry napes, and sat next to the Indian woman on the hay-covered ground. The huskies put their muzzles in Tom's face, licking his neck and cheeks. She spoke commands in Ojibwa. The eight dogs settled and formed a protective circle.

"Rather affectionate, aren't they?" Tom said, wiping his neck.

"They like you," she said. Tom thought he witnessed a brief smile, before she turned and added some wood to a fire burning in a stove. The smoke smelled of pine, sage, and sweet grass. The kennel was surprisingly warm and cozy. The walls were covered with deerskins. Mounted on the back wall were painted animal skulls, and from the ceiling hung fetishes made of bone and feathers. At the far end of the shed was a storage area for the dogsled. Tracking gear and snowshoe boots were arrayed neatly on the wall.

Tom remembered the day he first arrived at the fort. Master Pendleton had introduced Anika Moonblood, saying she would be Tom's personal guide for whenever he needed to travel outside the fort. She was a highly skilled tracker. She would also be his interpreter with the Ojibwa who lived across the creek. Tom had looked this small Indian woman up and down, observing her deerskin clothes with frayed sleeves, antler-handled knife on her hip, jet black hair, reddish-brown skin, and those wildcat eyes, thinking she was all savage. Now, as she sat back against the wall with a blanket wrapped around her shoulders and the orange glow of the fire highlighting her face, she looked so different, softer, more feminine, perhaps even pretty. Tom noticed deep within her eyes a beauty that her recent bruises couldn't tarnish.

"You have some questions?" she asked.

Tom realized he'd been staring. "Right, um..." He pulled his small detective's journal from his pocket and started writing. "What can you tell me about the windigo legend?"

"It is not just a legend. The manitou exists as you and I do."

"Okay, assuming that this beast is real, what do your people know about it?"

"My people?" Her face hardened again and she shook her head.

"What's wrong?"

"Tom, when are you going to see that the Ojibwa are your people, too?"

"What in God's name are you talking about?"

At the rise of his voice, the dogs all perked-up their ears. Anika picked up a knife and stick and started whittling. "Chris told me your mother was Ojibwa, and that you were born among the tribe. Why haven't you ever talked about that?"

Tom's jaw muscles tensed. "That's not a matter for discussion."

"And why not?"

"I'm here to get facts on the case, not get sidetracked. Now, if you can just answer my question..."

She grumbled. "You are the most stubborn man I've ever met. You want to understand the spirits the Ojibwa fear, yet you won't admit that you share the same blood." Anika sliced the wood with intense strokes.

"Why are you so upset?"

"Because for weeks I've watched you trying to solve your case like an arrogant white man from the city, insulting my tribe, treating us like we are heathens. You think what we fear is nothing more than superstition. Well, Inspector Hatcher, we have survived in these woods for many winters, because we understand the nature of the manitous and respect their territory."

"Anika, that's why I came here tonight. I'm trying to understand."

"Then tell me why you hate my people so much." She stared at him, the muscles around her high cheekbones tense. Her eyes looked as furious as the morning after Anika and Tom had slept together and he rushed her out the back door. The Indian woman was so full of anger. No matter what he said, something was always setting her off.

He sighed and gazed into the fire that popped in the stove. "I have no memories of being born among the tribe. My father, who was a soldier at the time, thought very little of Indians. He took me from my mother when I was a toddler and brought me to Montréal. Growing up, I always knew I was different than the other kids, but Father wouldn't tell me anything about my tribe or my mother. Her name was Spotted Fawn. That's the extent of how much I know about her. I never learned which band of Ojibwa I was born into or where they are located. My father, who became an inspector in Montréal, raised me to be like him. He was a highly respected man and a good father, but I always thought he was cruel that he wouldn't tell me about my mother." Tom looked back at Anika. "The more I get to know you, the more I realize everything Father told me about tribal people was wrong."

Her face softened, the green of her eyes brighter than he'd ever seen them. She touched his hand. "I can show you so much, if you will only open yourself up to that part of you that is Ojibwa."

140

Father Xavier blessed the chapel's nave, exorcising the evil presence that lingered after the infected woman was killed. *When the host's body is destroyed, the evil spirit lives on.* He thought of the words his mentor, Father Jacques, had spoken back when Father Xavier was training to become an exorcist. *In places where unclean spirits dwell, an exorcist must trust only the righteous and the signs from God, for evil hides behind many faces.*

At the prayer altar, tributaries of dried blood stained the Virgin Mary's eye sockets, cheeks, and outstretched palms. Father Xavier was no stranger to witnessing the miracle of stigmata. The sight of it brought back a memory of when young Xavier was ten years old and the exorcists were trying to save his sister, Mirabelle.

141

The Goddard Mansion
Montréal, 1830

For two weeks, the demon had a hold over Mirabelle Goddard. Xavier's thirteen-year-old sister cursed and flopped and spoke in strange tongues. The priests performed ceremonies day and night to exorcise his sister. Ten-year-old Xavier vigilantly prayed outside her doorway.

Then abruptly, the possession ended. Mirabelle returned to normal, settling into a deep calm. Satisfied, the exorcists left. The doctor prescribed some sleeping pills, then left, as well, patting Xavier's head on the way out. His mother returned to planning her next party, and his father remained absent, unaware that Satan had entered his home and nearly taken his daughter.

One evening, while lying in his bed, Xavier heard Mirabelle calling him from down the hall. "Brother, help meeee..." He rushed into his sister's bedroom. There was enough moonlight lancing through the windows to see her bed was empty.

"Mirabelle?"

"In here," her voice moaned from the washroom. She was crying.

"Are you okay?" Xavier padded through the gloomy bedroom. He stayed clear of her four-poster bed, afraid that it might rise up from the floor again.

Water splashed.

He pushed open the door to the washroom. Silver glass from a broken mirror covered the tile floor. Mirabelle was sitting upright in the tub, staring straight ahead. Her thin arms were propped up on her knees. One hand gripped a mirror shard that resembled a dagger. Black liquid trickled from two slashes in her wrists into a tub of dark water. Mirabelle twisted her head, facing him. Her eyes were solid white.

"I belong with him now." She giggled and floated upward, rising out of the water. "He wants you to come with us, too."

"No..." Xavier stumbled back into her bedroom. The bed and dressers shook, tapping the floorboards, the vibration pulsing up his bare feet.

"Come play with us, Brotherrrr..." Mirabelle's stick-thin silhouette stepped into her bedroom, her bones popping. Her neck cocked toward one shoulder. Her hands curled into raven claws. Dark water dripped onto the floor. Her red-soaked nightgown clung to her jutting bones, pronounced ribs, and small breasts that pressed against the transparent fabric. "Don't be afraid. Let me take you where the children play forever." She reached out a blood-covered hand.

Xavier bolted down the hall and locked his bedroom door. He pulled his crucifix off the wall. He prayed to Jesus and the Virgin and every saint he could remember. Fingernails scratched the door from the other side.

"She's mine now, Little Lamb," spoke a guttural voice. "And I'm coming for *you* next!"

The following morning he found Mirabelle lying in the hallway, her stiff arms jutting upward, the hands curled like bird talons. Her eyes were open, staring at nothing.

His sister was laid to rest inside the family mortuary behind the garden. After the funeral, he prayed each night that the thing that took his sister would never find him.

A few weeks after Mirabelle's death, Xavier visited her grave. A statue of her stood atop her crypt. He swore an allegiance to God and promised his sister vengeance on the Devil. Mirabelle's stone eyes began to stream red tears. The miracle was confirmation that Xavier was to join the Jesuits and become an exorcist.

Now, Father Xavier extinguished the dozen candles that had been lit by an unholy force. He relit them, praying, "Holy Lord. All-powerful

Father. Eternal God. Father of our Lord Jesus Christ. Cast out all devils and unclean spirits. Return this house of God to a sacred and holy sanctuary." Father Xavier blessed every corner of the nave, flicking holy water onto the walls and floor. He concentrated heavily on the bloodstains where the native woman had been shot in the head.

When he was done, the air inside the nave felt lighter. Father Xavier looked around, realizing he was alone. Where was Brother Andre? He had been missing for quite a while. Father Xavier went into the bedchamber behind the front altar. "Andre?"

His room was empty.

Andre had been acting strange ever since they arrived at Fort Pendleton. And he was keeping secrets. Last night, Father Xavier had gotten out of bed to relieve himself. He heard voices coming from the nave. He was shocked to find Andre talking intimately with Willow Pendleton. They kissed and embraced one another for a long spell. All day today, Father Xavier had waited for his novice to fess up, but he never did. When Willow collapsed earlier, Andre had worried over her.

Has another succubus latched onto him?

Father Xavier noticed something black protruding from beneath Andre's mattress. Father Xavier pulled out a diary. As part of his excamen, the apprentice was ordered to journal his thoughts at the end of each day.

He flipped through Andre's diary, skimmed the passages and saw the name "Willow" repeatedly. He shut the book.

No, this is wrong. His private thoughts are between him and God.

But now Father Xavier couldn't help wondering if his apprentice might indeed be cast under a she-demon's spell. *Better the Devil you know...* He sat down on the bed and began reading Andre's journal:

The nightmares torture me still. If I do not conquer these feelings of lust, I fear I may grow mad from desire...

142

At Noble House, Andre entered Willow's boudoir and set a candle on the nightstand. She was still in bed. Her face seemed to glow in the candlelight. An angel's face. Andre felt tempted to kiss her soft, rosy lips, as Prince Charming might awaken Sleeping Beauty. Last night's kiss had been the most delightful sensation he had ever experienced. Willow had held him so desperately, kissed him so feverishly, Andre feared he would burst. As he lay in bed afterwards, he couldn't sleep. His entire body had tingled as it did now. He fought the urge to climb

Brian Moreland
into bed with Willow.

He sat on the edge of her bed, held her hand.

She opened her eyes halfway. "Andre..."

He caressed her cheek and whispered, "Everything's going to be all right. I thought you might want this back." He tucked the charred Indian doll under the covers beside her.

Willow smiled and closed her eyes.

143

Tom, Anika, and her two favorite dogs, Makade and Ozaawi, stepped into her cabin. "I'll make us some tea," she said.

Tom stacked logs in her fireplace and built a fire. It wasn't long before Anika had a pot boiling and the cabin smelled of sweet herbs and berries. As Tom watched her move about her tiny kitchen, he felt tingles in his chest. He couldn't believe the change in Anika's face, as if she had shape-shifted into an entirely different woman. Every so often she looked up and smiled, and Tom imagined what it would be like to hold her, kissing her lips, caressing her skin... _No, stop._ Desiring the native tracker was the last thing he needed. She still belonged to Master Pendleton, and judging by Anika's bruises, the chief factor was not a man to cross. Tom had already slept with her once, but had been too drunk to remember anything. As much as he wondered what it would be like to make love to Anika sober, he knew that an affair would only bring on more abuse to her and cost Tom his job.

I'm only here to solve a case, he reminded himself. He pulled out his journal. "You were going to finish telling me about the windigo."

Anika brought over two steaming mugs of herbal tea and they sat at her table. "The windigo is an evil spirit that has been here longer than our people. It lives on one of the islands at Makade Lake, hibernates there in a cave during warm seasons. It comes out each winter to feed. It used to hunt only in Manitou Forest. But since the white settlers began trapping around Makade Lake, killing off the game, the windigo has begun to hunt these woods. That's why my tribe migrates down river every winter."

Tom jotted notes in his journal. "When Kunetay killed several tribe members, was he feeding the windigo?"

Anika nodded, sipping her tea. "It normally hunts alone, but this year it has turned others into cannibals. I believe the missing people from Manitou Outpost are hunting with it. If Kunetay wasn't eaten, then he may also be among them. As long as there is prey, the windigos will hunt as a pack."

Tom said, "Last night a soldier saw shadows just outside the stockade. They left behind footprints and scratches on the front gate. Will they keep trying to get in?"

"Their hunger never stops, so they seek food day and night. The more they eat, the hungrier they get. If the windigos run out of food, they turn on each other. Some will split off on their own and travel far away. I have spoken with Huron and Cree who have their own windigo stories. Eventually, the windigo of Makade Lake will eat all the smaller ones and return to its island. But we have a long winter yet. I'm afraid that eventually the windigo will find its way in."

Tom pictured the open gate to Manitou Outpost. The blood on the snow. The ghost village. "How do we kill it?"

"Spirits cannot be killed, they can only be sent away. The only people who have the power to banish evil spirits are a group of Ojibwa shaman known as the Grand Medicine Society. The Mediwiwin."

"Where are they?"

"A half-day's journey down river. I wish there was a way we could get to them."

Tom considered this. "No, it's too risky."

Anika said, "I know a place not far from here where some canoes are stored. We could get there in less than an hour."

"I'll suggest it to Master Pendleton. Speaking of which..." Tom checked his watch. Eleven o'clock. He closed his journal. "I need to report back to the officers."

Anika walked with him to the door. Before he knew it, her arms were around his waist. "I wish you could stay longer."

The feeling of her against his chest brought back the tingles. Tom hugged her back. "You keep safe tonight."

She brushed his lapels. "I hate this coat."

Tom looked down at the gray overcoat that had been his father's. "What's wrong with it?"

"It's too thin. It can't possibly keep you warm."

"Well, no, but it's the only one I own." Tom opened the door, and a frosty gust blew into the cabin, chilling him to the bone.

"Wait." Anika went to a wardrobe and pulled out a thick parka and mittens made of brown fur. She handed the coat to Tom. "This used to be my husband's. It's made from caribou and rabbit. I want you to have it to keep warm."

Tom slipped on the parka, pulling the bushy hood over his head. The inner lining was made of soft rabbit fur, the outer layer caribou. The mittens were equally soft. "What do I owe you for these?"

235

Brian Moreland

"Nothing. They are gifts."

"Thank you." As Tom stepped out into the cold night, he discovered the coat and mittens were the warmest he'd ever worn.

144

In the back bedroom of the chapel where the Jesuits resided, Father Xavier turned another page of Brother Andre's journal:

The nightmares torture me still. If I do not conquer these feelings of lust, I fear I may grow mad from desire. I keep wondering if I am fit to be a priest. I fear deep down I am just a common sinner like all the rest. And yet I question what is truly sinful. Entering the priesthood has been my greatest passion, and now every day a part of me asks, why I am giving up all that life has to offer? Especially the touch of a woman. How can a man stay sane in the presence of such power that the woman wields? Willow's scent, her laugh, her bright eyes and smile fill my body and heart with so many heavenly sensations. How can it be a sin to desire to kiss those lips and hold her close, naked and vulnerable as Adam and Eve? Why does the Church insist a priest deny himself the bond of a woman? Is her feminine essence really the plague of the Devil? Surely Willow, the most radiant angel I have ever met, can't be the embodiment of evil.

Father Xavier heard footsteps and looked up as Andre entered the room. His jaw dropped. "Why are you reading my journal?"

Father Xavier stood, towering over his apprentice. "Why didn't you tell me you have feelings for Willow?"

Andre's cheeks flushed. "I... She is my friend."

"Don't lie to me. Last night I saw the two of you in the nave. *Kissing.*"

"It was a moment of weakness. I'm sorry. I was going to confess—"

Father Xavier raised his palm. "You have lied to me and kept secrets. And last night you broke one of your most sacred vows. This behavior is intolerable. I'm afraid you and I have reached a crossroads. I don't think you are fit to be a priest."

"No, please, Father. You have to forgive me. I want to be a priest more than anything."

"Then you must honor *all* vows. Kissing a woman will only lead you down a dangerous path. And as an exorcist, you must always question if the Devil is leading you to sin, and his most powerful deception comes from the temptations of a woman."

236

"I won't let her tempt me again, I promise. I'll spend all evening doing excamen. Whatever you ask of me, I'll do it. Just let me prove that I am worthy to be your apprentice."

Father Xavier studied the young missionary's eyes to see if he was speaking with conviction. "Andre, if you truly desire to be a priest, then you must devote yourself to God, above all people." He pointed to the wall at a small painting of the Madonna. "And *she* is the only woman whom you should hold sacred in your heart."

"*Oui*, Father." Andre's eyes teared up.

"To be my apprentice," Father Xavier said, "you must confess every temptation, every sin. Exorcists hold no secrets from one another. If you and I are going to survive a holy battle, then we must form a bond that Satan can't break."

145

At Noble House, Pendleton entered his fourth-story home and was startled by the sound of hammers pounding against wood. He hurried into the parlor, where several Indian servants were gathered. They all seemed spooked. From down the hall, the hammering changed to grating sounds, as if someone were pushing furniture across the floor.

"Who's making all that bloody racket?"

The butler came over, holding up an oil lamp. "Lady Pendleton, Master."

"Everyone wait here." Pendleton took the oil lamp and marched down the dark hallway to his wife's boudoir. As he reached the door, it slowly swung open, the hinges creaking. "Willow!" The bedchamber was pitch black, except for where a few blades of moonlight slashed through the curtains.

The scraping stopped.

"Willow, darling, what's happening?" He eased across the threshold, holding out the lamp. The flickering flame offered a small circle of light. Torn pillows and feathers were strewn across the floor. White down floated in the air like snow. The four-poster bed was turned at an odd angle. The tall wardrobe had somehow slid out from the wall. Had there been some kind of earthquake?

The shelves that had displayed all the dolls were now empty.

"Willow?" Pendleton raised the lamp to her bed. She was in her nightgown, sitting cross-legged with her back against the headboard. Her long hair, frosted with pillow feathers, hung over her face. She rocked back and forth, her hand rubbing the face of an Indian doll in her lap. Willow whispered a phrase over and over. *"Fais ce que tu voudras. Fais ce que tu voudras. Fais ce que tu voudras…"*

Pendleton approached her. "Darling, what's happening?"

Above the bed came a strange knocking. He raised the oil lamp. A hundred porcelain faces with bejeweled eyes reflected the candlelight. The dolls were stuck to the ceiling, their little legs kicking the wood.

Pendleton gasped.

A doll flew down from the ceiling and struck his shoulder. Willow giggled. More dolls came down, floating over her bed. The room filled with whispering voices.

Pendleton backed away. The candlelight blew out. "Shit!" He fumbled through the darkness. Another doll smashed into his back. Another shattered against the doorframe. As he left the room and bolted down the hall, he heard a chorus of snickering little girls.

Part Fourteen

The Devil's Plague

146

Father Xavier and Andre each carried a black case as they followed Lt. Hysmith into the parlor of the Pendleton home. Master Pendleton was gathered at the fireplace with the other officers. Inspector Hatcher and Dr. Coombs were also present.

Father Xavier tensed at the sound of a door banging from down the hall. The air felt thick and oily with the presence of evil.

Pendleton said, "What the hell's happening?"

"A demon spirit is present." Father Xavier pulled out a silver cross. "Andre, seal off the room."

The apprentice drew chalk lines on the floor along every threshold to the parlor.

"Everyone stay within the chalked lines." The exorcist splashed holy water on the walls and whispered a prayer.

From down the hall, Willow moaned and wailed like a woman in the throes of sex.

Pendleton paced in front of the fireplace, cursing. "Damn it, do something, Doc!"

Dr. Coombs held up a syringe. "She needs a sedative."

"We need to strap her down," Inspector Hatcher said.

Pendleton shouted at the butler to fetch some rope.

The noise from the slamming door was maddening. Father Xavier tried to concentrate on his ritual, but the men in the room were frantic, talking all at once.

"I need everyone to stay quiet!" Father Xavier continued praying and dousing the walls.

The butler returned with some rope. Inspector Hatcher took it and gave some to Lt. Hysmith then turned to Father Xavier. "Okay, you lead us in there."

Father Xavier glanced at his apprentice. "Are you ready for this, Andre?"

The young man's eyes were wide. "I'm ready."

"Remember, keep your mind clear and your thoughts on God." Father Xavier crossed himself and stepped into the narrow hallway. He flicked holy water across the walls. The pink paint sizzled and flaked off. The door slammed at the end of the hall. Shrill screams came from Willow's boudoir. As he reached the bedchamber, her shrieks turned to giggles. The door stopped banging and slowly creaked opened to a void of infinite blackness.

This demon wants to play, Father Xavier thought.

Stretching out an oil lamp, he entered the room first. His shoes crunched over broken porcelain. On the floor, dozens of dolls lay across one another, their faces jagged holes, their arms and legs shattered. A massacre only a little girl's tantrum could cause. White down floated in the air like dandelions ushered in by an evil wind.

Father Xavier stepped deeper into the long, narrow room. He saw his fragmented reflection in a cracked mirror. The furniture was in disarray. The four-poster bed was now positioned in the center of the room. Willow was missing. The Indian doll was propped against the pillows, its head spinning. From the darkness behind the bed, a little girl sang, "I am the secret keeper, I know all your little secrets..."

Father Xavier motioned Andre and the other men into the room. "Demon, come out and face us."

Willow crabbed out from behind the bed, her body arched in a backbend, walking on hands and feet like a carnival contortionist. Her head twisted at an odd angle. She looked at the men with solid black eyes and grimaced. "Do I smell the fear of eunuchs?"

"I cast out this demon in the name of God!" Father Xavier splashed her face with holy water.

She screeched and scuttled spider-like toward a corner.

Father Xavier yelled, "Grab her!"

Tom, Hysmith, and Dr. Coombs rushed Willow, seizing her arms and legs. She thrashed and snarled, bucking and kicking, as they tossed her onto the bed. Father Xavier and Andre stood at the foot of the bed, chanting prayers as the men tied her to the four posts. Dr. Coombs jabbed a needle into Willow's arm. She cried out, her eyes once again blue. Her face returned to that of a young woman with undeniable beauty. For a brief second she stared at Father Xavier with pleading eyes, and he saw her face shift into Mirabelle.

An illusion, he reminded himself and continued exorcising Willow's demon until the sedative took effect and she passed out.

147

In Pendleton's study, Tom tossed the Indian doll into the fireplace. The flames engulfed the deerskin dress. The leather face peeled back and the wood skull beneath caught fire. The single green eye popped out of the socket with a spark of embers. Tom had first seen this hideous doll the day Zoé arrived. She had brought it from Manitou Outpost. After Zoé's death, Willow kept it on her bed. Tom later found the doll on the altar at Hospital House. He'd left it there to burn. How it found its way back to Willow's room, he didn't know. But seeing the Indian doll on her bed with its head spinning round and round made Tom wonder if he was going mad.

Now he watched the wooden figurine burn like a pagan's sacrifice. Its face was solid black, staring back at Tom with hollow sockets. Had the doll come with a hex? Tom had been told that many of these backwoods tribes had an Indian witch. He imagined an old medicine woman stitching leather skin over its wooden skeleton and then waving a burning root over her creation, chanting a curse. The crackling fire made the fiery doll move. Tom stepped back, half expecting it to hop out of the fireplace like a miniature demon and leap onto his leg.

Tom rubbed his stiff neck. *Maybe I am going mad.*

No, just in shock. He felt saddened that Willow was now infected. While he had tied her wrists to the bedposts, her face once again resembled his wife's, stirring up snakes of pain that knotted inside Tom's chest. She had looked at him with pleading eyes, whispering in Beth's voice, *You love me, don't you? Please, Tom, tell me you love me.* Then Willow laughed as her face turned sickly pale and sprouted blue veins.

She's turning windigo like all the others.

In a day or two, she would have to be put down and burned on a pyre like this wretched doll. Tom looked across the study at Master Pendleton. The fort chief was facing out the window. Tom felt a mixture of hatred and sympathy for his boss. The womanizing letch had whipped Anika. For that, Tom wanted to push Pendleton out the fourth-story window. But Tom also knew the pain and suffering of losing a wife, and his aching heart couldn't separate the conflicting emotions.

My enemy, my brother, bound together by fury and eternal loss.

When the Indian doll finally burned to ash, Tom joined the other six men at the conference table where they were quarreling over supper. Charles, the Cree butler, poured tea in everyone's cups, while a teenage maid—the same doe-eyed girl Tom had seen the officers take down to the cellar—served plates of food. She briefly made eye contact with Tom and then averted her eyes. Walter Thain, a corpulent man shaped like a walrus, put his hand on her back as the girl set a plate of toast covered with brown paste and sardines in front of him. Percy Kennicot fidgeted with his trembling hands. The officer had never been the same since his wife had been found butchered and half-submerged in a frozen stream. Brother Andre stared at the center of the table, deep in thought, while Father Xavier debated with Lt. Hysmith and Dr. Coombs.

"She has the lycanthropy disease," said the doctor. "And in a matter of hours or days she will become a werewolf."

"Nonsense," argued Father Xavier. "She is merely possessed by an evil spirit. Let Andre and I perform an exorcism."

"Gentlemen, don't listen to this charlatan," Dr. Coombs said. "She needs medical treatment, not Catholic witchdoctors."

"We can't just leave her in there," Hysmith said. "If Zoé could break her ropes, then so will Willow. Last thing we need is another beast loose in the fort."

"Enough!" said Pendleton from the window. The arguing men silenced. Their leader turned around, his eyes glazed from too much brandy. "I will not have any of you speak of my wife in with disrespect. Lady Pendleton is to stay in her bedchamber until we find a cure. Doctor, tell me there's a way to stop this disease."

Dr. Coombs shook his head. "Sir, I don't have an answer yet. The virus appears to be invisible. If I can't trace the viral cells, then it will be very difficult to find a cure. All I can do for now is explore the reactions of different medicines. See if any reverse the symptoms."

"Doc, how long will she sleep?" Tom asked.

"Through the night. I gave her a strong dose."

Tom said, "Then we have till morning to figure something out."

Dr. Coombs said, "I'd like to try some different elixirs—"

Father Xavier slammed his fist on the table. "If you men will listen to me, *I* have a way we can stop this disease." The priest's intense eyes held everyone captivated. "The Church calls the disease 'The Devil's Plague.' The Jesuits have been battling it for centuries."

Dr. Coombs glared. "Why didn't you tell us this?"

"As an exorcist, it is my duty to maintain secrecy until I have absolute conviction. After seeing the disfigurement of Jean and Nadia Chaurette's bodies, I am now certain that the cannibals were not infected by some microscopic organism, but by an evil spirit that possesses them."

Dr. Coombs expelled a husky laugh. "Priest, you think everything is the work of the Devil."

"And you found nothing in the blood samples to indicate the contrary."

The doctor sneered.

"Doctor, let him speak!" yelled Pendleton. "I want to hear his theory. Father, continue."

"The Jesuits faced an outbreak similar to Manitou Outpost back in the 1600s." Father Xavier opened his duffle bag and pulled out a book with a worn cover. "*The Jesuit Relations* from the journal of Father Paul Le Jeune. He was a missionary who came from France to Quebec to help convert the Montagnais-Naskapi tribe. He was the first to document this plague in Canada. In 1635, he reported a native man at Three Rivers as behaving cannibalistic and uncontrollable. He tried to eat his family. Later in 1661, the plague broke out again in greater numbers at a fort in Northern Quebec. This is what he documented." Father Xavier read the handwritten journal aloud:

At the outset, they are detained at Tadoussac several weeks, an epidemic sickness having arisen there which causes many deaths. Upon entering Lake St. John, they hear of the deaths of some Indians belonging to their party; these men have been put to death by the other savages, because they were seized by a mental disease which rendered them ravenous for human flesh. It is a sort of werewolf tale, which the missionaries receive somewhat cautiously. What caused us greater concern was the intelligence that met us upon entering the Lake, namely, that the men deputed by our Conductor for the purpose of summoning the Nations to the North Sea, and assigning them a rendezvous, where they were to await our coming, had met their death the previous Winter in a very strange manner. Those poor men were seized with an ailment unknown to us, but not very unusual among the people we were seeking. They are afflicted with neither lunacy, hypochondria, nor frenzy; but have a combination of all these species of disease, which affects their imaginations and causes them a more than canine hunger. This makes them so ravenous for human flesh that they pounce upon women, children, and even upon men, like veritable werewolves, and devour them voraciously, without being able to appease or glut their appetite—ever seeking fresh prey, and the more greedily the more they eat. This ailment attacked our deputies; and, as death is the sole remedy among those simple people for checking such acts of murder, they were slain in order to stay the course of their madness.

"The priest describes the infected as werewolves," Dr. Coombs said. "That supports my theory."

"Somewhat." Father Xavier handed the journal to Pendleton. "But unlike the mythical lycanthropes, those with the infection do not grow fur or shape-shift into wolves. Father Le Jeune was more accurate when he later described the infected as 'Devils.'"

"As in possessed by the Devil?" Tom asked.

"Yes," said Father Xavier. "The Jesuits believe Satan is possessing people through a spiritual disease, spreading his demon seeds in a way that is more frightening than any of the ten plagues prophesied in the book of Exodus."

148

"The Devil's Plague goes through four stages," said Father Xavier. "First, a person becomes filled with fear. If he confesses his sins to God and prays for guidance, then fearful thoughts pass on without effect. But in the absence of faith, fear and guilt cause someone who is spiritually weak to descend into a downward spiral. This makes him vulnerable to the temptations of evil spirit. This invisible force goes by many names: Satan, Lucifer, the Devil, Legion." The priest paused, his radiant blue eyes gazing across the table at Tom. "If the sinner acts on those temptations, then evil spirit leads them down a dark path of despair and clouds their mind with illusions. Stage two is when the sinner imagines things that are not really there."

Tom thought of the morning he had imagined his wife standing in his kitchen, not seeing that she was really Willow...the scratching sounds coming from his crate, as if the whiskey bottles inside were demons clawing to get out...Chris' ghost lying under the covers in his bed, then standing outside the window with his mother. Illusions. The Devil tempting Tom further into his downward spiral. His right hand trembled. "Are these illusions what finally drive a man to madness?"

Father Xavier nodded. "Belief in the illusions opens a doorway that evil can enter. Stage three begins when a demon spirit possesses a sinner's body. They are so lost at this point that they become puppets to the demon controlling them."

Tom said, "So the fourth stage the infected person becomes what the natives call windigo."

The priest nodded. "Stage four is called 'the Turning.' The infected grow claws, sharp teeth, their bones stretch, and their skin withdraws around the skeleton. They hunger for flesh and resort to cannibalism. At Manitou Outpost, the entire colony went through the stages from demon possession to physically turning into demons."

Pendleton said, "Father, can you save my wife?"

"Yes, when she wakes up, Andre and I can perform an exorcism on her demon. As long as a person is still in the early stages of possession, then they can be saved."

"And if they turn fully into a windigo?" Tom asked.

"Then death is the only solution."

149

"What I need to know is..." said Father Xavier as he studied the bewildered faces of the men sitting around the table. "Has any one of you seen peculiar phenomena or suffered nightmares?"

"What do you mean by 'phenomena?'" asked Inspector Hatcher.

"Ghosts, demons, strange visions, anything out of the ordinary."

Pendleton, Thain, Hysmith, and Dr. Coombs shook their heads.

Percy Kennicot's hands trembled as he set down his cup of tea. "I have, Father." Behind wire-rimmed glasses, he had gray circles under his eyes. Percy glanced at his fellow officers and then at Father Xavier. "My children have been suffering from nightmares. Last night my youngest woke up screaming. I spent half the night rocking Mary Kate to sleep. This morning she drew a picture of her nightmare."

"Not this again," Pendleton said.

"I think everyone should see it." Percy reached into his coat pocket and pulled out a folded sheet of paper. He opened it and placed the drawing in front of Father Xavier. Sketched in black charcoal was a stick figure with broad antlers. It was standing in the forest, almost as high as the trees. Father Xavier felt his heart drop.

Dr. Coombs said, "All kids have nightmares of the bogeyman."

Inspector Hatcher tapped his finger on the drawing. "I've seen this before, back in Montréal. When I tracked the Cannery Cannibal to his hideout. On the walls was a mural of a horned beast."

Pendleton said, "That's purely coincidental."

"What if they're connected somehow?" the inspector said. "Gustave Meraux performed Satanic rituals to a demon god. Now here it is again."

Pendleton said, "It's just a child's drawing."

"The inspector may be right," Father Xavier said. "The horned beast has shown up in countless places, everywhere from cave paintings to books on pagan rituals."

Percy said, "Last night I swear I saw this very creature." He pointed to the window. "Amongst the trees was a head with enormous antlers."

"You probably saw a moose," said Hysmith.

Percy shook his head. "I have been on enough hunts to know a moose when I see one. No, this beast was tall and stood upright, like a man. The eyes reflected the moon. I felt like the creature was looking straight into me. I blacked out for a spell, and when I awoke the beast was gone. Then this morning, after seeing my daughter's drawing, I began to ask myself, what if the thing that killed my wife was the windigo?"

"That's nothing but a legend," said Hysmith.

"The winter demon is real," said Father Xavier. "For over two centuries, the Jesuits have been searching for the windigo. It has stalked the Ontario woods, as well as Quebec, and become a part of the native legends. Father Jacques described witnessing this beast at Manitou Outpost before he and the others turned cannibal." He remembered a passage from the diary: *I have beheld the gaze of the Devil and feasted upon the beast's sacrament.* Father Xavier said, "I believe it was the windigo that turned Father Jacques and the trappers into cannibals."

"If such a beast indeed exists, then why is it stalking my forts?" Pendleton asked.

"That I am not certain," answered Father Xavier. "But in many cases where the Devil's Plague broke out, the attack was brought on by a curse from a medicine man or woman seeking vengeance."

"You think an Indian summoned the windigo?" asked Hysmith.

"It's quite possible."

"But who?" asked Walter Thain. "There are over a dozen Indians living inside our fort."

Master Pendleton slammed his fist against the table. "That fucking bitch."

150

Tom's blood pulse quickened as the soldiers surrounded Anika's cabin. Rifles aimed at her door and windows. *No, this can't be happening.* Tom tried to remain calm as he stood at the foot of her porch steps. *God, please let her be innocent.* "Anika, come out. We need to speak with you."

When she didn't respond, Master Pendleton approached the porch. "God damn it, woman, come outside this instance!"

The door remained closed. The light inside the windows went dark.

Shit, Tom thought. "Anika, please, we need you to cooperate."

Around the back of her cabin echoed frantic barking.

Pendleton shouted at the soldiers, "Bring me one of her dogs!"

Lt. Hysmith and a private went to the kennel and dragged Ozaawi out by the nape. The husky whimpered as Pendleton put a pistol to its head. "Anika, if you don't come out this bloody minute, I'm going to start killing off your dogs."

The front door opened, and Anika rushed onto the porch. "No, don't hurt them!"

The soldiers swarmed the native woman and threw her to the ground. She struggled against them. One soldier pressed her face into the snow. Tom shoved him to the ground. "Do not hurt her!"

Anika's face was half-covered in snow. She glared up at Tom. "What's this about?"

"Please, just do as they say. We're going to have to look inside your cabin." He followed Pendleton and Hysmith up the front steps and crossed the threshold. Tom was immediately struck by the odor of damp soil and garlic. On the kitchen table were bowls of feathers, bones, roots, and blood. Boiling in a pot was a red brew of twigs and crow feathers. Tom stirred the soup, and a bird's gray carcass floated to the top.

Hysmith grimaced. "Told you she's a bloody witch."

At a bench covered with baskets of herbs, Pendleton picked up a white fur mitten that matched Willow's coat. His face twisted. Growling, he brushed past Tom and stomped outside. Pendleton backhanded Anika hard across the jaw. "You cursed us, you fucking witch!" He pressed his pistol barrel to her head.

"Wait!" Tom rushed down the steps. "Don't shoot!"

"Stand back, Inspector!" Pendleton cocked the pistol. "Woman, why are you trying to ruin me?"

Down on her knees, Anika stared up with angry eyes. "If you're going to kill me, do it."

Tom said, "Both of you, calm down."

Pendleton's fiery gaze remained locked with Anika's. "She deserves to be executed."

"This is not the way." Tom spoke as a calmly as he could. "Sir, this is a police matter. Let me handle this."

151

At the soldiers' barracks, Tom took a seat across the table from Anika. Her wrists were bound. She stared down at the table, her fingernail tracing a groove in its knife-etched surface. Lt. Hysmith and his four gunmen stood around the room, all looking eager to be the one to shoot the medicine woman if she tried to run. Against the far wall, Master Pendleton sat in a chair with his arms crossed.

Tom stared at Anika a long while, trying to piece together clues from every moment he had spent with her. *Have I been played a fool? Was it Anika who put a curse upon Pendleton's forts?* If so, then she was not only responsible for the deaths of a few dozen people... Tom's jaw tightened as he thought back to the day at Manitou Outpost. He had sent Chris outside with Anika to gather up the horses. A windigo had attacked from the forest and killed Tom's son and a soldier. Miraculously, the native woman was only knocked unconscious. Why had the beast spared her?

Up to this moment, Tom had defended her, hoping to find a way to prove her innocence. But she had plenty of motive to seek vengeance on Pendleton, and if all the killings had begun with an Indian curse, then all the evidence of witchcraft in her cabin made Anika Moonblood's case look grim.

Tom said, "I need you to tell me the truth...did you summon the windigo to attack these forts?"

She kept her gaze on the table and shook her head. "It wasn't me."

"Bollocks!" said Pendleton. "Admit you bloody cursed us!"

Anika looked over her shoulder at him. "I didn't do this!"

Pendleton stepped toward her. "The bitch is lying!"

Tom said, "Sir, you're not helping matters. Let me ask the questions." To Anika Tom said, "Then explain what you were cooking on the stove."

"It's crow soup."

"You eat this?"

"No, it's for smudging the home. Evil manitous don't like it and keep away."

"How do I know you're not lying?"

"Tom, you have to believe me. My spells are only for protection." She spoke with conviction. Tom studied her face for any hint of a nervous twitch. Her cheeks and jaw remained taut, her eyes meeting his with equal ferocity. She seemed to be telling the truth. Her voice softened. "I believe someone else summoned the windigo. I've suspected it since the first killing."

"Who, then?"

"It could be anyone." She leaned back in her chair and glared at the chief factor. "Master Pendleton has plenty of enemies."

152

A soldier locked the cell door. From behind the bars, Anika stared at Tom, her eyes full of hurt and anger.

"How long will she stay locked up?" Tom asked Pendleton.

"Until I decide what to do with her."

"I say we hang her," said Lt. Hysmith. "That would boost the fort's morale."

"No," Tom said. "I'm not convinced she's guilty." He looked at Pendleton. "Sir, who else would want you dead?"

Before the chief factor answered, gunshots rang out from across the fort. Tom hurried outside with the others. More shots fired from Noble House. Tom, Pendleton, Hysmith, and two soldiers ran toward the four-story log house. Tom entered the front door first and charged up the stairs to the third floor. The butler and maids peered down from the landing.

"Get back upstairs," Pendleton barked.

Tom continued into the east wing. Up ahead, a man stepped into the hall, holding a candle and shotgun. Tom stopped and aimed his gun.

"Don't shoot," said Walter Thain. He was dressed in a long nightshirt and slippers.

"Who's been firing off their gun?" Pendleton asked.

"It's coming from Percy's quarters," said Thain.

Tom led Pendleton, Hysmith, and Thain down to the door at the end of the hall and twisted the knob. Locked. More shots were fired within. The kids inside were squealing.

"Stand back." Tom kicked open the door, then hid behind the wall outside, waiting for a barrage of lead. No one fired. "Percy, are you in there?"

"Go away, you sinners!" Percy yelled from somewhere in the dark flat.

Tom stood, gave the officers a quick glance, and then entered with his pistol aimed. Moonlight shone through the windows, offering enough visibility to see outlines of furniture. He smelled blood. He stepped into the first bedroom. The nanny was lying facedown in a crimson pool. The back of her head had a gaping hole.

"Oh Christ...the *children!*" Pendleton came out of the next room, pressing a hand over his mouth.

Tom peered in at the red-splattered walls. Percy's three children were lying in their beds with blood-soaked covers pulled over their heads.

Tom cocked his pistol. "Percy! Come out!"

"He's finally cracked," Hysmith said from a few paces back.

Tom eased into the study. Percy was sitting on the couch near the window. The moonglow lit up half of a red tribal mask that covered his face. His hands covered his ears. One hand tapped the pistol against his mask.

"Percy, put down the gun."

He looked up at Tom, Pendleton, Hysmith, and Thain. "It wants us." He sniffled and pointed out the window. "The beast out there. Can't you hear it?" He shook his head wildly, as if bees were swarming inside his skull. "The whispers won't stop."

Tom held out his hand. "Give me the gun."

"Get back!" Percy hissed with a voice that sounded like wind rustling dry autumn leaves. He raised the pistol and released a deep, guttural laugh. "The Dark Shepherd is coming for you all. One little lamb at a time." Then he placed the gun barrel under his chin. The shot boomed, ringing Tom's ears. The back of Percy's scalp blew outward. Red matter stained the wall. The clerk slumped back on the couch, his demon mask staring blankly at the window.

Part Fifteen

Brotherhood

153

"Take him to the Dead House," Tom ordered two soldiers.

"Aye, sir." They carried out Percy Kennicot's body wrapped in a bloody sheet.

Tom remained alone in the study, where the stench of death made the air almost unbreathable. Percy had released all body fluids as his brains exploded across the back wall. Blood dripped off several native masks. They looked back at Tom like a tribe of bodiless ghouls and demons. *False Faces,* Tom thought. He picked up the red visage Percy had been wearing. White dots traced circles around the eyes and mouth. Tufts of what looked to be ox hair hung off the sides. Tom recognized it as an Iroquois Indian mask carved from balsa wood.

A few years ago, in Lachine, Quebec, a group of Iroquois had entered a farmer's barn, wearing red demon masks and chanting. The disturbance had caused a scare among the white farmers. When Tom questioned the Indians, they explained they were members of the False Face Society. They claimed they were exorcising demons called *Ga-go-sa* that haunted the barn. These bodiless faces supposedly floated in midair and terrorized the Iroquois. Tom knew it was just another Indian superstition, but the Iroquois made monstrous masks with twisted faces and performed ceremonies to ward off the *Ga-go-sa.*

Tom frowned, his head full of questions. Why was Percy wearing an Iroquois mask? And what pushed him to murder his own children and then kill himself? On Percy's desk was the child's drawing of the stick figure with antlers.

It wants us, Percy had said. *The beast out there.*

Tom's hand began to palsy. He gripped his wrist to steady it. After his nerves finally settled, he went into the next room where Pendleton, Hysmith, and Thain waited with forlorn expressions on their faces.

Pendleton looked up from his seat. "Find anything, Inspector?"

"Percy left no suicide note. He appears to have emptied a bottle of Scotch. Was he a heavy drinker?"

Pendleton nodded. "Ever since he lost Sakari."

Tom leaned against the threshold, gripping the red mask. "Gentlemen, before Percy...took his life, he said some things that I find rather peculiar. I have to ask if any of you know what he meant by 'The Dark Shepherd is coming for you all.'"

The officers glanced at one another, shaking their heads, remaining tight-lipped.

Pendleton said, "Inspector, it's late, and we're all in shock at the sudden loss of our friend. We're going to turn in for the night. I suggest you do the same."

154

Tom went back to the barracks and told the guard on duty to go out for a break. In the corner cell, Anika rose from her seat. "Tom!"

He gripped her hands through the bars. "Are you okay?"

She nodded. "You have to believe I'm innocent. I would never—"

"I believe you." He squeezed her hands. "Anika, I'm so sorry for what we put you through. Pendleton was convinced you conjured a windigo to curse his forts. There's more that's been happening." He told her about Percy's suicide. "The officers are acting strange. They know something they're not telling me."

"They know they're cursed," she said. "It was only a matter of time before someone sought revenge."

"What do you mean?"

"The villagers all despise the officers. At Noble House, they have been making the servant women play sexual games down in the cellar."

"You've witnessed this?" Tom asked.

Anika nodded, her face a mask of anger. "Lt. Hysmith is the most dreadful, and all the women fear him. Last autumn, a servant girl ended up dead. I admit I wanted the officers to suffer, but I had nothing to do with the curse."

"Who then, one of the servants?"

Anika shrugged. "Anyone in this village could have paid a shaman to conjure the windigo."

155

Tom returned to his cabin and sat on his bed. Staring at the wall, he thought of all the strange events that had happened today. The cannibal attacks. The deaths of fifteen more colonists, the final ones being a triple murder and suicide. Percy's rampage had disturbed Tom the most. The voice behind the mask did not sound like Percy's, but one that had haunted Tom's nightmares for the past two years.

He reached under his bed and pulled out a trunk. Taking a deep breath, he opened it. Inside were mementos from a past he had wanted to forget. He picked up a black and white portrait of Gustave Meraux in a regal suit and top hat. Before going crazy, Gustave had been a high society libertine and an heir of the wealthy Meraux family. And then at the age of forty he started abducting and cannibalizing women.

What drives a man to go insane? Tom wondered. What makes him suddenly develop a craving for human meat?

Stored in the trunk were several newspapers. He read the headlines: INSPECTOR HATCHER CAPTURES CANNERY CANNIBAL; THIRTEEN WOMEN MURDERED; INSPECTOR'S WIFE CANNIBAL'S FINAL VICTIM.

The last headline brought a heaviness to Tom's eyelids, but he tightened his face and willed back the tears. He tried to remember Beth Hatcher when she was alive: her smile, her infectious laugh, the way she hummed when she cooked, one hand resting on the swell of her belly when she was eight months pregnant. But those memories were quickly torn away by nightmarish thoughts and distant screams. Tom quickly grabbed a fourth newspaper with the headline GUSTAVE MERAUX CONVICTED.

During the trial, the cannibal had been chained inside an iron cell in the courtroom, his arms wrapped in a straightjacket. As Tom gave his testimony, Gustave stared with feral eyes, his lips constantly moving. Upon the judge's summoning the death sentence, the killer rattled his cage and screamed, "As the Devil is my witness, alive or dead I will come back for you, Tom. I will eat your son's heart in front of you."

Tom had charged the cage. The bailiffs dragged Tom away as Gustave cackled. *"I am the Dark Shepherd! The collector of lost lambs!"*

Now, that raspy voice echoed in Tom's head as he tossed the newspapers and photo back into the trunk and shoved it under the bed. His right hand palsied. He began to hyperventilate. He went to the rinse bowl and splashed cold water into his face. He stared into the mirror. Behind his shoulder appeared a pale, grinning face. Tom jerked around. But like so many times before, the Cannery Cannibal wasn't there.

156

Tom stepped into the chapel. The nave was dark except for one corner where Father Xavier was kneeling at the altar. Candlelight and shadows rippled across the statue of the Virgin Mary. The blood tears had been cleaned from her face, but her cheeks now had a pink hue, as if the Madonna were blushing.

As Tom approached, the bald priest turned. "Evening, Inspector, what brings you to God's temple at this hour?"

"I couldn't sleep. I was wondering if you have time for a confession."

"Of course." The priest rose and led Tom to the confessional booths.

Tom sat inside a small closet and took a deep breath.

Father Xavier slid open the screen. "What is your confession?"

Tom crossed his chest. "Forgive me, Father, it's been a couple of years since my last confession."

"God loves you and forgives you."

Tom said, "Being from Montréal, you must have heard of the Cannery Cannibal."

"*Oui, oui,* he was quite notorious. Our cathedral was filled with people who lived in fear of him."

"I was the detective who finally captured him."

"What is your confession?"

Tom's stomach knotted as he recalled his days in Montréal. "I spent over a year tracking the Cannery Cannibal. I sinned a great deal during that time. I neglected my family. I drank heavily. I became completely consumed with the case. I spent most nights staking out the harbor docks. I visited brothels..."

"Did you sin with these women?"

"No, I loved my wife. I just went to the rooms with the women and questioned them. They were all on edge after several prostitutes had been found butchered." Tom envisioned skeletons with the heads left intact, the faces powdered with makeup. "I was so consumed with getting inside the mind of a cannibal, that I...I went so far as to break into a morgue. There was a fresh cadaver on the table. I stole small samples of flesh. At home I cooked the meat and tasted it. I knew I was sinning, but I had to understand what drove a man to cannibalize another person..."

"And..." said the priest.

"I was mortified by the effects of cannibalism. I felt stronger, more alert. The meat had a life force. I had a feeling of power like nothing I had ever experienced. As if eating human flesh awakened some animal nature within me. I felt a connection to some god that was far from holy." Tom clenched his fists. "I immediately craved more."

"And did you follow that temptation?" asked Father Xavier.

"No, I stopped myself, but it took all my will not to eat another piece of meat. I was disgusted with myself." Tom fidgeted with the sleeve of his coat. "After that I began to have nightmares. My relation with Gustave Meraux had gone beyond that of a detective hunting a murderer. I felt a strange brotherhood with him. Like we were two reflections walking on opposite sides of the same mirror. The cannibal began to target me, as well. I received three anonymous packages from him. Small sardine tins. Only they had fingers in them, one from each of his victims. He included notes goading me to track him down. The last tin he sent...one of the fingers was wearing my wife's wedding ring." Tom's chest burned with anger and sadness. "By the time I tracked Gustave to the Meraux Cannery..." His head filled with his wife's distant screams, as he relived the nightmare from two years ago...

157

A woman's tortured screams echoed across the rainy night.

"Beth!" Tom and his police squad raided the cannery with a half dozen bloodhounds. The complex was a labyrinth of docks and warehouses along the St. Lawrence River. Choppy waters splashed under the piers. Fishing boats bumped in their slips. The shacks groaned beneath the pounding of rain. Beth's cries of agony were drowned out by the endless torrents and crackling thunder. The hounds barked, stretching their leashes. Tom's heart pounded as he led his men along the docks, searching from building to building.

From the distance echoed a high-pitched cackle. Tom ran ahead of his men. His swinging lantern tossed the light across the rain-drenched dock boards and black river water. He half expected his wife's body to float up to the surface like all the others, her face eaten by fish, the skull covered in kelp and barnacles.

No, he'd heard screaming. Beth had to be alive!

The pier ended at a long warehouse set off by itself. The large shack was dilapidated, with peeling white paint and broken windows. Shimmering light glowed inside.

Pistol raised, Tom kicked the door open and burst into the warehouse. He ran past a fishing boat under repair. Beyond was a second door and a room where iron chains hung from the ceiling. As he entered, he was immediately pummeled by the smell of blood and offal. In a giant vat boiled some kind of red stew with chunks of meat. On a long table were hundreds of small soup tins and a machine used for canning.

Tom searched the shadowy warehouse for his missing wife, wary that the Cannery Cannibal could be hiding anywhere in the dark mortuary of broken boats. Whispers reverberated off the hulls. At the far end, beyond a thatch-work of fishing nets, glowed an altar of black candles. Kneeling before it was a naked man with blood smeared on his back and buttocks. His hands raised an object that was dark red and shaped like a cow kidney. He spoke something in a strange language and then set the glistening organ on the altar. "For you, Master." On the wall above loomed a tall mural of a dark-skinned beast with antlers.

Tom weaved through a maze of netting and chains that dangled from the ceiling. They chinked together. The killer remained on his knees, facing the Satanic altar. Tom gripped his pistol with a shaky hand and stepped up behind the cannibal.

"Don't move."

"I've been waiting for you, Tom." The Cannery Cannibal slowly stood and turned around. "Ahhh, at long last we meet."

The candlelight illuminated a rail-thin body painted neck to toe in blood. The outline of his ribcage pressed through his skin. His gaunt face was covered in white powder.

For a long, surreal moment Tom gazed into the eyes of the mass murderer he'd been tracking for over a year. The cannibal who had sent Tom tins of severed fingers. The beast who had abducted his wife. Gustave grimaced and Tom saw that all of the cannibal's teeth had been filed down to sharp points. "You're just in time to join me and Beth for supper."

Tom kept his pistol aimed at Gustave's chest. "Where is she!"

The killer's long-nailed finger twirled until it finally pointed toward a side wall. Hanging from the chains like a slaughterhouse carcass was Beth's stiff body. Her face had been made up like a doll. Her arms and chest were flayed to the bone. Her butcher had disemboweled her and removed the unborn fetus. It was in that horrifying instant that Tom realized what the cannibal had set upon the altar.

The room began to spin...chains...carcass...candles...cannibal.

Tom fell to his knees and vomited.

The warehouse filled with the sounds of barking bloodhounds and running footsteps as the other officers charged into the lair.

Gustave put his hands up in surrender and kneeled across from Tom. "Looks like you'll have to dine without me, Tom." The madman grinned as the police shackled him and lifted him to his feet. "Have you ever taken a bite of your wife's breast? I have. Ripped the nipple clean off."

Tom screamed and drew his gun, but several policemen grabbed him before he could kill the Cannery Cannibal. The maniac cackled as the police dragged him off.

158

Tom leaned back against the confession booth wall and looked at the priest's silhouette. "Father, I had wanted so badly to kill that son of a bitch. But the other officers wouldn't let me. The police chief was friends with the Meraux family and had ordered that Gustave be brought in alive. After Beth's and the baby's deaths, my life became a drunken blur. I cursed God and the Church. I verbally abused my son, Chris. Even though Gustave was behind bars, the nightmares persisted, as if the cannibal was imprisoned inside my head. I felt as if I were going mad. I brought my son here to start over, but shortly after we arrived...Chris was killed..." Tom choked. "And I feel...I feel as if God is punishing me. Beth, Chris, and my baby daughter are all dead because of my sins. I miss my family so much, I don't think I can go on." Before Tom knew it, he was weeping, and there was nothing he could do to stop the flowing of tears.

159

A half hour later, Tom sat in a pew illuminated by the flickering glow of votive candles. He whispered several Hail Marys to the Virgin statue. The knot in his chest began to release, and a euphoric feeling waved over him. He felt a lightness of mind, as if the Madonna had kissed his forehead. He wiped his eyes on his sleeve. At the sound of footsteps, he turned and saw the tall priest taking a seat next to him.

Father Xavier said, "How do you feel, Tom?"

"Like I've cried my guts out."

"You should confess more often. Bottling up emotions only summons the Devil."

Tom nodded. "There's something else that I haven't told you. Gustave still shows up in my nightmares. And I keep having visions of him here at the fort. Tonight, just before Percy shot himself, Gustave's voice spoke through him. He said the Dark Shepherd is coming after all of us. That was the nickname Gustave called himself during his trial. The collector of lost lambs. Am I going crazy?"

Father Xavier rubbed his rosary between his fingers. "Tom, I have my own confession. Because of my vow of secrecy, I have not been forthright with everything I know. But I need you as an ally as much as you need me."

Tom stared at the priest, not knowing whether to feel angry or intrigued. "If you can help make sense of all this, I need you to tell me."

Father Xavier took a deep breath and crossed himself. "Ever since you captured Gustave, I've been documenting his case for the Jesuits. I went to the warehouse where he performed his Satanic acts. I observed the mural of the horned beast. I sat among the congregation at Gustave's trial and saw what a monster he'd become. He wasn't just an insane criminal. He was possessed by a demon."

Tom pictured the madman wearing his straightjacket, sitting in his cage and staring across the courtroom at Tom. "I believe a man can be evil to the core, Father, but what makes you so certain demons exist?"

"I've been exorcising them for twenty years. I've seen enough bizarre occurrences to know there is a spirit world beyond anything we can imagine. And they have the power to influence our behaviors. They can bring out our fears." Father Xavier held Tom's gaze for a long moment and then said, "A few weeks ago, I visited the asylum where Gustave was being kept prisoner. The warden complained of mysterious happenings around the asylum. I performed an exorcism on Gustave, but his demon was the most powerful I have ever faced. It called itself Legion."

Tom said, "Gustave never spoke of that name."

"That is because demons like to remain hidden inside their hosts. It takes an exorcism to bring forth their identities. In Gustave's case, his demon had fully taken over. As I performed an exorcism, it got inside my head. It tried to use my fears against me, but I wouldn't succumb. So it rammed Gustave's body into the cell's door until he collapsed. I was tricked into believing he was dead, but later that evening Gustave murdered the warden and several guards and escaped."

"He's loose?" Tom's throat clenched. "Did the police find him?"

258

Father Xavier nodded. "They found his corpse at the cannery warehouse along with the skeleton of a missing prostitute. Both had been eaten by rats."

Tom released a breath.

"But I fear his spirit lives on," Father Xavier said. "Our final night in Montréal, we attended a masquerade party with Master Pendleton. I was being stalked by a man in a tribal mask. He spoke suggestive words inside my head that only Gustave's demon could know."

"How could that be possible?"

"The beast is a shape-shifter with many faces. It seduces people through their weaknesses. It can fill our heads with illusions. It can control animals. The entire journey to Fort Pendleton, I felt as if that demon spirit were following us through a flock of ravens."

Tom remembered seeing the swarm of black birds the day the priest had arrived. Today the cannibal at Hospital House had been covered in a squirming coat of ravens and rats. "Earlier, when I shot Jean Chaurette, I swore the killer was Gustave. I saw his face. I heard his laughter. Tell me those were just illusions."

"The cannibal you killed was undeniably one of the *voyageurs*, but the demon possessing him..." The priest squeezed his rosary. "I fear Gustave's demon and its legion are among us, hiding inside the bodies of the infected."

160

Black clouds drifted across the silvery full moon. At four in the morning, the last of the cabins finally went dark. The wind stopped, and a dead calm fell upon the sleeping village. The only sound was the *shuff-shuff-shuff* of fur boots running across the fresh powder. The disciple hurried with eagerness in his chest.

Tonight was the night.

The disciple entered an elongated shack that smelled of fur and slaughtered animals. The Skinning Hut. In the pitch darkness, he felt his way past a butchering table and stacked cages. He came to a door and knocked three times. It opened to a back room that was lit by candles. The bearded man who answered the door stepped aside. Several others turned to face the disciple. The group parted as their leader made his way to the front of the room. In the corner, two hogs paced inside a cage.

The disciple went to an altar. A bowl contained fingernail clippings and locks of human hair. He added his own clippings to the offering bowl. Then the disciple traced his finger around a red spiral on the wall. "We are ready for you, Master."

161

He dreamed of cadavers in a morgue. A naked woman on a slab, her dead eyes staring. Watching the knife carving into her thigh...please forgive me. Stealing a chunk of her flesh...I have to understand...cooking meat in a skillet. So hungry. Downing gulps of whiskey. So thirsty...craving more, more, more. Cannibal in the headlines...cannibal in the mirror...stormy night...tortured screams...chains...carcass...candles...cannibals...

So alone now. So cold. Racing through a blizzard. Howling wind. A boy screaming. Calling for his father. Tom yelling back, "Chris!"

Running faster now. Into the forest. Branches clawing. A whirling, white twister of fury. Shape-shifting into a hideous beast with antlers. Shifting. Face of a demon. Shifting. Face of a wolf. Shifting. Tom's face. Shifting. Gustave grinning.

"Dead or alive, I will find youuuuuu..."

Tom sat up in his bed, shivering. His bedroom took form. Gray and gloomy. Faint light seeping through the curtains. Another nightmare. Another morning headache. Did he drink last night? His head was foggy. He rubbed his face. His stomach rumbled. How long since he last ate? Yesterday. Breakfast. He had been so consumed by the case, he'd skipped meals.

I have to take better care of myself.

Hunger pains. Sharp, twisting his guts.

Tom dressed, went into his kitchen, and rummaged through his food stores. He gnawed on some salted pork. The shivers wouldn't quit. Neither would the hunger.

No...

A wave of nausea coursed through him, cold and slimy, like eels swimming in his stomach. He retched.

Please, no...

He tore open his shirt. Blue veins were visible through his skin. He looked thinner.

No, no, no...

He paced his cabin.

This isn't happening.

Tom looked into his oval mirror. His face was pale as a cadaver. His irises speckled with white flecks.

"No, god damn it!" He knocked over a chair in a fit of rage.

From within the mirror, a voice cackled, as a frosty shadow peered from behind the looking glass. Screaming like a lunatic, Tom grabbed his crowbar and smashed the mirror until his floor was covered in a thousand tiny fragments.

Part Sixteen

Red Spirals

162

At dawn, a gray mist drifted between the pines. The overcast sky rumbled as storm clouds approached from the distance.

"Christ, another damned blizzard." Private Wickliff sat up in the watchtower freezing his bollocks off. He sealed up his coat, pulling the hood snug around his head. The only warmth came from a small kerosene heater that barely heated his knees. He heard a whinny and looked out the tower window.

Just outside the fort, a black horse was tethered to a post. It ran in a circle, pulling at the rope. Wickliff hated that Hysmith had chosen Gussie to bait the windigos. But the old horse was too weak for riding and would probably die soon anyway.

There was a stretch of open land between the timberline and the fort, and Wickliff was ready to kill any predators before they reached the horse. With daylight creeping over the horizon, he was hoping to finally see the creatures that had clawed at the gates two nights ago.

The horse whinnied again and stood up on its hind legs. Wickliff aimed his rifle. Scanned the woods. Something ran in a fast blur between the pines, snapping branches. A rack of broad antlers. The animal disappeared into the mist.

Wickliff exhaled. "Just an elk."

163

Tom bundled up in the heavy fur parka and mittens that Anika had given him. No matter how many layers he wore, he couldn't rid himself of the chill inside his chest and stomach. He felt as if a large parasite were living inside him—a slick-skinned thing coursing through his guts. And it was hungry. Tom had devoured a week's supply of salted pork. He finished off leftover biscuits and jam, but nothing seemed to quell his appetite. And as he stuffed his mouth like a starving vagabond, he couldn't help imagining the ghoulish face of Doc Riley, the long-boned body of Zoé Lamothe, and the split-cheeked grimace of the native woman in the chapel, her mouth serrated with razor-sharp fangs.

How long before the infection begins to alter me?

Tom checked his own teeth in the mirror. They had not changed, but his gums seemed to be turning gray. If only there were some kind of remedy he could take. Dr. Coombs had failed to find any physical cause of the disease. No virus. No visible parasites. Only strange symptoms and cannibalistic rampages that brought on theories of werewolves and windigos and a plague the Jesuits believed came straight from the Devil.

Someone knocked at the front door.

Tom peeked out the window. Lt. Hysmith and a soldier were standing at his door.

Shit. Tom hid behind the wall, heart beating against his sternum.

Hysmith knocked again. "Inspector, you in there?"

Tom remained hidden, wondering what to do. If the soldiers saw he was infected...

"He must already be out and about," Hysmith said to his soldier. Their footsteps clumped down the steps, trailing off.

Tom peered back out the window and waited until the soldiers headed into the barracks. He released his breath. He pulled the hood over his head and covered the lower half of his face with a scarf. He shielded his eyes with a pair of caribou-bone goggles and stepped out onto the porch. The wind was strong today, with snow blowing across the village like swarms of insects, harrowing exposed skin with frostbite, causing temporary snow blindness. Everyone wore goggles on days like this. As he closed his front door, he saw something that caused him to gasp and stumble back.

The door was smeared with blood in the pattern of a red spiral. Had Hysmith and the soldier painted this? Tom wiped his finger across the marking. The blood had hardened into a crust and was edged with frost. Some vandal had probably done this after Tom had gone to bed last night. Sometime between 3:00 a.m. and dawn. Who among the villagers would mark his door? And was this some sort of curse? If so, why target *him*?

The village erupted with angry voices. Tom crossed the courtyard. On the snowy ground lay a couple of dead hogs, their throats slashed.

There were so many bloody boot prints, he couldn't discern a pattern of where they started or where they ended. Several people were standing in front of their cabins with frightened looks. On the doorways of every home he passed were more blood spirals.

Shit, we've all been targeted.

At the center of the courtyard, a mob was screaming at one another. Tom tried to slip past them.

"Ey, Inspector?" The throng of men and women circled Tom. Bélanger grabbed his coat. "Who marked our doors?"

"I don't know." Tom kept walking. The crowd kept with him, all talking to him at once, gripping his wrists, pulling him in a dozen directions.

"Beast's inside the fort!" someone shouted.

"It's that witch who done it," yelled another.

"We don't know that yet," Tom yelled back. "Everyone, go back to your homes."

Tom broke loose, marched away, leaving the frightened colonists to shout at one another. The cold inside his chest spread up into his throat. He coughed out white clouds. His hollow stomach ached. He craved meat, cooked rare and bloody.

The chapel had received the worst of the vandalism. The iron cross on the roof was tilted. The front walls and windows had been splashed with buckets of pig's blood. Father Xavier and Brother Andre stood outside, examining their door, which was marked with words written in French: ABANDON ALL HOPE EUNUCHS.

Tom approached the Jesuits. "Did you see who did this?"

Andre shook his head. "We were asleep."

Father Xavier frowned at the shouting mob. "The legion is taking over the village."

Tom noticed the Jesuits' faces seemed to be clear of the disease. "There's something I have to show you both." As Tom removed his goggles, icy claws of pain raked across his stomach. Groaning, he doubled over and collapsed at Father Xavier's feet.

164

Tom slowly opened his eyes. A blurry ceiling came into focus. Candlelight danced on the log walls, illuminating a crucifix that hung over the bed. He was lying beneath a heavy fur blanket. It warmed his extremities, but at the center of his chest and stomach the relentless chill made him shiver.

Andre said, "He's waking up."

Father Xavier wiped a warm, wet cloth against Tom's forehead. "You gave us quite a scare."

"What's happening?" Tom rasped.

"The demon has gotten inside of you." At the sound of Father Xavier's voice, the entity gestating inside Tom's belly squirmed. "Here, drink this." The priest pressed a bottle to Tom's lips. The liquid burned his throat like whiskey.

Tom coughed. "Jesus, what are you giving me?"

"Holy water." Father Xavier smiled. "It burns because the demon doesn't like it. Take a sip every hour."

Tom took another gulp. The icy critter beneath his skin retreated to the center of his chest. His hunger diminished. Feeling stronger and more alert, he sat up. "Amazing." He examined the bottle. It was plum-shaped with a cross engraved on the surface. "Will this cure the disease?"

"No," answered Father Xavier. "It will only release the demon's grip for a short while."

"I want this damned thing out of me," Tom said. "Can you perform an exorcism?"

"In due time. You're not the only one who became infected overnight."

"Inspector, we've got another crises on our hands," barked Master Pendleton's voice from the doorway. Tom's heart seized as the chief factor, Lt. Hysmith, and Walter Thain stepped into the room. The officers' faces were bone-white with veins branching across their cheeks. Like Tom, their eyes were flecked with white spots. Pendleton removed his hat. "The bloody plague is spreading again."

Tom slipped on his boots. "How many more are infected?"

"At least a third of the colony," Pendleton said.

"Everyone whose door was marked last night," added Hysmith.

"Except Andre and me." Father Xavier glanced at his apprentice. "So far neither of us has had any symptoms."

Pendleton said, "Inspector, do you have any idea who painted the doors with hog's blood?"

Tom shook his head. "Not yet. Did the night watchmen see anything last night?"

"Nothing," said Hysmith. "Private Wickliff was watching the woods. Private Simmons was supposed to be walking the grounds, but he's gone missing."

"That makes him a suspect," Tom said. "Is Anika still in jail?"

Hysmith nodded. "She's been there all night."

Tom stood and grabbed his coat. "By the looks of last night's rampage, there have to be several vandals, most likely men by the size of the boot prints." Tom turned to Pendleton. "Sir, I believe someone's trying to curse this fort, but I think we have the wrong person in jail."

165

Tom entered the barracks where Anika was still locked behind bars. "Are you all right? Did the guards mistreat you in any way?"

She shook her head. "No, they left me alone. I heard shouting. What's happening out there?"

"Bloody chaos. There's been another outbreak. I convinced Pendleton to release you." He found the keys and opened the cell.

She barreled into his arms, shivering. "I was so afraid I'd never hold you again."

Tom backed away. "Christ, I shouldn't be touching you."

"Why?"

Tom removed his goggles.

"No!" she gasped.

"It happened overnight." He told her about how Pendleton and the officers were also infected, as well as Willow and several others. And how, in the middle of the night, a group of vandals had slaughtered some hogs and painted blood spirals on the doors. "Anika, I don't know how much time I've got."

Before he could stop her, she hugged him, locking her arms around his waist. Anika pressed her head against his chest, sniffling. "I won't let you die."

Tom stroked her hair. "Right now, my sickness is the least of our worries."

Outside came the sounds of men yelling, dogs barking, and the crack of gunshots.

166

Tom and Anika ran outside. Four dogsleds packed with families dressed in fur parkas were riding across the courtyard toward the front gate. Lt. Hysmith and three nervous soldiers blocked the exit, aiming their rifles. The men on the sleds also held weapons. Tom's heart surged as he spotted women and small children amidst the deadly standoff.

Tom ran toward the gate. "Put down your rifles!"

Standing at the lead dogsled, Bélanger shouted, "Tell them to open the gate! We're leaving this godforsaken fort."

"That's not a good idea," Tom said. "The woods are dangerous."

"No more dangerous than staying here," Bélanger countered.

"He's right, Inspector," said Dr. Coombs, who was sitting on the front sled next to two Métis children. "There's nothing we can do to stop the outbreak. None of us is infected, so we're leaving before we catch it, too." The doctor pointed his own shotgun. "Now, if you'll kindly move out of our way, no one will get hurt."

Master Pendleton stepped toward the doctor. "Coombs, you bloody coward."

Dr. Coombs aimed his rifle at the chief factor. "You brought on this curse, Avery, not me. Now open the goddamned gate!"

Pendleton backed off and waved his hand at the guards. "Open the gate." To the families sitting on the four dogsleds, he said, "Anyone who leaves can never come back."

Bélanger cracked his whip at the huskies. Over half of the colonists rode out.

"Bugger off!" Pendleton yelled, kicking at the last dogsled as it exited the gate.

The soldiers and officers watched with solemn faces. Anika traded worried glances with Tom. He didn't know who had the better chance of survival—the people escaping into the wilderness or the infected still trapped within the fort's walls.

167

As Private Wickliff brought down the bar, sealing the gate's double doors, his heart wouldn't stop pounding against his breastbone. During the standoff, he had pissed his breeches. Now the red fabric around his crotch and thigh had frosted over and stiffened. He wanted to go back to the barracks and change uniforms, but Lt. Hysmith shouted, "Wickliff, Bowen, get your arses up the tower and keep watch on the forest."

"Aye, sir!" Privates Wickliff and Bowen moaned in unison. The two sentries climbed up through the trapdoor and into the central tower.

They both looked out the front portal and watched the four dogsleds loaded with men, women, and children vanish into the woods.

"Bloody fools," Bowen muttered.

"Maybe we should've gone with 'em," said Wickliff, as he stomped snow off his boots.

Bowen leered. "Wick, are you bloody crazy?"

"No, mate, did you see the officers' faces? They got the sickness. The inspector, too."

Bowen spat tobacco. "Well, I ain't caught it yet."

"Me neither." Wickliff crossed his chest. "Maybe we should've left while we had the chance."

"Yeah, and Hysmith would've put a bullet in our backs." Bowen opened the side door. "Before long it's just gonna be you, me, and a bunch of crazies running around here. If it comes to that, I'll be the first to start offing people." Carrying his rifle, the sentry started walking along the landing toward his perch at the corner tower. Halfway, Bowen turned around. "Oh, and Wick?"

"Yeah, mate?"

"Keep your floor door locked. One of them down there is bound to get hungry."

Wickliff latched the trapdoor. He lit up the heater and took a seat in the cold, hard chair. He looked out each of the three portals, scanning the woods. The four dogsleds were long gone. Even the distant barking had faded, and now all Wickliff heard was the hollow wind. He looked left toward the open field and jerked forward with his rifle. "Holy shit!" The horse that had been tethered to the post was now missing, and blood stained the snow all the way to the tree line.

168

At the chapel, Father Xavier blessed several containers of water. It took all his spiritual fortitude to keep his thoughts in the light. In his twenty years, he had never performed multiple exorcisms in a single day. Battling a demon inside one person sometimes took days and completely drained him and his assistants. Of the few remaining colonists, at least six were now infected, with Willow being the most in need of an exorcism. He prayed this holy water would weaken the Devil's Plague inside the others and give Father Xavier time to destroy each demon one by one.

His apprentice looked down at the bottles with the same distraught look in his eyes, as Father Xavier had seen in his previous apprentices. "What's bothering you, Andre?"

"I fear God is failing us like he failed Father Jacques. It looks as if we are all going to die."

"Perish such thoughts. An exorcist never gives up on God."

"But what if Our Lord has no strength here? What if the demon's legion is stronger?"

"There is no power greater than God. I need you to stay strong, Andre. Keep praying for deliverance."

169

At the open gate, Anika, bundled in her brown fur parka with the hood pulled over her head, tightened the harnesses of each husky on her dogsled. As Tom approached, the eight dogs snarled and woofed, the fur on their backs spiked.

"Makade, Mushcoween, shush!" Anika looked up at Tom, her face tight with determination. "Come with me. We can reach Otter Island before nightfall. Grandmother Spotted Owl is a powerful medicine woman. She can help you."

Tom shook his head. "No, your tribe would never let me bring this disease into the village." Tom's heart ached at having to let Anika go. He wasn't comfortable with the native woman leaving the fort, but now every infected villager posed a threat to anyone who stayed behind. Tom had no choice but to stay and help the Jesuits find a cure.

Storm clouds formed over the forest, and the wind picked up.

"A blizzard is coming," Tom said. "You should leave now."

They stared at one another for a long moment. He wanted so badly to hug her goodbye, to kiss her lips. It saddened him that he might not ever see the native woman again.

Anika tried to appear strong. "I promise to bring back help."

"Don't bother. If I survive the winter, I'll come find you." He reached into his pocket. "Here, I want you to have this." He handed her the flute he and Chris had whittled.

She held it to her chest, and her eyes gave way to tears. She wiped her cheeks, backing toward her sled. "I'm coming back for you, Tom Hatcher. You better still be here."

Tom started to protest, but the words choked in his throat.

She held up her palm. He held up his.

As Anika drove her dogsled downhill toward the river, Tom felt his chest go hollow. He stepped back into the fort and closed the gate.

"Inspector!" Lt. Hysmith and another soldier approached. The lieutenant looked as if all the blood had been drained from his face. "We found Private Simmons."

170

Father Xavier and Andre, now dressed in their exorcism robes and carrying black cases, entered Willow's bedroom. All the shattered dolls had been removed, the floor swept. The curtains had been torn away, and gray morning light filtered through the windows. Every picture had been taken down and all the furniture removed, except for the four-poster bed that sat in the middle of the room.

Lady Pendleton lay in bed, her arms and legs still tied to the bedposts. She appeared to be asleep. Her porcelain face was cracked with blue veins. Her hands looked like an old woman's, the bones prominent beneath a thin layer of skin.

Father Xavier nailed a crucifix on a wall. He noticed Andre standing at Willow's side, gazing down at her. "Andre, there's no time to waste. Perform your tasks."

"*Oui*, Father." His novice began drawing chalked lines across the floor. This would create a barrier that evil could not cross.

Father Xavier prayed at the foot of the bed and gesticulated. He then opened his black case and pulled out his holy instruments. He placed a violet sash around his neck. He pulled out a black book with a red cross painted on the cover—the ancient text of *The Roman Ritual of Exorcism*. On a shelf, he unraveled a cloth bundle, rolling out a set of silver crosses. The center cross had a daggered tip. He hoped it wouldn't come to using that one. He raised one of the blunt-edged crosses, kissed it then gesticulated. "In the name of the Father, the Son, and the Holy Ghost, I claim this chamber as a sanctuary of God."

171

Tom followed the lieutenant and private to the French *voyageurs'* corner of the village. The shacks were all nestled together. The private stood post, while Tom and Hysmith entered the long, rectangular-shaped cabin known as the Skinning Hut. In the back room, the missing night guard, Private Simmons, was hanging upside down from the rafters, gutted like a hog. On the floor were more than a dozen buckets of blood and paintbrushes.

Tom shook his head. "Damn it, we never should have let Bélanger's crew leave."

"They were performing some kind of Devil worship," Hysmith said. "Look at this." He raised his lantern. All across the walls and ceiling were red spirals and strange words painted in blood.

Tom felt his skin tingle, as if some kind of force emanated from the inscriptions.

At the back wall was a shrine. Tom struck a match and lit five black candles. There was a large bowl filled with coils of hair, nail clippings, bones, and teeth. The altarpiece was a large animal skull, from a giant grizzly bear, Tom suspected, only the jaw seemed human-shaped, with fangs that ran the full length of the bones, like a crocodile. Painted on the skull's forehead was a red spiral.

172

Dr. Coombs rode through the woods in the lead dogsled with Bélanger cracking his whip at the barking huskies. Behind them followed three more dogsleds packed to the hilt with families and luggage. Their decision to leave had been made with haste. They had no plan, except to get as far away from Fort Pendleton as possible.

"Where on earth are we going?" Dr. Coombs asked.

"Upriver," was Bélanger's only answer.

Dr. Coombs gripped his shotgun and held on tight as the sled barreled through the pines. He felt guilty for abandoning his mission to quell the disease. But with no visible virus in the blood, how could he save the infected? Mother Nature had won this battle, and now it was survival of the fittest.

Something moved through the trees off to his left. What appeared to be a four-legged animal with grotesquely long bones disappeared behind a wall of fog. "Did you see that?" he asked Bélanger.

"I saw it." The Frenchman brought the sleds to a halt in a field that was surrounded by thick spruce and pines. All across the clearing, half-buried in the snow, were bones and carcasses. A feeding ground. The huskies barked at a pack of animals moving inside the white mist. Dr. Coombs' scrotum tightened as he felt like a deer being circled by wolves.

He prodded his sled driver. "Keep moving!"

"This is as far as we go." Bélanger hopped off the sled and began singing in French. Several other men joined in, including the women,

271

singing like happy churchgoers.

"What is bloody wrong with you people?" Dr. Coombs asked.

Bélanger continued singing as he pulled out a large knife and cut the throats of each of his dogs.

Dr. Coombs felt his heart drop into his belly.

Women screamed as the other men began to slaughter their wives.

Dr. Coombs screeched and gripped his shotgun.

The children cried and ran off into the woods. Their fathers chased after them.

The mist closed in and swallowed the four sleds, until all Dr. Coombs could see was swirling white smoke and falling snow. Terrible shrieks rattled his ears. Gunshots fired. People screamed.

Bélanger and three of his backwoods brethren circled the doctor, holding up bloody knives. "It's feeding time, Doc."

"The hell it is!" Dr. Coombs fired his shotgun. The blast opened up a red hole in Bélanger's chest, knocking him backward. The others retreated into the fog. One man lurched upward into the trees. Some unseen thing tore him in two and hurled the bloody torso and legs in opposite directions. The other men's death cries were cut short, until the only sounds were of predators crunching sinew and bones.

A beast roared behind Dr. Coombs. He twisted around. A set of broad elk antlers jutted from the smoke. And then he saw it walked on two legs. Its face defied nature. He marveled at the bloodstained fangs—the long talons. The doctor stared with both awe and terror as the beast ripped him from his seat.

Part Seventeen

Demon Storm

173

Tom led Father Xavier and Brother Andre back into the Skinning Hut. Master Pendleton, Lt. Hysmith, and Walter Thain were already gathered here, wearing shocked expressions.

"Dear God in heaven," Father Xavier said, staring at all the red spirals and strange words painted on the walls and ceiling.

"Do you recognize these words?" Tom asked.

"It's *The Goetia.*" Father Xavier touched the strange name written in blood-red ink above the altar.

"You've seen this before?" Pendleton asked.

"I first came across this in my demonology studies," Father Xavier said. "*The Goetia* is the first book of a series called the *Lemegeton Clavicula Salomonis*, also known as the Lesser Key of Solomon. Legend is that King Solomon sealed seventy-two demons inside this book. Each leads its own legion."

"What does all this mean?" Tom asked.

The priest ran his hand along the passages. "The walls read like a grimoire. A book of black magic. The phrases are ancient incantations used for conjuring demons."

Tom looked at the three officers. "It was Bélanger's men who painted the red spirals on all the doors."

"Those bloody savages," Pendleton kicked over a bloodstained bucket.

"We never should have let them leave," Hysmith grumbled.

"They didn't give us much choice, now did they?" Pendleton snapped back.

"By the looks of their shrine," Tom said, "they were performing some kind of Devil worship. I've never seen a skull quite like this."

"It's clearly a grizzly bear," Pendleton said.

"Looks more like a gorilla," Thain added. "Except for all the teeth."

"No, it's not an animal." Father Xavier picked it up and examined it. "It's a demon."

Andre said, "Like the one you showed me back in Montréal."

Tom stared down at the massive skull, the broad jaw full of jagged teeth. "You two have seen this before?"

The priest nodded. "In the mid 1660s, Jesuit missionaries found a similar beast mummified in a bog in Quebec. Even dead, its bones have a power that resonates pure evil."

Tom could feel evil emanating from every part of the room. "What do the red spirals mean?"

"They symbolize doorways to the spirit world. They... Oh, Dear God..." Father Xavier's eyes met Tom's, then he looked to Andre, Pendleton, Thain, and Hysmith. "This building acts as a gateway for demons to cross through."

174

Tom watched as the soldiers torched the Skinning Hut. The demon skull, the buckets of blood, and Private Simmons' disemboweled body were all left inside. The rectangular cabin caught fire quickly, and soon it was nothing more than a frame with orange walls. Black smoke drifted up to the sky.

A hell mouth, Tom thought, as he pieced together all the times he'd seen red spirals: the cellar wall at Manitou Outpost, outside Kunetay Timberwolf's hut, at Doc Riley's house, as well as a shrine within Hospital House. The French Canadian *voyageurs,* the men who had canoed Pendleton to Montréal, had been conjuring demons inside their skinning hut.

At the opposite corner of the fort, the pounding of a hammer echoed off the stockade walls. Father Xavier and Brother Andre watched as Tom and the stout blacksmith nailed a large iron cross to the logs that made up the wall. Like the Jesuits, the blacksmith had not caught the sickness. He claimed it was due to his love of eating garlic and rabbit stew. He indeed reeked of garlic, but he had done fine work, making four iron crosses. The blacksmith backed away, looking up at the cross that now hung at the center of the stockade's back wall. "That good enough for you, Father?"

"That will do fine," said Father Xavier.

The blacksmith picked up three more crosses in his massive arms. "And these?"

"The same as this. Two nailed at the center of the side walls, and one at the gate." Father Xavier hoped that with God's blessings, these holy symbols would be enough to defend the fort against evil spirits and keep the demons in the woods at bay. As if Satan were mocking him, two black birds landed on the spiked-tipped fence and cawed at the exorcist and his apprentice.

Brother Andre said, "Father, are you sure these will be enough to protect us?"

"They have to. With our prayers, we will turn this fort into a holy sanctuary and exorcise the evil that haunts every cabin."

Lt. Hysmith and another soldier approached. The lieutenant's face looked more gaunt than before. "This Catholic superstition is a bloody waste of time."

Father Xavier said, "Only faith in God will get us through this. I urge everyone to keep drinking holy water."

"Bugger that," Hysmith scoffed at the suggestion.

Hysmith said, "Master Pendleton has ordered that everyone meet for supper at Noble House within the hour."

Father Xavier nodded. "We'll be done by then."

There was a flutter of wings, and all the men turned their heads, looking up. Several more ravens landed atop the stockade wall, lining up like sentries.

175

At the fourth-story balcony of Noble House, Avery Pendleton played Heinrich Biber's *Mystery Sonatas* on his red violin. He stopped occasionally to drink Scotch mixed with holy water. The throat-burning concoction tasted like kerosene and made him wince with each sip. He continued to play the melancholy sonata with tears in his eyes.

The village below looked like a ghost town as a careening wind blew snow across the rooftops of the empty cabins. A skeleton crew of a dozen people now remained within the fort. Willow, the last of the women, was still bedridden. When Avery got the news that Anika had left, he'd felt angry and then remorse. For the past two years, the native woman had been his mistress, and despite the fact that she was an ill-mannered heathen, Anika had been a better lover than his frigid wife.

Avery coughed, covering his mouth with a handkerchief. He felt the disease coursing through him like glacier water inside his veins. The boreal wind whispered in his ear, tempting him to do leap off the balcony. *Death will end your misery*, the gale promised. *With us you will be free.* He looked over the railing, feeling vertigo. The drop would land him on the front steps, sure to snap his spine.

"Not like this." He spoke back to the wind. If it came down to suicide, he would leave this world the same way his father had.

Avery stepped back inside his study and set the red violin gently on the shelf with a dozen others his grandfather had crafted.

His Cree butler brought another glass of Scotch and holy water on a silver tray. Avery smiled. "Charles, you have been more loyal to me than anyone. I don't believe I pay you as handsomely as I should."

The butler bowed and walked away.

As Avery sipped the fiery drink, calming the beast within, he heard a screech in the distance. Turning, he noticed a dark cloud approaching over the forest, then, as it exploded into a thousand black pieces, he realized the cloud was a swarm of ravens.

176

A massive leviathan swam across the sky, blotting out the light. Hundreds of ravens stormed the fort in a black cyclone of dark-winged chaos. The ungodly cawing deafened Tom. "Run!" he yelled at the other five men. And then they were running through the cemetery.

Tom felt a sudden wind at his back. The birds swooped down between him and the Jesuits, attacking with beaks and talons.

Whirring wings. Running legs. Burning lungs.

Tom fought his way through the maelstrom, getting pecked and scratched. He reached the front steps of Noble House, climbing up to the second story. Lt. Hysmith ran a few steps ahead. He opened the door. Behind Tom raced Father Xavier.

Back at the cemetery, men were screaming. Beaks ripped the flesh off the blacksmith's face. Andre and a soldier both collapsed beneath hordes of flapping birds.

"No!" Father Xavier tried to run back down the steps, but Tom pulled the priest into Noble House and slammed the door shut.

177

In the foyer, Tom caught his breath. His clothes were torn and his hands red with scratches. His forehead and cheeks burning, he knew his face must look just as bad. He stared out the window. Thousands of ravens swooped and swirled, surrounding Noble House like a black tornado. Black wings flapped against the windows. The thick panes held. Near the cemetery a feeding frenzy completely covered three bodies.

Father Xavier, who had cuts on his face and bald head, looked stunned. "Did Andre make it?"

Tom shook his head.

Lt. Hysmith swatted at a few birds that had gotten inside. They flew off into the ballroom.

"Is everyone all right?" Pendleton came downstairs with Walter Thain and their butler.

Tom informed them about the recent deaths.

"Who else was out there?" Pendleton asked.

Lt. Hysmith said, "Wickliff and Bowen were manning the watchtowers."

The six men looked out the windows at the black storm. Whether the sentries were alive or dead, Tom couldn't tell. With Willow upstairs, that left seven survivors taking refuge inside Noble House, five of whom were infected.

178

In the watchtower, Private Wickliff closed all the portals, blocking out the birds. They clawed at the roof and walls, cawing together in one maddening voice. Wickliff cowered in a corner, holding his hands over his ears.

179

Anika drove her dogsled through the pines with the river just off to her right. In the distance behind her, beasts howled. She whipped the huskies harder. They reached a bend in the river where several canoes lay along the bank. She loaded a canoe with gear. Her dogs barked, getting tangled with one another.

A white mist with whirling snow devoured the trees. The howls drew closer.

Anika cut loose her eight dogs and ushered them into the canoe. Her black wolf-dog ran back into the woods, barking.

"Makade!" Anika chased after him.

The dog vanished in the mist and yelped, followed by the sound of bones cracking.

Anika halted. In the snowstorm walked tall, skeletal creatures, with elongated limbs and faces that were all teeth and hungry eyes. *Windigos.*

Anika sprinted back, pushed the canoe into the river, and paddled away.

180

At Noble House, Father Xavier nailed a crucifix to the front door. His heart ached for the loss of Brother Andre. The young man had wanted so badly to become a priest. Maybe his fears had been portents of their imminent doom. Maybe God *was* failing them, just like he had Father Jacques.

That's what the demon wants me to believe. Keep your faith, Xavier. You have to be strong for the others.

Pendleton, Hysmith, and Tom nailed boards over the second-story windows. They each coughed. Father Xavier handed them more bottles of holy water. "Keep drinking." The priest then gazed out a window. Outside, ravens now stood along the stockade fence and covered the rooftops of every cabin.

Tom stood beside him at the window. "Is this also the demon's doing?"

Father Xavier nodded. "The legion has the power to possess the animal kingdom."

181

Anika swiftly paddled her canoe down the icy river. Snow fell heavily, the wind pushing against her back. Her seven huskies huddled together in the long canoe. Ozaawi moaned for the loss of Makade. As Anika's aching arms fought against the rapids, her thoughts had been reduced to the survival instincts of prey fleeing from predators.

Shrieks echoed from upriver.

Anika paddled faster through a narrow channel. The canoe slid over a sheet of ice and got lodged. She chopped at the frozen shore, but the ice was too thick. She struggled to guide the boat back toward moving water. The dogs yelped. The fog drifted around them.

A voice called out from Anika's left, *"Anikaaaaa."*

In the woods, the pack of human and animal forms was moving through the smoke. Her heart seized as a windigo that resembled Kunetay Timberwolf broke clear of the haze. It ran ahead of the pack, its stick-like limbs jutting at odd angles as it bound through the trees on all fours.

Anika pushed her oar against the ice. Her dog, Mushcoween, snarled at the windigos. The canoe shot downriver, just as the Kunetay beast leaped onto the ice and crashed into the river, shrieking as it sank.

Mushcoween moaned, thrashing his head violently. Anika gasped at seeing the claw marks on the dog's nape. Foaming at the mouth, Mushcoween bit into the throat of another husky, killing it. The other dogs ran to the far edge of the canoe. One leaped overboard.

"No!" Anika cried.

Mushcoween faced her. The dog's eyes were rolled back to solid whites. It leaped toward her, growling. She held back its fangs with her paddle. The canoe spun sideways over the rapids. The windigo dog snapped at her throat, drool falling against her cheeks. Anika grabbed the antler handle at her hip and drove her knife into Mushcoween's neck. Anika wailed as she pushed her dog overboard. She then jabbed the oar into the rapids and stopped the canoe from spinning. She paddled back on course, watching her four remaining dogs as they huddled together at the far end of the canoe.

Part Eighteen

The Hunger

182

At Noble House, all the second-story windows were boarded up. Tom peered between the slats that covered the window beside the front door. The flocks of black birds remained perched on all the rooftops and surrounding fence. They weren't all just ravens. Also among them were crows, jackdaws, and rooks. *Corvids*, Dr. Coombs had called them. Somehow the birds endured the wind and falling snow. In the dead gray sky, clouds formed over the forest, and Tom felt in his gut this was only a calm before another storm.

Cold fire burned inside his chest, the sickness once again spreading through him. He took another sip from his canteen. The holy water seemed to be working its miracles, restoring his strength each time he drank. He wondered how long the drink could hold back the sickness before it finally took over his mind and body.

He went into the large ballroom at the rear of the house. Christmas wreaths still hung on the walls between the windows. The tall tree with the star on top stood in the far corner with fake presents stacked around it. Tom had no recollection of this year's Christmas, as he had spent the holiday season floating in whiskey.

Gazing out the back window, he surveyed the shack at the rear of the cemetery. The Dead House. His son's winter crypt. Oddly, the door stood open. A white shape took form in the doorway's dark maw, and Chris appeared at the threshold, somehow alive, somehow beckoning Tom with a bone-white hand.

His head suddenly went dizzy. He rubbed his eyes. Looked back out the window. The door to the Dead House was closed.

183

Anika pulled her canoe onto the shore at Otter Island. The village was much larger than the one that neighbored Fort Pendleton. Here, several bands of Ojibwa gathered to endure the hard winters together. This island between two rivers was also a sacred place where evil manitous never trespassed. The windigos had stopped chasing her a few miles upriver. Her last image of them was a pack of stick-like creatures crouched at the shore.

Now, Anika's four huskies kept close to her legs as she entered the village. Ozaawi must have sensed the fear of her three siblings, for she took over as leader and led the way. Anika followed the sounds of beating drums. Snow continued to fall heavily, powdering huts and wigwams that were aglow with fires. She smelled venison cooking, and her stomach reminded her she hadn't eaten since yesterday. A few horses stirred, and some dogs barked, but no one greeted Anika and her dogs. It appeared that every tribe member was inside.

At the center of the village, she entered a large wigwam that thundered with drumming and chanting. Warriors were dancing backwards. A ceremony to ward off the windigos. Several elders were gathered in a circle. The shaman from several bands made up the Grand Medicine Society. The Mediwiwin. The elders passed around a ceremonial pipe. Grandmother Spotted Owl looked up. The drumbeats stopped as all heads turned toward Anika. Everyone looked at her as if a *wiitigo* had just entered the wigwam.

184

Tom joined four other men at the dining table. On his plate was elk steak cooked rare and bloody. The officers around the table were becoming a macabre lot with grayish-white skin and withdrawn cheeks. Tom dined with them, doing what he could to sate his voracious appetite and keep his strength up. He met eyes with Father Xavier. The priest looked nervous to be having dinner among the infected. He bit into a raw clove of garlic. He smiled as he chewed and offered some cloves to Tom. "Seems to help."

"Whatever works, I guess." Tom bit into the raw garlic, wincing at the burning flavor. The cold retreated. Evidently, the thing inside him didn't seem to like garlic either.

Lt. Hysmith reached for another piece of meat. Walter Thain

stabbed a fork into it. "Mine!" The obese man's white-striped eyes glared as fiercely as those of a hungry jaguar.

"You've had more than your share," Hysmith snarled back.

"There's plenty more." Pendleton rang a bell. The Cree butler came in from the kitchen with another plate stacked with bloody meat. Hysmith and Thain grabbed the meat shanks like barbarians.

The butler refilled their Scotch. Pendleton, who still had enough civility to eat with utensils, set down his fork and knife and raised a goblet. "Enjoy the feast, gentleman, for this may very well be our last."

Tom, feeling sick to his stomach, left the table.

185

Inside the wigwam, the chiefs and shamans gathered around Anika. She told them about the cannibal plague at Fort Pendleton and how the man she loved was turning windigo. She begged the Mediwiwin to save him.

Grandmother Spotted Owl shook her head. "Forget him. The white people conjured the tricksters. The disease is theirs to bear."

Anika said, "There must be something we can do."

An old shaman said, "There is no stopping the *wiitigo*."

"We can fight them with our spears and our magic!" shouted Swiftbear's voice. Anika's silver-haired uncle parted the crowd and stepped into the circle. He wore a bear-claw necklace. His broad chest and shoulders were engraved with scars that displayed his years as a warrior. Swiftbear also walked the path of a medicine man. "Together we can call in the spirits of the four winds and send the *wiitigo* back to Manitou Forest."

The Mediwiwin argued with one another. Those who were warriors wanted to fight, while those who were protectors feared the outcome of interfering with the spirit world.

Anika told the elders, "Every winter the *wiitigo* attack our trappers. We leave our land and they eat all our game."

Swiftbear said to Chief Mokomaan, "This winter they killed your daughter's husband and your grandson. It's time we fight back."

Grandmother Spotted Owl stepped between her son and granddaughter. "No, I won't allow this." The other elders joined in protest.

Chief Mokomaan raised his palm, silencing the crowd. "We have fled too many winters. Many of us have lost members of our family. It is time we call upon our good spirit Nanabozho to guide us. And the brothers of the four winds to fight the *wiitigo*." He offered Anika to take a few warriors with her to the fort.

Swiftbear gripped a spear that was etched with animal totems. He put a hand on Anika's shoulder. "I will go with you, also, Little Pup."

186

In the parlor of the Pendleton home, Tom helped Father Xavier assemble spiritual weapons on a table: crucifixes, bottles of holy water, silver crosses with dagger blades, and an exorcist's book of rites. Tom held up one of the cross-daggers. It was marked with a fiery sun: the Jesuit insignia. "I saw that Father Jacques had one of these. What is it for?"

"It is an exorcist's greatest weapon," Father Xavier said. "If a demon cannot be driven from a possessed one's body before the Turning, then the cross-blade is to be stabbed into the host's heart." He handed one of them to Tom. "This was Andre's. He won't be needing it."

Tom understood the pain that darkened the priest's eyes. "Father, I'm sorry for—"

Father Xavier raised his palm. "We must keep our thoughts pure. Sadness and anger will only strengthen the dark forces."

Tom slid the cross-dagger into his belt. "Father, if I may ask, what drove you to become an exorcist?"

"I got the calling when I was ten years old." The priest shared what had happened to his sister, Mirabelle. How she had been possessed by a demon that made her commit suicide. At his sister's grave, young Xavier swore to God he would avenge her. "I've been hunting my sister's demon my whole life. And now I've finally found it."

Tom heard the sound of cloth tearing. He looked up at Willow's portrait that hung over the fireplace. Invisible claws sliced through her painted face. From down the hall, Willow screamed.

187

In Willow's bedroom, ravens and jackdaws flew outside the windows, causing bird shadows to flap along the walls. The young woman fought against the ropes that bound her arms and legs to the bedposts. Her blonde hair was streaked with white. Her face, once beautiful, barely resembled the woman Tom had known. He gripped his dagger-cross as she reached for him, stretching the ropes. "Come to me, lover."

Father Xavier flicked holy water on her. "I cast out this demon in the name of Our Lord Jesus Christ."

Willow hissed and kicked her legs in a childish tantrum. "No, no, no, no, no!" Then she laughed, craning her head back toward Tom. She arched her back, heaving her bosoms. "Do you want me, darling?"

"Stop," Tom demanded.

Moaning, she licked her lips, spreading her thighs. "Don't you want to fuck me?" She lifted her pubic bone. Her nightgown slid down her heavily veined thighs, exposing her undergarments to him.

"Willow, stop!" Tom threw a blanket over her.

She scowled. "How dare you deny a woman in heat?" She bounced on the bed. "Somebody fuck me, fuck me, fuck me!"

Pendleton, Hysmith, and Thain entered the room.

"What the hell's happening?" asked Avery.

"Your wife's demon has taken over," Father Xavier said. She rolled her eyes back as the priest spoke. "You might not want to witness the exorcism."

Tom said, "Let us handle this."

"Don't worry about me," Pendleton barked. "Just get that goddamned spirit out of her."

As Father Xavier chanted, Willow's face rippled, the bones shifting beneath her skin. Before everyone's eyes, she turned several years younger, looking like the Métis girl, Zoé Lamothe.

"What is your demon name?" asked Father Xavier.

"I'm the Secret Keeper," Willow spoke in a child's voice. "And I know *allll* your sinful little secrets." She giggled.

"What secrets?" Tom asked.

"You kissed Willow." She snickered.

Pendleton glared at Tom. "What is she talking about?"

"I don't know. She's delirious."

"You're all a bunch of sinners." Zoé glared at Avery and the two officers flanking him. "I know about the cellar. The wicked games you play."

Pendleton said, "Woman, shut your mouth!"

Her face shifted back to Willow's. "You three betrayed my beloved, and now he's very, very angry." In a singsong voice Willow chanted, "*Fais ce que tu voudras. Fais ce que tu voudras. Fais ce que tu voudras...*"

Pendleton screamed, "Shut up! Shut up! Shut up!"

Willow chided, "You are a pitiful husband, Avery, always off fucking your whores. Well, I, too, have found a lover. His name is Gustave, and he pleases me like you never could."

"You bloody bitch!" Pendleton charged Willow. A force threw her husband against the wall. She cackled, kicking her feet.

Father Xavier held a cross to her face. "Gustave Meraux, if you are inside this woman, show yourself."

Willow's eyes went solid black. "Gustave is among us, yes, yes, the Dark Messiah's coming, he is. Coming for you all!"

Tom shuddered as he felt the Cannery Cannibal's presence in the room, along with many other damned souls. The entity inside his chest rammed against his ribcage like an animal trying to get out.

"What is your demon name?" Father Xavier said.

"We are *Legion*. We are everywhere. Inside each of you, feasting on your feeble minds."

"You are nothing but a cowardly demon," Father Xavier said.

"We are not!"

"You hide inside this woman, because you fear God above all!"

"There is no god here but us, you prickless eunuch!"

The exorcist threw holy water on Willow's demonic face. She growled like a wild beast. The bed slid toward the men, grating across the floor.

Pendleton and the other officers fled the room.

Tom and Father Xavier dodged the moving bed. It stopped in the center of the room. Willow fought against the ropes, laughing like a crazy-house lunatic, slamming her head against the headboard.

Father Xavier chanted in Latin as he crept toward the bed. Tom walked beside him, wielding the dagger-cross, ready to drive it into the epileptic woman's chest.

Willow sat upright. Her face shifted into Beth Hatcher's. "Please, don't let us die again." Her belly swelled.

Tom backed away. "Oh, Christ, that's my wife!"

Beth breathed short breaths in and out, in and out, as if going into labor. Her belly continued to expand. She doubled over, screaming in pain.

Tom stepped toward her. "Beth, no!"

"It's not her!" Father Xavier shoved Tom toward the door.

"I have to help her!"

Beth's belly kept swelling, threatening to burst.

"It's just an illusion!" Father Xavier screamed in Tom's face. "Leave, now!"

285

Tom left the room, tortured by the cries of his wife pleading him, "Tom Hatcher, don't you dare abandon me again! Tom, come back in here! Tommmmmmm!"

188

Father Xavier felt his arms shaking as he joined the men in the parlor. Everyone was in a state of shock. While Tom ranted about the woman yelling down the hall being his wife, Pendleton claimed he heard Willow's angry voice; Walter Thain swore it was his mother's; and Father Xavier heard his sister's. "Xavier, don't you dare abandon me again!" Mirabelle had screamed. "Xavier, come back in here!" She continued to yell and pound the headboard. He felt like he was ten years old all over again.

"Everyone ignore her," Father Xavier said. "The demon is trying to drive us all mad."

"It's bloody working," said Hysmith.

"I'm coming for you all!" Gustave's voice screamed from down the hall. "One little sinner at a time." Then he cackled like the flame-spitting clown from Xavier's childhood.

Pendleton yelled, "Father, do something to shut that thing up!"

The exorcist looked at Pendleton, Hysmith, Thain, and Tom. Hour by hour, the men were steadily changing, their features growing more angular, their irises more white. "Each of you is hosting a demon. And the legion won't stop until they have brought hell upon us all."

189

Anika, dressed in buckskins and boots, strapped weapons onto her body: tomahawk, throwing knives, and medicine bag. Grandmother Spotted Owl walked over with a bowl of burning sage. "Lift up your arms."

Anika stood with her arms out while her grandmother smudged her head and body with an owl feather and spoke prayers.

Swiftbear winked at Anika as he whittled a new animal spirit into his spear. Her uncle had fought outlaws and Iroquois Indians long before she was born. He had killed bears and moose and cougars with that spear. But he had never faced a windigo. None of them had.

The other warriors were sitting around the fire beating drums and chanting. They sang songs that summoned courage for battle. Anika took deep breaths as birds of panic flapped inside her ribcage. She grabbed her own totem spear and sat down in the heat of the fire next to her uncle.

Swiftbear touched her arm. "Do not be afraid, Little Pup."

She couldn't stop shaking. "We could all die tonight."

Her uncle looked around at the singing braves. "Then we will journey on to *giizhig-oon* and fly with the eagles."

"But what if the *wiitigo* turn us into their kind?" she asked.

Swiftbear gazed at the fire in the center of the wigwam. The rippling flames lit up the scars on his face. "If you die from a *wiitigo*, then follow the song of the Mediwiwin flutes. They will guide your spirit."

Anika nodded. She couldn't stop worrying about Tom. This Métis man who had hated her from the start. This man who had shunned his own people. This man who had more than once filled her with rage. Now all she could think about was his wounded heart. And the pain that Tom carried in his eyes. The moments they had spent sitting and talking. Now, a windigo spirit was inside him.

She pulled out the flute that Tom and Chris had whittled together. She studied the animal totems carved around the shaft—a white buffalo clashing horns with an elk, snow owls and ravens, and the faces of two women. One of them she recognized as herself. And Anika understood their destiny. And it gave her the strength she needed.

The drumming stopped. The logs in the fire popped. Anika gripped her spear as Swiftbear looked around the circle at the young braves. "For many winters our tribe has lived in fear of the *wiitigo*. They are beasts with skeletons made of ice. Some can walk as high as the trees. They crave flesh and their hunger never ends. They can possess a brave's mind, if he is not careful. If a *wiitigo* whispers your name, do not heed its call." Swiftbear rubbed a hand along his spear and looked at the elders who sat behind them. "Our weapons have been blessed by the Mediwiwin. Call in your animal spirits to fight alongside you. Trust your warrior instincts. Let the land that once belonged to our tribe be ours again." He shouted a war cry, and the braves raised their weapons and hollered with him. Anika felt a rush of adrenaline as her warrior spirit howled through her.

Later, as the men packed a canoe at the riverbank, Grandmother Spotted Owl gave Anika a medicine bag. She opened the pouch and pulled out white shells that had been carved to look like buffalos. Grandmother said, "They have been blessed and have great power against manitous. Use them wisely." The old woman hugged her granddaughter. "We will pray for your protection." Anika climbed into a canoe beside Swiftbear, and the two of them, along with six braves, paddled up the river.

190

The snowstorm finally reached Fort Pendleton. The black-winged minions flew off in droves as heavy wind and snow pummeled the fort.

The disciple ran across the cemetery and entered the Dead House. He lit a candle and set it on a barrel. Several rats fled for the darkness.

"I've done as you wished, Master."

The tool shed filled with the sounds of squeaks and chittering, the whir of flapping wings. Out of the gloom emerged a towering black mass made of ravens and rats. At the beast's massive head, the rodents and dark wings parted, uncovering the pale face of Gustave Meraux. His eyes were solid black. The Dark Messiah grinned down at his disciple with sharp teeth. *Do you worship me above all?* Gustave spoke in the man's mind.

The disciple kneeled. "Yes, Master."

The twister of fur and feathers circled him, caressing the back of the man's head with raven claws. He felt rats crawling onto his shoulders, down his back. The disciple shook with terror, afraid he might be eaten, then reminded himself of the glorious eternity that had been promised to him. "I will do anything you ask, my lord."

Even sacrifice your own body?

The man placed a knife to his own wrist. "I would drain my blood for you."

The dark mass whirled, once again spinning in front of the man. Gustave's black eyes gleamed. *Then you will have everything your heart desires. Now open your mouth.*

Black matter flowed from the demon's mouth to the man's. He began to choke, as if swallowing mud. His head and body shook violently, the spine popping, as hell's fury filled him. And then the disciple's awareness merged with many others full of hate and pain and suffering. And with them in this abyss of ice-cold blackness was their dark lord and savior. And the minions clung to the disciple, crawling across his body as he twisted and writhed inside his cocoon of fur and feathers. And finally he understood why the dark lord had come. When the metamorphosis was complete, the rats fell to the ground, scurrying off into the darkness. The ravens flew out the front door. The man stepped back outside. He touched his face and felt the solidity of his body. Grinning, the Dark Shepherd stared up at Noble

House with a new set of eyes.

191

At Noble House, the fourth-story windowpanes rattled. Tom stood in the parlor warming his hands at a fire burning in the hearth. With the chill that now resided inside his body, he relished any source of warmth. He stared up at Willow's portrait, her goddess-like features disfigured by five slashes that scarred her painted face. A short time ago Tom had lusted after this woman in sin. Had kissed her under the illusion that Beth had somehow returned. He had lied to his boss, denying his betrayal.

The only real truth, Tom now understood, was that everyone inside Noble House was slowly going crazy. In the dining room down the hall, the officers shouted at one another. From another hallway, Willow continued to wail and cry. And all Tom could think about was feeding his empty stomach.

Was this how the inhabitants at Manitou Outpost met their demise? Their demons slowly eating them from within until there was nothing left but animal hunger?

The demons seemed to know their weaknesses and fears. They filled their minds with illusions. In the final stages, when insanity reached its tipping point, the demons altered their flesh and bones. Tom couldn't stop seeing the image of Willow's face changing into Zoé's. That childish voice. *I am the Secret Keeper. I know all your sinful little secrets.* Willow had called Gustave her lover, taunting Avery. And then she had become Beth Hatcher, as real as if Tom's pregnant wife were lying there on the bed. She had glared at Tom with resentful eyes. His guilt over Beth's and his baby's deaths strengthened the entity within. It squirmed like a large tapeworm within his belly. The serpentine fetus sprouted a hundred centipede legs and crawled up into his ribcage. It demanded to be fed, filling Tom with unbearable cravings. He fed the thing another clove of raw garlic.

This only angered the entity as hot claws raked across the inner lining of Tom's belly. "Christ!" He doubled over, gripping his stomach. His face broke out in a cold sweat. When the pain finally passed, he squeezed his fists. He had to do something. The more he stood idle, the more the demon spiraled his thoughts down into a dark abyss.

He walked over to Father Xavier, who was reading from his exorcism book.

"Are we doomed, Father?"

"No, not as long as we fight on the side of God. You have to keep faith in your heart, Tom. Even when you are at your weakest, call upon the will of God to give you the inner strength to fight this. He will hear your call, and He will empower you to survive. Keep praying."

Tom didn't know how the priest could remain so righteous in the face of all that they'd witnessed. Father Xavier's spirit seemed unbreakable. Having the exorcist as an ally was the only thing that gave Tom hope. "All right, Father, I'll keep having faith."

Down the hall, the shouting match between the officers escalated. Tom said, "What do we do about them?"

"I can only exorcise one demon at a time." Father Xavier grabbed his holy book and a dagger-cross. "I must first attend to Willow. If the others start to turn…"

Tom checked the bullets in his revolver. "I know what has to be done."

"God be with you then." The exorcist headed back down the hall toward Willow's bedroom.

Tom turned his attention toward the shouting that came from the dining room.

"How could she know?" asked Pendleton. "Who told her?"

"Don't bloody ask me!" Thain yelled back. "I'm not your wife's keeper!"

"Zoé must have somehow known," said Hysmith.

"It's him, isn't it?" Thain said. "He's come back for us."

"God damn it, I won't stand for this!" Pendleton headed toward the stairs.

"Where are you going?" Tom asked.

"It's none of your goddamned business." He hurried down the stairs.

Tom waited a few seconds and then secretly followed his boss down to the stairwell that led to the ground-floor cellar. Pendleton entered and closed the door. Tom crept down to the foot of the stairs. Turned the knob. Locked.

Why had the chief factor come down here?

Tom lit a match. Carved into the door was the phrase the Secret Keeper had spoken. *Fais ce que tu voudras.* "Do what thou wilt."

192

Upstairs, in Willow's room, Father Xavier read from his exorcism book. "'Holy Lord! All-Powerful Father! You who sent your only son into this world in order that he might crush this Roaring Lion...'"

Willow, now resembling his teenage sister, Mirabelle, ranted with an angry scowl, "You abandoned me! You let the beast take me to hell."

Father Xavier struggled to concentrate as the claws of guilt gripped his chest. "'Snatch from damnation and from this Devil of our times, this woman who was created in your image and likeness. Throw your terror, Lord, over the Beast who is destroying what belongs to you.'"

Mirabelle rocked back and forth, shaking the bedposts.

Father Xavier continued praying, "'Give faith to your servants against this most evil Serpent...'"

Mirabelle's facial bones shifted into something monstrous, a long black tongue slithering from her mouth.

The exorcist chanted, "'Let your powerful strength force the Serpent to let go of your servant, so that it no longer possesses her.'"

Mirabelle's cheeks began splitting, as rows of fangs sprouted from the sinews that tore open from ear to ear. His sister released a cry that sounded like a squealing pig.

Father Xavier's eyes teared up as he raised his dagger-cross over her chest.

"Yes, Xavier, kill me!" The female demon shifted back to Mirabelle's teenage face. "Kill me, kill me!"

His mind was filled with a vision of him hacking the blade into her chest, spattering blood across the sheets and walls.

"No!" Father Xavier pressed the dagger-cross flat against her breastbone. His sister screamed and arched her back. He held her in a locked embrace. She bucked beneath his cross. The demon shrieked. The windows shattered. A snowy gust blew into the room.

Father Xavier's sister stared up at him with frightened eyes. He said, "God, release Mirabelle from this unclean spirit! Send her soul to heaven!" He felt a rush of warm air as Mirabelle's spirit passed through him. Her ghost floated above the bed, rising upward to the ceiling. Father Xavier met eyes with his sister one last time and then she was gone. The young woman spasming in his arms changed back to Willow. She curled into a fetal position, sobbing against his shoulder.

"And release Willow, Eternal God! Cast out her demon once and for all. Amen!"

The frosty wind sucked back out the window. The shattered glass flew back into the windowpanes, reforming into solid windows that didn't have a single crack. Willow fainted against his chest, her smooth, porcelain face looking normal again.

Father Xavier sat back against the headboard and cried over the miracles he had witnessed.

193

Tom returned to the fourth floor. In the dining room, Walter Thain was still stuffing his fat face. Lt. Hysmith rang a bell, and the butler brought out another tray of canned food. Tom's hunger was so strong, he felt the urge to join the gluttonous officers.

No, that's what the thing inside me wants.

Tom followed the butler into the kitchen. "Charles, I need your help."

The Cree servant looked at him suspiciously.

Tom said, "You must have witnessed some of the things that went on inside this house. What the officers did to the servant girls."

Charles' face hardened and he nodded.

Tom said, "Do you know where I might find a spare key to the cellar?"

The butler glanced toward the dining hall at the officers, then whispered, "Master's study." He waved Tom to follow. On their way through the parlor, they met up with Father Xavier. The priest looked as if he'd aged ten years.

"How's Willow?" Tom asked.

"Better. I think her demon's finally gone. How are you feeling?"

"Holding together," Tom said. "We have to act quickly. Pendleton took *The Goetia* down into the cellar. I don't trust him."

Charles led them into Pendleton's study. The butler opened the drawer of a curio cabinet and produced a key. "A skeleton key. This will open any door in the house." A bell rang from the dining hall. "Excuse me, gentlemen." Charles left to attend to the needs of the demanding officers.

"What's this?" Tom spotted a door behind a hanging bearskin. He unlocked it. Inside was another chamber, much smaller than the study. One of the dormer windows looked out over the village. The opposite wall was covered in masks from many cultures: African, Gaelic, Venetian, French, and Asian. There were also several Iroquois masks, like the demon heads in Percy Kennicot's study. The hollow-eyed false faces grinned as if they knew Avery Pendleton's secrets. *We know the wicked games he plays.*

Several costumes hung inside a wardrobe. On a table was an open crate full of daguerreotype photos: wealthy gentlemen wearing masks and posing with nude women.

"Oh, my lord," said Father Xavier.

"What sort of affairs was Pendleton into?" Tom asked, flipping through the photos.

Father Xavier said, "He invited Andre and me to a masquerade ball before we left Montréal. I saw Pendleton go into an orgy room with two women."

Tom knew that his boss was a letch with the women here at the fort, but had no clue of the chief factor's affairs back in Montréal. Evidently, he maintained the company of other rakes who were into parties of a sexual nature.

At the bottom of the crate, Tom found a portrait of a group of gentlemen in suits and top hats. It was the only one where they weren't wearing masks. Written on the photo was "Bacchus Ball, Montréal, October, 1866." Avery Pendleton stood among two dozen men, including several familiar faces: Pierre Lamothe, Percy Kennicot, Walter Thain, Lt. Hysmith, and Dr. Coombs. Tom's blood went cold when he recognized the man standing in the center of the front row...Gustave Meraux.

Part Nineteen

Hell Fire

194

Tom, gripping his pistol, charged into the dining room with Father Xavier. Lt. Hysmith was missing. Walter Thain was seated at the table, slurping stew from a tin. While most of the infected had wasted away to skin and bones, Thain seemed to have grown heavier. His clothes were splitting at the seams. His engorged cheeks were greased with red muck. He grimaced at Tom and Father Xavier. "Feed time, feed time!" The rotund beast released a low, guttural growl, revealing fangs. Thain started to rise. Tom aimed and put a bullet into his forehead. The back of Thain's head exploded red against the wall. The mammoth man collapsed across the table, scattering empty soup tins.

Tom eased toward the body, making sure Walter Thain was good and dead. His eyes lolled back. The back of his skull looked like a cracked-open gourd. He didn't move.

Father Xavier whispered a prayer, blessing Thain's corpse.

Tom picked up a can and sniffed. "Christ, he was eating human meat."

"How can you tell?" Father Xavier asked.

"My sense of smell has heightened." Engraved on the bottom of the can was a fancy letter M. "It's from the Meraux Cannery." Tom crushed the tin in his fist. His blood singed at the thought that Avery Pendleton and his officers had associated with the Cannery Cannibal.

A huffing sound came from the kitchen. Tom pushed open the door and found Hysmith hunched over the dead butler, tearing strings of meat from the Cree Indian's throat. The lieutenant's rail-thin body and misshapen head resembled a praying mantis in a red uniform.

Tom aimed his pistol, but Hysmith moved too fast, scampering on all fours out a side door. Tom chased the spindly-legged lieutenant down the stairs. He, *it*, roared as Tom fired shots, hitting the wall and banister. Before he could get off another shot, Hysmith bolted out the front door.

Tom ran outside, into the raging blizzard. "Lieutenant!"

Hysmith vanished in a bank of white fog that covered the fort. Only a few rooftops were visible now. Tom stopped halfway down the front steps. Wind whipped his hair and clothes, freezing his extremities. Snow pelted his face. Lt. Hysmith howled from somewhere in the storm. Tom hurried back inside and shut the door. He brought down the bar that barricaded the door.

Father Xavier came down the stairs. "The officers turned faster than I expected."

Tom pulled out his key to the cellar. "Come, Father. We have to find Pendleton."

195

The canoe filled with a band of Ojibwa braves paddled upriver against the storm. Anika chopped at the rapids with her oar. Snow flew into her eyes, making her squint. She watched the shoreline. As twilight faded, the forest grew darker.

"That's where I saw the *wiitigo*," she pointed toward the riverbank. "Kunetay was among them."

Swiftbear said, "They are upstream now. Moving toward the fort."

"How do you know?" Anika said.

"Hawk medicine gives me vision from the sky."

Like Anika's grandmother, Swiftbear had been born with a veil of skin over his eyes. He had the gift of second sight and could see through the eyes of animals. Hawk, who circled the sky, was his favorite totem. Anika wished she had been born with such a gift. But for her, practicing medicine had always been difficult. She knew a few spells to ward away evil manitous, but she had yet to discover the power to call upon the help of the spirit world as the elders of the Mediwiwin did in their ceremonies.

Anika was grateful to have such a powerful shaman as her uncle to journey with her. She prayed to Great Spirit that they reached the fort in time.

196

Tom unlocked the cellar door. A dusty chamber with a dirt floor stretched off into an impenetrable void. There were no windows down here. The ground floor acted as a vault. Avery Pendleton was somewhere in the multi-roomed maze that stretched the length of Noble House. Tom had visions of a spindly predator crouched in the darkness, waiting to pounce upon its prey. He cautioned Father Xavier to keep close. The priest carried his black bag and dagger-cross. Tom had the second dagger-cross on his hip, but preferred to carry his pistol. They had to exorcise Pendleton's demon before the chief factor fully turned like the others. Tom hoped they weren't too late.

He entered cautiously with the exorcist a step behind. Tom's oil lamp lit up numerous barrels and crates. Doorways led off in both directions. The powdery earth floor had too many boot prints to follow a trail.

A sound echoed from the room to Tom's left.

"This way." He led Father Xavier between pallets stacked with pelts—beaver, raccoon, muskrat, rabbit, otter, deer, and fox. The bounty of Pendleton Fur Trading Company. A rack of hanging wolf furs with the heads intact stared with hollow eyes. From each pelt, Tom smelled the musky scent of the skinned animal. His mouth salivated. His mind filled with images of chasing a deer through the woods, pouncing on the prey, tearing into its nape. He saw other creatures in this vision, half-human, half-animal, as Tom feasted among a pack of windigos. And then he saw the face of the Beast with antlers. Feeling dizzy, Tom stumbled and gripped one of the fur stacks for balance. A hand touched his shoulder.

"What's wrong?" whispered Father Xavier.

"More illusions. The demon's making me think like an animal." Tom's stomach ached. "Christ, the hunger's getting worse."

"Keep drinking," the priest urged.

Tom sipped from his canteen. The throat-burning liquid reminded him of his mission. He gripped Father Xavier's wrist that was holding the dagger-cross. "If it comes down to it, Father, I want you to use this."

"As long as we stick together, I won't let the demon turn you." The priest gesticulated the cross in front of Tom. He spoke something in Latin.

"You can exorcise me later." Tom kept walking. "We must first find Pendleton."

They continued exploring the dark cellar. Candlelight glowed up ahead. Tom entered what looked to be some sort of ceremonial room with pagan statues and benches that faced an altar. A fire burned in a large hearth.

Tom's stomach knotted as he saw a large bed with chains dangling from the posts. *The officers have been making women do sexual things down in the cellar,* Anika had said. Another wall was covered in whips.

Tom's throat filled with hot bile. He stepped into a ceremonial chamber lit by several torches perched on iron poles. Avery Pendleton was standing at an altar and appeared to be praying to male and female deities.

Tom pointed his pistol at his boss' back. "What the hell is all this?"

Pendleton turned around. The torch flames flickered shadows across his skeletal face. His skin had turned so transparent that all of his veins and arteries were visible. One of his irises reflected the light like a wolf. He frowned as Tom and Father Xavier stood shoulder to shoulder, holding out a pistol and cross.

"This chamber is off limits," Pendleton snarled. "Both of you, go back upstairs."

Tom pointed to the stained mattress on the four-poster bed. "You and your officers were sexually abusing women down here, weren't you?"

"That's none of you goddamned concern, Inspector."

"It bloody well is when there's a murder. Three months ago you killed a teenage girl. That's why your employees cursed you, isn't it?"

Pendleton started to protest, but instead waved his hand in gesture of concession. "Actually, it's much more complicated than that. Those men had a vendetta against us long before that girl's death. And for the record, it was Lt. Hysmith who killed her, not me."

"I don't give a damn about Hysmith, you sick son of a bitch. Tell me about these men." Tom held up the photo of two dozen gentlemen in top hats.

Pendleton's eyes widened. "Inspector, you have no business snooping in my—"

"Why didn't you fucking tell me you knew Gustave Meraux?"

"You wouldn't understand—"

Tom cocked his pistol. "Answer me!"

"Bloody well then!" Pendleton folded his arms. "If you must know...we are all members of a secret fraternity called the Hell Fire Club."

197

The Hell Fire Club. Tom swallowed hard when he heard the name.

As a teenager apprenticing with his father in London, Tom had learned about a secret society of elite aristocrats who gathered for drinking, orgies with prostitutes, and all sorts of debauchery. The Hell Fire Club had been founded around 1750 in England by a rebellious man named Sir Francis Dashwood. He was a womanizing rake and loved to throw lewd parties with other wealthy men. The club's meeting place was a Cistercian monastery called Medmenham Abbey, near Marlow. Above the door was the phrase, "Do as thou wilt." Secret rituals were performed in caves beneath West Wycombe Hill. According to rumors, naked women were used to represent nuns in Black Masses.

Tom said, "The Hell Fire Club was rumored to have disbanded in the late 1700s."

"The club only went underground," Pendleton explained. "It moved from England and was secretly established in Montréal."

"And all of your officers are members," Tom said.

Pendleton nodded. "As well as other business owners."

"And the Masquerade parties?" Father Xavier asked. "Is that how you engage with the Devil?"

"We aren't Devil worshippers," Pendleton said. "The club's meetings are nothing more than high society having a jolly good time. We indulge in wine, women, and pagan rituals to honor the Druids." He looked at his altar statues. "We worship Bacchus and Venus. It was Gustave who took up an interest in conjuring demons."

Tom looked at the group portrait—Gustave standing on the front row, wearing a suit and top hat, a sinister smile. "How could you associate with such a monster?"

Pendleton said, "Inspector, you only knew Gustave as a mass murderer, but before he went insane, he was a charismatic libertine and well-liked among his peers."

"Then what made him become the Cannery Cannibal?" Tom asked.

Pendleton exhaled. "It all started ten years back, when Lt. Hysmith, Walter, Percy, and myself did some fur trading with the Iroquois Indians. They are well known for cannibalizing their enemies. The Iroquois taught us that human flesh contains a spiritual life force that can be absorbed when eaten. It would give us more power and sexual potency, they promised."

"And you ate human meat?" Tom asked.

"We were adventure seekers, willing to try anything once. The Iroquois were right, our sexual appetites increased, as did our feeling invincible. After we returned to Montréal, I met Gustave. He told me about a club that engaged parties where any desire can be fulfilled. The four of us joined. We told our new brothers about our eating human meat with the Iroquois. Gustave became fascinated with the idea and began bringing soup tins to the parties. He called the marinated human meat *viande de pourvoir*. It was considered a delicacy, like caviar and tartar, only the power felt from eating human meat was highly addictive. We consumed it voraciously and demanded more."

"You fucking cannibal!" Tom gripped the lapels of Pendleton's fur coat. "You helped Gustave kill all those women!"

"My club had nothing to do with those murders!"

"Bollocks, he was supplying you human meat!" Tom shoved the barrel into his neck.

Father Xavier gripped his shoulder. "Don't, Tom, you'll only strengthen the demon inside you. It feeds off your anger."

Tom released Pendleton and backed away.

The chief factor straightened his jacket. "Gustave told us he was getting the meat from the Iroquois. It was only after his arrest that we learned he was abducting prostitutes and canning their meat at his cannery."

Tom squeezed the handle of his pistol until his knuckles ached. It took all his restraint not to bludgeon Pendleton's ghoulish face. He had known Gustave was the Cannery Cannibal and failed to report this to the police. If Avery had, Beth would still be alive today. He glared at Pendleton. "You son of a bitch, you have been lying to me this whole time."

"Be sensible, Tom." The chief factor raised his palms. "I was only protecting my interests."

Father Xavier said, "It was Gustave who summoned the legion to attack your forts, wasn't it?"

Pendleton nodded.

"Why is he coming after you?" Tom asked.

"Three years ago Gustave and I became bitter rivals. He tried to overthrow my leadership and turn our club into a Satanic cult. In one of our rituals, he used that skull. After that, Gustave told everyone to call him the Dark Messiah. My brothers and I attempted to have Gustave murdered. But he escaped and went underground. A few months later you arrested him.

"Shortly after, I received a letter threatening that Legion would hunt down every member of the Hell Fire Club."

Tom looked at the demon skull on the altar. "How did that skull end up here?"

"Gustave wasn't working alone. He had formed a cult. They've been sabotaging the forts."

198

Upstairs, an axe blade split the front door of Noble House. An arm reached through the hole and lifted the bar across the door. Cloaked in his new human skin, Gustave entered Noble House with the frosty wind at his back. He ascended the stairs. His blood-covered hand stained the banister with red mucus. His axe blade tapped the stairs with each passing step.

At the fourth floor, the Pendleton home smelled of death and echoed with the sounds of chittering. In the dining hall, rats and ravens were feasting on the bloated corpse of Walter Thain. His stomach erupted with gases. In the kitchen, the same frenzy was happening to the remains of the butler. While there was still plenty of flesh on the dead men's bones, Gustave was not hungry for meat. His lusts were fevered more by the floral scent of perfume that wafted from down the hall. Feeling fire in his loins, he entered the study. Inside Avery Pendleton's secret room, a dozen masks hung on the wall. Gustave pulled down an Iroquois warrior's mask. He waved a hand over it, changing the pattern to match the dreams of his beloved.

199

In the watchtower, Private Wickliff jerked at the sounds of howls coming from the forest. He opened one of the portals. Snow was falling heavily now, the wind blasting frosty air into his lungs. The white fog pressed against the fort.

Where are the others? Wickliff wondered. He hadn't seen or heard from his lieutenant since the birds attacked. Nor had he heard so much as a peep from Private Bowen in the corner tower. He called out to his mate, but the wind was so loud it snatched his words.

Wickliff opened the side door and crossed the landing that stretched between the watchtowers. The portals at the corner shack were pitch dark.

"Bowen, are you in there?" Wickliff peered into the portal. He heard the sound of chittering and chewing in the darkness. A rodent leaped onto the windowsill. A bloated thing with diseased white skin and a ropy tail. The rabid rat hissed and foamed at the mouth, baring bloodstained teeth.

A cry of pain issued from beyond the dark portal. A soldier's arm covered in more hairless rats reached out. Bowen's half-eaten skull jutted out the window. "Wicklifffffff!"

"Oh, shit!" Wickliff turned, slipping, and raced back toward the center watchtower. A column of white-eyed rats scurried after him.

200

Willow woke up from her slumber. Her room was pitch dark. "Avery?" she called out. "What's happening?"

Her last memory was entering Hospital House and seeing the man from her dreams offer her a snort of cocaine. After that, nothing.

She tried to rise but her arms and legs were tied to the bedposts. "Avery!"

Down the hall the floorboards creaked. Metal scraped along the wall. A flame suddenly flared up in the darkness and lit an oil lamp on a table near the door.

Willow looked past the foot of the bed. From the gloom of the hallway formed the shape of a man wearing a tribal mask—white with red circles around the eyes and mouth. "Hello, Little Lamb."

Willow's heart fluttered. Her dream lover had returned.

She gasped, "It was you all along."

"Yes, my love." The man entered her boudoir and leaned an axe against the wall. "I have wanted you since the day we met."

Heart beating wildly, Willow closed her eyes. The man from her dreams gripped her shoulders. She moaned. He tore open her nightgown. She arched her back. Then, what felt like sharp blades carved into her bare bosom.

Willow cried out. In her dreams there had never been pain. She opened her eyes.

Things squirmed behind the man's mask. His eyes were chasms of infinite blackness. "We will rule our legion together, you and I."

"Noooooooo!" Willow ripped off his mask and screamed at the sight of his face.

201

At the front of the fort, Wickliff fled from the rabid rats. His boots slid along ice that covered the stockade's landing. He gripped the spike-tipped wall to keep from falling. A rodent leaped onto his leg and bit his calf.

Wickliff screamed and swatted the critter off. Two more rats ran up his legs. He hurried along the landing. The blizzard howled. Snow blurred his vision. Just outside the fort he saw shapes moving within the fog. Creatures clawed at the front gate. A giant with a long, white arm reached a skeletal hand over the fence. Talons swooped, ripping Wickliff's coat. He dashed back into his watchtower and shut the door.

"Oh, Jesus!" He fought back rats trying to climb in through the open portal. He closed the panel, crushing several rodents.

Heart hammering, Wickliff slid down on his rump, praying.

The shrieks outside were maddening. Down below sounded the clack of a bar being lifted and the gate's double doors swinging open. What followed was the thundering footfalls of a stampede, as if a herd of cattle had been let into the fort. Directly below Wickliff, someone climbed up the ladder and knocked on the trapdoor.

"Bugger off!" Wickliff screamed, aiming his rifle at the floor.

"It's Lt. Hysmith. Open up!"

"Lieutenant?" Wickliff felt confused. Inside the fort, beasts were howling.

The hammering rattled the floorboards. "Open the goddamned door, soldier!"

Wickliff removed the bar. The trapdoor flew open, knocking him back. Dozens of squealing rats flooded the tower. Wickliff backed to a corner, stomping and kicking. The horde crawled up his legs and chest, a dozen greedy mouths biting into him.

"*Hungrryyy...*" A beastly form dressed in a red soldier's uniform climbed into the tower.

Paralyzed with fright, Wickliff watched helplessly as Lt. Hysmith burrowed his monstrous face amidst the feeding rats.

Part Twenty

Legion

For Jesus said unto him, "Come out of the man, thou unclean spirit."
And Jesus asked him, "What is thy name?"
And he answered, saying, "My name is Legion: for we are many."

Mark 5:8-5:9

202

The night echoed with the howls of the damned. Tom turned around and faced the cellar's front wall. Outside approached a sound like a cavalry charging in on horses. "What the hell is that?"

Father Xavier said, "The legion is inside the fort."

Creatures shrieked and scratched the outside walls.

"Christ!" Pendleton bolted out of the room.

"Quick, Father, upstairs!" Tom grabbed one of the torches and hurried back through the maze of pelts and up the staircase to the second floor. The ballroom was pitch black, except for a fire burning in the hearth. Tom and Father Xavier ran into the foyer, where frosty air was blowing through the open front door. A wall of fog pressed against the doorway. Beyond howled the windigos.

Tom shut the door, brought down the bar to barricade it. Snow blew in through a wide crack in the center of the door.

"That will never hold," Tom said.

Father Xavier opened his black bag and handed Tom a canteen. "Splash the door."

Tom saturated the door with holy water.

With a stick of chalk, Father Xavier drew a white line on the floor at the threshold. "*Ad Maiorem De Gloriam!*"

Beasts roared just beyond the smoke. Claws scraped the outside walls.

Tom backed away, aiming his pistol.

Father Xavier held up his cross-dagger at the entrance and chanted in Latin.

203

As the Ojibwa braves pulled their canoe onto shore, Anika ran up the snowy hill.

"Wait for us!" Swiftbear yelled.

She stopped, her heart beating wildly. She tried to locate Fort Pendleton in the whirling sleet and fog. Only one corner tower was visible. Manitou shrieks echoed from the fort.

The eight warriors, clad in hooded fur parkas, gripped their spears and gathered around Anika. She glanced at Swiftbear. His nod filled her with courage she desperately needed.

"Stay close to me." Swiftbear pointed with his spear and hollered. The warriors charged up the hill, their battle cries clashing against the storm winds.

204

Avery hurried up the four flights of stairs. He stopped at the landing outside his home, fell against the rail, coughing up spittle of blood. His joints popped, and he screamed in agony as his forearms and hands stretched. His elongated finger bones broke free from the skin, the tips shaping into claws.

He cried out in pain. The hunger returned, more ravenous than before, the demon within him craving blood and meat. Avery ran into his home. Found Walter Thain's skeleton crawling with rats. Ravens cawed at one another over the flesh inside the ribcage.

Meat! Meat! Meat! chanted the preternatural thing taking over Avery's mind. It wanted to rip into what was left of Thain's innards and suck the marrow from his bones.

No! Avery bit into his own hand, fighting back with all his will. He went into his study. The snowstorm blew the balcony doors open. He stepped outside and looked over the railing. Moonlight reflected off a swirling fogbank that enshrouded the fort. He could barely see the rooftops of the cabins. A horde of skeletal beasts moved within the smoke. They clawed at the walls of Noble House, their elongated arms shattering second-story windows. Windigos that had once been his employees howled up at their boss.

We have come for you, spoke Gustave's voice inside Avery's head. *Jump! Offer us your flesh.*

"No..." His mind spun with vertigo. He gripped the railing.

Remember your promise to me, Avery?

He had a vision of himself ten years ago. A man who had lost a fortune in the fur trade. Standing on the Victoria Bridge overlooking the St. Lawrence River. Ready to jump. Until, out of thin air, Gustave Meraux approached and offered Avery Pendleton a dream life. Wealth, power, women. Every lust and insatiable need fulfilled. All Avery had to do was join the Hell Fire Club and do business with a group of gentlemen who had sold their souls to the Devil.

Your soul belongs to me. Along with Willow's.

"No, you can't have us!" He went back into his study. Shut the balcony doors. He would never surrender, nor would he allow that Satanic libertine to have his wife.

"Avery?" Willow called out from down the hall. "Help me!"

"Coming, darling!" He found his pistol in the study. Checked the chambers. Two bullets.

You are a failure like me, son, whispered his father's voice.

Avery stared up at the gray family portrait of his parents. His father pressing his hands down on young Avery's shoulders. The boy frowning as he gripped a red violin. When he was thirteen, Avery found his father and mother lying dead in their bed, dressed in their fanciest ballroom attire. The side of his mother's head was blown out. The back of his father's head was a gaping hole. Blood stained the headboard and pillows. A marriage immortalized by death. Avery always knew he would end up a failure like his father. Suicide was the Pendleton legacy.

You can't escape from the demon inside you, crooned Gustave's voice.

As Avery raced down the hallway, he fell forward, loping with one knuckle against the floor, the other hand gripping the pistol.

You belong to us now.

"No!" Avery entered his wife's bedroom. "Willow!"

He could smell her in the darkness—perfume, feminine musk, and blood pumping through her fast-beating heart. He struck a match and lit an oil lamp. Willow was lying on her bed, wearing a red ball gown and white porcelain mask. The same masquerade costume as the night he had met her.

Avery's clawed-tipped hand stroked her hair. Of all his lovers, Willow had been the most beautiful. His precious doll. And with the kiss from two bullets they would spend an eternity together. He removed her mask and jumped back, releasing a scream that echoed throughout the Pendleton home.

205

Anika and her warriors reached Fort Pendleton. The front gate's double doors stood wide open. The snowy ground had been trampled, leaving behind dozens of footprints. She crouched, observing several that were larger than a bear's. The fog was so thick, she could barely make out the buildings.

Swiftbear made hand signals. One by one the warriors crept through the gate.

Anika held her breath as she walked close behind her uncle.

Up ahead, animal shapes moved through the mist, some hunched over, others walking giants. Two of the braves charged into the whirlwind and were yanked off the ground, their screams cut short.

"Keep to the fence!" Swiftbear shouted.

The warriors fought against windigos that were half human, half animal. A spindly child ran toward them on all fours, snarling. Anika gasped as her uncle impaled it.

A guttural voice called from above, "Anikaaaa!"

A rattleboned creature in a red uniform leaped down from the watchtower. Lt. Hysmith growled, his sharp teeth stained with blood.

Anika ran down the fence. He lumbered toward her on stilted legs. "Come back here, you little whore!" His elongated arms swooped, talons slicing the air just above her head.

She backed into a corner. Hysmith swatted at her spear, taunting her. His eyes were the color of maggots. His face split into a ripsaw grimace that stretched from ear to ear. He opened his arms out wide. "How about one last shag, for old time's sake, ey little whore?"

Anika burned with rage for all the nights Hysmith had raped her down in the cellar. She howled like a she-wolf, yanked a knife off her belt, and threw it into the lieutenant's throat. He gripped the handle, choking on his own blood.

She charged, spearing the Hysmith windigo in the chest. It released a guttural sound as she shoved it against the fence, driving the point deeper. The beast flopped, its flesh sizzling from the spear that had been blessed by the Mediwiwin.

Thinking of all the native women who had suffered like her, Anika pulled out a tomahawk and chopped off Hysmith's head. The lieutenant's body collapsed like a fallen scarecrow.

Anika, shaking with adrenaline, pulled her spear out of its chest, her other fist gripped tight around the bloody tomahawk.

Swiftbear and four braves emerged from the fog. Her uncle looked down at her kill and then nodded for Anika to follow. Thinking of Tom, she ran with the warriors along the stockade wall, wary of the animal shapes moving inside the snowstorm.

206

At Noble House, Avery backed away from Willow's bed. "Jesus Christ!"

Her glistening red face had no skin. Her mouth, no lips. The teeth opened in a skeletal smile. Bulging eyeballs turned toward Avery. "I've been waiting for this night."

"No..." Avery dropped the oil lamp on the bed. The sheets caught fire, lighting up the room.

Willow rose off the bed, reaching for him. "Let us take you to where the children play forever." Blood gurgled in her throat.

"Get back!" Avery aimed his pistol, shooting her in the chest.

She stumbled backward, but somehow remained standing. She cocked her head. "Did you really think my lover would let you kill me, darling?"

Avery backed away, aiming at her head. His shot was knocked wild by a sudden blow to his arm. A fiery pain erupted as his gun hand snapped loose and flew across the room. Blood spurted from his severed wrist. Avery wailed, turning around.

Gustave Meraux grinned as he gripped an axe. "Hello, old friend." His rail-thin body was covered in rats.

"No..." Avery backed away, holding his bleeding wrist against his chest.

"It's time to pay the piper." Gustave swung the axe. The blade snapped Avery's knee. He collapsed against his wife's beauty table. Another chop severed both his legs.

Avery screamed in agony.

Gustave cackled as his body fell away into a chittering horde of rats. They fed upon Avery's bleeding stumps, crawled up his body. Avery's back arched violently, his spine popping, as his ribcage stretched. The corners of his mouth tore open, and he felt teeth cutting through his gums.

The spreading flames caught the wall on fire. Avery clung to consciousness, his eyelids drooping.

"Don't drift off now, darling." Willow's silhouette approached. The blaze highlighted her hair, the red sinews of her cheek and neck. She picked up a rat, petting it. "You need to eat. You'll need your strength where we're going." Her exposed teeth grinned as she shoved the rat into Avery's mouth and fed the hungry demon within.

207

Downstairs, rabid beasts snarled at every boarded window. White hands shattered the glass. Tom fired his pistol as bony fingers jutted between the clapboards and tore at the crack in the front door.

Father Xavier stood at the threshold, chanting, "We exorcise you, each unclean spirit, each power of Satan, each Legion!" He doused the clawing hands with holy water. The flesh smoked, burning the skin like acid. "Be uprooted and put to flight from the Church of God!"

The hands retreated from every window. The blizzard raged around Noble House, rattling the clapboards. Gusts of freezing wind and snow blew in through the broken door and windows.

Tom leaned against a wall, catching his breath. "Can you hold them back?"

"For the moment." Father Xavier's face looked haggard. "We have to seal off every window on this floor." The exorcist went down the wall of the fur-trading room, chalking lines on the floor.

Tom coughed, shivering. The cold thing inside his torso shot out frosty tentacles through his arms and legs. His bones felt as if they were turning to ice. He drank from his canteen, but only a few drops fell onto his tongue. "Damn it!" He hurled the canister. His body shook with a primal hunger. He gazed at Father Xavier. The exorcist had his eyes closed as he stood at a window, whispering a prayer. His flesh began to smell like honey-cured ham, like marinated venison.

Eat the priest! commanded Gustave's voice inside Tom's head.

"No, I can't!" He growled and ran into the ballroom. Most of the wide-open chamber was pitch dark. The only light came from a fire burning in the hearth. He went to it, relishing the heat against his shivering body.

He rolled back his sleeves. Blue veins sprouted across his pale skin. The bones became more prominent.

"God, get this thing out of me!" Tom pulled out the cross-dagger from his belt. The metal felt hot in his hands. He dropped the cross. It hurt his eyes to look at the Christian symbol. He kicked it into the darkness.

Tom leaned against the mantle. He searched inside for something to cling to. Something to ground him in his body. He thought of Anika. The savage woman who had repelled him. The medicine woman who made crow stew and read Jane Austen novels. The whittler of flutes and animal totems. He pictured her wildcat green eyes. Her rare but precious smile. Anika Moonblood was the strongest, most defiant woman he had ever met. Her native ways clashed with his own, and yet somehow she penetrated all of Tom's defenses. Thinking of her now gave him a reason to live. And then he remembered something she had given him. He reached into his breast pocket, pulling out a flat, white stone carved into a buffalo. His totem.

It is your guardian, Anika had said. *You can call on its medicine for strength.*

He pressed the stone to his chest and connected to the half of him that was Ojibwa. "I call in the spirit of White Buffalo."

His mind flashed with a vision of a massive, white bison charging through the trees. His body filled with strength.

The beast within recoiled.

208

Anika sprinted between the cabins. Behind her ran the others, fleeing from an eight-foot-tall windigo. It looked like a skeletal bear. A paw with long talons lashed out from the mist, grabbing one of the scouts. He wailed as the beast pinned him to the ground and ripped open his belly. A pack of smaller carrion eaters joined in the feast.

Anika continued running between the houses, leading the hunting party into Tom's cabin. She bent over, catching her breath. Only Swiftbear, herself, and two young braves were left. They looked scared after losing their brothers and cousins. Anika felt sadness that four men had lost their lives for her mission. She touched her necklace, praying for the Mediwiwin to protect the others.

Outside came screeching. Everyone ducked in the shadows as more jackal-faced creatures ran past the windows. When they were gone, Anika searched the bedrooms, but Tom wasn't here.

Her uncle met her eyes, and she looked away, trying to hide her sorrow.

Swiftbear whispered, "He must already be a *wiitigo*."

"No." She shook her head. "I can feel him. He's alive."

He touched her arm. "I'm sorry, but there are too many for us to fight. We must retreat."

"Go if you must." Anika gripped her spear and tomahawk. "I'm staying."

Swiftbear frowned. "This is no time to be stubborn."

A brave named Squawking Crow pointed out a window. "A fire! A fire!"

Anika peered outside. At Noble House, part of the roof was on fire. Her heart lunged with fear and hope.

209

In the ballroom, Tom picked up the cross-dagger. The silver metal was no longer hot. Nor did the Christian symbol offend him. He slipped the blade under into his belt.

The entity inside him had pulled back its frosty tentacles and burrowed deep within his belly. He ached as if he'd swallowed a snowball. What he'd give right now for a hot cup of tea.

He realized he had abandoned Father Xavier, leaving him in the fur trading room. As Tom went to check on him, the ballroom echoed with squeaks and cawing. At the staircase, a waterfall of rats poured down the stairs. The horde turned the corner and went down the stairwell that led to the cellar. Before Tom could make sense of what he was seeing, a swarm of black birds flew down from the upper floor and followed the rats.

Tom's skin sprouted gooseflesh. *What the...?* He ran to the staircase and peered down. The descent to the cellar was a black chasm. He could hear chittering and scratching and the rustling of feathers.

He had no idea how they got in. He became more concerned by what drove them down there. Tom sniffed, catching a whiff of smoke from upstairs. Then he heard the sound of crackling. "Christ, a fire!" He raced up the stairs.

210

In the fur trading room, Father Xavier sealed off every window with a chalked line and a prayer. He could hear the demons circling Noble House. They scratched the boarded windows, then pulled back with cries of agony. Father Xavier released his breath. The holy shields seemed to keep the evil out. But for how long?

He sensed an evil spirit out there in the blizzard. A higher intelligence far superior to the bloodthirsty cannibals. The legion's ruler probed his mind, searching for his weakness. With Mirabelle's soul set free, the dark forces no longer had a hold on Father Xavier. "My mind is a sanctuary of God, demon, I cast you out!"

The evil spirit backed off.

Father Xavier went into to the ballroom and searched the surrounding darkness. "Tom!" He had run off in a fit of rage. *His demon was taking over and I neglected him.* Father Xavier became burdened by guilt and sadness. He didn't expect Tom to return human.

It's just me now, alone against Satan's legion.

Father Xavier couldn't fathom how he could possibly survive. An entire fort village had perished. His own mentor, Father Jacques Baptiste, had died trying to fight this legion. Father Xavier felt the enemies of fear and doubt begin to wear away his faith. He crossed the ballroom to the glow of the fireplace. On a small table sat his holy book, *The Roman Ritual of Exorcism*, along with an arsenal of cross-daggers. Engraved at the center of each was the fiery sun. The insignia of the Jesuits.

I will not go out without a fight.

The exorcist chalked a half-circle along the floor around the fireplace. "I bless this space as a sanctuary of God." He then picked up a silver cross. "I call upon the Immaculate Virgin, Mary, Mother of God, the Apostles, Peter and Paul, and all the saints." With each name he kissed a cross and gesticulated. He then called forth his patron saint, the Jesuit soldier. "I invoke the bravery of his holiness, St. Ignatius Loyola." Father Xavier picked up the last holy dagger. "Fill me with the divine warrior spirit of Archangel Michael. Give me the strength—"

"Your saints and angels can't save you now," a voice echoed off the wood floor.

Father Xavier spun around, holding out the cross-dagger. "Who's there?"

Brother Andre stepped to the edge of the fire glow. "Hello, Mentor."

211

At the fourth floor, Tom ran through the Pendleton home. Smoke filled the parlor. The paint on Lady Pendleton's portrait melted and dripped. Tom coughed and hunched over, covering his mouth. "Willow!"

"Help me!" she cried from down the hall.

He ran to her bedroom. At her doorway, a wall of heat knocked him back.

A fiery blaze consumed the bed, walls, and ceiling. The floor was covered in blood and the remains of a skeleton with severed bones. Avery Pendleton's misshapen head was propped against his lap.

Willow sat at her beauty table, brushing her hair and humming. She wore a red ball gown. The cracked mirror reflected a crimson face. Lidless eyes. "I've been waiting for you, lover." She turned, facing Tom. Her facial bones shifted into a demon.

Tom backed away, stumbled down the hall.

Willow appeared at the threshold, silhouetted by a wall of fire. "This time you're all mine."

212

Down in the ballroom, Brother Andre remained in the gloom that bordered the chalked line. He was wearing a priest's cassock and white collar. "Surprised to see me?"

Father Xavier gasped. "How on earth...?"

Andre just smiled, his radiant blue eyes gleaming with arrogance. There was not a bird scratch on his face.

Father Xavier felt the sting of betrayal. "I trusted you."

"Sorry to disappoint you, Father, but I've found a new mentor to follow."

"Whatever demon is influencing you, don't give in. Remember your vows, Andre. You took an oath to be a soldier of the Society of Jesus Christ."

The young missionary laughed. "Frankly, Father, I find Catholic priesthood to be too frustrating. I mean, the Church takes away our primal desires? Castrates us? And then expects us to live in a world of lustful women without giving in to temptation? I just don't understand the purpose." He ran a hand down his black robe. "I've found a new religion to follow. And on this path I don't have to vow to forego sex."

"I knew your spirit was too weak," said Father Xavier. "Willow's succubus seduced you, didn't she?"

"For two years I flogged my thighs to hold back my desire for her. I've endured enough pain on behalf of the Church." Andre smirked. "Now that Pendleton is gone, Willow and I will spend an eternity together."

"You ignorant fool," Father Xavier spat. "You have been tricked by Satan. Your eternity in hell will be spent suffering for your sins."

"We disagree." The young Jesuit suddenly spoke in dual voices, "Under Lucifer's rule, hell shall finally come to earth, and all mankind will know true ecstasy!"

Father Xavier said, "Lucifer holds no power in the kingdom ruled by our Lord and Savior Jesus Christ!"

"I admire your passion, priest." Andre's cheeks grew thinner as he walked the edge of the chalked border. "We are a lot alike, you and I. We were both sent here to carry out missions to serve our gods."

"And what is your mission, demon?"

Andre twirled his bony hand. "To make sure every man finds the pleasure he seeks. Such as your cravings for caviar and crackers, and your father's needs to have affairs with teenage girls."

Father Xavier felt as if he'd taken a blow to the chest. He raised his cross with a shaking hand. "What is thy name, demon?"

Andre's eyes went solid black. "I am the one you've been seeking your whole pathetic life, eunuch." His face shape-shifted into Gustave Meraux.

213

Upstairs, Tom raced through the smoke that filled the Pendleton home. Behind him ran Willow. Her dress and hair were on fire. She ripped off the tatters. Pulled out her hair. She slapped at her scorched flesh, unleashing screams like a coven of burning witches.

Tom dashed through a maze of corridors and hid behind the dining room table. His lungs burned. He crouched down low, sucking in air. On the floor lay Walter Thain's bones, picked clean. Tom ignored this fact and jammed fresh bullets into his revolver. He spun the wheel and cocked the hammer.

The flame-covered succubus shrieked as it ran past the dining room. Her bare feet thumped along the floorboards down the hall. Tom considered chasing the demon, but the haze was too thick. His biggest concern was finding his way back to the stairs. Fire was spreading into the parlor. Orange tongues licked the ceiling over the dining room table. A heavy beam came crashing down.

Tom rushed out into the hall. Heard thumping along the floorboards. He turned as the succubus pounced, knocking him to the floor. His pistol skidded away.

Willow straddled him. Tom grabbed her wrists. She was bald and naked, her black and pink skin clinging to her frail bones in patches. She smelled like boiled tallow and charred meat.

The cannibal within Tom hungered to tear his teeth into her half-cooked breasts.

Willow gripped his jaw. "You want to eat me, don't you, lover!"

"No!"

"*Ravage me!*" She clamped her thighs tight around his waist.

"No, damn it!" He fought to push her off, his fingers sliding down greasy skin.

She roared inches from his face. "Then I will eat you!" Her mouth ripped open. A dozen shark's teeth sprouted from her dripping gums. She cackled like a madwoman.

Tom reached for his belt, gripped the cross-dagger, and drove the blade into the back of her skull. Willow arched her neck, wailing at the ceiling. Her eyes caught fire. Her face turned black with orange cracks. And then the demon's head burst into an explosion of charcoal. She slumped across his body. Tom rolled her off.

He picked up the holy dagger. His pistol with the Hatcher family crest was lost somewhere in the fire and thickening smoke. Coughing, he made his way to the stairs.

Orange-blue flames snaked across the floor, torching the railing. Tom hurried down the winding staircase with an even greater sense of doom. Somehow, he and Father Xavier had to get the hell out of Noble House.

214

Gustave's cassock transformed into an upper-class business suit as he casually walked the arc of the chalked line. Flames from the fireplace rippled in his jet black eyes. "Xavier, did you ever wonder how your father made his fortune?"

"You leave my father out of this!"

"He was never there for you, was he? Always traipsing off with his young mistresses. Little sluts not much older than your sister."

Father Xavier remained paralyzed as his childhood flashed before his eyes...living in a giant mansion...his father always away on business trips...Xavier's mother drinking heavily...his sister, Mirabelle, becoming possessed by a demon and slashing her wrists in the tub.

Father Xavier's throat constricted as he remembered the thing that had clawed at his bedroom door. *Let me take you to where the children play forever.* "It was you..."

"Yes, I took your precious Mirabelle. I would have taken you, as well, had you not been so damned righteous."

Father Xavier felt his rage building. "Why...why did you take her?"

"Your father failed to fulfill his agreement with me." Gustave grimaced, showing sharp teeth. "And the sins of the fathers always fall upon the children."

"Father!" Tom ran into the ballroom. "Upstairs there's a...!" He froze.

Gustave grinned. "Welcome to the party, Tom."

215

Tom nearly choked on his own breath. The entity in his belly shot out cold spikes at the sight of the Cannery Cannibal. Gustave Meraux and Father Xavier stood opposite one another, the crackling fire in the hearth at the priest's back, the shimmering light reflecting off Gustave's high-boned cheeks. His black and silver hair was slicked back. His eyes gleamed like polished black stones. "At last we meet again."

Tom's hunger returned. So did his rage. He tried to speak, but his words came out in a harsh growl.

Gustave smiled, blinking his eyelashes. "I wouldn't be happy to see me either."

Tom walked toward him, pumping his fists.

Father Xavier held out a palm. "Stop, Tom. Don't come any closer."

"I'm going to strangle this fucking cannibal."

"He's feeding off your anger," Father Xavier said. "Keep your thoughts on God."

Tom halted, his entire body shaking.

Gustave folded his arms. "I'm afraid you can't save this one, priest. He and I have a contract to settle."

Tom said, "What the hell are you talking about?"

"Remember the human flesh you ate?"

Tom recalled the woman's cadaver on the slab at the morgue. Stealing small samples of flesh and cooking them at home. The rich, juicy flavor. The sudden surge of power in his body.

"I had to understand what drove a monster like you to cannibalize women."

"And you took pleasure from it." Gustave twirled his hand as he spoke, his long-boned fingers making gestures. "You devoured every piece of her meat, didn't you? Then you felt the rush and craved more. In essence, you became a cannibal like me."

"No, I only ate those few bites. You murdered over a dozen women."

"One bite of human flesh is all it takes to seal a contract with me." The cannibal grinned, exposing a mouth full of razor-sharp teeth. "The dark lord whom I serve is waiting for you right outside. It owns your soul, Tom, and I'm here to claim it."

216

At the first light of dawn, Anika and her warriors ran through the fog toward Noble House. A fire consumed the entire roof and top floor. The dormer windows exploded with gusts of flame. Black smoke drifted over the fort.

Anika and Swiftbear ran side by side, the two braves right behind them. As they neared the log mansion, the mist thickened. A fierce wind knocked Anika sideways, and she fell to one knee. Snow blinded her eyes.

Beasts howled from every direction. The warriors hollered, their voices trailing off. Anika stood, bracing herself against the storm. She wiped sleet out of her eyes. And found herself alone. "Swiftbear!"

Amidst the fog echoed a maddening clash of growls and battle cries. A man's wailing voice was cut short.

Anika raced toward Noble House, using the burning sky as her guidepost. A stench of carrion pummeled her senses. She froze like a rabbit wary of a predator. As the haze drifted, she saw a monstrous shape. She made out the skeletal back of a giant, man-shaped beast with broad shoulders. It was sitting cross-legged at the bottom of the steps to Noble House, its bony arms resting on its legs. Elk antlers jutted from the sides of its enormous head.

Anika crouched behind the well, quivering. Sitting before her was the creature she'd seen painted on petraglyphs. The Ancient One. The first winter manitou. Her heart nearly stopped when the windigo turned its head, facing her.

217

The raging thing inside Tom expanded ice-cold hatred up into his chest. His forearms and finger bones stretched. He twisted his head, snarling.

"That's it," Gustave said. "Give in to the beast."

"Fight it, Tom!" Father Xavier yelled. "Keep praying for salvation."

Tom's mouth salivated. His stomach caved inward. He circled Gustave and Father Xavier like a predator sizing up its prey.

"Eat the priest," chided Gustave. "Eat the lamb's sweet meat!"

Father Xavier's flesh suddenly smelled like juice-dripping lamb. His blood, like the sweet aroma of port wine. His bone marrow, like honey.

The priest opened his exoricsim book and waved his cross. "God the Father commands you! God the son commands you! Christ orders you, he who is the eternal word of God, become man!"

Tom growled.

"You're becoming one of us now," said Gustave.

Tom squeezed his fists. "No, I won't give in!"

At the staircase, the railing crashed down as the fire from upstairs reached the landing. Smoke and serpents of flame drifted across the ceiling.

Gustave held out his arms. "We will be brothers in hell, you and I."

Father Xavier shouted, "Fear take flight, when the holy and terrible name of Jesus is invoked by us!"

Gustave reeled and grabbed his ears. "Shut up, eunuch!"

Tom's fury unleashed. He loped like a wolf and charged his prey.

218

Outside, the horned beast's eyes penetrated Anika. Its shredded lips pulled back in a wide grin, exposing racks of icicle fangs. She felt petrified as a claw as long as a knife blade pointed in her direction.

A dozen windigo cries erupted in the storm. Stick-like bodies charged through the fog. Anika turned, gripping her spear and tomahawk. A decrepit old man with pale white eyes loped toward her. She impaled his brittle chest and shoved him into the well. The spear fell with him.

A hairless wolf leaped for her throat. Anika swung her tomahawk, shattering its muzzle. The next attacker was a giant with stilt-like legs that stretched up into the swirling black smoke. She sprinted across the courtyard through the fog. A pack of windigos ran behind her, roaring.

She reached a corner wall. Climbed up the ladder. A snarling child windigo scurried up after her, grabbed her ankle. She kicked its face. It fell down upon a horde of others. She hurried up the ladder, her eyes on the watchtower. She climbed inside the hole in the floor. More beasts were leaping onto the ladder, ascending at an incredible speed.

Anika shut the trapdoor and slid across the metal bar. More windigos ran along the landings on either side of the guardhouse. She closed all the portals, latched the door. Claws scratched at the floorboards and walls. Fists pounded on the roof.

She reached into her medicine bag and pulled out a handful of white shells. Each was carved with a snow owl. She dropped them across the floor. As the windigos wailed all around the watchtower, Anika squeezed a shell in her hand and prayed to Grandmother Spotted Owl.

219

Tom tackled Gustave, knocking him to the floor. The beast within raged as Tom pounded the cannibal's face. Drove his thumbs into his eyes, pushing them back into his skull, squishing them. Gustave screamed. A force knocked Tom back. He flew ten feet and skidded across the floor.

Gustave leaped to his feet. Blood hemorrhaged from his eye sockets. "Surrender yourself to me, Tom."

"Never." He stood, gripping his bruised ribs.

"Let your demon take over."

Tom's skeleton felt as if it were turning to ice. His spine lengthened. "No!" Tom pulled the cross-dagger from his belt. It burned his hand, but he didn't let go. The demon caged within Tom's bones released a wail of terror.

Gustave stepped forward, blindly. "What are you doing?" His face was streaked with blood, his eye sockets hollow red pits.

Tom squared up to the Dark Shepherd. The beast who had murdered his wife and unborn child. "I am not going with you."

"Then we will take you by force." The madman cackled. The ballroom echoed with a chorus of squeaks and cawing. Rats crawled up from the cellar. A swarm of black birds flew into the ballroom. Satan's scavengers formed into a black twister of fur and feathers. They roared together as one enormous beast, standing as high as the ceiling.

A force knocked Tom back.

Father Xavier charged out of his sacred space, waving his cross. "God of heaven! God of Earth! God of Angels! Creator of all invisible beings!" The exorcist stepped between Tom and the oncoming swarm. "From the ambushes of evil spirit, free us, O Lord!"

The black spiral of claws and talons exploded outward, circling Father Xavier, Tom, and Gustave like a cyclone. Orange-blue flames spread across the ceiling, rolling in waves of scorching hot air.

Trapped within the whirling black funnel, Tom stood back to back with Father Xavier. The priest kept praying, "Our Father, Who art in heaven..."

Rats and ravens hopped off the spinning wall, clinging to Gustave's rail-thin body, gathering around his head until the only thing visible was his red-streaked face. He spoke in multiple voices. "Your fate is sealed, Tom. Kill the priest and join us or our minions will feast upon you for an eternity."

The exorcist continued shouting at the swirling black mass. "...May your kingdom come! May your will be done on earth as it is in heaven..."

Gustave pointed to the priest. "Eat the holy Eucharist, and you will be saved!"

Tom's cravings for meat returned, more ravenous than before. His leg bones stretched until he towered over Father Xavier and Gustave by two feet.

"Eat or be eaten!" the legion commanded.

Tom slowly turned, raised the cross-dagger above Father Xavier's back.

"...lead us not into temptation! But deliver us from evil! Amen!" The exorcist spun around, aiming his cross. "God have mercy on this man's soul!"

Tom, growling, turned around and rammed the holy dagger into Gustave's eye socket. The cannibal demon shrieked. Shafts of white light shot out of his eyes and mouth. Vibrant rays lanced through cracks in his face until Gustave's head glowed like a fiery sun. The cries of lost souls released from the Dark Shepherd's throat.

"Tommmmmm..." Beth Hatcher's voice drifted upward.

Tom backed away, reaching toward the ceiling with a long bony arm. "Beth!"

Her voice faded into the cacophony of a thousand other souls.

White flames engulfed Gustave's body. The rats and ravens squealed and disintegrated as the holy fire spread through the spinning swarm.

Then the room exploded with blinding white light.

220

Inside the watchtower, Anika heard a loud *boom* like dynamite going off. A force rocked her back against the log walls.

The windigos stopped clawing at the walls and roof. She heard them hopping down to the ground. Their running feet thundered like a stampede of buffalo toward the gate. She peered out a crack in one of the portals. The howling snowstorm seemed to be retreating from the fort. The fog rolled across the snowfield, back into the forest. The pack of windigos sifted between the pines. Among them ran the Ancient One, its antlers snapping the branches. The storm clouds kept retreating over the treetops, until they were a far distance away. Along the horizon appeared the glow of the waking sun. The snow stopped falling. The wind died down. The only sound was a crackling fire.

Anika opened a portal facing the village. A giant blaze consumed Noble House. The roof crashed in.

"Tom!" She climbed down from the ladder. Ran toward the towering bonfire.

Anika's heart leaped, as Swiftbear and a young brave came running out of a cabin and ran alongside her.

At the second floor of Noble House, Tom burst out of the smoking door with Father Xavier clinging to his shoulder. The two men ran down the steps. When they reached the ground, they collapsed at Anika's feet. Her heart dropped at the sight of Tom's gaunt face and elongated body.

221

Lying on a bed of snow. Shivering. So cold. Tom's body spasmed. He coughed. Opened his eyes. The sky was burning. A tower of flames.

Black smoke.

Father Xavier was standing over Tom, praying. Two Indian warriors gathered around the priest with spears aimed at Tom.

"Get back!" the priest yelled.

"He must be killed!" spoke an Indian with silver hair.

"No, don't hurt him!" Anika stepped between the braves. She jumped to her knees and touched Tom's face with a furry glove. His eyes welled up at the sight of her.

Part Twenty-One

Phoenix Fire Woman

222

Anika paced on the porch outside her cabin. She clutched the prayer bundle around her neck, praying to her grandmother and the elders of the Mediwiwin.

In the courtyard, Father Xavier argued with Squawking Crow. "Let me see him! He needs my help!"

The young brave kept pushing the priest back, blocking him with a spear.

Swiftbear came out of the cabin and put a hand on Anika's shoulder. "I have done all I can with my medicine. I'm sorry."

Anika shook her head. "No!"

"He is lost. He is almost *wiitigo*."

"Then I will save him." She walked toward the door.

Swiftbear blocked her. "No. We must burn down the cabin before he wakes up."

Anika paced, searching her mind for the right medicine. "I will perform the Phoenix Fire ceremony."

He shook his head. "Too dangerous."

"Grandmother gave me her medicine bag. I can use her magic." She pulled out a handful of white shells.

"It takes a seasoned shaman to use owl medicine." Swiftbear scowled. "If you fail, he will kill you."

Anika gripped her uncle's forearm. "Tom is my destiny. If I am to die, then I will die with him."

"You are as stubborn as your grandmother." Swiftbear looked toward her cabin door and sighed. "Go to him, Little Pup."

Anika hugged him and stepped into her cabin. She closed the door and took a deep breath.

Tom lay on her bed, covered in buffalo hides. He tossed and turned. Anika fought back tears when she saw his face had grown even more angular, his pale skin stretched around the skull, all his veins exposed, like blue branches under a sheet of ice. His body was longer, his legs hanging off the bed. He moaned and cringed as if having nightmares.

Anika undressed. With an owl feather, she stirred up smoke from sage burning in a bowl and smudged her nude body. "I call in the spirit of the Phoenix."

On the bed, Tom's bones made popping noises. His head shook on the pillow.

Anika put a hand on his bony chest. His skin felt so cold. She pulled out the flute that Tom and Chris Hatcher had whittled together. Her fingers felt the carvings of a white buffalo clashing horns with the antlers of an elk. She played a sacred song. This calmed him.

From her medicine bag, she poured white shells around the bed. Then she chanted an Ojibwa prayer and imagined a bird of fire flying into her chest. Her entire body filled with heat. She placed a flat stone in Tom's hand and closed his fist. Then she climbed under the buffalo hide and embraced him, warming his naked body with her own.

223

Tom was running through the foggy woods, half man, half animal, searching for something to feed his hunger. His keen sense of smell picked up the scent of pine and snow and, from somewhere, blood. He loped faster between the trees, snapping branches, and came to a clearing. In the center was a snow mound with a red spiral.

The symbol was familiar, but he couldn't recall where he'd seen it.

"Father!" a boy's voice called.

The windigo shook his head and suddenly remembered he had once been a man. A father who had lost his son. "Chris!"

The boy was standing in the mist at the edge of the clearing. He appeared transparent against the trees. A ghost. He beckoned Tom. "Come with me." Chris' spirit ran into the forest.

"Wait, where are you going?"

"They're coming for us," the boy called back. "Hurry!"

Tom followed, wondering who was coming after them. Inside him, man and beast were battling to take over this body. The animal in him wanted to run the opposite direction, continue to hunt for prey. What was left of the man clung to his memories. The good years he had

323

spent married to Beth and raising their son. The family shattered by their untimely deaths. And all the drunken nights that follwed as Tom's life had gone into a downward spiral.

Chris was leading him to heaven, where they could all be together again.

The boy stopped at the edge of a lake covered in white ice. The mist swirled around an island of jagged rocks and pine trees. In the cliffs were several caves.

Tom stopped. "This doesn't look like heaven."

"It's your new home." Chris' ghost evaporated.

Tom shouted, "Son! Wait, come back!"

Howls echoed from the island. And the beast within Tom howled back.

The fog drifted over the frozen lake. Within the mist formed the broad antlers of an enormous beast with fiery white eyes. And Tom somehow knew that this was the Ancient One, he who was older than old. Behind the windigo loped dozens of smaller skeletal creatures. Their bodies were marked with ragged holes and exposed bones as if the pack had been feeding off one another.

Tom started toward them and was stopped by the sound of flute music. It seemed to come from the sky. A flock of snow owls swooped between Tom and the horned windigo. It shrieked at the birds.

Stay with me, Tom, whispered a woman's voice.

He felt a sudden warmth against his skin.

Call on your totem.

He opened his fist and saw a white stone etched with a buffalo. And he remembered where he came from. "By the powers of my ancestors, I call on the spirit of white buffalo." In the woods behind him came the sound of thundering hooves.

The antler-horned windigo stopped in the center of the frozen lake and roared. The other windigos retreated into the fog.

Tom turned and stared into the peaceful eyes of the white buffalo. It snorted and bowed its head. Tom walked up to his spirit guide and put his hand on its forehead. Snowflakes speckled its thick white fur. Tom felt a warmth course through his body as he drew power from the sacred bison. He felt his long bones shrinking, his muscles growing thick. His claws pulled back into his fingers. His cravings for flesh dissipated. His strength returned.

The antler-horned windigo shrieked, then turned and disappeared into the mist that surrounded the island.

Tom's heart filled with heat. He woke up to find Anika's warm body entwined with his. He embraced her.

224

A week later, at the village on Otter Island, Tom stepped out of a wigwam. He was feeling whole again. His body had returned to its normal size. His stomach was full from a delicious breakfast Anika had made him. She joined him, taking his hand. They walked together to the river, where several braves were packing a long canoe. Father Xavier stood at the shore. He looked ten years younger.

Tom put a hand on the Jesuit's shoulder. "Thank you, Father. I owe you my life."

Father Xavier smiled. "I owe you just as much. You, too, Anika. Tell your grandmother I said thank you again for my new hat." He patted the coonskin that covered his bald head.

As the priest climbed into the center of the canoe, Tom asked, "Is the nightmare really over?"

"For Gustave's legion... *Oui.*" Father Xavier set his black bag at his feet. "But the battle against evil is far from over. Satan has many legions."

"We will be ready," Anika said.

The brigade paddled away from the shore. Father Xavier waved goodbye. "Tom, if you ever find yourself in Montréal again, you know where to find me."

Tom put his arm around Anika. "Thanks, but my life is here now."

Part Twenty-Two

The Four Winds

225

As Tom spent the remaining winter living on Otter Island among the Ojibwa, he learned that the Four Winds bring upon the change of seasons. In the dead of winter, the tribe always migrates to stay clear of the hungry windigos. The evil manitous have been around since the beginning of man and will still be here long after man makes his journey to the afterworld. But winters come to an end. And with the coming of spring, the tribe returns to their northern village to enjoy all the riches that the sacred land has to offer. Friendly manitous appear in the forest to help the tribal people find good places to fish and hunt and harvest rice. These manitous become their totems that connect them with the spirits of Father Sky and Mother Earth.

At long last, the sun shining in the bright blue sky warmed Tom's skin. The snow melted. All up and down Beaver Creek, ice fell into the trickling water. A herd of deer drinking at the stream watched the Ojibwa walking through the forest. Tom walked among them, dressed in buckskins and moccasins. He had a full beard now, and his hair had grown well past his ears. Anika walked beside him. Her belly was already starting to show. By autumn, they were due to have their first child. Anika, who was still just as stubborn as ever, had never looked happier. While Tom was looking forward to being a father again, he would never forget his first born. Thinking of Chris now once again brought Tom's grief to the surface.

The tribe gathered around the burial ground, where small spirit houses covered the graves. Grandmother Spotted Owl led the ceremony, chanting a native song. Anika, Swiftbear, and the other shaman joined in on the singing. Tom watched with teary eyes as a group of braves set a spirit house over a body wrapped in fur blankets. Then everyone fell silent and looked at Tom. He pulled out the flute that he and his son had whittled together.

From the forest came a hooting sound. A white snow owl was perched on a branch above the burial ground. As Tom pressed the flute to his mouth and played sweet music, the owl spread its wings and flew upward, into the clear blue sky.

SAMHAIN
PUBLISHING

It's all about the story...

HORROR

www.samhainpublishing.com

CPSIA information can be obtained at www.ICGtesting.com
Printed in the USA
BVOW011056260112

281450BV00001B/139/P